I0819883

Praise for
I Am Cardinal Wolf

I Am Cardinal Wolf by Roderick Kenney II is a must-read for anyone seeking a candid and intimate portrayal of the struggles and challenges that come with life after sexual abuse. Kenney's raw, authentic and deeply moving storytelling takes the reader on a journey of pain, triumph and self-acceptance that is truly remarkable. The cardinal wolf serves as a poignant metaphor for the author's own journey toward recovery, adding depth and complexity to the story. Kenney's courageous and honest storytelling is a true testament to the strength of the human spirit and the transformative power of literature.
—Chad Herold, Pastor at *Richmond Point Church Missouri City, Tx*

***

I am Cardinal Wolf is an amazing read! The worlds created in this story are so vivid and yet so full of insightful nuggets of what it's like to grow up in the world after a traumatic event like (but not limited to) sexual abuse. I truly believe this book can help the process of healing for not only those that have sadly gone through this as children, but also ones who have experienced all the pain of being taken advantage of at any point in life. Through the characters in the story, the author accurately describes the different stages of processing trauma. I truly enjoyed how the struggles of trauma were personified into beings with thoughts, plans, and most importantly in my opinion; weaknesses that can be overcome. The real fight with trauma is completely internal, so giving "the opponents" qualities we can all see was genius in my opinion. That's very encouraging to me for the struggles in my life that I'm currently trying to overcome. It's FULL of fruit the entire way through. Reading two chapters back to back is so filling you may have to take a

step back to fully digest what you're chewing on! It is a definite must read!
—Za Smith, Music Artist

***

Roderick C. Kenney II takes readers on an insightful, relevant and creative journey into the perilous world of overcoming trauma. It's a self-help inspired novel!
—Deborah Watkins, minister at *This is Pentecost Sacramento, Ca*

***

An exploration of the heavy issues that plague the heart and mind resulting from trauma. This novel walks through the plan of the dark forces that war to destroy the heart; and the power that is found in the light through the power of confession and forgiveness. A timely story that deals with the traumatic issues of life that have been silenced for too long.
—Rafael Fi Portillo, Pastor at *The Hill Vallejo Vallejo, Ca*

**

Everyone has had times in their life when their decisions and the decisions of others cause a ripple effect. This doesn't just affect the external world but the mind, heart, and spirit with lasting consequences. Cardinal's character's struggle to combat the war within shows how tough the battle can be but also that you are never alone and there is always hope.
—Portia Kenney, Youtube influencer

I Am
Cardinal Wolf

Overcoming Childhood Abuse and Exposing the Tuxedo

Roderick C. Kenney II

Published by KHARIS PUBLISHING, an imprint of
KHARIS MEDIA LLC.

ISBN-13: 978-1-63746-227-0
ISBN-10: 1-63746-227-1

Library of Congress Control Number: 2023945511

All KHARIS PUBLISHING products are available at special quantity discounts for bulk purchase for sales promotions, premiums, fund-raising, and educational needs. For details, contact:

Kharis Media LLC
Tel: 1-630-909-3405
support@kharispublishing.com

Table Of Contents

DAY 21

Today marks the twenty-first day of a new year. A lot has happened since the year started. Twenty one days ago to the average person, nothing happened that was out of the ordinary. Many celebrated the start of the new year with luscious kisses to a friendly stranger. Some danced the night away while downing tasty and strong spirits to commemorate the shift of another calendar year. While others celebrated by seeking refuge in their churches and tabernacles to give praise and worship to their deities for creating another year. Many watched from the rooftops of their homes the explosive and colorful dancing lights across the sky. Yes, twenty one days ago was the start of a brand new year, it would seem. We made promises to ourselves that we would soon not keep. We made promises to others that would soon become nonexistent. Twenty one days ago started the year twenty-nineteen, but to a select few there was a dynamic shift with the transition of another year. The shift has created a paradigm, one that is not only obscure but also perplexing, it was almost as if the world was getting ready for something.

"Aye Cardinal wassup man, how you doin bruh?" The voice over the phone asked

"Man, I'm chilling, how's everything with you?"

Cardinal asked

"I'm cooling out. Man partied last night and have a hangover, why you ain't come out with us last night mayne?" The voice over the phone asked.

"Man I couldn't because I had to work that night man, remember I told you that. You must have been super faded if you don't remember." Cardinal responded jokingly.

"Not gonna lie, I did start pregaming early yesterday. Hey we still on to play a round of golf this weekend? Right?" The voice over the phone asked.

"Yeah man I will be there, our tee time is at 5:30 am right?" Cardinal asked.

"Naw man it's at 6, I ain't waking up that early." The voice over the phone started while letting out a little chuckle.

"Okay, bet. Hey man, can I ask you something?" Cardinal sincerely asked.

"Wassup dawg." The voice over the phone acknowledged.

"You feel like this year is different in comparison to the other years we have lived through? Like seriously, it's a different numerical year but it just feels like something is off this time. You feel that?" Cardinal probed.

"IDK what you talkin bout player. Did something happen to you?" The voice over the phone questioned.

"It's just like, okay, so I am sitting on my porch staring at a sky that seems alien to me. Everyone knows this revolving rock to be called Earth. But this planet isn't what it's imagined to be. It's so funny we call this place Earth. The definition of the word Earth is the substance of the land's surface. The comedy of naming this planet Earth is that the planet was made up of 71% water and only 29% of land. I know this all seems like arbitrary chit chat and you're wondering how could this possibly equate to the depth of the year? You see, we as people floating through the void of space and time create meaning and reality based on the perceptions and notions that resonate with us. So naming this planet Earth was a decision based on the existence of humanity on what we know to be, but is that really true? Do we really exist on this planet as we know it? These are some of the things I have been thinking about." Cardinal answered.

"You know that's kinda deep bro, it always astounds me that you don't smoke because you're on some other stuff right now." The voice on the phone jokingly stated.

"The reason I bring this up is that for the past twenty days I have been seeing things and hearing voices that I am sure no one else is seeing nor anyone else is hearing. I will try and describe these things to the best of my ability. There are these "creatures", these "beings" that look like humans. They have all the same physical features as the common man and woman: a head that sits atop their bodies, a neck, arms, hands, fingers, a torso, legs, feet, even a personality. They have voices too, but they do not speak from mouths. At first glance, there is literally nothing that would differentiate them from you, your best friend, or a neighbor. That is until you look them in the face. They have no facial features whatsoever. They are blank faced individuals, and the strangest thing is they all dress alike. They all wear a two piece black suit. Their suit jackets are as black as night, and their pants are darker than the void of space, and their shirts are white with a black tie. It is ironic that nothing differentiates them from one another, but yet and still there are seeable differences with each one. I have been seeing these "beings" everywhere for the past twenty days. I have even seen them in my own house. I have tried to ask them who they are and why are they just showing up now and I receive no answer. Strangely enough, I do feel that I know them. Like you would know the face of a childhood friend you hadn't seen in decades. I have come to know these "beings" as Suits. These Suits are extremely powerful for they know your every weakness, and because they know your weakness, they will exploit that weakness in you. I have seen it myself." Cardinal continued.

"What do you mean you have seen it yourself?" The voice over the phone asked immediately.

"Ight so twenty days ago, a day after the change of the year, I traveled to Pineland. While I was there, I saw a man sitting on the sidewalk with his head between his knees. His hair was matted, he had a flannel shirt on that was blue and white in pattern. His skin was smooth and was the color of an old rusted penny. He had gray sweatpants on that were discolored and stained. He did not smell too pleasant for life was extremely hard on him and left him homeless. This man was broken as he seemed to let out a bellowing chuckle. He laughed so hard that he urinated on himself. Those that passed by on the street walked around this man as he sat in his own urine. Sitting on both sides of this man were two Suits. Both with their arms around the seemingly psychotic man. As I got out of the car to walk into the taco shop, I then realized what I was looking at. The Suits that were sitting beside this man were not a loving man and woman trying to console this man but two nefarious beings. They both forced his hand to a bottle of liquor that lay beside his body and with gentle seduction caused the man to sip from the bottle. As I stared at the three of them the two suits gazing at the man both turned around and looked me in the eyes. At that moment, something came over me as I walked into the shop to grab my food. A feeling of uneasiness and fear. When I came back outside, I realized that these Suits did not just sit with this man, but they were walking amongst and with many of the people on the streets. Who were they? Why did I feel some form of connection to the ones that I was looking at with the man on the street? These were questions I did not have the answer to." Cardinal finishes with defeat in his voice "to keep it a stack bro I think you got a wild imagination. Like what pillies you poppin cause I need those in my life. Fa real." The voice over the phone interrupted.

Cardinal starts again now even more confused than before, "And it's like, now it's the twenty first day of January and I still have no answers to what I saw and why those two suits seemed so familiar to me. I have seen many more Suits that I feel that I know but yet I cannot grasp their intention or identity. I have myself been confronted with Suits that frequent my home, my room, my existence. The voice that I hear is one in particular that has been calling out to me in my sleep. It sounds like a familiar voice, one that I've heard before, but it only speaks during a certain part of my dream. I have this dream that I am standing with someone in a room, we are having some sort of conversation. I cannot really make out the words being exchanged between the two of us, everything sounds muffled like he is speaking from the other side of a water wall. Surrounding us is a bunch of concrete walls and graffiti sprayed on one directly behind him. We continued to talk until I noticed him backing up completely horrified, unaware of why he was so spooked. I look to my right and see another arm growing from my shoulder. I look left and see the same thing. The arms begin to rotate until the palms on the excess arms are on my shoulders, the arms begin to push on me hard, it feels as if my body is being cut in half. Then suddenly, there is another dark figure in front of me. He smiles and says my name, just once. I turn to look at the person I was just speaking with and the horrified look on his face just disappears. He just stands there looking at me almost as menacing as the other blackened individual does. Before I can make out the next part of the dream I wake up because they both lunge at me. I generally wake up in a cold sweat, confused and that has been happening literally since the year started. Everything about the dream is so weird because it feels real. I feel that the person standing in front of me is a friend of mine, but I just cannot understand why he turned on me and why something came out of my body. I feel that it may have something to do with all these Suits walking around here." Cardinal finished.

"Aye yo bro that's nutty. Not gonna lie to you, I need a blunt to listen to everything you saying right now cause this some FX movie ish you talking right now." The voice over the phone mocked again.

"Whatever bro you treating me like I'm crazy fa real. Anyways I'm bout to head over to my parent's house and chill. Maybe they can grant me some answers about everything that I am seeing and hearing. They are the smartest people that I know, I just hope they don't think I'm crazy like A LOT of other people do." Cardinal condescendingly stated into the phone.

"Aye bruh you good, I just sparked one up, you can keep talking." The voice over the phone chuckled.

"Ight bruh I'll holla at you later," Cardinal responded friendly.

"Ight G. See you on Saturday." The voice over the phone reciprocated.

"One Hunid. Deuces." Cardinal said. "Peace." The voice over the phone hangs up.

Cardinal Wolf was not the only person that was able to see these Suits. In fact, there were many in society that had the gift to see these beings. The change of the year created newer eyes in select members of the world. Cardinal was not the only one that was blessed with a gift. This gift is known as discerning vision. However, Cardinal was particularly different because his gift did not develop because of the change of the year. Cardinal's encounter with the suits goes back to his childhood.

CARDINAL WOLF

Twenty years ago, Cardinal experienced a life changing experience which opened his eyes to discern the suits. It all started when Cardinal was seven years old.

It was a hot summer day and Cardinal was outside playing with his sisters and his cousins. The sun was beaming down, hugging the brown skin of the young children. The wind, desolate, selfish to withhold the blessings of its cool nature. They enjoyed the vivacious innocence God blessed every child with during this time of the year. This was a time of play, no school, and no worries. A child's wonderland. The birds chirped with excitement to see the youth in their natural innocence and imagination. The grass swayed with the anticipation of supporting the games to be held on the surface of their course and luscious majesty. The asphalt scorching with passion to be incorporated with the plans of the children. This was a special time in history because children only had their family, friends, imagination, and nature to satisfy their curiosity. On this particular day, Cardinal, his older sister Aurelia, his younger sister Jade, and his two female cousins Aspen and Dove all decided to go outside and play.

"Hey Grandaddy can we go outside and have a water fight?

Pleeeaaasse!!!" they all asked emphatically.

"Ok, OK just make sure you shut the water off when you are done." He said with a bright smile on his face. Happily willing to be interrupted from watching the horse races on television. "Aaaaand they're off. Smarty Jones takes the lead by a head. Uh oh snatching second by a tail is Admiral. As they come around the bend, we have Seattle Slew stealing the front by a nose." The television penetrating the ears of the young and old.

They screamed with joy and excitement as they ran to their rooms to prepare themselves for battle. Eager to partake in the adventures of the day.

"Stop running in the house!" Grandaddy scoffs as he turns back to the television. "And It's going to be Foolish Pleasure taking the win by a head."

The racing commentator says from the television. "Doggoneit!" Grandaddy lets out with disappointment having lost the money that he gambled on one of the horses.

Once they were all in their clothing to fight, they rushed through the front door to begin the war.

During this summer Cardinal's parents Alpha and Omega had purchased water guns for him and his sisters so they were excited to use them. They were accurately named Super Soakers for they were the perfect weapon to ensure victory in any water fight. Their massive 78 fluid oz chamber held more than enough water to keep the wielder of the weapon on the offensive against their enemy.

"Okay these are the rules, it is going to be girls against boys." Explained the elder cousin Aspen. Aspen was a fair skinned young girl with soft flowy hair that barely reached past her shoulders. By this summer her age reached the double digits, something most children aspired towards. She was quite tall and thin. Her age and intellect is what gave her the privilege to be commander in this war soon to ensue.

"Heeeeeyyy that is not fair, that means I will be all alone," exclaims Cardinal.

"I will be on Cardinal's team." proclaimed Jade. Jade was Cardinal's baby sister. Jade and Cardinal were very close. Some would even say they were two peas in a pod. They had the likeness of twins even though they sat with two years of age difference. Jade was a very small and cute child. Her skin likened to the smooth chocolate of an irresistible chocolate bar atop a mountain of ice cream. Her hair thick and beautiful, the epitome of the royal bloodline she had been birthed through. Knockers and barrettes in her hair accentuated the youth of the young girl. Her smile was infectious and her charm could bring down an entire kingdom, this is probably why Cardinal and Aurelia would use her to ask their father, Alpha, for things.

"Okay that's fine. So Cardinal and Jade, you two will be on a team. Me, Dove, and Aurelia will be on a team. We will put the water guns in the center of the yard with the water balloons. On the count of three, we will all run to the guns and balloons to grab our weapons, whoever gets the wettest after the first round is out." Explained Aspen.

Dove was the younger sister of Aspen. Life only separated Dove and Aspen by a couple of years. Dove was a lively and energetic young girl. With strong thick hair, and brown skin that was healthier than the bark on a mighty pine tree and just as tall as a pine tree as well. She and Aspen were much like Cardinal and Jade in relationship for they could always be found one with the other. Aurelia was the elder sister of Cardinal. She was a very clever and intellectual individual even at her young age. A year of life is what separated her from Cardinal. She was strong and tall.

"OK." all agreed.

They all worked together to fill the water in the guns and the balloons. As soon as the weapons were prepared, they went to opposite sides of the battle ground. Cardinal and Jade were definitely outnumbered but Cardinal had a huge advantage because he was faster than everyone. His strategy was to grab weapons for him and his sister and take out the oldest cousin first.

"OK, three....two.....one...GO!" Yelled Dove.

All kids rushed the battlefield to grab their weapons. Cardinal did get to the guns first but because he was there first, he was wide open for attack. Aurelia was next to the battlefield. Rather than go for the guns she went right for the ballons and the water bucket. Strategically, this was a better option because it would distribute more damage. Cardinal gave his baby sister one of the bigger guns and as he went to grab another one Aurelia unleashed on him. At this time, Dove and Aspen had grabbed a gun and some water balloons and they all attacked Cardinal. They formulated the plan to get Cardinal out first because he was a bigger threat. Once the guns were empty and the balloons were all gone it was time to determine who was going to sit out.

"Well, it looks like Cardinal is going to be sitting out this next round because he is wetter than everyone. So now Aurelia and Jade will be on a team and it will be me and Dove on a team." proclaimed Aspen.

Sad and defeated Cardinal goes to sit on the porch to wait for the battle to end before going back in. Water covered his body as the sun started to work its magic, gradually drying off the young boy. As his shorts hit the pavement a small sizzle let out from the untouched blazing rock.

"Hey what are you guys doing out here?" questioned Jay.

Jay was Cardinal's cousin. He was staying with the Wolf Family unbeknownst to Cardinal. Jay was much older than the younger kids. Jay was a teenager. He was a strong built individual with many problems from his childhood. Cardinal looked up to Jay because he was the closest thing to an older brother that Cardinal had. Jay could do no harm in the eyes of the young Cardinal.

"We were having a water fight but I lost so now I have to sit and wait for the next round." Cardinal expressed sadly.

"It's okay kiddo. Hey there is something I want to show you." Jay said, patting Cardinal on the shoulder.

"Ok." Cardinal agreed. Rising from the hot porch and taking his socks and shoes off before stepping on the carpet inside of the house.

Both Jay and Cardinal walked inside the house towards the back room. This was where Alpha and Omega slept. Cardinal had been in this room before but today the room seemed foreign. Cardinal walked into the room with enthusiasm to see this surprise that Jay promised to show.

"What do you have to show me?" questioned Cardinal. "What I have to show you is a new game that I want us to play. Now this game is going to be between you and I. I do not want you to tell anyone about this game because if you tell them they will die and then we will not be able to have fun playing this game anymore. After the game is over you will get a nice surprise and I will get you some candy or ice cream. How does that sound?" Jay asked.

"Candy! I love candy!" eagerly expressed Cardinal. "How do you play this game?" Cardinal asked.

"Well first because you are all wet you need to take your clothes off," ordered Jay "OK" said Cardinal.

"Well, it wouldn't be fair if you got undressed and I didn't." Jay said while removing his clothes. "Now I want you to lay on your stomach and we can watch cartoons together."

"But my parents said that we can't watch TV during the day," Cardinal said worryingly.

"It's okay Cardinal, remember we are not going to tell them about this game because they may die if they know and we won't be able to have fun anymore."

"OK." Cardinal said with naivety.

Jay then turned on the TV and changed the channel to the cartoons and Cardinal was happy to be watching one of his favorite shows. He felt guilty because he was going against what his parents told him, but at the same time Cardinal really wanted an elder brother and Jay was the closest thing to a brother so he wanted to build his relationship with him. How exciting. Watching his favorite show with his honest, trusting, role model, what could be better than that, were the thoughts that circled through the mind of the young Cardinal.

"Ouch!" Cardinal painfully expressed. "You can't do that Jay that hurts."

"I know it hurts a little bit but this is how you play the game. If you do not want to play this game, I have another game that we can play. I have a lollipop you can suck on and there is a special surprise when you suck it for a little bit."

"Really? Okay." Cardinal reluctantly said. "Wait, you want me to put that in my mouth? I do not think that I should be doing that." Cardinal expressed hoping that this role model of his would sense the fear and prevent the young boy from playing anymore.

"If you want me to buy you ice cream and candy afterwards then you are going to have to put this in your mouth for a little bit then you will win the game. You want to win the game?" Questioned Jay.

"Yes I want candy, OK I will do it" answered Cardinal.

During this time Cardinal reluctantly did what Jay had asked him to do. He finished the game and that surprise that was described before did emerge. Cardinal was told to take that surprise and once he finished it then he would get his candy. Cardinal did and at that very moment he noticed something different about the room. He remembered only going into the room with Jay, but for some reason, there was another figure in there as well. In the corner stood a figure adorned in what Cardinal recognized as 'church clothes."' This being scared him because he had no face. That love and respect that he had for his cousin Jay then became disdain and every fond memory became horrifying. Every time after they played this game, Cardinal would see the faceless figure. The once loving place that was known as a home soon became a prison for Cardinal. Every joyous memory that was had with Cardinal laying with his father watching Karate movies then became perverted. A room once seen as a full embracing joy now became a dark empty void. Cardinal that day had seen a suit for the very first time. The horror that he felt that day was a feeling that he did not want to ever feel again. So Cardinal tried to put up many blockades in his mind so that he would never have to see or experience that fear ever again. Cardinal thought he was successful at blocking out the incident until one night he had a nightmare.

"Hello Cardinal" spoke the faceless individual.

"Wait I know you. I have seen you before. You were in the room with Jay and I the day we played that game. Where is your face? Why didn't you say anything that day? Why do I see so many of you guys now? Why are you here?" Every question flowed from the mouth of a dreaming little boy.

"Well Cardinal, I am not going to answer all of your questions. But I will answer a few of them. First, my name is really irrelevant. But if you would like the answer to this trivial statement. My name is Abuse. I have existed far longer than you can imagine. You seeing me for the first time is an anomaly. Not many people can see me and my brothers and sisters. We exist because of humanity. When you get older you will understand what that means. I do not have a face because that is how I was designed. We will continue to haunt and affect humanity from the day you are born to the day you die. We all have different characteristics and names but you can call us Suits. You can never get rid of us. Just because you can see us now does not mean anything. We will still do what we were designed to do and there is nothing you can do to stop or impede our mission. By the way, it's not just suits out here there are also……."

Cardinal snapped out of his dream, woke up and ran to his parents' room. It was from that night on Cardinal decided his parents would never know of the game played in this room. Ever.

WANNA PLAY A GAME

The days after this recent event were very different for Cardinal. He lost the sense of respect that he had for his cousin even though he could not holistically determine if the game he was playing was wrong. All Cardinal knew was that he did not like the rule of not telling his parents about the game. He did not like hiding things from his parents. As much as Cardinal would prefer not to see his cousin it was difficult because his cousin would pick him up from school and when they would get back home, they would be the only ones there. Just Jay, his Grandaddy, his Mamama (who would typically spend her days downstairs in solitude), and himself. Cardinal was also very unsettled by the faceless being that he met the other day. Why was this all happening to him? Cardinal was unable to pander his thoughts on why Jay chose him to play the game. Cardinal couldn't even consider whether he truly enjoyed the prizes he acquired for playing the game because when he would try to wrap his head around what was happening, his cousin Jay would manipulate him into playing again.

"Hey Cardinal, do you wanna play a game?" Jay asked. "Can we just watch TV instead, without playing the game?" Cardinal responded also fearfully observing the faceless creature in the corner of the bedroom.

"Cardinal, I know you didn't just ask me to watch TV on a school day. Oh if your parents knew you were doing that, they would definitely give you a whoopin. Do you want me to tell them that you have been watching TV on a school day all this time?" Jay asked.

"No! Please do not tell my mom and dad they would not be happy at all." Cardinal begged and pleaded.

"Well, I guess I can just keep this between you and me as long as you are willing to play the game with me," Jay said knowing that he had manipulated him. "I will even let you choose the show you get to watch. How about that?" Jay asked.

"Okay. Instead of candy, can I have some ice cream? Also, instead of making me swallow the stuff that comes out of you, can I just spit it in the toilet? I do not like the taste of it." Cardinal pleaded.

"Cardinal, you know the rules if you want the Ice cream then you are going to have to swallow it, just think of it as milk," Jay stated while pushing Cardinal into the back of the home to start playing the game.

"Ok fine," Cardinal answered reluctantly.

They both walked into the back of the house and closed the door just slightly enough not to raise suspicion but also enough to where if someone did walk in, they would not get caught doing anything. Jay picked up the remote and gave it to Cardinal and instructed him to turn it on and chose something that he wanted to watch, all the while Jay started pulling down his pants and his boxers.

"Hey look Bananas in Pajamas. I love this show." Cardinal exclaimed with excitement "Okay, say ah." Jay instructed.

5 minutes passed and Jay and Cardinal continued with their game until Jay heard someone walking down the hallway. He panicked because he did not know whether the person would be coming into the room or going to another room in the house.

"Hold on." Jay whispered to Cardinal. Simultaneously pulling up his pants and throwing a blanket over Cardinals nearly naked body. A few seconds after Cardinal was ushered to stop the door swung open to the bedroom. It was Grandaddy.

"What are y'all doing in here?" Grandaddy asked. Cardinal's heart began to beat quickly because he was not only nervous about the fate that his Grandaddy would ensue by finding out about this game, but also he was relieved that a knight showed up to protect him from the monster laying beside him.

"Nothing, I just picked Cardinal up from school and now he is watching his favorite show." Jay responded.

"I do not think his parents want him watching TV during the week. Y'all come out of this room and Cardinal if you got homework you need to do I recommend you go do it before your parents get home and get mad at you. Jay, go take that trash out." Grandaddy commanded.

"Yes sir," Jay responded. As quickly as Grandaddy had opened the door and came into the bedroom was as quickly as he left and it appeared that the game had suddenly ended. Cardinal was elated that his grandfather saved him from completing the objective of the game. Cardinal tossed the blankets off of him and started to put his pants back on and walk out of the room until he felt Jay grab his arm and bring him back to the bed.

"We are not done playing yet Cardinal." Jay forcefully proclaimed.

"But grandaddy said that we cannot be in here anymore and I have to go do my homework," Cardinal informed Jay trying to exit the room.

"Don't you want the Ice Cream? Come on, we are almost done." Jay responded bringing cardinal back to the bed but turning off the TV so as to not alert Grandaddy a second time. 2 minutes elapsed and the game they had been playing had come to an end. Cardinal had completed the mission and won his prize: an ice-cold bomb pop from the ice cream driver who promptly showed up in the neighborhood around 3 pm every weekday. Cardinal got his ice cream and ate it in the corner of the yard and consumed his ice cream, after eating it he went inside the house and started doing his homework. This cycle continued every Wednesday because that was the day that all the kindergarten and 1st grade kids got out a lot earlier than the rest of the school. All the other days of the week Cardinal would be accompanied by his sister Aurelia who would walk with him back home from school since they got out at the same time. This became Cardinals new life.

One week during the lunch hour Cardinal met up with his neighbor who also attended the school with him, his name was Forest. Forest and Cardinal were not really friends because they did not share much in common. The only thing that partnered them was merely their age. They hung out here and there but for the most part they did not really hang out with each other. So Cardinal was ushered by Forest to meet him in the back of the school during the lunch break because there was something that he wanted him to see. A game that he wanted to play. Cardinal was a little bit nervous for the fact that he did not know whether the "game" that his neighbor wanted to play was the same game his cousin had been playing with him at the back of the house for over a year now. When the lunch bell finally rang, Cardinal exited the door and walked to the playground where he saw Forest standing there waiting for him.

"Hey Cardinal, come over here. I got someone that wants to meet you." Forest led him to the corner of the yard behind the really large sequoia tree which impeded the view of all the adults watching. There was a small circular table with 2 benches over in that corner, and based on the drag marks in the grass it appeared that Forest moved the table over to keep people from seeing what they were planning on doing. At this point Cardinal's heart began to beat fast because he did not know that his neighbor knew this game. Was his cousin Jay also playing this game with him? Would he get no rest from this game? He thought. Just before he panicked out of his skin he saw a young lady behind the tree, also hiding from detection. Was she going to be playing this game as well? Cardinal thought?

"Maybe I'm overreacting," he thought. "There was no way that she and him both knew the secret game that his cousin taught me." Cardinal continued his deductions.

Just before Cardinal could be assured of his deductions Forest informed Cardinal why he was brought over to the side of the yard.

"Now Cardinal you are my man so I didn't want you to miss this opportunity. We always play together outside and my brother told me that you become more mature when you mess around with a girl. This lady right here is Chardonnay. She also wants to be a woman and from what her uncle told her she will become a woman when she plays this game with another man. We are here to become older. All we have to do is touch on each other, kiss a little bit, and then we will be men. Don't you want to be a man?" Forest asked.

"Yes." Cardinal answered reluctantly "So are we going to share her or something? I mean it seems kinda strange that we are both going to play this game with only one girl." Cardinal rebutted.

"Yeah man come on it will be great," Forest assured as he grabbed the little girl and ushered her to the table. She laid down on the table and allowed Cardinal and Forest to touch on her and she touched on them. After feeling her hand on his body Cardinal felt cold and weird. He looked up from her and saw Abuse standing around all 3 of them, and that scared Cardinal, so rather than playing the game with Forest, Cardinal ran. When Cardinal got from around the large tree one of the adults saw Cardinal running from the perimeter of the school and shouted.

"Hey what are you doing over there! You know you are not supposed to be off school property." The adult yelled.

"Sorry I thought I lost something over there so I had to go get it." Cardinal quickly responded.

"Were you over there with anyone?" The adult questioned stepping closer in the direction of the tree.

"No, it was just me." Cardinal quickly rebutted to keep the teacher from finding Forest over in the trees with the girl. Cardinal remembered that the first rule of the game is to make sure that no one finds out about the players in the game, so even though he was not playing with them anymore he felt obligated to protect them from being found out. The adult then hurried Cardinal back onto the playground and Cardinal finished his lunch break by playing with the other kids on the play structure.

The bell rings indicating that lunch was over. Cardinal hops down from the monkey bars and glances over at the sequoia tree that Forest and the girl were just playing at. After a few seconds of staring in the direction, Forest and the girl walk out from behind the tree holding hands, it appeared to Cardinal that Forest had become a man that day. Some day he will too.

Once school was over Cardinal and Aurelia met up at the back of the school to begin their descent back to the house. Cardinal upon making his arrival to the gate at the back of the school waves at Aurelia. He starts to jog to catch up to her.

"Hey! So how was school for you today?" Aurelia asks "Oh man it was good. I learned how to count." Cardinal responded. "How was your day" He asks.

"It was also really good we learned about the solar system and all the planets…" Aurelia began explaining her day but as she spoke Cardinal's attention began to slowly turn towards the sequoia tree. He remembered how much he hated the game that he played with Jay but this time he felt that he may have liked the interaction he had with the girl. Maybe the game was not so bad after all. Cardinal began to think that maybe he should try playing the game he had been taught with girls. Maybe the game they were playing wasn't all that bad afterall.

"...homework to do?" Aurelia finished her statement about her day by asking Cardinal a question. Unbeknownst to Cardinal, who was still thinking about the game realized that she was asking him something.

"I'm sorry. What did you ask me?" Cardinal asked.

"I said, do you have homework to do?" Aurelia seconds.

This time much closer to the house.

"Yes, I do have some math homework that I have to do. Since we just learned about counting, the teacher wants us to write out our numbers." Cardinal responds. "What about you?" Cardinal asks "Yeah I got some work I have to get done. I want to watch some TV before mom and dad get home." Aurelia responds.

"Well grandaddy won't let us watch TV either so how would we do that?" Cardinal asks.

"We just have to keep the volume down low. Jay taught me how to get away with it." Aurelia responds while walking into the driveway of the house.

Cardinal followed her into the house but he couldn't believe that his sister may have played a similar game with Jay that he played. He couldn't be sure; he also could not see the suits that he had previously observed floating around Forest and the young girl from the school. No way this happened to her too.

"Hey shuga. How yall doin?" Grandaddy asked as they both walked in the door.

"Good." Aurelia answered "Good." Cardinal answered.

"I went to the store and got you all some cakes. You can have one. make sure to leave one for your sister when she gets home from school." Grandaddy said over the background of the TV.

"Thank you grandaddy!" Aurelia let out with excitement "Thank you grandaddy!" Cardinal let out with excitement. "You're welcome baby. Now go downstairs and say hi to your mamama before you go eatin those cakes." Grandaddy commanded.

"Okay!" They both responded. Cardinal ran over to the garage door and opened it to see their grandmother sitting in her favorite seat watching her westerns.

"Hi Mamama!" They both engaged her bosom with enthusiasm.

"Hello! How are the babies doing?" She asked. "Good." Aurelia answered.

"Good." Cardinal responded. "How are you doing?" He asked.

"I'm marvelous darling," she responded. "Did you see those cakes your grandfather got for y'all up there on that table?" She asked.

"Yeeeessss. I can't wait to choose one." Aurelia responded. "Me too." Cardinal seconded.

"Well y'all better get up there and get your snack and do your homework before your parents get back home. I do not want them mad at you." Mamama responded.

"Ok. Love you mamama!" They both yelled as they climbed the step bringing them back into the kitchen.

"Ok baby. Don't forget to close the door when yall leave." She responded.

They closed the door behind them and went back up to the kitchen and got their cakes and traveled into the back room to start watching TV. On an average day their cousin Jay would not be home until their parents got there, because he was in high school and due to its proximity to the house, he typically got picked up by Omega on her way back home from work. So Cardinal and Aurelia were by themselves in the back of the house without adult supervision. Cardinal began thinking about what Aurelia said about watching TV with Jay and he wanted to know if they had been playing the same game he was playing with Jay. So when Aurelia turned the TV on, Cardinal looked at her and asked. "Hey Aurelia. Do you want to play a game?" "What kind of game?" Aurelia asked.

"It's a really fun game, the only thing is you can't tell mom and dad about this or they will get killed." Cardinal informed.

"Oh ok, do I get some ice cream or candy after it." Aurelia responded.

Cardinal knew what that meant. From then on, he started to notice His cousin Jay taking patrons into the back room to play this special game. Something would need to change to get them away from this monster.

THE HEART OF MAN

"You mean I get to have my own room?" shouted Cardinal in disbelief "Almost correct. You will no longer have to share a room with your sisters. Now you will just share a room with Jay. How does that sound?" informed Alpha and Omega "PLEASE NO. PLEASE DO NOT MAKE ME SHARE A ROOM WITH JAY!" Cardinal rebutted fearfully.

"Whoa son, what is the problem? I thought you loved your older cousin Jay?" questioned Alpha. Alpha was Cardinal's father. He was a tall strong man. His presence radiated with purpose, love, and conviction to protect and provide for his family. Cardinal cherished every moment that he got to have with his father because he worked so much.

"It's nothing. He just scares me." Cardinal confessed. Still petrified from the years of keeping their little game a secret. He imagined the fate that might succumb to his parents if he were to dispel their game. They could never know about their game.

"I just don't want to share a room with him."

"Okay son if it is that big for you then we will just leave him here with your grandparents," Omega said calmingly. Omega was Cardinal's mother. She was a young beautiful woman full of love and warmth. It was no wonder that Alpha married her because she was the ideal woman. Alpha knew that he was lucky to have her and Cardinal knew he was lucky to have her as a mother.

This new move was the start of a new journey for Cardinal because he believed that now that he was moving away from Jay, he would now stop seeing the faceless suits. His youthful mind had not fully come to grips with the dream he had about Abuse those years ago. What did that suit mean when he said, "there were not just suits." Were there other beings out there, more horrifying than what he had experienced? All Cardinal knew at this time was that he was going to be leaving this prison and actually enjoying the place people called a home, in a new city called Mariano City. Mariano City was a beautiful city on the water with a naval base not too far away. One of the greatest things about this new city is that right at its center was a place of wonders for any child. A place called Marine Planet. This place was amazing. This park housed the most amazing marine life dolphins, penguins, sea lions, and walruses. They also had live performances on the water including fireworks and an amazing Batman show. This seemed like the ideal place for a new start. A place where the innocence of a young body and mind can be rebuilt.

As Cardinal slept that night, anticipation of the next week's move lingered fresh in his mind, Abuse met with his colleagues. The Suits all met in a place known as the Heart of Man. This place existed with no walls, no roof, no floor but yet was a space that could be filled. It was a dark space only illuminated by the dimmest of lights. Time was a mere spectrum in this place, and did not have the same uniform principles that existed on Earth. This empty void was filled with the noise of distant cries and regret. Out of the chaos a voice spoke. "Stress! Where are you?" Abuse spoke.

"What do you need with Stress, Abuse?" questioned Addiction.

Addiction was a slightly smaller Suit in comparison to Abuse. It was frail and short but what it lacked in stature it made up with enumerable deeds and the monstrous reputation it had.

"Why don't you try and mind your own business. I know you have an affinity of no self control, but why don't you try and control your mouth and stay out of this." sneered Abuse.

"You know it's not in your nature to be so aggressive, Abuse.

That's more my speed." exclaimed Violence.

Violence was a more muscularly built Suit with a small head. It thrived on hostility and ignorance; these two characteristics caused his massive build.

"Look I just need to talk to Stress because of the turn of events I was told we will be facing very soon." Abuse answered. "Now that I think about it, it would be more advantageous if Fear were here too. Where is Fear?"

"I know where they are. I'll go get 'em." Proclaimed Addiction.

In that moment Addiction vanished just leaving Violence and Abuse to idly talk.

"You know we should team up; we could do a lot of damage, you know." Violence exclaimed.

"When will you learn," Abuse snickered, "Not every situation involving me requires you. I am more than capable of accomplishing my goal without you being there. Just because we do some exquisite things together doesn't mean I need you now. I need Stress and I need Fear."

Instantly Addiction returned with Fear and Stress. Fear entered the void shaking, biting its nails. Fear walked with a limp and stood like a giant. A very tall Suit with no self esteem completed its best work by impressioning its perspective on people. Stress shared many of the same characteristics of Fear for they were conceived at the same time. They were twins. While Fear limped on the right side, Stress limped on the left side. Typically, where you would look for one you would see the other. They worked very closely together because once Fear attached itself Stress would then attach itself in a revolving relationship with one another. At that moment Violence decided to leave for he was not needed for the coming conversation.

"Stress. Fear. I have been calling for you guys where have you been?" Asked Abuse.

"We were out having some fun creating nightmares. Most of the terror we have spread has been stifled by Addiction because she brought us back here. What do you want?" Fear questioned.

"Yeah, what do you want?" seconded Stress.

"Look I understand you guys were busy, but I need your help because something has happened that may be problematic later. A young boy has knowledge of our existence." explained Abuse.

"Wait, wait, wait. You mean someone has seen you? How did this happen? This is not good. Did you tell.......you know who." whispered Fear.

"You know if he finds out that could be a problem." Furthered Stress.

"I know that! This is why I have called for you two. We need to team up against this little boy because we know what could happen if he figures out how to purge us. Not only will we be powerless against him but potentially everyone. I have the perfect plan though. Okay so, I have already done what I needed to do to afflict the boy and that will be good for a season, but it will not be enough to hold him over. Right before I showed up, I used one of your tactics' Fear. I told him that if he ever tells anyone about what will happen his parents will die. I created some fear but I need you to put an impression on him. Once you.."

"Wait. This kid wouldn't happen to be the kid having those nightmares about the dark figure in the bedroom taking advantage of him, would it?" Questioned Fear.

"Yeah, that is who I have been talking about. A boy by the name of Cardinal Wolf." answered Abuse.

"Funny. I did not know his name but I have been working on that boy since that day. I didn't quite understand why he was having nightmares about the stuff he was. Typically, I am able to scare young boys with less intricate and detailed dreams. But that was heavy. Now I understand that it was your doing that created that image in his head. I must say Abuse, you did some good work on that boy. It makes my job a lot easier." Fear said, praising Abuse.

"I appreciate the respect, but like I was saying once you apply your impression on that boy then I will have a better chance of sticking around." finished Abuse.

"Wait, are you saying that you will be purged?" probed Stress.

"That's the thing, I do not know. I can only see up until a certain point in his life. It's like I lose perspective the further I look into Cardinal's future. But what I am certain of is that if we work together then this perspective may change." answered Abuse.

"Well, you seem to have a good reason for wanting my twin Fear, but why do you want me?" Stress stressed.

"It is obvious. The work that you will do will make it impossible for Cardinal to deal. You are the cherry on top. Without you, we create situations, but with you, we now have a lifestyle." Abuse said smiling. "I believe that we will do great things together."

"Hey I know you guys have a plan and everything but maybe you could use my help too. I'm telling you I have quite the impression you guys should…" Addiction states before being cut off.

"No Addiction we do not need you, why don't you go try and figure out how you can be useful elsewhere" snarkily expresses Abuse.

At that moment a loud voice bellows out of the void. "What are you three doing? And who told you to meet up?

Bellowed the ominous figure.

"I know that voice is that you Sel...Selfishness?" Staggered Abuse.

"I didn't think you would merely remember my voice. Again I ask, what are you three idiots doing?" Selfishness asked a second time.

"You are not our superior so we do not need to answer you." Fear and Stress answered in unison.

"True as that may be, I am still superior. Know your place. This is exactly why you two were never elevated." Selfishness proclaimed.

"Actually, we were just building a plan on how to deal with Cardin…." Abuse stumbles

"Look, I already know what you three are doing and I personally do not care. Just as long as you do not get my way. Cardinal is a tough cookie but I have had my eye on him for a while and soon I will have my way with him. See you vagabonds later." And just like that Selfishness had gone.

Selfishness was not a Suit; in fact, it was something far more powerful. It once existed as a Suit but had been elevated beyond that of the faceless beings. It did not wear the same attire that the Suits wore, in fact it wore a tailored coat with intricate designs and a skirt. Its appearance was quite beautiful and full chest with definitive curves. Its hips were round and its face had a distinctive feature that the Suits did not have. It had eyes. Deep, penetrating green eyes with silky smooth eyelashes. Its eyelids were covered with dark lace styling.

Now that Selfishness had vanished, Fear, Stress, and Abuse finished their conversation.

"I really cannot stand Selfishness, always making everything about her." stated Fear.

"Yeah, we should have elevated before her. Right twin." stated Stress

"Look, forget about her. Do I have you guys help?" Abuse asked with its hand out to formulate a handshake.

"I'm in." Fear said, reaching out its hand. "Me too." Stress said, reaching out its hand.

All three shook hands and disappeared from the Heart of Man.

The deal had been done and three powerful Suits had been united with the intention to solidify their place in Cardinal's life. Cardinal arose from his slumber the next morning anticipating the new journey he would soon embark on.

NEW HOME

The time had finally come for Cardinal, Jade, Aurelia, Alpha, and Omega to move to this new city of promise. Excitement overcame the three Wolf children. Unable to silence the inner screams and passion of the children bouncing around in the back seat of the van, Alpha and Omega conspired a plan to keep the children occupied. As they pulled from the driveway of Wealthland to make their way to their new house in Mariano City, Alpha and Omega turned around to the children and asked, "Hey do you guys want to play a game while we are driving to our new home?"

"Yaaaaaaaay." the three children screamed with youthful anticipation. "What's the game?" they each asked, unable to contain themselves not only for the new house but for this new game.

"Okay your father is going to be the driver of the car okay. He is the captain. We have to look out for the dinosaurs that are going to be chasing the car. We cannot let them get close because if they do, they will eat us." explained Omega.

They all watched as Omega spoke eager to hear the next explanation of the game. At this time Alpha put his blinkers to signal he was about to merge onto the freeway.

"So in order to protect the vehicle it is up to you three to tell us when you see a Dinosaur and when you see it call it out so that we can navigate away. Each one of you has guns to shoot the dinosaurs as well. If we get eaten then we will not be able to make it to our new house. The dinosaur will only be cars that are silver. Whenever you see a silver car shout out to "There's a dinosaur" so that we can get away. Okay." Omega Said finishing up the explanation of the game.

"Yeah, we got it." they all remarked.

Alpha seeing the light turn green he then hit the gas and got onto the ramp to take the family to the new city. Driving up the ramp to get onto the freeway Alpha and Omega began to count down resonantly. "Three...Two...One....The game has started."

Aurelia and Cardinal had an inherent advantage in pointing out the dinosaurs over Jade because they both had the window seats. Due to the size of the young Jade, she sat in the middle seat, but her booster seat did give her just enough elevation to see over the heads of her older siblings.

"There is a dinosaur approaching fast from the right side of the car!" yelled Aurelia with excitement. "We have to shoot it before it gets too close and eats us."

"Pew pew pew pew! Bang! Pop!" They all let out a myriad of onomatopoeias.

"That dinosaur is down but look out dad we have a dinosaur gaining on us from your side you have to speed up or else it will catch us!" yelled Cardinal.

With this information Alpha once again put on his blinkers to signal he needed to merge into a different lane, simultaneously stepping a bit firmly on the gas to outrace the car approaching from the left.

"Aurelia, that is your side of the car, you have to shoot it before it gets us.

"Oh no!" expressed Jade. "Behind us we have three dinosaurs. I will shoot them down before they catch up to us."

"Come on Dad, you have to go faster or we will be caught!" The three Wolf 's anxiously expressed.

The game continued for several minutes, dinosaurs slayed and evaded. Their drive continued until they reached the bridge that would separate their old life and bring them to a new one. Mariano City. The forest green colored sign greeted you the moment you crossed over the bridge. Lines of countless cars began to become more evident as many cars waited in line to pay the toll of crossing the bridge. Tall, sharp, rocky ledges surrounded the toll booths. The sound of honking and the peaceful humming of the engine of many cars merged with the noise of the children finishing up their game.

"Okay guys you ready. Once we pass through this booth we will enter into our new home. Are you guys ready for that?" Questioned Alpha as he gave the money to the booth attendant.

"Yes!" they all said with excitement.

"Welcome to Mariano City." Alpha and Omega said.

As they passed through the toll booth it seemed that the sun that had been shining on the car the entire day had a different warmth to it. The flavor of the snacks that had been consumed during the journey to the new city seemed to taste a bit different. The sound of the revving engine became a melodic symphony. At this point the game had ended and the family began to discuss the new things that they saw as they were entering the city.

"Oh look, it's a McDonalds!" Aurelia said with excitement.

"Wow this place has a McDonalds too!" Cardinal and Jade both expressing similar excitement. "This city is amazing." they all began to proclaim with full acceptance of the new city they would soon call home. Ten minutes went by effortlessly and the Wolf family finally pulled into the driveway of their new home.

"Welcome home Wolf family." Alpha and Omega said to their young children.

The van doors opened up much more swiftly today for the young Wolfs could not wait to claim the place they would be staying for what they would deem to be forever. "Slam." the sound the van doors made as the children closed the vehicle doors to conclude their long journey. The front door swung open and the smell of a once foreign house filled the nose of each of the children and the parents. They breathed in the smell and they took in the emptiness that this house held. Eager to fill the house with memories the children ran right into the rooms and began to unpack. Aurelia and Jade got the bigger room while Cardinal received the smaller one. The texture of the walls embraced Cardinal, begging him to transform the blankness with the posters of Bruce Lee that he had brought with him. The sun eager to shine through the dusty shades pierced through the small crack letting in just enough sunlight to hug Cardinal's skin. Cardinal then reached up and swung the shades open to let in all the glory that was shining in on his new fortress, one free from terror, "games", and Suits.

The Wolfs unpacked all of their things from the clothes to the furniture that they needed and began to fill the house. Their new home. The summer ended fairly quickly. Jade, Aurelia, and Cardinal were able to make new friends with the neighbors. They would play tag and hide and seek for most of the day. Catch, skating, and riding bikes were other activities that they enjoyed during that summer. It was a glorious time to be alive. But as the sun became less intense and the leaves began to fall, so was the end of summer. It was time to go back to school. A time of dread for every child.

"The school is right down the street. I want you three to walk together. Do not leave one another. Make sure you are at school on time. If you are not in school when you are supposed to be, I will spank you. Are we clear?" asked Omega, releasing her children on their first day.

"Yes!" answered Aurelia "Yes!" answered Jade "Yes!" answered Cardinal

"Okay go grab your lunches. They are in the kitchen. I love y'all. I have to go to work but be safe and try to make some friends." Omega said, kissing each one on the forehead before getting in the car to drive across the bridge.

"Come on guys, let's go before we are late. I ain't taking a spanking for not one of y'all." exclaimed Aurelia.

The three of them left the house. Today was particularly cold. The fog swallowed the visibility to the point that the Wolf children could not see more than two houses down the street. Their backpacks full of supplies and food, and their brains eager to learn they continued their way into the school. After several minutes of walking, they finally arrived. Nickel Elementary School. A beautiful school full of possibilities and potential friendships; unfortunately for Cardinal, ever since the day his innocence had been stripped from him, he became more and more withdrawn from meeting new people. Cardinal for most of his life had been a very silly and outgoing individual, although now that personality has become more and more dissolved. He thus came to know his sisters as his closest friends. Meeting someone new would yield some new challenges.

"Okay guys, I'm headed to my class. See you after school. Let's meet right here in front of the school. Okay guys, bye." Words spoken by the eldest sister as she separated herself from her younger siblings. Cardinal and Jade stayed together as Cardinal humbly walked his younger sister to her class before making his way to his classroom. Classroom 23. "Room 23? Where is room 23?" he began to ask himself as he continued walking through the hallways. Every step he took was a step of anxiety as he did not look forward to introducing himself to all of the new people. Each step erupted with the sound of one hundred nuclear warheads going off in the mind of the young Cardinal. Eventually, he found the correct room and he stood in line behind all his classmates.

"Welcome in children, my name is Mrs. Crow and I will be your teacher. Come in and find your seats. I have name cards on your tables, go inside and find your name and sit there quietly. Once everyone gets to their seat, we will go through the room introducing one another okay. Come on in." Instructed

Mrs. Crow.

Mrs. Crow was a very short lady. She had thin black and gray hair curled at the top of her head. She was an older lady and the wrinkles around her eyes indicated that she did not sleep very well the night before. She had an enormous mole on her nose that made her look like the wicked witch in many iconic movies.

Cardinal came in and found his seat and sat down. The moment he situated himself he felt someone tap him on the shoulder.

"Hey man can we switch seats because you are sitting next to my best friend and I want to sit with her." the random child pleaded.

"Yeah, ok." Cardinal answered without hesitation.

Some time elapsed and Mrs. Crow opened up the floor for the kids to start introducing themselves to one another. "I want each one of you to stand up at your table and tell us what your name is, where you are from, and something that you like to do. We will start over here." At that point each child spoke up and introduced themselves. It became evident that Cardinal may be one of the only people that was not from Mariano City. Stress began to overwhelm Cardinal and his heart began to beat fast for now it was his turn to introduce himself to the class.

"Hi my name is Cardinal Wolf, I am from Wealthland, and I like to play outside with my two sisters." Cardinal then sat down with speed and conviction. A couple more kids stood up to speak and then one of the last kids stood up and spoke.

"Hi my name is Azure Bear. I am from Florida. I like to play with my brother and my sisters outside."

What were the odds? Someone else that was not from this city that also may need a friend. The possibilities raced through the head of Cardinal as he contemplated how he would talk to Azure. Before he could it all through Mrs. Crow informed the kids that it was time for recess. They were ushered to go out to the yard and play. All the kids yelled with excitement and they ran outside. The only two that slightly hesitated were Azure and Cardinal. "This was the perfect opportunity to introduce myself." Cardinal thought. It must have been a shared thought because as Cardinal went to approach Azure, Azure was approaching Cardinal.

"Hey, my name is Cardinal." "Hey my name is Azure."

They both shook hands and began to talk about their move from their hometowns to this new place they would now have to learn to call home.

After befriending Azure, it seemed that time no longer stood still, in fact time moved relatively fast. Before Cardinal even knew it, time had come for him to meet with his sisters in front of the school. He gathered his things and as he was leaving, he found Azure.

"Hey Azure it was nice meeting you. Where do you live?" Cardinal asked.

"I live right around the corner. That way." Azure pointed.

"Wow, that is amazing we do not live top far from one another. I live right around the corner too; I live that way." Cardinal pointed.

"Cool. Maybe we can play together this weekend?" Azure stated hopingly.

"Yeah, that would be awesome. Why don't you tell your mom my mom said it was cool." Cardinal conspired.

"Yeah, and you tell your mom that my mom said it was cool." Azure conspired.

"Okay sounds good. I have to meet my sisters at the front of the school. I will see you again tomorrow. Bye." Cardinal said running towards the front of the school.

"Ok see you tomorrow." Azure responded.

Cardinal met his sisters in front of the school and with a smile on his face he questioned them about their days. They talked while they walked home and he learned they also met people that were friendly and they looked forward to coming back to school. They continued walking up the windy hill until they got home. They entered the house where they began doing their homework. Alpha and Omega had not returned home from work yet, and the kids knew that they had chores that they needed to do before their parents got home. Cardinal took out the trash that had piled high. Jade cleaned the bathroom which just needed some attention to the toothpaste drying on the sink. And Aurelia simply organized the kitchen. Several hours elapsed and Alpha returned home from work.

"Daddy!" they all screamed with excitement to see their dad walk through the door.

"Hey little ones, how was your day?"

The four of them began talking about how awesome each one of their days were when they heard another car pull up to the front of the house. Omega was home.

"Mommy!" They all ran to embrace her. With groceries in hand, Omega began asking about their day. The Wolf kids disclosed their day and how awesome it was and before they knew it, dinner time had come. They all sat down at the table and Alpha instructed everyone to close their eyes so that he could pray over the food.

"Thank you Jesus for this food that we are about to receive. I pray that you will bless the nutrition of our bodies and our minds. If there is anything in this food that shouldn't be, I pray that you take it out. Thank you for the hands that prepared this food. In Jesus' name we pray. Amen."

"Amen!" they all said in unison.

After dinner had concluded, the Wolf's finished their homework, bathed and then were ushered to bed.

"Well done today Stress and Fear we successfully applied ourselves today." Abuse congratulating his companions.

"Yes and the best part is that Cardinal has worked hard to forget about us so now we have nothing to fear." Fear proclaimed.

"I don't know if I would say that twin. We should probably still stress the fact that Abuse was not able to see past a certain point in this boy's life. That is concerning." Stress stated.

"Yes true, but did you see how scared he was when he had to go into that classroom all alone. That charismatic boy is no more. We have successfully defeated him." Abuse further gawked. "I don't know what selfishness was talking about. Ha. Tough cookie that boy is a mere shell of what he used to be and it's all thanks to me."

"You are starting to sound a lot like Selfishness, Abuse. "Hey, quiet. I'm just saying."

"Well, I would love to stick around here and talk with you Abuse but Stress and I have got some work to do tonight. We have to scare Cardinal." Fear stated just before vanishing.

"Selfishness was wrong about me. I will get promoted and I will forever be with Cardinal. Forever." Abuse proclaims to himself.

A VIVID DREAM

"I don't know why they treat me like a little fish in here. Did they forget that I was a Jacket before I was demoted to being a Suit. Shoot, the amount of damage I can do to Cardinal would be legendary, in fact I could have him trapped for years. I probably could do a lot more damage with Abuse working with me, but he is so stupid." Addiction spoke in the void.

"Honestly, I have done some good work on Cardinal's Father, did they forget about that? It was because of the work that I did on that man that I got promoted to be a Jacket. I will show them. I will connect with Cardinal, and I will do some fine; lasting work on him." Addiction spoke.

Addiction knew that her time to wreak havoc on Cardinal was soon to come, but first she had to be patient. She sat quietly for a few moments observing the void of the heart of man before vanishing. As Cardinal slept in his warm bed that night he was confronted with Fear, Stress, and another being he had not yet met before. This night was much different than many other nights because Cardinal did not have a nightmare, he had a vivid dream.

"Hey Omega, is it weird that my finger hurts? it feels like someone is beating on my left finger with a hammer." Alpha stated "I don't know! But I told you that you need to air yourself out before coming to bed because the smell of cigarettes makes me sick. You know what, you can have the bed. I'm going to sleep on the couch." Omega proclaimed upset.

....Wait, did you say your finger was throbbing?" Omega questioned as she walked away.

"Yeah. It feels like someone's beating on it with a hammer" Alpha confessed.

"Let me call the advice nurse to see what they have to say about that." OMEGA claimed.

"Thank you for calling the Kaiser help desk. If you have a medical emergency, we recommend that you call 911." Narrated the automated messenger.

"Thank you for calling the Kaiser advice nurse line, how may I help you?" Questioned the nurse.

"Yes my name is Omega and my husband is stating that his finger is throbbing." Omega responded.

"What other symptoms does your husband exhibit?" The nurse proceeded to probe.

"He says that his chest is also hurting and it feels like he has indigestion." Omega further explains.

"Is your husband there with you right now?" the nurse asked with concern.

"Yes he is in the other room." Omega said.

"Can you put him on the line for me please." Asked the nurse.

Omega pulled the warm sheets back from her tired body and placed her swollen feet on the ground. She cautiously maneuvered through the darkness of the room to get to the light switch. She flipped the switch, and instantly the light cut through all the darkness. Her eyes fluttered as she tried to adjust to the change. Once she had her bearings, she navigated through the hallway to get to her husband who was standing in the kitchen drinking a cup of water. She then explains to him that the advice nurse wanted to ask him a few questions. She hands the phone over to Alpha and goes to sit down to rest her feet. At that moment Alpha began to speak.

"Hi my name is Alpha. I told my wife that my finger hurts, my chest hurts, what is wrong with me?" He questioned.

"Sir, do you have a history of heart attack and stroke and your family?" The nurse asked.

"None at all." Alpha responded with confidence.

"Do not panic sir, but I think it would be in your best interest to take a few aspirins and come to the hospital. I think you may be exhibiting symptoms of a heart attack." The nurse advises.

"You guys are Trippin!" Alpha fearfully proclaims.

Alpha then hangs the phone up and walks over to his wife to discuss what the advice nurse just said.

"Hey babe those people were Trippin they said I'm having a heart attack isn't that crazy." Alpha snickers as he attempts to lay on the couch.

"You need to get your clothes on and go to the hospital right now!" Omega aggressively demands.

"You cannot be serious." Alpha remarks

"Do exactly what she said and go now. You are not gonna leave me a single mother. Go now!" Omega demands.

Alpha begrudgingly puts his clothes back on, then takes the car and drives down to the hospital where he checks into the emergency room. Alpha walks up to the counter and says to the clerk why he is there.

"Hi my name is Alpha Wolf; I called the advice nurse and they said to come in because they think I'm having a heart attack." Alpha said jokingly.

"Sir, let's get you into a room ASAP." The clerk states with urgency.

The clerk disappears behind a door just leaving Alpha to stand at the counter. As he stands tapping his finger on the desk, he looks to see all the patients waiting to be seen. Before he could make up his mind to go take a seat the clerk rushed back out to the lobby with a team of doctors and a stretcher. They then called his name.

"Alpha please lay on the stretcher, we need to roll you back" one of the doctors instructed.

Alpha followed the instruction of the doctor and laid on the stretcher. Still in disbelief that his young 35-year-old body could even be susceptible to a heart attack. They then began rolling his body back to a room where they could take his vitals. In that moment Alpha expressed a difference in his body.

"Wait something is happening, I feel like my chest is gonna explode. I think I just need to close my eyes." Alpha says with a lack of energy.

The doctors then began to rush through the vacant hallways of the hospital to get back to the empty room they prepared for Alpha. The urgency they exhibited had their white and blue coats flowing in the wind as they looked at him with concern. They then arrived at the room; the moment they entered Alpha's eyes began to close. The clear vibrant words of the doctors and nurses began to fade into murmuring and mutterings. The doctors and nurses expeditiously worked as they attempted to take his blood, temperature, and pulse. Alpha, unable to keep his eyes open, drifted into a deep sleep. His breathing shallowed and his heart stopped. At that point a dark figure emerged from the chest of the lifeless Alpha. The figure was cloaked in all black, and in his right hand he held a dagger. This figure was none other than death himself. Surrounding death were several Suits, each one reflective of the life that Alpha decided to live. Addiction, Stress, Fear, and Violence all gathered around the lifeless body and celebrated their victory.

Cardinal woke up with a gasp unable to comprehend what he just experienced. As tears swelled up inside of his eyes, he sat there in the dark trying to make sense of what he had just dreamed. Was it a nightmare? Was it a vision? What did he just witness? These would be things Cardinal would think about for years to come. Finally finding some peace, Cardinal fell back asleep. Several hours later the sun emerged from behind the hills. Cardinal woke up that morning and made it a mission to go and hug his father. He woke up and rushed to his father who was sitting on the couch eating a donut and drinking his coffee. Cardinal embraced the chest of his father and squeezed tightly. Alpha looked down at the curly head of his young son and was confused as to why his son seemed to be so passionate about this hug.

"What's going on son?" Alpha asked concerned.

"It's nothing, I just love you dad." Cardinal responds, "Well OK just make sure you're not late for school." Alpha stated just before going outside to smoke a cigarette.

Cardinal Put on his favorite T-shirt. The shirt was black containing three dogs; a Pitbull, Rottweiler, and a Doberman Pinscher each one had a long gold chain. He put on his blue jeans and his black tennis shoes. He then went inside the restroom to wash his face and brush his teeth. Once he finished, he cupped his hands and filled it with the crystal cold water that ran from the faucet. He then splashed all the water on his face. After leaving the bathroom, he walked into the kitchen where his younger sister Jade was making lunches for everyone.

"Hey Jade how did you sleep last night?" Asked Cardinal. "I slept really good! I am so excited to learn some new stuff in school!" Jade exclaimed "Me too." Stated Cardinal. This would be the day that Cardinal and his new friend Azure would make their plan for their family to meet each other.

"What kind of sandwiches are you going to make for our lunches today?" Aurelia asked "PB&J" proclaimed Jade "I am tired of PB&J why don't you make us turkey sandwiches." expelled Aurelia "Because all we have is PB&J." Jade responded. "Whatever" Aurelia scoffs.

They packed their lunches in their backpacks and grabbed their homework from the previous night. Once they were all ready to go Jade Aurelia and Cardinal all walked down to the school. They walked like they did every morning until they arrived to the front of the school. They stopped at the mural at the front and Aurelia said her goodbyes and walked to class. Cardinal did what he did every morning and walked Jade to class. After dropping Jade off to class, he then rushed over to his class. He stood in line and waited for the teacher to open the door. At this time Azure walked up and greeted Cardinal.

"Hey, did you talk to your parents about me coming over this weekend?" Azure questioned "Yeah, I told my mom that your mom said it was OK for you to come over." Cardinal responded.

"Awesome! I told my mom the same thing." Azure seconds "OK kids, time to come on inside." Instructed Ms. Crow.

Cardinal and Azure talked for the rest of the day to plan out their hang-out scheme. RING! The last bell went off to let the kids know that now it was time to enjoy their weekend. Cardinal and Azure gathered their stuff and walked outside and continued to talk about how they would get their parents to meet one another. At that moment, Cardinal had seen something that he had never seen before. It was not a faceless being dressed in a Suit, it was a hooded figure engulfed in white. Around the brim of his hood was gold, and his countenance was kind and sweet.

"Hey dude. Do you see that guy's white hoodie over there?" Cardinal openly expressed pointing in the direction of the faceless being.

"Naw man, what are you talking about?" Azure responded. Cardinal, being quick on his feet made something up so as to not shock Azure.

"Oh man, you were just too slow he just left. It was a pretty sick hoodie though." Cardinal lied. This being existed in the same realm as the Suits. Although I did not dress like a suit nor did it react like a suit it was still something that Cardinal could only see. Cardinal became confused. He said goodbye to Azure and Azure began to walk to his house. At that moment the hooded figure began to walk away.

"Wait who are you? What's your name?" asked Cardinal "Young man my name is Friendship." Introduced the hooded figure. "I am what is known as a Virtue, but you can relate to us as Hoodies. We Hoodies exist in the same realm as the Suits. We do not exist in the same home for we are opposites. Today you have made a friend out of the young boy Azure. He will be your friend for a lifetime. I am proud that you have broken through your shell and have found someone to call a friend. There are many hooded individuals like me but I cannot tell you, their names. Through your journey of life, you will endure a lot. You will see many Suits and many Hoodies. Do not block us out, embrace that you can see us because whether or not you admit we're there, we're there." Friendship spoke with conviction before turning around and vanishing before Cardinal. Azure turned around yelled back at Cardinal to verify he did not need anything else.

"Hey buddy did you say something to me?" Azure asked. "Naw man, you're good. I'll see you soon!" Cardinal yelled back.

Cardinal amazed and excited by what just happened, he ran to his sisters at the mural. Out of breathe Cardinal said, "You guys won't believe what just happened."

FRIENDSHIP

"What happened?" Jade asked "Yeah, what happened" seconds Aurelia "I made a friend. This guy is pretty cool, he is from Florida. He wants to come over this weekend and we have devised the perfect plan to get our parents to meet each other." Cardinal said with enthusiasm.

"What are you guys gonna do?" Jade questioned, intrigued to hear the plan.

"I am gonna tell Mom and Dad that his Mom and Dad said it was cool for him to come over. He is gonna tell his mom and dad that our mom and dad said it was okay for him to come over. Then I am just going to tell mom and dad that he is going to be coming over at 6. He is going to tell his parents that we will be expecting them at 6. It is the perfect plan. What do y'all think?" Cardinal asked with a big smile on his face.

"That does not sound like the best plan. What if mom and dad say that he cannot come over? What is his name anyways?" Aurelia asked.

"His name is Azure and even if mom and dad said that he cannot come over it will be too late anyways because he will already be on the way. So this is why it is the perfect plan because one way or the other he will come over. Now I may get a spanking for doing this but that is the risk I am willing to take." Cardinal explained.

"Ok, well it seems like you already have your mind made up. We better start walking home or else dad will get mad at us." Aurelia instructed as they made their way home.

The three Wolfs started their journey home. They walked past all the familiar houses and distinctions that made this walk similar to many others. Today for Cardinal this walk home was extremely exciting and stressful for he did not know how his plan would turn out. Every step closer to the house yielded anticipation for the move that he was going to make. As they came around the last house in the neighborhood the three Wolfs ran to the house like they usually did. The moment they crossed the threshold of the home they yelled out, "We are home." Alpha emerged from the back of the house where he usually would be playing video games and watching television. He approached his kids and hugged each of them.

"Hello children. How was school?" Alpha asked.

"School was amazing we……." Aurelia began to speak. At this point Cardinal was so worked up because of what he was going to say today that time began to move in slow motion. He looked at the mouth of his talking sister only to find that he could not really hear her voice. All he could distinguish is a few words here and there. "And that is how you can solve for X." Aurelia concluded her lesson learned from the day.

"Wow you are so smart." Alpha recognized. "Okay who is next? Cardinal, how was school?"

"School was cool. I made a friend whose name is Azure and he is from Florida where I learned from him that there are alligators that walk around the streets. Isn't that cool. They are like little dinosaurs. I also learned how to count money and how to give change. Like if something costs 50 cents and you give a dollar then you get 50 cents back." Cardinal shakingly stated.

"Wow, son that is amazing and you made a friend today that is wonderful." Alpha remarks. "Okay Jade your turn. How was school?"

"School was nice. I learned about colors." Jade expressed. "That is amazing baby. Now that you all have expressed to me the day you had, I need you three to go grab a snack and do your chores. Aurelia since you did not do the dishes last night get in the kitchen and go clean the dishes. Cardinal go take out the trash and the recycling then vacuum the floor. Jade go clean the bathroom. When you are all done with that, go and clean your rooms. It's a pigsty in there. Make sure you guys have this done before your mother gets home cause I do not want her yelling." Alpha instructed them before going back into the back of the house to finish his movie.

Cardinal walked into the kitchen and opened the fridge. The cool breeze of the fridge brushed over the arm of Cardinal. The smell of freshly prepared taco meat from last night's dinner waffed in the nose of Cardinal. He bent down and opened the produce bin to grab an Apple. His favorite fruit. He pulled the apple out and carried it over to the counter to cut the apple into 8 slices. The slices he would then dip into peanut butter, his favorite snack. Jade and Aurelia during this time grabbed a much more simplistic snack. A bag of chips. They filled their small sandwich bags with well-seasoned nacho cheese chips and sat at the table. The three of them began to eat their snack. Crunch Crunch Crunch came from the mouths of the three young Wolfs as they consumed their snacks. The sounds persisted for 5 minutes before the snacks had fully been consumed, the time had come for them to knock out their chores. Aurelia disappeared back into the kitchen where she began to wipe off the kitchen counters. Jade walked in the opposite direction where she entered the bathroom to prepare working on the toilet. Cardinal walked into the kitchen right behind Aurelia and picked up the recycling and the trash and walked it outside into the backyard. He threw the trash into the gray bin and the recycling he pretended he was on the court of a famous basketball game and was being defended to make the finishing shot.

"Cardinal is being guarded by two players now. Oh no the clock is counting down. Will he get enough space to make the shot. 10. 9. 8. 7. 6. 5. 4. 3. 2." Before saying the number one Cardinal turns around and throws up the bottle. The bottle turns end over end as it floats through the air. At that moment Cardinal finishes the final count,

"One. eeeeeeennnnn." he lets out just as the bottle began to descend into the bottom of the recycling bin.

"And the crowd goes wild. Aaaaaaaaaa." Cardinal pretends as he screams and dances in the backyard. He then places the remaining recycling in the bin before returning into the house. He walks past his sister Aurelia as her task changed from cleaning the counters to cleaning the dishes. He walked past her and picked all the shoes, socks, and other miscellaneous items off the ground so that he could complete his tasks. Today he made sure to do them even more perfectly so there could be no reason he could get into any trouble with his parents. He walked across the house to where the front door was and pulled out the vacuum. Cardinal untangles the cord and plugs the vacuum cleaner into the wall and began to vacuum the floor. He pushed and pulled the vacuum across the floor until the brushes of the vacuum created strokes of cleanliness in the carpet. After the entire room was vacuumed, Cardinal moved from the living room to the hallway. He continued this room to room until his task was complete. Several hours had passed and Cardinal had realized that it was almost 5:30 and his mother would be home any moment. He had to pick up the pace and finish his work so that he could tell his parents what was going to happen by 6.

Cardinal ran to his room and picked up all his clothes and threw them in his hamper and cleaned up all his toys. He could not help that he was getting more and more nervous. Stress then entered the room. Stress stared Cardinal right in the face and reached out to Cardinal. Cardinal flinched as he did not know what Stress was planning. Suddenly, he felt his stomach start to turn. He looked down to see that stress had his hand in his belly. Stress turned his hand in a circle and with each turn of his hand Cardinal felt more and more sick. Stress also had his hand on Cardinal's heart and began to squeeze it rapidly. Cardinal could feel his heart rate increase. Before he could open his mouth to confront Stress, his mother opened the front door.

"Honey, I'm home." Omega shouts as she walked into the house with groceries in her hands. "Y'all go outside and get the rest of the bags out of the car." she instructed.

The three Wolfs came out of their rooms to see their parents in the living room kissing each other on the lips passionately.

"Eeeeeewwwwww! That's nasty." The three Wolfs said in unison.

"How do you think yall got here? Ha..Ha." Alpha says separating himself from his wife. "You heard your mother go out there and get those groceries."

Before walking outside to get the rest of the groceries Cardinal decided this would have to be the perfect time to tell his parents Azure was coming over since it was almost 6. Stress knew its playtime with Cardinal was coming to an end so it made a final effort to paralyze Cardinal. Stress gripped Cardinal by the legs and began to shake, Cardinal could feel the strength in his legs begin to go. He mustered up the courage to finally speak.

"Mom, guess what? I made a friend today. His name is Azure and he is from Florida. He is so cool. His mom said it was okay for him to come over tonight at 6. Is that ok?" Cardinal stated with Stress still tormenting him.

"Why did you make plans with that boy today and only give us a few minutes to decide whether or not we want another child in the house?" Omega questioned. "If we were to say no then what is going to happen? It is a good thing we do not have any plans for this Friday night. Yeah, it is okay for him to come over but I need to talk to his mother first." Omega concluded.

It seemed to all be going to plan, Cardinal thought. But wait she had to talk to his mother first, this would thwart his attempt to get him over. Cardinal then confessed that he did not have his friend's number and they already discussed 6 o'clock. Omega looked intently into the eyes of his son and said.

"Well, I will still have to talk to her before he can come into the house."

Omega finished before walking into her room and closing the door.

Cardinal joined his sisters outside. They gathered the groceries and ran back into the house. They brought the heavy bags into the kitchen where they began to unpack the bags and put away the food. Omega emerged from her room where she entered the kitchen and started preparing dinner. 6 o'clock hit and there was no sign of Azure. Maybe he forgot, or worse, maybe Azure's mom would not let him come over today. Perhaps I made a mistake planning this get-together, Cardinal began to think. 6:30 rolled around and still nothing.

At this point the dinner was ready and Omega called out, "Dinner is ready. Everyone to the dinner table."

They all ran to the bathroom to wash their hands to eat dinner. As they waited one behind the other, they began to chant. "Wash your hands…..so you can eat….wash your hands….so you can eat." After they had finished washing, they all sat down at the dinner table.

Alpha spoke. "Okay everyone bow your heads and close your eyes. Thank you Jesus for this food that we are about to receive. I pray that you will bless the nutrition of our bodies and our minds. If there is anything in this food that shouldn't be, I pray that you take it out. Thank you for the hands that prepared this food. In Jesus' name we pray. Amen."

"Amen!" they all said in unison.

They then picked up their forks and began to eat. Slightly defeated that his friend did not show up, Cardinal picked up his fork sadly. Before placing the food into his mouth, the doorbell rang. "Ding Dong." "Could it be," he instantly thought. Cardinal slammed his fork on the table and ran to the front door.

"AZURE! YOU'RE HERE! COME IN!" Cardinal spoke excitedly.

"Before my son steps foot in the house I need to speak to your mother, young man." said the Mother of Azure.

"Okay I'll go get her." Cardinal said incandescently happy. "Mom, Azure is at the front door and his mom wants to speak to you."

Omega got up from the table and began to walk to the front door. Cardinal followed slowly behind to see what was going to happen with this encounter. Omega reached the front door and opened her mouth and said.

"Hello my name is Omega Wolf and my son tells me that you agreed to let your son come over to our house today, is that right?"

"It is wonderful to meet you Omega my name is Carolina Bear. Azure is my son. You know it's funny because my son told me that you agreed to let him come over." Carolina said confused.

"Why don't you come inside." Omega said while opening the door more to let them in the house. "Here sit down on the couch. Are you hungry we are just finishing dinner."

"No, it is okay we just finished eating ourselves." Carolina confesses.

"Boys, why don't you go play so we can talk." Omega proclaimed.

"Yes, we definitely need to talk." Carolina agreed. "Okay" replied Cardinal.

"Sweet" seconded Azure.

"Let me show you my room." Cardinal urged as they ran to his room.

After being in his room for some time Cardinal realized that he had not yet introduced Azure to the rest of his family.

"Let me introduce you to my sisters." said Cardinal "You have sisters too?" Azure asked.

"Too? You mean you have sisters?" Cardinal questioned.

"Yeah, I have 2 older sisters and 1 younger brother." Azure responded.

"Wow, that is cool. Yeah, let me introduce you to my older and younger sister." Cardinal stated.

The two boys ran back down the hallway. As they turned the corner to go back into the dining room, they passed Omega and Carolina sitting on the couch. Neither one of them knew exactly what was being said but they did notice the smile that was on the face of their mothers. At that time, Cardinal witnessed in the center of the room Friendship standing with its hands on both of their shoulders. It was at that time Cardinal knew that they created a bond with one another. They walked into the back of the house where Jade, Alpha, and Aurelia were sitting watching TV.

"Guys this is Azure my friend. This is the guy I had been talking about." Cardinal said.

After introducing Azure, they all began to talk and laugh.

Time elapsed and Carolina called for Azure.

"It was so nice meeting you Omega, but it is getting late and I have to get him back home so that he can take his medicine." Carolina confessed.

"No problem, it was my pleasure meeting you and your family is welcome in this house anytime." Omega said giving a hug to Carolina. "It was also nice meeting you Azure, you can come over anytime you like."

Cardinal and Azure said their goodbyes and the Bears left the house. The moment the door closed Omega turned and looked at Cardinal and ordered him to go grab a belt. He was going to get spanked. In that moment he felt the joy of what happened leave his body. He walked slowly through the hallway. Each step he took towards his parents' room was a step closer to his demise. Sweat began to pour down the side of his face. Just before he touched the door knob to grab a belt Omega opened her mouth and called him back.

"Cardinal Wolf, come here. I am going to ask you one time. Did Azure's mother actually tell him that he could come over?"

Terrified of the punishment that would ensue if he lied, Cardinal told her the truth.

"No, she didn't. We both made the whole thing up. We did it because we really wanted the family to be friends and we thought this was the best way to get him over here."

Omega smiled and patted Cardinal on the head. "Son you did not have to do that to get him over here all you had to do is ask. They seem to be a fantastic family and I could see why you two are friends. You both share a common mind. To be honest his mom is pretty Awesome." Omega says jokingly to make Cardinal more at ease.

"Okay." Cardinal confirmed before being dismissed to go back to watch TV with his siblings.

The night ended well and as Omega and Carolina had said, Azure came over often and Cardinal visited their house as well. The girls met one another and became friends. The Bears and the Wolfs were now a strong unit. A year elapsed and nothing had really changed until one day. The Wolfs came home from school like they normally did, they had their normal snack, they did their normal chores, and their mother came home at her normal time. The one thing that the Wolf children could not answer is why wasn't their father present in the home. They did not dwell on the thought for too long because they had things that they had to do. Omega came through the door at her normal time but rather than expressing her joy of being home she instructed each of the Wolfs to sit down.

"Guys today I have some bad news."

A CHILD'S PRAYER

"Thank you Jesus for the day. I pray that you will protect us as we sleep tonight. I pray that you give my Dad the strength and the courage to stop smoking cigarettes. I pray that you will give me a brother. In the name of Jesus I pray…..Amen."

This was a prayer that Cardinal prayed every night since he was six years old. He loved his sisters and the relationship he had with them but more than anything, what he really wanted was a brother. He prayed this prayer fervently and religiously for years, since the time he lived with his Grand Daddy. It was now two years later and a lot had changed. He no longer lived with his Grand Daddy, he now had a place that he could call his own, he had now accepted the fact that he could see beings that no one else could and he had made a friend that he would categorize as a brother. The one thing that Cardinal was jealous of Azure was that every night he got to play and spend time with his little brother, Spectrum. Cardinal wanted that interaction but he knew that he may never get that because his parents vowed they were done having children. 3 was the maximum; nonetheless, Cardinal still prayed this prayer because just as much as he believed that a miracle could make his dad stop smoking, he also believed that a miracle could give him a brother.

"Guys sit down, I have some big news for y'all." Omega said.

The Wolf 's sat on the couch with anticipation for what their mother could have for them. Are we getting a new puppy? Are we moving again? Am I finally going to get that snake? These were all the thoughts circulating in the mind of Cardinal.

"I'm pregnant."

Silence fell over the room the moment those two words left Omega's mouth.

"Wait, did you say pregnant?" Questioned Cardinal. "Meaning you are going to give birth to another baby?"

"Yes son. Your father and I gave it a lot of thought and we decided to have another child." Replies Omega.

"So are we having a sister or brother?" Jade asks. All the other Wolf 's sitting waiting for the words to escape Omega's mouth.

"I don't know." Answered Omega Alpha suddenly interrupts

"Your mother does not know because she chooses to not know. She wants to be surprised. Little ones, there are but so many things in life that can really give you an honest surprise and one of them is revealing the sex of the baby the day they are born. So your mother has chosen to find out the day the baby is born. That being said I cannot wait that long so I have decided to find out what we will be having. Do not ask me what the baby is because I am not telling you, cause y'all don't know how to keep a secret and someone is going to tell your mother."

"Okay answer me this, am I going to have a brother?" Cardinal asks emphatically.

"I guess you will have to wait and see." Replied Omega.

IGNORANCE

Cardinal waited patiently for the next 9 months for the birth of the new member of the family. He had prayed for a brother for so long and it seemed that God had heard his prayer and gave him what he wanted. He did not have a certainty that this child was a boy, but he knew that prayer worked and that his prayer had been answered with this new baby. The names began to flow through the mind of the young Cardinal because as far as he was concerned this child was his. He cleaned and managed his room for the new baby to be born. He sectioned off sides of the room that would undoubtedly be the living quarters for his new brother. Cardinal had Joy.

While Cardinal was preparing for the birth of a new baby the Heart of Man also took in a new member to the enterprise. This day for Abuse was a bit different than most days because normally the heart of man would be crowded with noise and screams, but for some reason today was silent.

"What is going on here?" Abuse questioned.

His voice bounced around the empty void. As he stood there bewildered by the sight of emptiness he began to pace back and forth thinking about his plan. He seemed to be doing a great job trapping Cardinal with the help of his new compadres but he needed a guarantee of a sure fire way to know that he would have Cardinal forever. As he paced back and forth, he noticed a small fragile looking Suit sitting by themself. The Suit looked like a small child and it appeared to be weak. Something about this Suit was different from the rest of the Suits. The countenance of this Suit seemed pleasant and soft but something about it confused Abuse. Why was this Suit alone and where was everyone else? Abuse approached the sitting Suit to question why it was there.

"Hey what are you doing here by yourself?" asked Abuse. "I don't know?" responded the suit.

"Where is everyone?" Abuse seconded. "I don't know." the Suit seconded.

"Who is your superior, and why haven't I seen you before?" Abuse probed.

"I don't know." The Suit answered.

"Do you know anything?" Abuse asked irritated by the back and forth.

"I don't know." The Suit responded even more melodramatically.

"Well, what is your name?" Abuse continued. Before the Suit could answer, Abuse interjected "Lemme guess. I don't know." The suit shook its head in agreement.

"Well, we need to figure out where you belong cause I need answers and clearly you do too. Come on get up and let's go find out where you came from." Abuse said reaching out to grab the young suit's hand. The Suit reached back and took the hand of Abuse and they walked through the empty hallways. The darkness consumed both of their bodies as they walked and Abuse began to notice something about this Suit. He wore the same attire as the rest of the Suits but he looked like he was developing characteristics of a Blazer.

Blazers were much like Suits for they shared similar qualities. The difference is that Blazers were much more powerful and they had redeeming characteristics. Abuse feared one Blazer in particular named Selfishness. Selfishness started off as a Suit but due to the damage that it produced, it grew and became more powerful than a Suit. One thing that Abuse noticed about Selfishness was that when she was about to get promoted certain things changed. No Suit has any human type facial features but Selfishness began to start forming eyes. Ones that had clearer vision than any suit could even ask for, and this was something that Abuse was pushing for. He needed the ability to be able to see things clearly so that he could see the day of his demise and try and change the outcome for good.

As he began to look at this young Suit, he noticed that some small pupils began to form. Why did this Suit that I had never seen before look like he ranked higher than me? Abuse began to ponder in his own head.

They continued walking through the halls and the rooms and to no avail no noise and no Suits. What was going on?

"Hey I didn't notice back then but it looks like you have some pupils. Tell me, are you ranked?" Abuse began to ask.

"Ranked? What is that?" the Suit questioned.

"You really are dumb, aren't you? Know what, that is what I am going to call you Dumb." Abuse stated before letting out a small chuckle. "Ok Dumb let's keep walking let's sneak into Blazer hall and see if we can find your superior there."

Abuse took the Suit called dumb by the hand and they began to walk through the void. Every step they took echoed in the emptiness that was the Heart of Man. *click clack click clack click clack* every step echoed. They walked for what seemed forever until they came to the stairway of ascension. No suit could walk up this stairway unless accompanied by a Blazer, but Abuse had planned for this. Because Dumb had specific characteristics that mirrored that of an established Blazer, he would be able to gain access to walk the Stairway.

"Ok, so this is what we are going to do Dumb. We are going to walk up that stairway and we are going to see if we can figure out where you came from so that we can get you back there. We also need to......" before Abuse could finish his statement, he noticed that the hand he was holding of the young Suit began to tighten up. "Hey what's wrong with you Dumb?" Abuse asked.

"It's something about this stairway...I have been here before...and it is because I've been here before that I know exactly what you are trying to do with me." Dumb responded.

"Wait. Wait. Wait. Wait just a minute were you playing me the entire time." Abuse rebutted at the situation.

"No, it is not in my nature to play, if you are looking for a suit like that you should speak to Folly she is good for jokes. No see, I was in a place I had never been to before and that room left me lost and confused. Thank you for helping me to find my bearings because seeing this stairway has helped me to remember who I am. My name is Ignorance and contrary to what you believe about me I am the furthest thing from dumb; in fact, I was able to deduce your simple little plan the moment we got here."

"And what is my simple plan then?" Abuse snarled.

"You saw some small, helpless and broken looking Suit sitting in the middle of the floor and you thought this would be a good opportunity to try and acquire another member to help you with your mission. Once we started walking and talking, you saw how "dumb" I was and you thought that I wouldn't be suitable for your plan. It wasn't until you noticed that I had been in the process of getting promoted that your plan of action switched from recruiting me to using me; thus, you decided that you would infiltrate the upper floor. You do not have access to the upper floor. You were going to try and use me to go up there and uncover who I am but also to try and figure out a way you could snake and slither your way into the Tuxedo's room and grab files to help you deal with the little issue that you are having with Cardinal. You want to try and elevate and the only way you can do that is if you impress by succeeding with Cardinal; your final test. Does that sound about right to you Abuse?" explained Ignorance.

Clap, clap, clap went the sound of the hands that clapped together as Abuse stood in awe of the explanation, he heard from the now revealed Ignorance.

"Bravo! Bravo! You my friend are very smart and you seem to have a lot of data, but you see the issue with you is you have all that data but you are still just Ignorant. My final test is not Cardinal and double cross the boss is not something I would ever try but great job on noticing that I definitely attempted to abuse this relationship with my own personal agenda." Abuse stated.

"Wow now I can see it so clearly. Selfishness has an impression on you that is so strong that you even do some of the things she does." Ignorance claimed.

"What do you know about Selfishness? And don't give me that "I don't know" spill that ain't gonna work with me now." said Abuse.

"Selfishness was the one that elevated me. My eyes now are all thanks to her. I could not have gotten where I am now if it wasn't for her." Ignorance said with gratitude.

"That's right he has been my project for quite some time now." Selfishness proclaimed while descending from the stairway.

"Have you been listening to what we were saying?" Asked Abuse

"Now why would I have to do that when I knew that you would ultimately try and scheme on the little Suit Ignorance who is more powerful than you and I. I knew you would try and operate in your own fruition because you and I are alike." Selfishness proclaimed.

"Just you wait I will ascend to a higher rank than you and your little boy toy Selfishness." Explained Abuse

"Come now Ignorance we have some work to do, we want to get you out of that suit and into a blazer as soon as we can." Selfishness spoke before grabbing Ignorance by the hand and ascending up the stairway.

"Wait before you go there is something that I would like to know. Where is everyone?" Abuse asked.

"You don't know what just happened, Cardinal has just been baptized. His heart is at peace right now." Selfishness explains.

"Wait then why haven't we been wiped out yet?" Abuse asked concerned.

"Because there are depths to this Heart that not even Cardinal knows anything about so we are safe for now, but I would advise that you do something before you are one of the ones that gets expelled next Abuse." Selfishness states before disappearing.

Abuse stood at the bottom of the stairway thinking about who might have been lost after this event. It was oftly quiet in the Heart of Man but if he was able to find Suits and Blazers still here then he knew that his time that he envisioned had not quite come yet. Work needed to be done. Abuse began to walk away from the stairway and back toward his room to plan for his next entrapment.

Some time had gone by in Cardinal's life and he was having a great time with his new friend and preparing for the birth of the new baby. The month was now July 2000 and Cardinal woke up late from his sleep. He was rested and ready to make his usual routine of going and talking to his mother's belly so that the child could hear him speak.

"Wait, where is Mom?" Questioned Cardinal towards Alpha.

"Your mother is fine; she is at the hospital. She went into labor last night so I took her to the hospital. I came back home because I knew y'all would be waking up soon." Alpha assured him

"Sooooooo…..is it a Boy?' Cardinal Probed.

Alpha looked down at his son and smiled and said…...

OMEPHA

In that moment Cardinal had a rush of emotions. His throat seemed to have closed up and his heart seemed to beat at one hundred miles an hour, while also not beating at all. He looked at his father's mouth as he began to speak the words. Silence filled the room and it would appear that the words missed the ears of the young Cardinal. He pleaded with his father to say what he confessed again.

"Get your clothes on, we are going to the hospital to see your new brother Omepha." Alpha said.

In that very moment all the words penetrated Cardinal's heart. The word brother echoed in Cardinal's mind. This was the moment that he constantly prayed about and reality had finally begun to forge. Cardinal's consciousness finally allowed him to process the words of his father and he let out a loud yell in excitement. His octaves bounced off the hallway walls as he ran to his bedroom to gather his clothes so that he could see the new addition of the family. In that same moment Cardinal's sisters arose from their slumber and congregated into the hallway to figure out why Cardinal let out such a loud scream.

"What's wrong with Cardinal?" Jade asked.

"Your mom went into labor last night and has delivered a new member of the family. Y'all now have another brother." Alpha answers.

"It is so close to my birthday though. Are we still going to celebrate my birthday?" Questioned Aurelia.

"Don't worry, just because you now have a brother born just before your birthday does not mean we will not celebrate your birthday. Each one of you will be celebrated individually." Alpha assured his eldest daughter. "Now I need y'all to get dressed so we can go to the hospital so we can go see your mom and new brother." Alpha instructed.

The Wolf 's children got dressed quickly and in no time were sitting in the car waiting for their father to come out and drive them down to the hospital. They lived on a hill. The hospital was a thirty second drive from their house but the drive that day seemed like it was 30 minutes away. Alpha emerged from the house holding a bag full of their mother's belongings. Some crochet needles, some yarn, and a halfway put together blue hat and blanket. He placed the bag in the center counsel of the car and placed the car in reverse and pulled out of the driveway. As they began to roll forward Cardinal looked at the partially completed garments and began to think, how did his mother not know the sex of the baby being born but still started to crochet clothing and blankets in a traditional color for baby boys.

Alpha put the blinkers on to signal that he needed to take a left turn into the parking lot of the massive hospital. The Hospital glistened bright as the rays of the sun bounced off the large glass window panes. The multitude of people entering and exiting the large building resembles that of an ant hill. Deep in the center of this huge building was the queen that the young ones were going to see. Alpha pulled into the parking lot and let the little Wolf 's out of the back seat. They all grabbed each other's hands as they pushed towards the big sliding doors of the hospital. The doors slid open and anticipation grasped the hands of not only the Wolf 's children but also Alpha. His face glowed with happiness and pride that his bride ushered into the world a gift that the whole family would appreciate and love. They all shared the same excitement to see the new addition.

"What floor number are we getting on Daddy?" Asked Aurelia as she eagerly waited to push the button to take them to their mom.

"It's floor 12." Responded Alpha.

Aurelia pressed the button for number 12 and watched as the button illuminated red. A sudden jolt shook the inside of the elevator as it began to ascend to floor number 12. Boop boop boop the elevator spoke as it moved past each floor. The elevator let out a long Beeeeep to notify the family that it had finally reached the floor they wanted. The doors flew open granting freedom to the family to walk through the hallway until they reached the reception desk.

"Hello and who are you here to see?" questioned the nurse at the reception desk.

"Omega Wolf." Alpha answered.

"Okay she is in room 7. You all can go right in." The nurse said while pointing in the direction directly behind her.

The moment that Cardinal, Jade, and Aurelia saw the number on the wall they ran right into the room.

"Mommy!!!" They all let out a yell in unison.

"Keep it down guys, the baby is resting. He has had a long battle and needs to rest."

"What long battle?" The Wolf 's asked in unison."

"Well there were some complications during his birth. When I was pushing your brother out, he got entangled in his umbilical cord and it wrapped around his neck. It got to the point that once he was born, he was a blue color. The doctors thought that he would die because of the lack of oxygen to his brain. They took him away from me and while they had him in a separate room I just began to pray with your father. We will not allow the devil to steal this child from us. He will be healed and he will live. The moment we finished the baby breathed a breath and cried for me. I gave him some milk and he passed out. It is time for him to sleep. He has fought valiantly through life and death." Omega Testified.

"The idea of life and death is incredible. How could the entrance and introduction of someone's life also put them so close to death. That's quite the paradox." Cardinal pondered. In the midst of him thinking about this paradigm he did notice something that he overlooked when he first walked into the hospital. The light that he saw emitting from the hospital was not the light of the sun shining from the windows, but rather it was the light from the promise and purpose of all the new life in the building. He turned and looked at his new brother Omepha and he saw the brightness of his being cutting through this darkness that was also present in the corners of the room. It was a darkness that Cardinal knew and had seen before. It was almost like….

"MY DREAM." Cardinal remembered.

The darkness he saw in the corners of the room looked like the darkness that emitted from the chest of his father in the dream he had those years ago.

"This darkness, was it death, was it evil, was it pain?" Cardinal contemplated.

While he began to think what it was, he was seeing, he noticed one of the dark corners of the room swiftly conform into a hooded creature and glide over the head of his father. The darkness remained there ominous for several moments before vanishing. Fear hit Cardinal hard in that minute.

"Was this my dream? Did my mom bring in new life just so one could be snatched from the family. God forbid." Cardinal thought

Before Cardinals fear and thoughts could manifest into concern a cry let out in the room. Omepha was finally awake. The fear melted and the concern left as Cardinal knew this was the moment that he had been waiting for his entire life. The opportunity to be able to ask his mom a four worded question.

"Can I hold him?"

"Let me feed him first then you can hold him okay." Omega answered.

Omega placed her nipple on the lips of the crying baby and without thinking the baby just latched on and began to feed. It was a crazy sight to see. Something so small could eat so much. He must have really fought a hard battle. After several minutes Omega told Cardinal it was finally that time for him to be able to hold his baby brother. She wrapped him up in his blankets to the point that he looked like a small human burrito.

"Okay so you are going to cup your arm around his body then you take your other hand and cradle his head. Make sure you support his head. Babies do not have strong enough necks to support their own heads." Omega instructed.

"I got him." Cardinal responded with confidence.

"Wow, I am holding an answered prayer in my hands right now. This is a powerful feeling." Cardinal began to think.

He held the baby for several minutes before he had to give Omepha to his sisters. This was literally the best day of his life. After spending several hours in the hospital with his new family it was now time to go home and eat dinner.

At the Heart of Man the Suits began to rejoice for the new life that entered into the Wolf 's family.

"Every new birth, we get to prove our worth. Every new birth we get to prove our worth." The Suits began to sing and dance. Each one of them proud and in anticipation for the damage they could cause to a new life. Each one was happy except for the small legion of Abuse, Stress, and Fear who knew that the time for Abuse to reign in Cardinal's life was diminishing day after day and they were no closer to figuring out how to keep Cardinal entangled.

"They're all out there partying and they have no idea that anyone of them at any moment could lose grasp over someone, they are such simpletins." Abuse snarled.

"Well, my brother and I have done a fantastic job at keeping Cardinal enchained. You like the stunt we pulled today that was all Stress's idea. We used the dream that he had and we made it look real. The amount of sweat that poured off his forehead was priceless." Fear chuckled.

"Aww stop, you are giving me too much credit. I was only doing my job. confounded on what to do in that moment and I was inspired by the touches you placed in the room. The darkness that he saw freaked him out and it was all thanks to you." Stress remarked.

"Can you both stop it; you are making me Sick." Abuse stated.

"You do not look like Sick. He is over there partying." Fear pointed.

"Whatever. What about my problem?" Abuse asked.

"Like I said we are doing everything we can to keep him from moving forward, and because we are doing all the heavy lifting, we were able to get into the upper room and figure something out." Fear confessed.

"What? When? It doesn't matter, what do you now know?" Asked Abuse.

"Well, it is nothing about Cardinal, it's more so about you. Did you know that you have a sister? I bet you didn't know that your existence is actually based around another Suit that was born the same time you were and her name is Addiction. We think the reason that you are not succeeding in making any headway is because you are trying to create another big moment for yourself when all you have to do is utilize the moment you already had and capitalize on it with your sister. Addiction can be the link you have been missing." Stress emphasized.

"Wait? You mean to tell me that Addiction is my sister?

How did you fools figure this out?" Abuse questioned.

"It was easy. We are privy to certain information because of the headway we have been making. Maybe if you were more focused on moving forward you would know some things as well." Fear confessed.

"Well, anyways, Thanks for the idea guys, that's something I will consider." Abuse thanked both Stress and Fear.

"We are gonna go join the party. Come on Fear." Stress instructed.

"Right behind ya." Fear said.

"Every new birth, we get to prove our worth." The Suits sang out in unison.

That moment Abuse sat alone again and began to think. "Does this mean I am a lot like Fear and Stress? Is the reason they are making such great progress because they are both tormenting together? Is what they said about me even true or are they just trying to confuse me even more? How would I even confirm this information, it's not like I can just come out and ask Addiction if she knows this to be a fact." The questions just began to flow from Abuse. He continued to sit there and consider the possibilities as the Suits continued to party.

Cardinal returned home with Alpha, Jade, and Aurelia. They all talked about the baby for the rest of the day and remarked how excited they were to see the baby again.

A few days passed and Omega was released from the hospital with baby Omepha and he was brought into Cardinal's room to sleep. Nothing could stop the joy that Cardinal felt.

"Now I lay me down to sleep. I pray dear lord my soul to keep. If I should die before I wake, I pray dear lord my soul to take. Thank you God for another awesome day. Thank you for answering my prayer and blessing me with a baby brother. Thank you, thank you, thank you. I knew you would hear my prayer, but God could you please deliver my father from smoking. That is what I want more than anything. In the name of Jesus I pray. Thank you father and Amen." Cardinal prayed.

Time went by and they celebrated the first birthday of Omepha. Cardinal had graduated into middle school and things were looking up until God decided to answer Cardinal's prayer one night.

AMEN

Thank you Jesus for the day. I pray that you will protect us as we sleep tonight. I pray that you give my Dad the strength and the courage to stop smoking cigarettes. Thank you Lord for answering my prayer for my little brother but God I have been praying for my father to stop smoking and he has not stopped yet, Why? God I am so scared that he is going to kill himself. Please help him. In Jesus name I pray AMEN." Cardinal prayed.

This prayer had changed slightly through the year of Omepha being alive. Omepha had finally celebrated a birthday. He was now 1. He was walking around; he was talking and he was lively. Everything that Cardinal looked for in a little brother, Omepha exhibited, although, playing outside and sharing similar interests in video games seemed to be taking much longer than cardinal anticipated. For the mind of a young child, time traveled much slower than they anticipated. Even though it seemed that time took a back seat and let experience drive, Cardinal loved the moments he spent with young baby Omepha. He cradled him in his pubescent hands day and night, he fed him from his bottle, he changed his diaper, and he even became the focus for the baby to walk to.

A change had come this year as well Omega was pregnant again. It seemed that the prayer for life released an overflow rather than the singular blessing that Cardinal had asked for. Was this baby a boy or a girl? Time would tell. Friendship and Family stood in the living room of the house most days. They smiled and observed the bond expanding between the two boys and were excited for what the future held for them. Aside from the two Hoodies, there was another entity that stood by and observed the changing of the time. Abuse. Abuse stood confused because even though he was not purged yet he couldn't understand why he did not have the same effect that he used to on Cardinal. He knew that the memory from the night of his molestation still gave Cardinal nightmares, but it wasn't enough to cease and neutralize Joy.

Joy was a very beautiful Hoodie. Her hoodie was whiter than fresh snow falling from a winter sky on the east coast. She had long black hair that stood strong and round on her head. The curls and kinks demonstrated strength and her skin was richer in color than the most potent chocolate. Her lips were full and moist. She followed Cardinal very closely since the day that Omepha was born because his birth was not just an answered prayer but also something that represented the growth and development of Cardinal's new mind.

Since the day Joy showed up, Abuse had been trying to find ways to battle her and this was a crucial mistake that Abuse made to lessen his grip on the life of Cardinal.

"I do not get what I have to do to get Cardinal away from that witch. She is ruining everything. She is the only Virtue that follows so closely to him. She is impending my mission. Everything I try she just rubs his head and pats him on the back and he goes back to normal. It seems that I am not able to disrupt like I used to. I need help! Where the Hell is Fear and Stress?" Abuse's thoughts spoke loudly through the void.

In that moment Stress and Fear showed up.

"Why are you stressing Abuse? It's not like you." Stress asked.

"Yeah and why are you asking for us? Have we not been doing what we promised we would by helping you?" Questioned Fear.

"You have been doing an exceptional job helping out but this stupid Virtue has been impending my mission. I do not know how to deal with her and Cardinal at the same time and I feel that my time of purging is coming closer every day. I have no idea what I have to do." Confessed Abuse.

Fear and Stress looked deep into each other's faces. Without words being exchanged or any gestures being made it was like Fear and Stress had come to an agreement about what to do. Abuse could tell that they had come up with something by the energy that they gave off.

"What have you discovered? Tell me." ordered Abuse.

"So you have been doing everything you could to try and vandalize the heart of Cardinal but you have been using the things of Cardinal and not looking for another way." Fear disclosed.

"Yeah have you thought about maybe going to see a neutral and propositioning them to what you want. You might have to make a case for them being with us this time but Cardinal has been setting you up literally for this perfect scenario. Have you not been hearing the prayers?" Stress said.

"Wait, prayers?" Asked Abuse. "What are you guys talking about? I typically tune that stuff out but if you know something that could help my case then out with it. I do not have the time to decipher your cryptic language."

"I pray that you give my Dad the strength and the courage to stop smoking cigarettes. This is something that Cardinal has literally been asking for since he could speak. This helps you because he is not being specific. He just wants his Dad to stop smoking but consider what would happen if his Dad died. See he would be getting exactly what he prayed for and at this point, we would be able to enslave him forever. Not just that but you would most certainly be elevated for the work that you put in. The only thing you will have to do is convince a neutral to follow suit with your plan." Explained Fear.

"Yeah not to mention I would have to get into the neutrals plane and the only way to do that is to get direct consent from the head honcho and I do not know if he will just give me access to that realm just because I do not want to be purged. I have to make a compelling argument for why I need to be there. So I appreciate the plan but if I can't even get into the upper room and get information about my demise, what makes you think I will be able to convince Him that I need to be granted access to the land of the neutrals?" Abuse complaints to Fear and Stress. They stood there in disbelief that Abuse would even make a case for why he could not save himself from being purged. They stood there looking at a defeated Abuse for what seemed like a hundred years. The time seemed to pass by extremely slowly, just before Abuse could turn and walk away Violence and Addiction popped out of nowhere.

"Hey wassup Abuse we hear you have been having some issues with your human. You need to pull the reins on that boy before you get purged." Violence proclaims.

"Yeah V, if he only knew that if he hadn't rejected us years ago, he would be getting promoted tomorrow as well." Addiction boasted.

"Promoted?!?! Excuse me. How did this happen? I haven't heard anything about you two in a while. How is it that you're becoming Blazers? Abuse murmurs under his breath, "It's just not fair."

"Oh it's not just us, there are a few of us elevating tomorrow. And due to the confused look on your face, I am shocked that these two withheld this information from you." Addiction said pointing at Fear and Stress.

"Waaaaait a minute, you mean to tell me that the two idiots that have been helping me on my human are getting elevated tomorrow too. Why?" Questioned Abuse.

"Well, it is quite simple Abuse. It is because we do not fantasize or become stagnant on one human. We do our damage and we frequent them in their darkest moments and lastly, they cannot see us so it makes it much simpler to manage their behavior. You started off really strong with the work you did on Cardinal but you have become fixated and this fixation has made you sloppy, but here is the thing Abuse, I am not here to patronize you I am here to help you. That idea that Fear and Stress gave you was actually something that I proposed for one of my humans in the past. They prayed for their grandmother to come to peace in her time of Cancer and I was able to convince the neutral, Death the Reaper, to take her life. We were able to keep him Neutral because he was only responding to the prayers of the family. Just so happens, due to this death, the family turned to Alcoholism and drugs. I used the neutral…"

"Wait, that generational issue was something that you caused a Neutral to do?" Abuse interjects. "I heard about that situation."

"Yes, that was something I was able to accomplish. The only reason I was able to make this happen was because it did not jeopardize the neutrality of Death the Reaper. Now you are probably wondering why I am so willing to help you right now?" Addiction asked.

"It's because you are going to take me to the land of the neutrals. You have been there and you are going to get me there. What I cannot figure out is why does it matter to you?

Why are you helping me?" Questioned Abuse.

"You are right I am going to help you get to the land of the neutrals but it is not that simple. I am helping you because Cardinal is now my human." Addiction confessed.

"And mine" Proclaimed Violence "And mine" Proclaimed Fear "And mine" Proclaimed Stress.

"So what, they don't think I can handle him on my own?"

"Those answers you will need to get from the head himself." Violence stated.

"Okay well there is no changing this order. So how are we going to get to the land of the neutrals?" Questioned Abuse.

"With this." Addiction handed over a red card with several numbers on the back of it. The card was thick and heavy but had no name except one "HIM." The word was written in big letters pressed into the card. Abuse took the card and held it tight.

"So how are we going to get to the land of the neutrals? I do not exactly have the directions," snickered Abuse.

"You are so funny. You really think just because you have that card you have free access to the gate of the land of the Neutrals, you cannot get in unless you are accompanied by someone of a higher rank. That is how you are going to get there because we 4 are going to get you in there." Violence explained.

"So have yourself ready tomorrow because that is when we are going to be making your case to the Reaper." Addiction furthered.

Abuse overwhelmed with being belittled this entire time just put his head down and shook his head in agreement to the terms.

"See you tomorrow." Addiction stated before vanishing "Deuces Bruh." Violence saluted.

"Hey why don't you come by the ceremony tomorrow and watch us obtain our eyes. That way we can go to the gates right after." Fear instructed.

"Do I even have a say now? After tomorrow you will be my superior." Abuse lifted his head up just to see that he was standing there alone.

The next day Abuse showed up to the ceremony to see his fellow Suits obtain their eyes. He saw as the Heart of Man ushered in 4 new blazers. Abuse had never physically been to a ceremony for elevation because he vowed that the only one that he was going to attend would be the one for his own elevation. He stood there waiting for the ominous voice of the Tuxedo to announce the elevation of Violence, Addiction, Fear and Stress.

"Violence please step forward and look up to the ceiling please." The voice spoke from the void.

Violence stood up and walked forward to look up. As he looked up a dark light engulfed his face. The only thing that was visible was his black suit. The darkness seemed to shudder when this light flashed over the face of Violence. After about 5 seconds violence dropped his head with what seemed like blood flowing from his countenance. The entire void went silent while Violence attempted to open his eyes for the first time. Little by little the eyes peeked through the lids. Violence moaned as he directed his focus over to an intrigued Abuse. His eyes zeroed in as he saw the chains around the ankle of Abuse that led directly into the hands of him and all the other blazers. At this point in time, Violence understood the power that the Blazers had over the Suits. They literally had control over where they walked and how they orchestrated their practice. With this understanding, he also realized why the blazers were developed without mouths. It was to control the flow of information of the new lieutenants. Violence squinted his eyes and shook his head in acceptance, he turned around and walked back into the darkness. The other 3 Suits repeated this process and turned into the darkness and accepted their new robes. They traded in their Suit jackets for their new Blazers specific to their energy and purpose. Violence received a blazer engulfed with red velvet. The pattern and design mimicked that of a burning inferno from years of war. Addiction was covered with a golden blazer for the first look of the beauty of her blazer was quite pleasant but her ultimate features left you trapped forever. Fear and Stress looked very similar due to their twin-like characteristics. They both had black and gray blazers, plain looking, but the depth of the simplicity is what encapsulated their human.

"How do we look Abuse?" Addiction asked.

"I'm surprised you have the features of a humanistic female. I thought you were more male? Not that that matters at all,

I'm just a little shocked." Abuse confessed.

"Some of the most dangerous Blazers have feminine distinctions. You should know this considering that your once handler Selfishness was Feminine." Addiction combatted.

"You did not need to bring her up." Abuse responded in disgust.

"Well, it seems that you have been around Ignorance for a little while because he is starting to rub off on you." Addiction rebutted.

"So y'all ready to take off now?" Abuse questioned.

"I don't see why we all need to be there. I am going to stay here and take in all the festivities and go see what my new assignments look like. Maybe I'll start a war in the middle east." Violence stated "Deuces." Violence saluted before walking away.

"Honestly, there was something that I saw when I got my eyes and I think that you two need to talk." Fear said before ushering Stress to walk with him away.

"Okay so I guess it's just the two of us, let's get a move on Abuse." Addiction started moving forward.

"What did Fear mean when he said we need to talk?" Abuse asked.

"Honestly, it's nothing you do not already know. We are just your superiors now, and to be more specific I am your commander." Addiction confessed.

"So that is what you meant when you said "once handler?" You were talking about me getting pulled from under Selfishness and now working for you. What do you mean by handler? I mean I know that we have to report to y'all but it's not like we are under lock and key or something. Right?" Abuse remarked.

"Exactly that would mean that your success or failure would be on the account of the Blazer, and things are much more complex than that. Anyways, let's keep going forward. We still have some time before we cross the threshold of the Heart of Man.

The two of them walked through the dark void. Step after step the sound of each step echoed in the void. They walked until they reached the gate to the Heart of Man.

"Okay now listen very closely to me Abuse, it is imperative that you stick by my side the moment we leave this gate. If you stray too far from my being you can be eradicated by a seraphim. The other reason they require you to come out here with a Blazer is because you will need eyes to be able to circumnavigate this land. Now don't get it confused, if we are not strong enough to overcome a seraphim, we would need a nephilim and we do not have the ability to summon them. So just make sure you stay with me okay, I do not need you getting killed on my first day being a Blazer." Addiction instructed.

"Okay I got it, but what if we run into a Seraphim? What do we do?" Abuse asked.

"We do have a failsafe and it's a declaration that was made a long time ago that basically keeps us alive but not for long because this decree does not necessarily apply to our travels to and from the land of the neutrals but just keeps mindless fighting at bay until the great war."

"What great war?" asked Abuse

"Don't worry about that, just know that there will be a point in time where there will be a fight between the Seraphims, Nephilims, Virtues, and the Coats, Blazers, Suits, and even Tuxedos." Addiction explained.

"Tuxedos? That's plural, are you saying that there is more than one master?" Abuse confusingly asked.

"Ever since I got these eyes, I have been endowed with so much information. It honestly would not make any sense to you if I tried to explain it so let's just get going. We have a deadline with this card. In a little while the card will be rendered useless and we will not be able to gain entrance into the Land of the Neutrals and this journey will be worthless." Addiction said.

"You are not making any sense, but I am ready, let's go." Abuse agreed and moved forward.

Abuse pulled out the access card and swiped it at the gate and the doors flew open. The moment Abuse and Addiction crossed over the threshold they both heard angelic sounding music flood their being. Horns, flutes, snares, harps, violins engulfed this new world. There was next to no light but the sound of the music created a thick atmosphere that seemed to make both Abuse and Addiction freeze in their tracks. Addiction came back to her senses and grabbed Abuse because he was unable to shake off the vibes of the atmosphere. They rushed through this world as quickly as they could. Addiction activated her sense of sight to be able to navigate without detection. She got to the gate of the Neutrals and inserted the card. The gate consumed the card and asked for further authorization. Addiction placed her eyes to the gate and the eye reader scanned to verify the clearance.

Access Granted The Gate opened up and allowed Addiction and unconscious Abuse to enter the building. The moment they walked into the building, Abuse started to regain his sanity, but not to the extent to understand what was going on. Addiction dragged the stumbling Abuse to the directory to determine what area they needed to go to. They walked across the clean marble floor to the directory where they saw the name Death the Reaper displayed on a plaque.

Clank The door behind them closed firmly with a lock.

Now knowing where they needed to go to see the Reaper they pressed firmly against the name on the wall and they were instantly transported to the desk of the Reaper.

"Hello Death. How goes it?" Addiction attempts to make small talk.

"You are clearly a Blazer so you should know how this works. State your case and I will consider whether or not I can abide by your request." Death spoke.

"I'm sorry Death, I am brand new to being a Blazer. You see, not before long I was exactly like this Suit, discombobulated and dazed. I was just elevated today and I am learning many things. My name is Addiction"

Addiction stated.

"Well congrats." Death uncaringly responded. "Now what do you want? I have many things to do today."

"Yes, so my request is to respond to a prayer." Addiction came out and started without hesitation.

"Now Addiction, you should know that I need much more information than that. I cannot just go around killing people just because they wish they were dead. In fact, Suicide is one of your people, isn't it?" Death rhetorically asked.

"Yes, she is and of course I understand all too well the power and stance you have being a Neutral. You see Death, you once helped me before. You took away the pain of a family that begged for relief for their aged grandmother with Cancer. So I know you can answer my request." Addiction responded.

"You are funny if you think I could remember you and your specific scenario. Many people have been touched by my hand; I do not know you Addiction. I find my job much easier if I do not build these superficial relationships with you Iniquities or Virtues. So how about we do this, you stop wasting my time and tell me what you are requesting." Death ordered.

"So my human has been praying since he was a child that he wants his father to stop smoking. It has been years since the first time that boy uttered those words, and to keep it real with you I have seen his father's health deteriorate for years. You and I both know that the principles placed on the earth are in your favor for this one. The father has squandered the body that he has been given and if you touched him this would be in your nature. Also, because he has prayed for his father to stop being in pain, then this gives you the right to take that man's life and cease his pain." Addiction disclosed.

"This is an oddly specific request. You do understand that I cannot just go take this man's life. I have to check in on the validity of your statements." Death remarks.

"Of course. We will wait here until you get back." Addiction states.

In that moment, Death puts on his cloak and disappears from the realm. Addiction stood there with Abuse staggering in and out of a stable mind. Abuse could not remain in this realm for too much longer. As quickly as Death left, he returned with his twin Life.

"This is my twin Life and we see that your claim is valid but I cannot just go down there and forcefully take this man's opportunity at life. So Life and

I will visit Alpha together and give him an ultimatum. He can perish from his world or stay and fight another day, it will be up to him."

"That sounds wonderful. Thank you Death and it was a pleasure meeting you Life. Until we meet again. Now if you could be so kind and…"

Before Addiction could finish her statement, Death snapped and transported her out of their realm back to the Heart of Man's gate.

"What happened? All I remember is a directory and two cloaked beings. Did we do it?" Abuse asked.

"Well now that you are up why don't we go and find out." Addiction responded.

In that moment, Addiction and Abuse listened from the ear canal of a sleeping Cardinal.

"Hi my name is Alpha. I told my wife that my finger hurts, my chest hurts, what is wrong with me?"

"Let's take a look" the doctor says.

"It looks like it has begun. Tonight is the night that Alpha has a heart attack. Cardinal dreamed about this before and this vivid dream was actually a view into the future. Now all we have to do is wait." Addiction informs Abuse calmly.

"It doesn't matter whether or not he lives or dies. I just need to make sure that we do not get purged." Abuse states.

"Speak for yourself Abuse. I have been working on Alpha for a long time and to be honest, if he lives that could cause me some issues. I would much rather see him dead." Addiction says.

"Hey since he is your human, do you think we can view what's going on through his heart?" Abuse asks.

"First of all, it would be impossible for me to go in there with you, secondly, did you not hear what I said. He is having a heart attack and we cannot force our way in there now. It would be dangerous because if he does survive, we will be eliminated for good. We just gotta wait for a good time." Addiction declares.

Cardinal slept through the night without the knowledge of what was going on with his father. Hours go by as he rests in his bed while his father did the same in a hospital.

The sun crept up over the horizon and the light shining through the blinds caused Cardinal to wake out of the bed. He goes from his bed to the bathroom to brush his teeth and clean his face like he did every day.

Something was different today though. Why wasn't the TV broadcasting its lies and entertainment? His father was usually up before all the kids. That moment, Fear gripped the heart of Cardinal and Stress strangled his brain. Cardinal then rushed to the master bedroom to find no one there. He did not need to hear it from anyone, he knew something was wrong. He picked up the closest phone and called his mom but nothing happened, the phone call went right to voicemail. He called his father's phone and he heard the ring from the bedroom. His father's cell phone was still there and his mom was not picking up. Was this his dream? He panicked until he heard the front door open. It was his mother.

"Mom, where were you? Where is Dad?" Cardinal asked with concern.

"Son, I need you to be strong. Your father is in the hospital. He had a heart attack and is in the hospital getting surgery. He had a blood clot in his heart." Omega said.

"Is he…...going to die?" Cardinal asked nervously.

"Of course not sweetie. People have heart attacks all the time. He will be okay, what I need for you to do is to continue praying for him because he needs that more than anything." Omega said calmly.

The moment Omega said that Cardinal rushed to his room and got to his knees and prayed a very simple prayer.

"GOD PLEASE DO NOT TAKE MY DADDY'S LIFE. IN JESUS NAME. AMEN."

COATS

Cardinal rose from his knees thinking that the pain he was feeling would subside but the truth of the matter was he couldn't stop the fear that gripped his heart.

"Why is my father suffering like this? Why would God let this happen? Do my prayers even mean anything? What if he dies? Will I be fatherless for the rest of my life?" The questions just began to flow from Cardinal's mind. He wanted to be brave but it was all too much for him to deal with.

Meanwhile at the Heart of Man the blazers gathered to talk about the news concerning Cardinal and his father's condition.

"You see how I have thrown his head into a frenzy; he doesn't know what to believe, his faith is shattered." Fear exclaimed.

"Be happy that you can do something; it seems that Cardinal is not quite ready to let me run wild in his heart just yet. I can feel that he will embrace me soon. How goes it with you Selfishness?" Violence asks.

"I will always be at the center of everything he does because I am literally the toxin of humanity, never mind the work I have done." Selfishness scoffs.

"Yeah, you guys know nothing, and I thought that was supposed to be a trait of mine. I guess I'm rubbing off on all of you." A newly promoted Ignorance proclaimed.

"It's okay my child, they are just trying to get under my skin." Selfishness states calmly.

"Hey does anyone know who called this meeting anyways?" Stress asked concerningly. "Yeah cause we do have some very important work to do." Fear agreeably states.

"I did." a dense strong masculine voice claims from the shadows.

In that moment a figure steps through the shadows into the presence of the blazers. This being stood tall and strong. His eyes deep and dark as the ocean floor. He sported a menacing smile. His teeth sharp as daggers. His face has skin that mirrored that of a snake. His coat was the color of a setting sun or a freshly exploded nuclear warhead. On his coat were many badges that had little symbols on them. Even though none of the Blazers knew this being, the one thing they did know was that it was a Coat. Coats are one of the most powerful beings in the Heart of Man aside from the Tuxedo. In fact, they were considered the assassins to the Tuxedo. The damage that they did to human race was so lasting that many could not shake the habits and snares inflicted on them by these beings.

"And who might you be?" Selfishness asked without hesitation.

"Know your place low life. I would hate to see you disappear for no reason." The being promised.

Coats had an uncanny ability to devour the Blazers and Suits for nutrition if they needed. This would in turn create a more powerful Coat with many abilities. This is precisely why many humans inflicted with Coats seldomly could overcome them.

"Allow me to introduce myself, my name is Pornography. I know that can be hard to remember so just call me Porn. I know you'll arc wondering if these badges are my……." quirks"...... let's call it that. They were once Suits and Blazers like you'll. This one here, this is Masturbation. He was a difficult Blazer to digest. This one is called Pride. She was just born when I devoured her. Oh, and this one, this one is my favorite, this one is called Perversion. Thanks to them I am what I am. I know you are all wondering why I have decided to call this meeting and in part, it has something to do with what is going on with Cardinal. The other part is what is to come. Wait…..we are missing someone. Let's see, Selfishness, Ignorance, Violence, Fear, Stress, where is Addiction? Can someone tell me where she is?" Porn asked

"Yeah, she is with Abuse and they are observing Cardinal duress with the situation with Alpha." Violence answers.

"That is the reason why we are here. Can someone please go and get her? NOW!" Porn aggressively orders.

In an instant, all the Blazers disappeared from the meeting place to grab Addiction.

As Addiction and Abuse observed the tears flowing from the eyes of Cardinal, Violence appeared.

"What are you doing up here in the brain? Do you have any idea what is going on right now?" Violence asks.

"Yeah man, one of the Coats is having a meeting and he is furious because you are not there. We need to leave right now." Fear orders.

"What are all 5 of you doing here? Which Coat sent for me?" Addiction asked.

"Do y'all not see me here? What is going on?" Abuse asks.

"Don't worry about it, this is far above your pay grade. By the way Addiction, it was Pornography. I guess we were all just so nervous about getting absorbed we just all came to get you but we need to go back." Fear ordered.

"Sorry Abuse I gotta go, do not leave from this spot I will be right back." Addiction promised.

Fear, Stress, Ignorance, Violence, and Selfishness all disappeared back to the meeting place. Just before Addiction disappeared back to the Heart of Man, Abuse stopped her.

"Hey Addiction there is something that I wanted to know. I know that because you have been promoted you are privy to certain information, I have a question that I hope you can answer for me."

"I only have a moment, what is it?" asked Addiction.

"Do you have a brother? You know, like how Stress and Fear were conceived at the same time and share similar qualities. Do you have a brother like that?" Asked Abuse.

"Yes." Addiction states before vanishing.

At that moment Abuse stood there thinking about what that simple answer meant.

"Was Addiction in fact my sister? Was that why I was reassigned to her squadron?" All these thoughts flowed through Abuse.

"GET UP OUTTA BED NOW JADE AND AURELIA, YA'LL NEED TO GET READY FOR SCHOOL!" Omega yelled into the bedroom attempting to wake the two sleeping girls.

Cardinal did not know how they were going to react to the news that their father was in the hospital but he knew that at this time he had to dry his tears and be strong for his sisters when they did find out.

Cardinal put on his uniform for school and walked to the kitchen to make the lunches for his sisters. He pulled six pieces of wheat bread out, the strawberry jam from the refrigerator, and the peanut butter from the cabinet. He started by rubbing the jam on the bread, a task usually easy; however, today the task was very challenging because Cardinal's hand could find peace. He shook with the force of an earthquake. The jam spilled on the counter and floor. With speed, Cardinal rushed to the wall where the napkins were and ran a couple of napkins under the sink water to wipe up the mess before anyone could see it. After cleaning the mess, he tried once more to complete the simple task of making a peanut butter and jelly sandwich for lunch. From across the room, Omega saw the challenge that Cardinal was having so she graciously walked across the floor to grab the butter knife from his hands to complete the lunches for him.

"Don't worry about the lunches, I will do them for you. Go get your backpack and homework ready. I will finish this." Omega said softly.

"Okay Mommy." Cardinal agreed.

He walked back through the house into the hallway to get to his room when he saw his sister Jade waiting for her sister to come out of the bathroom so she could brush her teeth and wash her face.

"Good morning Jade." Cardinal said, walking through the hallway. Jade, still halfway asleep, did not respond.

Cardinal finally reached his room and put his books and binders into his backpack as he got ready for another day at school. He was ready to go to school hoping that being in a new place would make him feel better, but yet and still his heart was still fearful from the possibility of losing his dad.

Back at the Heart of Man Addiction finally arrives at the meeting.

"Sorry about that guys, I guess I did not get the memo that I was supposed to be here. Now where is......" before Addiction could finish her sentence Porn grabbed her by the neck and stopped her from talking.

"I could swallow you right now for your tardiness and lack of concern for being late. If you make a habit of this, believe me, I will turn you into one of my badges. Now take a seat maggot." Porn aggressively threatens before throwing Addiction into her seat.

"Now the reason we are here is for me to give you some instruction from the master himself. You six will be under me from now on. We coats have been known to be very much hands off when it comes to you lower leveled beings, but because you all think you can do what you want, now we gotta keep you in check.

"Wait what are you talking about? None of us move on our own fruition. We can only do what we are allowed to do by the master's approval." Selfishness attempts to correct Porn's statement.

"Do you really think I am Ignorant Selfishness?" Porn sarcastically asks while pointing at Ignorance. "The reason I am even talking to you dimwits is because the master has seen someone enter into the land of the neutrals with a card without his approval. Now, personally, I don't want to point out anyone in particular for what they did so I am going to ask you to speak up." Porn orders.

"It was me. Abuse and I went to the land of the Neutrals and spoke with Death the Reaper. No harm was found and not only that, look at the mayhem we created in Cardinal. He is so unstable now, we definitely helped you all out." Addiction made a case for herself.

"You know what else you did Addiction, you caused a ripple effect that might not be good for any of us. Do you know what is going to happen to Alpha when he has to choose whether he wants to live or die?" Porn asked.

"No, I had not thought about that." Addiction confesses. "Because he is going to have to make a choice, his eyes are going to be opened to the realm we all exist in. Iniquities, Hoodies, Tuxedos, Seraphims, and Nephilims alike will all be visible. If he decides to choose life then he will always be able to see us. If he is able to see us too, then by being the head of his family he could snuff us out of his entire family. You are so determined to help your freaking brother you have risked all of our existence." Porn explains.

"What have you done, Addiction." The Five Blazers all began to expel with grave concern.

"It looks like Alpha is having his second heart attack as we speak. For your sake, you better hope he doesn't pull through. Porn says to Addiction. I have called this meeting to let you Blazers know I am your new leader." You are not to go to the land of the Neutrals without my say so." If I find out that one of you has gone there without my consent, believe me when I tell you, your days will be short." Porn threatens with a maniacal smile. "That is everything that I had to say to you. I have got to get back to the Master. If for any reason you need to reach me all you gotta do is resonate your frequency at this location and I will meet you here. Goodbye." Porn finishes, and just like that he leaves all 6 Blazers sitting there.

"Can you all explain to me why you'll act like we didn't plan to go to the land of the neutral together?" Addiction questioned.

"Did you see the way he looked at us while he was talking? There was no way in the universe I wanted to start any problems with that Coat." Violence confessed.

"Violence you have nerves! You literally start wars, but now you want to act all scared of that Coat because of how he looked at you? You're acting like Fear." Addiction says with disgust. Looking at the rest of the blazer, Addition asked, "What's ya'lls excuse?"

"Honestly Addiction, each one of us considered that going there was not the best idea. Why do you think at the last minute we all just decided we weren't coming? It's because we figured by not getting approval we would get into trouble. You know you are so much like your brother it's scary." Selfishness states.

"Well you would know, considering that you were once his Blazer. You sorry sack of….." Addiction starts before getting cut off by Fear.

"Hey, watch it! Profanity is not going to come back because Porn consumed her. So just stop it Addiction." Fear says.

"Look, all I'm saying is you guys could have backed me up okay." Addiction says.

"Hey you guys hear what Porn said though, right? Alpha is on heart attack number 2 which means that his chances of survival are lower." Addiction continued

"Yeah, well I guess we will have to see with time. Don't you think it's a bit strange that the Coat Porn is our leader? It's not like he has done anything in Cardinal's heart." Ignorance spoke.

"Right, I did think that was an odd pairing. If we were going to be led by a Coat, I would have thought that it would have been Depression." Selfishness agreed.

"Well guys, since this meeting is over, I have to get back to Cardinal's brain and speak with Abuse." Addiction said before vanishing.

Back at the brain Abuse sat peering through the Eyes of Cardinal as he sat in his English class filling out the paragraphs his teacher prescribed the class to do.

"I see that you have stayed." Addiction jokingly says. "Yeah, I have to do what my superior tells me to do." Abuse responds.

"Well Selfishness told me you were the rebellious type. You didn't really listen to the orders of your superiors." Addiction rebuttals.

"I despised Selfishness because she thought the world revolved around her. You're different." Abuse proclaims.

"And what exactly makes me different?" Addiction questions "You're my sister." Abuse states.

"Who told you? I am curious." Addiction asked. "It was Fear and Stress." Abuse answered.

"Somehow I knew. Well now that you know does it make sense why we have vested interests. If you are able to get promoted like I was, then who knows the amount of carnage we could cause? Cardinal would be a shell of himself, a defeated creature. We have got to get you on our team."

"Wait what team are you talking about?" Abuse asked "Oh that's what the meeting was about. We are now being managed a bit more closely by the Coats because of something that I did for you." Addiction remarked.

"Was it going to the land of the Neutrals?" Questioned Abuse.

"Yeah. So now Selfishness, Fear, Stress, Violence, Ignorance, and I are all under their watchful eye." Addiction responded.

"Wait, that little twerp Ignorance is a Blazer now?" Abuse asked, shocked.

"Yeah, although he is not little anymore. He has gotten bigger, and don't even think about asking for details. I will not be able to tell you anything."

Abuse and Addiction sat there as Cardinal finished up his day at school. The sound of the school bells went off signaling the end of the day. The school Cardinal attended had not been successfully built so the children all had classes between tarps underneath the bleachers of a race track. Cardinal and Aurelia met at the end of the parking lot right next to the amusement park that was across the street and began their walk back to their home.

"Do you think Dad will pull through?" Cardinal asked his older sister Aurelia.

"Of course he will, Dad is the strongest person on the planet. You cannot lose faith bro. He will be okay." Aurelia spoke with confidence in her eyes, unbeknownst to Cardinal that she was also struggling with unbelief of her father's ability to pull through. That walk home felt like it took days as Cardinal's heart seemed to drop to his stomach and his throat tightened. He could see the grip of Stress wrapped around his throat but there was nothing he could do. He was broken. Step after step they both took to make it back to their home. One foot after the other was the only thing that circulated through the mind of Cardinal. They turned the corner with anticipation to hopefully see a sign that their father was home. A car in the driveway would be enough. As they approached the top of the hill, they received the confirmation they were eagerly looking for, in the driveway sat the minivan, which meant that their father Alpha had to be home. In that moment the virtue Joy and Peace carried the feet of Cardinal as he ran faster than he ever did in his life to reach his house. Stride, Stride, Stride was the simple thought process of Cardinal. As he reached the door, he burst through to find his sobbing mother in the middle of the living room.

"Oh God, please no." This was all Cardinal could think as he saw what he saw. Had his father died? What other reason could his mother be sitting in the middle of the floor crying.

"Mom, what's wrong?" Aurelia asked as she came through the door.

"My children it's nothing, how was school?" Omega asked drying her eyes.

"Mom please just tell us, is dad dead?" Cardinal asked with no hope in his eyes.

"Baby no your father is okay. He has to have surgery on his heart but he is okay. The surgery is a simple operation they will not have to crack his chest open or anything. The doctors say that after the surgery he will be a lot better but he had a second heart attack today." Omega confessed.

"What? Another one?" Cardinal remarked.

"Yes but the reason that I was crying baby is because I spoke with your father today and the doctor told him that if continues to smoke and eat fast food then he will not live to see his 40s. Your dad has promised to never smoke another cigarette." Omega stated.

In that moment a rush of emotion came over Cardinal's body. He felt Joy rubbing his back, he could see Peace abound in the room, he could feel the tears forming in his eyes. At that moment, all he could do was look to the ceiling and say.

"Thank you, Jesus, for answering my prayers."

ABUSE AND PORN

After receiving the information that his father would ultimately live, Cardinal felt the immense pressure of Stress subside from his being. At that moment, Peace wrapped her loving arms around his body and Cardinal felt the weight of fear being lifted.

Back at the hospital, Alpha laid lifeless on the hospital bed waiting for his procedure to start. He laid with his eyes open staring at the flickering light on the roof thinking about his family. Moments later, the doctor walked into the room with his snow white coat and his clipboard and paperwork.

"Mr. Wolf, are you prepared for the minor procedure we are going to put you through?"

"Yes, will I feel any pain?" Alpha asked concerned "To be honest you won't feel a thing because we are going to give you anesthesia, so, I'll explain how the procedure is going to go. We are going to cut a small incision in your thigh. that will in turn allow us to run a stent through your artery into your heart. Once that stint is in place, then we will be able to remove and bypass the blood clot in your heart. This should not take us longer than a few hours to complete. Now you have several options: we can subdue you completely, you can be awake for the procedure, or we cannot go through with the procedure?" the doctor asked.

"I definitely want to go through the procedure, I think I will stay up and watch." Alpha responded.

"Alright then Mr. wolf I'm going to put this needle in your leg and we will go ahead and get you started. Once we are done you can invite your family over to see you." the doctor spoke.

"Awesome let's do this." Alpha said energetically.

It didn't take long for the anesthesia to kick in. Alpha felt his leg tingle then start to go numb. Even though he was excited to get the procedure done and finally go home he was a little nervous, so he tilted his head back and said a quick prayer. Mere seconds felt like hours as Alpha whispered his prayers under his breath.

"I now know how Jesus felt when he was praying In The Garden of Gethsemane. "Alpha stated in his head.

In that moment, he let out a little laugh with the thought that he just had. Time ticked slowly while he sat and waited for the nurse to come in and roll him into the operation room. Eventually, the nurse walked into the room and asked Alpha.

"This is it, are you ready to go Mr. wolf?"

The nurse navigated herself to the back of the bed and released the brake. She then pushed Alpha through the double doors to the back of the hospital where the operation room was. As they moved through the heavily lit hallways the tires under the bed began to squeak thus creating a rhythmic tune that soothed Alpha.

* squeak.....squeak......squeak* all the way to the operation room. As they approached the doors the nurse used her hip to hit a button which opened both doors wide so that they could push Alpha into position. The doctor stated the procedure took no more than a few hours, and Alpha courageously watched as they placed the stent into his heart.

Abuse sat still in his corner defeated by Alpha's choice to choose Life instead of Death. Abuse was disgusted by the Joy that now embodied Cardinal when his father returned home. In the distance Abuse could hear the other Suits and Blazers congratulating each other for the opportunity that they seized while Alpha was in the Hospital.

"Did you see how I was choking Cardinal while he was walking home? Did you see that?" Stress asked with excitement.

"Yes I did my twin, did you see the amount of fear that I was able to possess in that little boy?" fear expressed.

"Yeah, yeah, yeah. Can you guys take that somewhere else." Abuse snickered.

"Looks like someone is having a rough day. Come on guys, let's get out of here." the group of Suits and Blazer said to each other.

"Those Blazers are so pretentious. They walk around here with their heads high like they don't have anything to prove. They must have forgotten that they were Suits just like me not too long ago. If I cannot do something to keep Cardinal Shackled and chained then I will become useless." Abuse sat there thinking to himself.

In that moment a voice echoed from the darkness.

"Wouldn't you like to be able to command those silly and pretentious blazers?" the anonymous voice spoke.

"Who goes there?" Abuse asked.

"Oh that's right I forgot you lowly Suits cannot see someone of my stature. Just stand there and I will momentarily grant you permission to have a discussion with me." The voice spoke.

Abuse felt something abide on his face and instantaneously eyes grew out of his head.

"What is this power that I'm experiencing?" Abuse pondered "That is the power of a Blazer. And what you're looking at is a coat." The anonymous figure said.

"A coat? I have heard about you guys. You are way more powerful than the Suits and the Blazers combined. Why are you here talking to me? And why did you grant me the power to be able to see and talk to you? It's not like I've done anything worthy of having a discussion with you." Abuse stated with lack of esteem.

"You know Abuse, you could be so much more advantageous if you weren't so critical of yourself. The amount of damage that you could cause in Cardinal's life will soon come to fruition, but only with my help. Pardon me, where are my manners? Allow me to introduce myself, my name is Pornography. Since we are going to get to know each other really well you can just call me what everyone else calls me. Porn."

"Wait, I have heard about you. My sister Addiction told me that you all had a meeting not too long ago and you are now the lead of all of them. So you still have not answered my question. Why are you here with me?" Abuse asked.

"Oh Abuse, you have to learn how to read between the lines. I just told you that the Carnage you will enact on Cardinal will soon come to fruition with my help, so what do you think I'm here to do." Porn asked.

"Help me. But why?" Abuse asked again.

"Frankly, because you and I have a lot in common. Through the accounts of humanity, I have constantly doomed many great men and many great women. You see, sex was a gift given to humanity for good. The thing is, Humanities hearts are dark and because of the darkness I was able to infiltrate them, this is a very important and pertinent gift. Mankind embodied Selfishness…here is the truth I bet you never considered, the power that you have over your host fails in comparison to the power that you have in mankind. Just let that sink in for a second. You and selfishness are vital and not only my survival but my growth. To make it more plain, once mankind embodied Selfishness they then abused their own physical bodies by pleasing oneself, rather than using their gift in the appropriate fashion. That's where I was born, in the exacerbation of Selfishness and Abuse. That's why I need you to do something for me. I have just granted you with this immense power of a Blazer, that's why you have eyes. I am going to temporarily grant you the power of a coat. What you're going to have to do in order to permanently retain this power is consume a Blazer." Porn instructs.

Porn reaches with his hand and covers the face of Abuse. In that moment a dark swirl swallowed Abuse and from his face grew fangs sharper than daggers and a mouth for consuming Blazers and Suits.

"Does it matter who I consume?" abuse asks.

"Clearly based on the explanation I just gave you about my coming into existence you cannot consume Selfishness, but anyone else is fair game." Porn further instructs. "Understand this, whoever you consume they will permanently become a part of you. So make sure that you are certain on whom you want to consume." Porn finishes.

"I have just the Blazer for the job." Abuse States.

"Perfect. Well Abuse, I will be seeing you soon; whether it's you being elevated or me consuming you myself. You have 24 hours in human scheduling." Porn states before vanishing into the void.

"I can feel all the power endowed on me. If what porn was saying is true then I will be able to surpass everyone that overlooked me before. I'm still a bit confused about the history stuff Porn was talking about. Time to go consume me a Blazer."

Abuse sat for a second considering the havoc he was going to reach at the Heart of Man. His eyes wandered through every nook and cranny. Every room and every hallway. Through the blackness until his eyes fixated on the Blazer that he had been looking for.

"There you are." Abuse traveled through the void in an instant to the chambers of Addiction.

"Hey sis." Abuse whispers from the darkness of the abyss. "That voice sounds familiar but it couldn't be Abuse because

I would be able to hear and see him, who are you imposter?" Addiction questions.

"What type of devilish trick is this coat playing?" Selfishness asked.

"The day of reckoning has finally befallen you. I considered making this quick and easy but after careful consideration, I do have 24 hours to get this thing done and I think I will use twenty three of those hours making sure that you experience every amount of torment I could execute on you." Abuse aggressively proclaims.

"Selfishness it appears that this coat has underestimated the powers we have, together we could cause him to fall in line." Addiction responds.

"Even though I could do away with this garbage myself, I do believe that us two should be enough to do away with this scum bag." Selfishness seconds.

"I'm sorry, where are my manners? Allow me to reintroduce myself." Abuse sarcastically exclaims.

In that moment he steadily makes himself visible to both Selfishness and Addiction.

"Tada." Abuse expresses.

"Wow you look so powerful! How did this happen to you?" Addiction emphatically expresses.

"That joke wasn't funny. You cannot go around doing that to people Abuse." Selfishness authoritatively states.

"You no longer have the right nor the authority to tell me what to do Selfishness." Abuse snarls while staring into the eyes of his victim. "As for how I got like this, do not worry too much about that, just know that YOU" abuse says while pointing at Addiction. "Are safe from my wrath. In fact I did not travel all the way here to see you. I came here so that I could wreak havoc on Selfishness and like I said I have a whole twenty three hours to do it." Abuse finishes before taking steps towards Selfishness.

"Wait, wait, wait. What is going on?" Addiction questioned.

"I think it's time for you to go sis. Or better yet I think it's best that you and I got outta here." Abuse calmly says before rushing towards Selfishness with great speed. Abuse rushes past the still body of Selfishness, who was not competent enough to visualize the movements of Abuse. Abuse then reaches his hand up to the face of Selfishness and grasps her face. The speed and pressure executed on Selfishness's face nearly killed her, she engaged every muscle that she could to prevent from dying on the spot. Abuse travels through perceived time to a place where neither one of them could be disturbed.

"Welcome to your funeral Selfishness. I'm sorry that no one could be here to see you depart, but worry not after you are consumed your essence will still be felt through me." Abuse addresses.

"Since I am going to die here answer two of my questions. What happened to you and why did you choose me?" Selfishness asks.

"Choosing you was simple, once I was instructed that the only way that I would retain this power was if I consumed one of the Blazers in Cardinal's life, I knew immediately that you were the one. After all the times you undermined me, the times you could have assisted me in my plans, the times where you kept me down. I considered no one else to be fit." Abuse explained. "Since you are going to die soon, I guess I can tell you why I was hand chosen for this task. Porn came to me and…" Abuse began to explain before getting cut off by Selfishness.

"Wait so Pornography did this to you?" Selfishness asked.

"You said you only have two questions, it appears that you have many more than that. To keep it frank, Porn needs me and in order for me to be effective I need to become a coat and the only way I can sustain this form is if I consume you. You know what though, I want this to be entertaining, so, why don't you run, I'll track you down with these new powers." Abuse casually instructs.

"How about this." Selfishness says. Before letting out another word, Selfishness puts up her fists and charges directly at Abuse. Selfishness cocks back her right fist. She then steps down, twists her body and throws a strong punch. Abuse stood there in bewilderment as the punch swiftly moved towards his face. He could not understand why at this moment he was not worried. A punch from a Blazer could literally knock his head off if he were still a Suit. The idea came to his mind that because he was powered up at the time that maybe the punch would not hurt. Inch by inch the fist moved closer to his face. He could see the punch coming every millisecond that passed, but he did not move. Just before the punch connected with his face he glanced into the eyes of Selfishness and noticed that she was not looking at the side of his face where the punch was going to land but at his chin. She was simultaneously throwing another punch from beneath. In that moment the first punch lands. "Boom" Abuse had sadly underestimated the severity of the situation he had gotten himself into. The punch just about knocked the energy out of Abuse. He was not just fighting against a Blazer but against one that had much more experience than he did. The second punch just about landed but Abuse was able to snatch his head back to prevent from being hit in the chin. Abuse jumped back and stroked his face to feel that a portion of his face was now gone.

"You see, you brought me here with the idea that you were just going to consume me and I would just let you do it, but you have underestimated my experience in combat. I was not just promoted to a Blazer because I am effective at creating a self-centered human the moment, they are born but also because of the combat skills that I have acquired through the years. You have just locked yourself in a dungeon with a monster." Selfishness states before putting her guard up.

"My…...Face…." Abuse remarks with confusion. "You are right, I did greatly underestimate your abilities, and even though I am far more powerful than you now, I do lack the experience that you have, but all I have to do is consume you in the next twenty two hours." Abuse states before putting his fists up and charging back towards Selfishness. While Selfishness and Abuse waged war on one another Cardinal sat in his third period math class feeling weird.

He typically had days like this, where it seemed like time traveled slowly and every small issue was an enormous problem. Not only could he not figure out the math problem that his teacher placed on the board but he suddenly began to perspire and he never had this happen where an odiferous odor came from his underarms. Puberty had finally come for him. Maybe it was the war raging on the inside causing heat to swirl in his body thus causing him to sweat. Maybe it was the math problem he was struggling with; all he knew was he could not walk around like this all day. He approached the front of the classroom where the teacher was and asked if he could go to the restroom. After permission was granted, Cardinal walked to the restroom to wash his underarms with the bathroom soap and paper towels. This would have to do until he could get home to ask his mother for some deodorant. As he walked to the restroom one of his female friends walked to the ladies restroom from another classroom.

"Hey Cardinal!" She expressed her excitement to see her friend. She ran over to give him a hug. But in that moment of awareness, Cardinal realized that if he hugged this girl with his arms smelling like this, he may never get the opportunity to hug her again. So rather than embrace her as she approached, he put up one finger to indicate that he needed a second and he vanished into the restroom.

"How embarrassing." He began to think.

Cardinal put his hands under the running water to test for temperature. Once the water was warm enough, he placed a few paper towels under the water to soak them. Once the paper towels were wet, he placed the towels under the soap dispenser and applied a favorable amount of soap on the towel. He did not want to experience the embarrassment of having a classmate come into the bathroom and see what he was doing so he took the paper towel into the stall and closed the door. He then removed his shirt and wiped back and forth under his arms to eradicate the smell. Once the smell seemed to have dissipated Cardinal walked back to his classroom. Some time went by and math class had come to an end and it was time for lunch. Cardinal picked up his backpack and rushed out the door to get to the lunch line. While he ran down the ramp to get into the lunch line, he saw a few of his friends running down to the lunch line as well.

"Hey wassup Forest. Wassup Seltzen." Cardinal greeted.

These were two of the friends Cardinal met while he was in middle school. All three of them were in the same grade and around the same age.

"Yo we need to hurry otherwise the line will be super long." Forest addresses.

"Hey I gotta tell you guys something that I found last night while I was watching anime on the computer." Seltzen says.

"Okay, but let's make it to the lunch line first." Cardinal says. The three of them ran until they arrived at the lunch line, which to their chagrin was already long.

"Dang it, now we are going to spend half of the lunch waiting in line for food." Forest states.

"Yeah but you guys have to hear about what I found on the internet." Seltzen brings up again.

"Well since we are not going anywhere for the next twenty minutes, tell us what you found." Cardinal orders with slight irritation.

"Okay so I was on the internet watching some Dragon Ball Z. The episode was almost over and this ad popped up right over the video." Seltzen suddenly stops to build suspense. "What was the ad?" Cardinal and Forest ask.

"The ad was to a website. A super crazy website." Seltzen informs, but pausing again to build suspense.

"What was so crazy about this website?" Cardinal asks "Dude there was a bunch of girls, like anime girls having, like real sex with other anime characters. Dude the one I watched was Android 18 and Krillin. Dude it was a crazy scene. I masturbated until I sprayed all over the place. It was all over the roof and walls." Seltzen whispered.

"Dude, there is much better porn out there. If you type in this website, you can see real people doing it." Forest emphasized.

"Hey guys what exactly is Porn, and what does masturbation mean?" Cardinal asked.

"Dude are you serious?" Forest asks.

"You mean to tell me you have never touched yourself or watched porn before?" Seltzen asks.

"I was just joking, come on guys, of course, I know what that is. Shoot, I was on the site last night and I did it in the bathroom." Cardinal began to lie.

"Wait, how were you able to do that, I thought you did not have a cell phone?" forest asked.

"Oh, it's because I used my dad's laptop." Cardinal answered. "Did you remember to delete the history and clear the cookies?" Seltzen asked.

"Of course I did, I am no rookie at this." Cardinal said with confidence.

"Good cause if he were to find out that you were looking at that type of stuff on his computer, he would probably kill you. Knowing your dad." Seltzen said.

"Yeah true." Cardinal agreed.

Cardinal at that moment made his mind up that he would need to do some research on this thing they called porn.

At the moment that Cardinal decided that he was going to watch porn that night, Porn transferred himself to the brain of Cardinal where he made sure to infect and plague his mind about the decision he was going to make. For the rest of the day that would be the only thing that Cardinal would focus on. Porn's influence caused Cardinal to plot on how he would watch the videos, how he would sneak his father's laptop into the bathroom, and also to remember to clear the history and delete the cookies to avoid future detection.

Back at the Heart of Man Selfishness and Abuse continued their battle. By this time both of them had become fatigued by the battle. Abuse took on more damage from Selfishness than Selfishness had taken from Abuse. Her battle experience definitely gave her the upper hand.

"You know Abuse, once you said that you had twenty three hours to consume me, my goal was to just time you out. We have been at this for twenty two hours and you still have not completed your goal of consuming me. At this point you won't, and I just want you to know that once you go back to being a lowly Suit, I will personally make sure that you never, ever, see ascension in this heart." Selfishness proclaims.

"You know what I have noticed the entire time we have been fighting in here. That I have no chance of consuming you on my own. So instead of me trying to defeat you in the next hour I had a thought. Why not just use the powers that I have been granted that you clearly do not have the access to." Abuse smirks

"What are you talking about?" Selfishness questions

"I do not have to fight you. All I have to do is condemn you, and condemnation literally puts you at the chopping block of a Coat. As of today, I have become a Coat so now all I have to do is say the words in front of a witness." Abuse informs.

"Well, you made a critical mistake and brought me here where there are no witnesses, so your luck is up." Selfishness chuckles.

"Not at all. Just before Porn left me after our conversation, I asked him what were the powers that I had been introduced to, and this was one of them. He also told me the conditions for which my powers worked, and once I was privy to the information, I asked Porn to be present here, and in just a moment he will be here to accept the reasons for which you will be condemned. Once that condemnation is in place, I will devour you." Abuse further explains.

In that moment Porn appears in the void.

"Porn I would like to condemn Selfishness for the crime of battling against her superior." Abuse spoke.

Selfishness stood there in disbelief and she knew that her time as a Blazer had come to an end.

"Well, she actually cannot be condemned for that reason because you started this battle. Also I explicitly stated that you could not consume Selfishness because she plays a vital role in my existence and my plan." Porn addresses.

"I know that this is what you commanded of me, but consider that the reason that I think she should be consumed by me is because it will be easier for you to control the powers of me and her if we were in one vessel" Abuse retorted.

Selfishness then finds relief in the fact that she was not going to be consumed. It appeared that Abuse's plan had backfired on him.

"Look at you now, Abuse. Now when you revert back I will make sure to keep you under my feet forever." Selfishness expresses authoritatively.

"Shut it, I'm still a Coat for a few more minutes. So can she not be condemned?" Abuse asks again.

"Not for the reason you are trying to condemn her. As for you consuming her....You make a pretty valid point. It will be simpler to manipulate one of you versus two of you so I will allow this, but considering that you only have a mere few minutes before your time runs out, I don't see how you will successfully consume her. To be honest, if you fail I may just give her your abilities for a few minutes, have her consume you, and I still get what I need out of Cardinal." Porn states

"So she can be condemned, and I don't have much time left." Abuse thought to himself.

"I got it, I am requesting condemnation on Selfishness on the grounds that while I was a Suit, she did not report my activity to the higher authorities when I navigated to the stairway of ascension." Abuse started staring directly into the eyes of Selfishness. "You should have taken me out when you had the chance." Abuse retorted.

"Well that certainly is enough to condemn Selfishness." Porn proclaimed. Porn stretched out his hands and pointed at Selfishness. In that moment immense chains bounded towards her body and wrapped themselves around her. Selfishness could not move her body for she had become caged. Abuse walked with haste to her still body. He opened his mouth wide and swallowed Selfishness. Abuse then felt his clothes and body regenerate back to the full strength and a badge then grew on the coat pocket of Abuse.

"Great job on devouring your first Blazer. There will be many more opportunities for you to gain immeasurable power. You have done what you needed to do and with optimum timing for I have enchanted Cardinal's mind. He is currently about to make a decision to welcome me into the forefront of his heart, and now that you have ascended, we will be able to trap him." Porn explains and places a hand on Abuse's shoulder. "Welcome to the Ascension."

Cardinal's day began to slowly come to an end. It was 2:50 pm. The end of school, Cardinal and his sister Aurelia and Jade all had a two mile walk in order to get back home. They commenced with the small talk about how their day was and the things they had learned, all the while, Cardinal was still thinking how he was going to indulge in this new experience. Each step he took closer to his house the intensity built. He could feel and see Anxiety and Stress gripping his throat, turning his stomach, drying his mouth. Cardinal just took step after step as he began to approach his house. As he turned the corner to ascend the hill to his home he saw a hooded figure, brightly lit, appear to him on the corner. The Figure was only there for an instant to give him some information.

"Cardinal, my name is Conviction. I am what you know as a Hoodie. I have been here with you since your conception and will continue to be here for you until the day you die. I am here though not to educate you but to inform you. You have the freedom of choice so choose ye this day. If you decide to yield to your corrupted mind then you will spend years trapped. Hurt, Pain, Distrust are a few of the things that are going to become a part of you. DO NOT GO INTO YOUR HOUSE AND WATCH PORN." Conviction urged before walking away and vanishing.

Cardinal was so fixated on the choice that he felt he already made that the Blazer Justification began to whisper in his ear.

"It's definitely not all that. Porn is only to you. How could you be hurting someone else when all you are doing is pleasing yourself. You are really just overthinking this. It's gonna be fun. Just remember to clear the search history and the cookies and you'll be fine."

Cardinal heard both utterances and made his way to the bathroom with his father's laptop in hand. He had a small gap in between his father coming home from the school so this was the best moment to do his research. He sat down on the toilet seat cover and cracked the laptop open.

"Of Course, it's password protected," Cardinal said.

This really was not a problem since his father used the same password for all of his accounts. He typed in the first password and like it was not protected at all the computer welcomed him back. Cardinal took his index finger and scrolled to the icon of the flaming fox, known as Firefox, and double clicked. He worked the cursor up to the tab and opened a discrete tab so that he could not have the information he typed in to be tracked. He memorized the site that his buddy told him at school so he then used the rest of fingers to punch the keys to spell out the website in the search bar. Once everything was punched in, he hit enter. In that moment a warning message popped up which ushered a response of maturity.

"The user must be 18 or older to view content. Please hit the check box if you would like to continue." the message stated.

Cardinal hit the box and hit "I Agree." In that moment an influx of provocative images and videos flooded the eye gates of the young man. As his mind began to process what he was seeing his body began to have a reaction to the images. He felt his blood pressure rise, his body got hot, his mouth salivated, and an erection started. He then found something that seemed to fit his appetite and commenced with feeling himself. Porn now empowered by the decision Cardinal made began to flow throughout Cardinal's being. Porn created his home in Cardinal's womb. Beyond his stomach, beyond his internal organs, and rested in his soul. This now became the home of the Coats. It did not take long for Cardinal to finish his investigation. Once he was done, he wiped up his mess and flushed the toilet and walked out of the bathroom. He made sure to clear the history and delete the cookies so that his father would not figure out what he was doing. He felt really weird though. His stomach hurt and his head was pounding. The only thing he could think about was the next time he would be able to indulge in this sexual act again. Not too long after he finished watching the sexual videos his dad walked into the house and asked each one of them how school was. The day concluded like any other day did, except that Cardinal convinced himself that he would stay up until everyone went to sleep to look at that website again.

The time had finally come. It was extremely late in the night and both Cardinal's parents had gone to bed and all of his siblings had been tucked in. Cardinal went to the place where he hid his father's laptop and took it into a corner of the room in the back of the house to enact his pleasure. He opened the laptop and used the same steps as he did before but this time it seemed that the same video did not have the same effect it did the first time. Cardinal's Lustful appetite grew. He scrolled through the website to find something more enticing. As he began to scroll, he saw images and videos that were even more explicit and provocative than the last one.

"This one look good" He began to think. He clicked the video and watched.

After he was done, he closed the laptop and placed it on the couch in the living room, which was a common place for his father's laptop. He cleaned up himself and went to bed.

That night at the Heart of Man and Man's Bosom two coats Abuse and Porn met with another coat.

"Guy's, we did it, we enslaved him just like we planned to. Abuse now that we have a permanent hold over him you will be able to create triggers that will affect his interaction with others for the rest of his life." Porn energetically states.

"What do you mean?" Abuse asks

"It's evident what Porn is saying. Now that we have become a part of his DNA then something as small as a shoulder touch or someone standing behind him will create panic, Anxiety, Stress, discomfort." Lust explains.

"I see what you are saying, I do not believe that we have had the pleasure to meet. I am Abuse." Abuse introduces himself.

"Yes I know who you are because you becoming a Coat was spectacular, in fact many of us Coats know you here. My name is Lust and Porn and I work very closely with one another. We are kindred if you will."

"Man Lust you getting fat, Cardinal fed you a lot today." Porn jokingly said.

"Come on now Porn this body is just a premonition I can look how I want to. I just value the power I have acquired and I see it more appropriately depicted this way." Lust rebuttals.

"Wow I didn't know my ascension was that renowned." Abuse thought to himself.

"It is seldom that someone just jumps rank like you did so yeah kind of a big deal. I would like to think it was more my plan to give you those momentary powers than it was Porn's." Lust informed.

"Wait, you mean you had a hand in this?" Abuse Questioned.

"Of course I did, like I told you Porn and I are kindred spirits, but also it's because this was the same process that I tried on Porn when he was a Blazer, but Porn had the support of some powerful individuals, and because of this I could not devour Porn." Lust furthers.

"You attempted to devour Porn? Wow!" Abuse exclaims. "You can't just say stuff like that Lust and not give the entire story. Lust was here before I ever was. In existence I mean. When I was finally conceived, Lust was very arrogant and undermined my power and abilities. So much so that at one point we were ranked the same. Blazers. I do not know who authorized Lust's new powers for the time but she got them all of a sudden and she tried desperately to consume me. Thankfully because of the plans for Cardinal's life our Tuxedo did not allow her to consume me. It's all because of the relationship that the Tuxedo and I have with one another. It is nothing special, it is simply he has favorites and I happen to be one of them." Porn addresses. "But let's keep it real Lust even if you could have consumed me you never would have gotten the opportunity to do it because I am too much for you to handle." Porn finishes.

"Please you were a pup back then, nothing I couldn't have handled." Lust schoffs.

"I guess the history runs deep with you two. The question that I have is what does this new home mean for the three of us?" Abuse asks

"Don't be so dense, have you not seen how big this place is and how many rooms there are in here. We are not the only three that will reside here, in fact the other 2 coats will be here soon." Porn informs.

"That's right. Now just because we have now been issued a place outside of the Heart of Man does not mean that your responsibilities change. In fact now we have even more work to do. We have to be diligent in keeping this place intact because this place is commonly where hoodies reside. We have just won the battle to reside here. So not only will we have to administer protocols and missions for our teams at the Heart of Man but now we will have to battle for this place. Since you are the newest of the Coats, is this something that you think you would be able to handle Abuse?" Lust questions.

With a maniacal grin Abuse responds. "Absolutely."

That night Cardinal slept uneasily. He tossed and turned while his Coats and Blazers were at work putting in play the plans and plots, they had for his life; all the while, his hoodies Peace and Mercy soothed him into deep sleep.

DESTINY

Cardinal woke up the next morning ready for an eventful day. His eyes were heavy from a night of mediocre sleep, but yet he was somewhat excited to educate his friends on the discovery he had just made. He wiped the eye boogers from his eye and went to the bathroom to brush his teeth and wash his face. He looked down at the bathroom toilet seat cover and remembered the day that he had yesterday sitting there.

"When I get home from school, I have got to do that again." Cardinal thought to himself.

He then finished brushing his teeth, then cupped his hands together to reserve a place for the warm sink water to form. He puckered his lips and sucked the water into his mouth. He swished the water around for a few seconds then spit it all back into the sink. After he was finished with his teeth, he cupped his hands one last time and splashed the water into his face. He closed his eyes to prevent the water from going into his eyes. He blindly reached around to the towel rack to acquire a towel to remove the water from his face. Once Cardinal had finished his morning routine, he exited the bathroom and went to pack up his things for the day. Once all his books were packed, his lunch was placed in his backpack, and he had his homework in the appropriate folders, his father drove him and his sisters to school.

Cardinal had processed and practiced exactly what he was going to tell his friends the moment he saw them. He was going to tell them how the euphoria felt from watching Porn. He knew he would not see his friends until either lunch or the first break, so Cardinal was looking forward to meeting up with them the entire morning. He entered into his first class for the day which was English. This was a subject that bored him because he hated reading, he would much rather walk through the step-by-step process of an equation any day.

Ring, went the bell, indicating that the time to transition from this class to the next was at hand. Cardinal picked up all his books and backpack and started to walk to his next class which was his favorite, Computer class. This class consisted of the students learning the ins and outs of using Microsoft products and familiarity with other processing capabilities. This class was especially favored by Cardinal because this class included a girl that Cardinal had become smitten with. Her name was Coquelicot.

"Hey Cardinal." Coquelicot yelled as she ran from across the courtyard.

"Hey Coquelicot. Did you finish the assignment for this class today?" Cardinal asked waiting for Coquelicot to reach him.

"Wait, there was an assignment for this class?" Coquelicot asked.

"I can see that you didn't do it, but hey you still have time." Cardinal informed.

"Okay what do I have to do?" Coquelicot asked.

"All you have to do is…Give me a hug." Cardinal smirking responded.

"Woooooow. You really had me there." Coquelicot said chuckling.

She reached out her arms and embraced Cardinal as they waited outside the door of the classroom for the teacher to open the door for all the students to come inside.

"Man, it's cold out here. When is she going to open the door?" Cardinal attempting to make small talk.

"You know she is always late." Coquelicot says while turning her head and spotting someone. "In the meantime, I'm gonna go buy some candy before class so I have something to snack on. You want something?" Coquelicot asks.

"Yeah. I'll take a few sour strips. Thank you." Says Cardinal

Thankfully in their class there was a boy that sold candy from his backpack. His mother worked at Costco so he was able to grab the whole box of candy for a low cost. She fronted her son the first few boxes then he went out and paid for his own inventory after. It was quite a lucrative business for a teenage boy just trying to earn some money; however, selling goods from your backpack was against the school policy so students knew to keep the business low key.

"What's up Drew can I have some gummy bears, some sour strips and some chocolate please. I have a 5 dollar bill." Coquelicot orders.

"Yeah no problem." drew responds as they orchestrate their transaction. And in perfect timing because just as the candy exchanged hands from Drew to Coquelicot the teachers opened the door.

"Good morning class, come on in." The teacher instructed.

Today was no special day for class, except for the fact that within the hour Cardinal could discuss the discovery of his research with his buddies. Each student walked in the classroom one after the other. As Cardinal stepped foot in the room one of his classmates brushed past on his right side and in doing so placed their hand on Cardinal's back. Cardinal spooked by the gesture, jumped a little. In that moment he felt his stomach jump and heart beat erratically. In that moment Stress and Abuse smiled simultaneously from different places. Class went by fairly quickly and like clockwork the bell rang indicating that it was now time for the students to make their way outside for break. Cardinal logged off his computer and picked up his backpack. As he placed his backpack on his shoulder he realized that his friend Coquelicot was waiting for him outside of the door.

"Hey what class do you have after this?" Coquelicot asked Cardinal.

"Math, with Mr. Nixon." Cardinal responded.

"Wow you got him. He is such a good teacher. Well I will see you then because my class is on the other side of the campus." Coquelicot said.

"Okay I'll see you around lunch." Cardinal spoke with some relief. He was slightly nervous about her being there with him and as he talked to his classmates about the discovery that he made that night. As he made his way up the steep hill to get back to the main part of the campus one of his classmates Forest yelled out his name from the other side of the campus.

"Cardinal! Hold up man!" Forest yelled out.

"Hey what are you doing down at the principal's office dude?" Cardinal asked.

"Oh I'm not in trouble or anything, it's just, I forgot my lunch and my mom had to drop it off to me." Forest responded.

"Wow you mom really cares for you. Shoot had that been me, my parents would have called themselves teaching me a lesson and I would not have eaten for the day." Cardinal jokingly proclaimed with an anxious giggle.

Forest and Cardinal made their way up to the deck where Cardinal and Forest's classroom were after the break. It was also the meeting place for their friend Seltzen. Right after they approached the stairs to ascend to the deck, they heard Seltzen's voice from up above.

"Hey what's up guys." Seltzen greeted.

This was the moment that Cardinal had been waiting for, the time to tell his friends about the things he had seen that night.

"Hey did you guys watch that episode of Dragonball Z last night?" Cardinal questioned, attempting to start the conversation with something a little more tame.

"Yeah man it was another one of those filler episodes where we do not get to see the fighting until maybe next week. I really hate when they do this, why can't they just give us what we want to see?" Seltzen spoke with passion.

"Yeah man I did not get the opportunity to watch it last night because of all the homework I had to get through. Maybe I will catch the rerun on Thursday." Forest remarked with disappointment.

"Yeah well my parents do not let my siblings and I watch television during the week so I will have to catch it this weekend......Oh man guys you should have seen the videos I watched last night with this girl and this guy it was crazy." Cardinal said as he went into grave detail about the video he watched and over exaggerating the euphoria and feeling that he had in his bathroom.

"Dude that sounds gnarly, what site did you go to?" Seltzen asked.

"Oh you know the site that everyone goes to." Cardinal stated.

"Dude you know there are literally hundreds of websites on the web that show porn right?" Forest informed.

"Well since you seem to be the expert why don't you educate me on all the websites you use." Cardinal snerked.

"You know Cardinal I'm starting to get the impression that yesterday was the first time you even watched porn. How did you say that you came across it again?" Forest probed.

At that moment Cardinal realized that he needed to remember someone else's story to authenticate his lie. He remembered people talking about finding dirty magazines under their brothers' beds. That wouldn't work for Cardinal because he was the older brother. He began to think how he could spin this story, and without even a second thought Cardinal said.

"Dude my older cousin had these playboy bunny magazines under his bed and triple x magazines that I saw one day. I looked them up on the internet and that's how I came across it. I am just saying I am not a veteran like you are." Cardinal spoke.

"Dude, that's like me, although I saw some magazines in my dad's closet. He almost caught me last night on my cell phone but I was able to close it before he came upstairs. Hey if you go to this site, you see all the crazy stuff. If you go here, you can watch celebrity tapes. And if you go here, you can watch all black girls. Dude there is literally so much." Forest said.

"I will have to look at that stuff tonight." Cardinal and Seltzen both agreed.

Ring went to the bell to indicate that the next class was soon to start.

"Alright guys I will see you at lunch." Cardinal proclaimed. "See you dawg." Forest responded.

"See you dude." Seltzen also responded.

Cardinal walked over to where his classroom was to prepare for his instructor to let him in. Cardinal used all of his concentration to try and remember the websites that Forest told him just minutes ago. Never before was he so willing to go inside of class so that he could jot down the information that he learned.

"Wassup kids, who's ready to get down on some math?" Mr. Nixon asked. Mr. Nixon was one of those cool younger teachers. He was always hip to the latest fashions and slang and advocated for the black men in the class to never sag their pants and to get their education. As soon as Cardinal sat down at his desk, he opened up his notebook and jotted down the websites that he heard so he would not forget them for later. As Mr. Nixon taught the class about the new equation that they would be using for the next few days, Cardinal's mind drifted into the wonders of what he would find on the computer when he got home.

Back at Man's Bosom, Porn continued to link the chain that he would soon wrap around the mind, heart, and soul of Cardinal.

Cardinal's school day wrapped up with little to nothing happening. Surprisingly this was a day that his father came to pick up him and his sisters.

"Hey Dad, we get a ride today?" Aurelia asked "Yeah, get in the car." Alpha ushered.

They drove for a few minutes until they pulled into the driveway of their home. As they were all getting out of the car Alpha reached back and said.

"Not you Cardinal, you stay in the car."

At this point Cardinal's heart started to race.

"Why did my father only want me to stay in the car? Did he find out what I did the other night? Am I in trouble?" These were the things that went through his mind as Alpha orchestrated him to get into the front seat of the car. Before Cardinal could even panic anymore his father opened his mouth and asked.

"Do you have any homework to do today?"

"Yes." Cardinal said with hesitancy for he was still confused and nervous for why his dad asked him to stay in the car.

"Well the reason I asked you to stay in the car is because your granddaddy called me today and asked me if I had taken you to the golf course since we came back from that Washington trip, and when I responded to him that I had not. He questioned why I did not, I further responded to him that I did not because I did not have the money to pay for the equipment and the lessons. He told me to take you today to the moment you got out of school to the golf course, but I have to ask you a question before we go up there and you waste my time and your grandfather's money; Do you want to play golf?" Alpha asked.

Relieved by what his father asked, Cardinal began to feel more and more relaxed. Cardinal responded. "Yes I do."

"Okay then let's go." Alpha said while turning the car back on and putting on his seatbelt.

Cardinal wanted to play golf since his parents could remember. In fact it was told that Cardinal had asked his parents if he could play golf at the ripe age of 6; however, the perspective of his father at that time was that "Golf is a white man's game." So Cardinal did other things instead. It was not until one day when Cardinal was much smaller than he is now that Cardinal and his family made a trip to Washington to visit his parents' family friends and two cousins, one of which shared a birthday with Cardinal, and were the same age. They spent an entire week in Washington in a massive house on acres of land. One of those days that they were there, Cardinal escaped from the house into their backyard where he found just sitting on the side of the house some old rusted golf clubs and some old water stained golf balls. Cardinal picked up one of the clubs in his hands and positioned one of the balls in the grass and swung and hit the ball with good form and precision. Little did Cardinal know there were a few people watching him at this time, His father, mother, uncle, and a hoodie known as Destiny.

"Hey, I didn't know your son played golf." Cardinal's uncle asked.

"He doesn't." Alpha responded.

"Shoot you may want to consider putting him into it. His swing is elegant and did you see how far he hit that ball? That boy is talented. You might want to consider putting him into golf." The uncle praised.

"Man look here, the moment we get back to the bay area he 'gon be the next Tiger Woods." Alpha said with pride.

The three adults walked outside to where Cardinal was hitting golf balls, and they watched intently as he struck another ball into the grassy field. From that day Destiny took a back seat in Cardinal's life because in order for Cardinal to experience the fullness of this lifestyle he would need the assistance of his father, who, after they returned to the bay there was no golf to be played until this day.

The drive to the golf course was so exciting for Cardinal. He could feel Joy and Happiness close by as the car passed another stop light. They drove for a few minutes before they finally arrived at the golf course Blue Stone Lake. This was a very large course. There were two sides, one course on each side of the street. The side that Alpha had pulled up to was the driving range. Cardinal could barely hold in his excitement as he prepared to jump out of the car. The moment his feet hit the concrete he could feel the energy, joy, elation, euphoria all grace his presence. Destiny also got out of the car with Cardinal and with a pat on the head stepped foot after foot with Cardinal and Alpha as they made their way to the driving range pro shop. Alpha opened up the heavy metal and glass door that led to the inside of the driving range where they were met with an extremely rude and disgruntled elderly man.

"What you boys need?" The elderly man asked with an attitude.

"I have never played golf before, and my son really wants to play. Can you help me in figuring out what I need to do in order for him to start? Could you also direct me to someone that can instruct him because, like I said, we are new to the game." Alpha transparently and politely asked.

The elder man with irritation in his voice said, "Does your son have any clubs?"

"No, like I said we….." Alpha started before being interrupted.

"Is he right-handed or left-handed?" The old man asked. "Right." Alpha responded keeping it direct and short this time.

"Okay if he is right-handed, he will need a glove for his left hand. Here take this club down to the driving range. Do you have money to pay for some golf balls?" the old man asked.

"Yes." Alpha responded.

"Okay it's going to be 8.50 for the balls and 6.75 for the glove. Now when you get down there just start hitting balls and I will send someone down to give you lessons." The old man instructed while taking the money and giving Alpha some tokens for the driving range machine.

"I'm sorry, what am I supposed to do with these?" Alpha asked.

The old man rolling his eyes said, "You take these to the machine on the outside. You put one token in at a time. Make sure the bucket is under the feeder before you stick the token in. The balls will dispense. Any more questions?" The old man asked.

Without responding to the old man, Alpha lovingly cupped the back of Cardinal's head and ushered him to the door. When they got to the machine Alpha followed the old man's instruction to the T. While the balls were dispensing into the bucket Alpha looked at his son and asked.

"Did you sense that?"

"Yeah. What was wrong with him? Why is he so rude? We did not even do anything." Cardinal answered with confusion and hurt in his voice.

"Son, don't let that get to you. Some people are just like that. In fact in this game, you will experience a lot of that, so just build your mind and prepare for what is to come because that is just the start." Alpha warned Cardinal.

Once all the balls had been filled in the bucket Cardinal carried the balls and the 2 clubs down the steep hill to the bottom where 25 mats lined the driving range. A sea of men stood atop each mat sending the little white balls flying for what seemed like miles. It was almost like the verbal exchange that Cardinal witnessed with his father and the old man did not happen after the wonder and amazement flooded Cardinal's eyes.

"Wow!" Cardinal thought, seeing everything in all its glory.

Once they descended down to where the mats were they looked for an empty stall to position themselves to strike their own freshly cleaned golf balls into what seemed like an endless field.

"Look dad there's one!" Cardinal expressed with enthusiasm and excitement.

They both walked to the empty stall. Cardinal placed his clubs down on the mat and looked into the field of green and saw numbers that lined certain sections of the land. 100, 150, 200, 250.

"What are these numbers? A point system? Distance?" Cardinal began to think to himself.

Atop the 150 number was a fetish looking metal sign with an individual bending over and their red polka dot underwear showing, and atop the 200 there was the same sign except the underwear was blue with polka dots.

"How silly." Cardinal giggled in his mind.

"Go ahead, show me what you got." Alpha said while sitting down on the bench behind Cardinal.

With his heart racing and excitement building Cardinal put on his glove and picked up the club with the number 7 on the bottom of it. He placed a golf ball with the word "pinnacle" on the rubber tee protruding from the artificial turf. He set up his stance, gripped the club, and swung at the ball with all he had.

Smack The ball flew all the way to where the 100 number was. "Whoa, dad did you see that?" Cardinal asked.

"Yeah that was awesome son. Keep hitting balls." Alpha smiled.

Cardinal placed another ball on the tee and swung again. This one he topped and the ball rolled a few feet in front of him. He picked up another one and placed it on the tee. As he was getting ready to swing an elderly Mexican guy approached Alpha and Cardinal.

"Hey, were you the guy who was inquiring about lessons? JoJo up at the Pro shop was telling me about it" The elderly Mexican guy asked.

"Yeah that is us. My name is Alpha Wolf and this is my son Cardinal Wolf." Both of them reach out their hands to shake the stranger's hand.

"My name is Francisco Fernando. It's a pleasure to meet you both. Okay kiddo, let's see that beautiful swing of yours." He instructed.

Cardinal gripped the club and approached the ball. Before he could even step up to swing at the ball Francisco stopped him.

"Okay Cardinal, before you can swing, we have to make sure that your grip is correct. If you hold the club like that then you will have no control over the ball. You want to make sure that your left hand is positioned on the club like this." Francisco taking the club in hand showing Cardinal how to hold it. "Then once you have your left hand on the club then you can unite the right hand like this." Francisco then placed his right hand on the club showing how it should look to Cardinal and Alpha.

Once Cardinal placed his hands on the club like his instructor asked him to do, he swung at the ball and felt a totally different sensation. It seemed like he could feel everything connected.

"Great Job kiddo. This is your first lesson today. Your grip needs to be perfected before you come back for another lesson. As for today, enjoy your time hitting balls and always check your grip to make sure it's correct. Now dad you have some homework of your own, you have to make sure that he is practicing otherwise this teaching will be in vain. Bring him back next week and we will see how he is doing." Francisco said while preparing to leave.

"How much are your lessons?" Alpha asked.

"Do not worry about it today, if he is serious about golf and I see you next week we can talk about fees." Francisco said while leaving.

"Thank you!" Cardinal said loudly to express his gratitude for the interest the man had taken.

"No problem kiddo. Enjoy." He responded while walking down some stalls to grab baskets and go back to the Pro shop.

Cardinal hit the rest of the balls and after finishing looked at his dad with a smile and hugged his torso.

"Thanks dad for taking me to the driving range, this was so awesome." Cardinal expressed.

"Yeah no problem, just make sure you practice what your instructor has instructed because if this is something you want to do, we are going to make sure you get what you need." Alpha said.

"Well how can I practice griping if I do not have any clubs?" Cardinal asked.

"We are going to Big 5 to go pick up some clubs for you right now." Alpha quickly responded.

"Ouch. My hands hurt." Cardinal stated as he played with the newly formed bubble on his hand.

"Just don't pop that because I can guarantee that it will hurt much more. This is your first step to gaining callus on your hands. It will make it to where when you do this again it will not hurt." Alpha remarked as they walked up the ramp back to the car. "Oh snap, I forgot to give this club back, go get in the car while I run this back inside." Alpha instructed. Cardinal listened to the instructions of his father and walked back to the car with his new friend Destiny. They sat in the car for a few minutes when Alpha got back into the car.

"Sorry Cardinal, I was trying to get some information from your coach about what would be the best stuff to get you to start playing golf. He wrote me a little list so that when we go to Big 5 we know what to look for."

"Ok. So are we going to Big 5 now?"

"Yes. Call your granddaddy and tell him thank you for investing in you. Cause to be honest, I do not know if this would have happened had it not been for him." Alpha said while passing over his cell phone.

Ring ring ring. Ring ring ring. Ring….click "Hello." An elderly man spoke from the other side of the phone.

"Hey granddaddy, it's me Cardinal." Cardinal introduced himself with a smile on his face.

"Well hey suga. How you doing today? It's so good to hear from you today!" Grandaddy said with unwavering joy.

"It's always good to hear from you Grandaddy. I was just calling to tell you thank you so much for paying for me to go to the golf course today. It was a lot of fun. I really enjoy it. In fact my dad and I are going to the store right now to get me some gear so I can practice at home." Cardinal detailed.

"That's good to hear suga. I was gon' ask if your dad took you up there today. I gave him the money to get you started on your way. I just want you to do something that you enjoy baby." said Grandaddy.

"I know Grandaddy. How are you doing today?" Cardinal asked.

"You know I am doing alright. I really can't complain. I'm alive and breathing and that's all you can really ask for. Just sitting here watching these horses run." Grandaddy informed.

"Oh did you win anything today?" Cardinal asked.

"Well, I got a lil' somethin' somethin'. Nothing too major. Now you know Grandaddy gotta come up there and watch you hit them balls right?" Grandaddy questioned jokingly.

"Yeah, I can't wait for you to see me swing, but you have to wait until I actually get good at the game first." Cardinal said with little confidence.

"Okay, will do son." Grandaddy said.

"Okay we are at the store now. Thank you again Grandaddy and I love you." Cardinal said, exiting the conversation.

"Okay suga. I love you too. Bye."

Click went the phone as they hung up with one another.

Cardinal and Alpha shopped in the store for a few minutes knocking off all the items on the list that the coach had given him at the course. Once everything had been obtained and paid for, the two of them drove just a short 3 miles back to their house. By this time Omega had made it home from work and it was pretty close to dinner time. Before Cardinal was able to go into the house Alpha had one last thing to say to Cardinal.

"Now look, just because you were out there having fun does not mean you start neglecting your responsibilities at the house. The moment you start slipping up in the house or in school will be the moment we cut your little golfing. Do you understand me?" Alpha authoritatively said.

"Yes." Cardinal responds.

"Now get in there and do your chores and your homework." Alpha ordered.

They both exited the car with the bags of the newly purchased equipment in their hands. Cardinal reached for the door handle and turned the knob. As soon as the door swung open Cardinal was bombarded by the sound of many voices screaming, "Daddy." It was all his siblings and even the dog aroused by the entry of Alpha. What a beautiful joyous noise. Cardinal knocked out his chores quickly so that he could go into the backyard and swing with his new clubs. After dinner Cardinal finished his homework with intensity and speed and was right in the backyard practicing his grip and new swing. While Cardinal was swinging his club, he heard a small voice beckoning from the pits of his bosom.

"Don't forget about me." The voice whispered. It was Porn reminding Cardinal of his new habit. Cardinal placed the club against the wall and went back inside of the house. He realized at the moment he would not be able to indulge in his sinful pleasure because his sister was still up doing the dishes. So Cardinal went on the computer in the back of the house and started to do some reading from his textbook to guarantee he was fully understanding all his reading material. A few hours passed and his older sister had finished the dishes and the entire house fell to silence. This was the opportunity that Cardinal had been waiting for the whole night. He went to the living room where his father kept his laptop and carried it to the back of the house. He made sure to mute the volume so that he would not be discovered. He cracked open the laptop and entered his father's password to gain access to the computer. Once he successfully had access to the internet Cardinal went to his backpack to grab the notes that he took from today about the best websites to visit. He tapped the keyboard with the succession of letters to get to the first website. The moment he hit enter he was flooded with many images and videos that would be nearly impossible for anyone to forget. And he didn't forget.

CONSEQUENCE

The rest of the school year flew by like a light leaf on an autumn day. Cardinal's 8th grade year had come to a close and the next chapter of his life was beginning. High School. This was a difficult moment to deal with for Cardinal because all of the bonds that he made from this school were also coming to an end. All his friends, all the experiences, all the fun would be lost to memories. The day of the promotion from Eighth grade was a great occasion. Cardinal was able to get dressed up in his best clothes, got a fresh haircut, and now that puberty had started to slow down, he was feeling himself. He placed his gown over the top of his clothing and sprayed his cologne over his gown. Now he was ready to walk the stage.

"You look so handsome." Omega emphatically stated while grabbing her camera.

"Come on mom, no cameras." Cardinal expresses with a smile.

"On three. One. Two. Three." Omega says while clicking the picture of Cardinal standing in a funny pose.

"Come on y'all or he is going to be late." Alpha yells from outside of the house.

Cardinal grabs his cap and runs to the van. He grabs the handle and slides the door open and climbs in the back seat while his sisters and his brother get in the van behind him. They all click their seatbelts on and Alpha turns the key to start the car. They back out of the driveway and begin to drive to the park where they were hosting the promotion. Once they had pulled up to the park, Cardinal turned around in his seat and noticed the long white van that had been following them was Carolina Bears.

"Hey dad can I get out here so that I can meet up with Azure? He is right behind us." Cardinal asked.

"Sure thing let me turn on my hazards so they know you're getting out." Alpha informed.

Alpha turned on his Hazard lights and Cardinal got out and ran to Carolina's van. When Carolina saw Cardinal, she put her car in park. Cardinal could see Azure getting out of the back seat of the van to get to the door. Once he reached the door he hopped out and they ran to one another and embraced each other with a hug.

"What's good bro, you ready for today?" Azure asked. "Yes and no." Cardinal confessed.

"Why not bro. We are finally going to be in high school. That's exciting." Azure reasoned.

"Yeeeeaaah. But the thing is I am not coming back to the same school district in the fall. My parents are moving me to a better school district. One where the education is supposedly more advanced and where I can practice golf for the school as well." Cardinal confessed.

"Hey bud, don't sound so gloomy. It's all good it's not like we do not live right around the corner from one another. We will still see each other. All you gotta do is come over whenever you want to hang out." Azure reminded Cardinal.

"True; although we will not have the same friend group or even share the same experiences anymore bro." Cardinal still unfazed by the conversation.

"Yeah but dude it is okay. We are family. Maybe I can convince my mom to transfer me over to your school district. Honestly, she might because I want to play football and they do not have that program in this high school." Azure said thinking.

"Yeah man that would be cool if she could make that happen." Cardinal admitted.

They walked and talked until they came to the building where a woman began instructing children to separate according to their last names. Since Wolf and Bear were at opposite ends of the alphabet Cardinal and Azure had to depart from one another, with a quick hand shake they separated from one another. Cardinal walked down the hall until he ran into his classmate with the same last name as him.

"Falu what's up. Is this where we are supposed to be standing?" Cardinal asked.

"Yeah man. You ready to do this?" Falu asked.

"Yeah I was just talking to Azure about that, and to be honest I am ready but I am going to miss everyone." Cardinal confessed.

"I hear you man. So do you have any plans for the summer?

Any trips?" Falu asked.

"Honestly, if this summer is like any of my last summers, then I gotta say no. Probably gonna be at home the entire time just playing and practicing my golf game. Gotta prepare to try out for the high school team. What about you?" Cardinal asked.

"This year my family is traveling to Japan. I'm so excited. I always wanted to go there, and this summer we are going to go. In fact we are supposed to hop on a plane right after this promotion is over." Falu confessed.

"Wow man lucky you. That is going to be one heck of a vacation. I always wanted to go to Japan myself. Maybe one day I'll be able to go." Cardinal exclaims.

"Alright students in line. We are going to start walking one after another when you get into your row, just go down until you get to your seat and just sit down. Please do not get out of order because if you do, they will call the wrong name as you walk out. Thank you. Let's go." The school attendant instructed. Each child walked out one after the other just as instructed, while they walked out to the crowd of parents, each one let out a scream when they noticed their child was amongst those that were attempting to go find a seat. One by one the young men and women walked out with gowns and caps on their heads until the last student emerged from the back and sat in their seat. At that moment the speaker of the promotion approached the microphone to give touching words about why they believed the group of students sitting there would be the next cure for the world. Cardinal and surely many of the other eighth graders had tuned the words of the lady speaking out, all they could think of was the amount of fun they were going to have this summer.

"And now let's welcome the graduating class." the announcer announced as she began reading the names of the students approaching the podium to ascertain their certificates.

"Azure Bear." The announcer spoke into the mic. "Wooooo that's my dawg! That's my dawg!" Cardinal yelled out along with many of Azure's siblings and family.

Some time went by as the names were read from a long list. Eventually the time had come where Cardinal's name would be called.

"Cardinal Wolf." The announcer spoke.

"Wooooo. Let's go Cardinal." Cardinal could hear Azure screaming out amidst the sounds of his family screaming and praising his accomplishment.

More time slipped by and eventually the announcer announced that the promoted class could arise and walk back out the side door that they had emerged from an hour ago. Each row stood up in order and walked out the side door to meet their family who were waiting outside of the building. Cardinal and Azure met up after the ceremony and with an arm over each other's shoulder and back, they confessed to one another the love that they would eternally share as brothers.

"Hey man don't forget." Azure nudging Cardinal. "Forget what?" Cardinal asked.

"That even though you are moving to another school, we are still gonna marry twins and live as neighbors. That's the dream." Azure reminded.

"Dude ooooffff course. That's the dream." Cardinal assured as he echoed back the words that they shared early in their friendship.

While Cardinal and his family were celebrating, back at the bosom of man Abuse saw a vision that concerned him.

"Porn, how good is your grip on Cardinal's life?" Abuse questioned.

"Fantastic, in fact I grow stronger each day of his life. I am constantly on the prowl adding more Suits and blazers to my rank. In fact, I have a meeting set up with Stress and Fear later today to grant Depression head of their ranks. He is definitely much more equipped to deal with them. Why did you ask me something like that?" Porn curiously questions

"Because I just saw a situation arise that might be problematic for you, that will in turn make me much more powerful." Abuse confessed.

"Well what happened?" Porn asks.

"You will be discovered by Alpha before the summer is over. I do not know when that will happen but I suspect that if you are discovered then you will also be purged." Abuse confesses.

"Yes I do know of this event that you speak of Abuse, but understand that I am not concerned at all. You see, by my presence becoming known to Alpha I have a rare opportunity. I can slip through his eye gates and perhaps infect him as well. Now, there is a chance that I can become purged, and if that were to happen then I would be forever gone from Cardinal's life. The uncertainty is thrilling wouldn't you say?" Porn asks, smiling.

"So, what, are you telling me that you don't have a plan to overcome this?" Abuse questioned.

"Of course I have something planned. In fact we are going to visit our good friends the Neutrals and see if there is anything they can do in my favor. You are more than welcome to accompany me in my journey to their land,

Abuse." Porn invites.

"Yeah I'll go, but who are we going to see?" Abuse asks confused with the lack of information.

"We are going to see Consequence." Porn informs. "Consequence? Yes I do remember seeing that name on the directory when I was in there the last time. How do you figure that you will be able to convince Consequence to help you in this endeavor? I thought Neutrals were called neutrals because they were not for or against humanity. They are just principles? Right? At least that's what Death the Reaper told me." Abuse confessed.

"That's the thing with the Neutrals, they are based around causality, and they do not inherently cause anything to happen but they are the effect of an action but my dear Abuse there is a loophole to dealing with the Neutrals." Porn admits.

"Really!? What's that!?" Abuse asks confused.

"You will have to wait till we get there and I will show you what I'm talking about. You ready?" Porn asks.

"Let's go." Abuse responds.

Abuse and Porn both vanished to the gate between the realms to head into the land of the Neutrals. Before they made their way into the headquarters of the Neutrals, Porn turns his head and looks at Abuse and says, "Now Abuse when we get in there no matter what happens, I need for you not to get involved and just let whatever happens happen." Porn says with a smile on his face.

"Sure thing but what is that supposed to mean?" Abuse asks.

"Consequence and I have a pretty good relationship but there are some things that have not been resolved yet and because of that Consequence might want to eradicate me." Porn confesses.

"But how? I thought Neutrals could only be reactionary." Abuse asks confused.

"I'll tell you if we make it out of here alive." Porn states as he pushes open the door to the massive building. Porn and Abuse step over the threshold of the building and Abuse makes his way over to the directory to see where they need to go in order to meet with Consequence. As he starts walking over to the directory Porn interrupts his motion by placing his arm around his shoulders.

"Since you have been here before you know exactly how to get up to their offices, but this time we are not going to be using the directory to go upstairs. This time we are going to be going a different way." Porn states while leading Abuse away from the directory. Abuse followed while under the arm of Porn, all the while extremely confused.

"What other way is there up there? There are no stairs here. There is no elevator. There is no other way upstairs Porn. I don't know if when you were here the last time things were different but I do not see another way up there." Abuse vocalized his confusion.

As soon as Abuse finished talking Porn removed his arm from Abuse shoulder and punched him directly in the stomach. Abuse not only shocked but also in pain collapsed in the middle of the floor. He gasped for breath and after his lungs were filled to the capacity necessary, he let out a scream that seemed like it would shatter a rift in space. At that moment two figures appeared out of nowhere, and before Abuse could even look up to see who they were they were both escorted through the building at speeds equivalent to that of when he saw Death the Reaper. As Abuse formed a thought of where they could be going a few cloaked individuals sat before them at a long glass like table. The room was almost as prestigious as the lobby was, floor made of onyx, ceilings flowed with satin, walls made of marble. The Cloaked individuals did not speak they just sat in silence as they stared at Porn and Abuse. Porn smiling looks over at Abuse and began to talk.

"Good evening Council. How is everyone doing today? Good I hope." Porn being facetious.

"Porn why are you here? You know well that you are not welcome here, especially after what you tried the last time." One of the cloaked individuals stated.

Abuse began to stand up coughing, "Wait a minute, what was done the last time?"

"I'm so sorry where are my manners, This is one of the newest Coats. His name is Abuse. He actually came here before with…." Porn expresses before he is abruptly stopped by one of the cloaked figures.

"Pornography, why have you not told him why you are not allowed in here?"

"Wow my full name, someone must really be upset by what I attempted the last time." Porn interjects.

"Can you all stop speaking in code and just tell me what is going on please." Abuse says with frustration.

"Isn't it pretty obvious what is going on here. Porn needed you to get in here, and the reason that he assaulted you was because he needed a council meeting, otherwise he would not be able to meet with any one of us. You see Abuse, the last time Porn was in here he went to see Consequence and Pain. After leaving the office of Pain he ventures into Consequence's office to try and propose a union between the two of them. After Consequence explained to Porn that a plan like that would never work because of their distinctions Porn attempted to devour Consequence. This is why he is not allowed in here. He cannot see any of us Neutrals on a one-on-one appointment so he caused some ruckus to make us all gather so we would have to address him." The cloaked individual explained.

"Y'all are way too sensitive. It's not like it actually worked. The way I see it, no harm no foul. Am I right?" Porn announces jokingly.

"Look Porn, you got what you wanted, you got us all here to meet with you, what do you want? You do know that there is no bargaining with us. Whatever happens, happens." The cloaked figure states.

"Of course I know that. You think I don't know that. I wasn't made a coat yesterday. I know how the rules work. What I need is for Consequence to present herself. Where is she. I need to speak to Consequence." Porn proclaims.

One of the Cloaked individuals reaches up to the hood over their head and removes it to reveal themself to be Consequence.

"Ah there you are Consequence, I do not need you to unite with me, clearly that was a mistake I made the last time and I have grown a lot since that day. What I need for you to do is I need you to be you. There is an event that will soon happen much sooner than I care to admit, but this event will be a cataclysmic one for me. All I need you to do is when this event happens to force judgment on the person responsible for the affliction. Make sure they get what they deserve." Porn advocates.

Abuse shocked by what he just heard. "That doesn't make any sense why would Porn advocate some form of justice to an action that is literally in his DNA. It makes no sense. He is literally asking to be discovered. We do our best work in the shadows. By not being discovered why would he want to be known. Why?" Abuse began to think. Similarly, Consequence was equally as shocked by the request.

"Why do we seldomly get visits from the Hoodies?" One of the cloaked individuals asked.

"Porn, let me get this straight. You came all the way here to tell me to expose you? Are you sure that is what you want? You do know that you can be destroyed if you are discovered right?" Consequence asks.

"I know how this whole thing goes Consequence. You do not have to try and educate me. I asked for something specific. Can you do it?" Porn asks.

"If it's in my nature then it is something that I can do. Is there anything else we can do for you?" The council asks.

"Well since I do not know who the rest of you are there is a once in a lifetime opportunity for you to unite…." Porn attempts to finish before being transported back down to the lobby.

"With me." Porn concluded his statement. "Those neutrals are really something I tell you." Porn addresses Abuse.

"What the heck are you thinking? You really think that what you are asking for is a good idea. You want Consequence to expose you? Are you insane?" Abuse frantically questions.

"One thing you gotta understand Abuse is that vision you saw is not something that we can just wish away; this is something that will happen. It will happen. There is nothing I can do about it, except accelerate it. What you do not understand is that I have accessed this whole scenario. I have been working with our neighboring suits and blazers in order to attain the best success for myself. What you have not experienced yet is a war. I have been through many and this is going to be one of them. If I can enrage Alpha and keep Cardinal consumed by Fear then I will still be here. I will just go dormant for a little while. This will not be the end of me." Porn answers

"You think by doing it, this way you will have a more favorable outcome?" Abuse asks.

"Look in human psychology anytime someone is corrected in a violent way then they will typically become more susceptible to repeating the same action. Like I said I have been communicating with our neighboring Suits and Blazers and I have a pretty good profile on Alpha. I know who he is and what he is capable of. This will work" Porn confesses with confidence.

"Oh yeah Porn one more thing." Abuse says. "Yes." Porn responds

As soon as Abuse noticed that Porn was no longer paying him any attention Abuse wound back his fist and punched Porn right in the back with enough force to level the entire building. Porn absorbed the punch to the back and fell to the ground flat on his face. Abuse regained his stature from the last punch thrown and made his way back to the Bosom of Man, while

Porn laid unconscious in the middle of the lobby of the Neutral Headquarters. The neutrals, completely aware of the altercation that just transpired, relocated the unconscious coat back to the consciousness of Cardinal. Cardinal all the while had no idea what to expect in the coming days. Once back at the Neutral headquarters the Neutrals Consequence, Pain, Life, Death the Reaper, and Time all decided to meet about the coming of the Coats to their location.

"So what are we going to do about Cardinal. We do not interfere with the behaviors and decisions of the humans. I do not know why we keep getting visited by those coats as if we could honestly oblige their requests." Time scoffs

"To be completely honest, Porn was not too out of pocket to ask me to do something. He is in the right. Cardinal had been looking at pornographic images on his father's computer and due to his father's oversight behind the internet, he implemented a firewall to track movement through the internet. This experience is going to happen when? Time?" Consequence spoke.

"According to my watch he will be confronted in the next few days." Time educates.

"So a few days from now Alpha will have an inclination to check the log of all the recent activity on the internet and that will be when Cardinal will have a decision to make. Depending on his decision will dictate whether I need to be there as well." Pain added.

"Indeed. You know we do a lot of work together, Pain." said Consequence.

"Yes it's because like our nature we are reactionary, and I work directly with you according to the event." Pain educated.

"Well we have some work to do. Was that everything?" Death the Reaper asks.

"We still have not talked about what we are going to do about all of our unwelcome guests. There should be some type of protocol in place so that they just don't randomly show up here. They are going through the field of the sleeping nephilim and seraphim now like it's a stroll in the park." Life states.

"I thought we worked out something with the Tuxedo's and the Hoodies about the established protocols of coming here?" Death the Reaper asked.

"Yeah we did, it appears the only ones that seem to leave us in our neutral realm seem to be the Hoodies." Consequence chuckled.

"It would appear to be that way. We should move." Time suggested

"Where would we move to?" Death the Reaper asked out of frustration.

"It was just a thought." Time responded.

"Maybe we establish a binding law that prevents anyone who is not neutral from coming here." Life advocates.

"That is the best idea I have heard thus far, and to be completely honest I do not know why we don't have something like that now." Death the Reaper confessed.

"Well, I hate to cut this short but whoever does not have anything to do can work on creating that, but I have somewhere I have to be." Consequence blurted.

"Okay, fine we will reconvene on this topic shortly." Pain added.

A few days had passed since the graduation and Cardinal celebrated his accomplishments with his family and friends. Cardinal joyously filled his face with cake, ice cream, chicken wings, and soda. "What a day to be alive" he thought to himself. The weather was perfect outside, his taste buds danced with every flavor that dropped on them, his family laughed and played. Everything seemed perfect, juvenile, playful, all the while Cardinal could feel the tug on his gut to sneak in the bathroom with his dad's computer to watch one of his favorite films. "Why are my urges so bad today? Is it because I am having a really good day and I want to have more fulfillment? What is wrong with me?" Cardinal thought to himself. He knew that this was definitely not a good time to indulge in his secret sin, he knew he would have to follow the protocol and watch his video once everyone was sleeping, but even with that knowledge, it did not change the overbearing sensation that he could feel building up inside of him.

"I bet ill scrape you in this videogame." Azure yelled over the music blasting from the other room.

"Dude consider yourself a misbehaved child because you are about to get spanked." Cardinal yelled back with confidence as he ran across the house to get to the controller sprawled out on the floor. The moment Cardinal picked up the controller from the ground he thought about how fleeting this moment would be in the grand scheme of time. Some time from now he would not see his best friend all week like he was used to, things were changing. Azure and Cardinal sat waiting for the Menu screen to pop up for the video game. The colors of several developers popped up and swirled on the television. Finally, the game was ready to be played. Tekken Tag. Cardinal loved fighting games and this was one that he particularly liked to play. They pressed start on the controller and navigated to the character select screen where they chose the 4 characters that would battle each other. Cardinal chose his two favorite characters, a guy named Brian Fury and another guy named Law, who favored the fighting style of the deceased Bruce Lee. Azure chose his two characters who he admitted he chose because they looked strong. A simple and yet accurate deduction.

"Okay now press "A" to select the stage so I can destroy you." Cardinal instructed with confidence.

"Dude I'm trying to tell you I am gonna beat you this time." Azure responded with greater confidence.

"Round 1. FIGHT" The announcer from the video game announced. At that moment the clicking and clacking of fingers navigating buttons on the controllers seemed to be the only sound that filled the room as the two young boys went to work trying to defeat one another.

"K.O." The announcer announced as the seemingly strong character went down. "Round 2. FIGHT." The announcer announced. Again the room filled with the sound of the clicking and clacking of the boys' fingers pressing buttons stringing together what seemed like seamless combinations to program their televised characters.

"K.O." Says the Announcer "Brian Fury Wins." The announcer proclaims the victor.

"Let's Go. I told you I would whoop you like you stole something." said Cardinal arrogantly.

"Chill out, I was just getting warmed up. To be honest those two guys are not even my mains. Let's run it back and I guarantee you won't be so lucky." Azure responded.

They returned to the character select screen where Cardinal chose his second string characters, an alien looking samurai and a white haired martial artist. Azure chose the American icon Paul Phoenix and a kapoeta professional known as Eddie. Since Cardinal won the last round, he was the one who was able to choose the stage. He navigated to a stage on the streets and pressed the select button. They waited for a little while then were transported to their stage.

"Round 1. FIGHT." The announcer announces. Instantly the boys went to fighting one another on the screen. This time it did not seem as effortless for Cardinal to vanquish Azure's characters. Cardinal's second string were characters that he did not practice much with so Azure became quite the contender for this round. Click click clack went the sound of the buttons as they were frantically pressed to control the characters on screen.

"K.O." The announcer proclaims. Eddie wins. "Let's Go!" Azure lets out.

"Hey don't get too excited, that was just the first round we have another round to go." Cardinal quickly rebuttals.

"Round 2. FIGHT." The announcer announces. Again the boys went to tapping and pressing the buttons on the controller. All the while behind the eye lids of Cardinal the Blazer Violence sat smiling because he knew that the seed was being planted in Cardinal.

"My time will come, soon." Violence said. Click Click Clack the controllers said.

"K.O. Yoshimitsu wins." The announcer announces. Cardinal looks over at Azure with a face to say, "This isn't over yet."

"Final Round. FIGHT." The announcer announces. Both the boys' fingers go back to work putting together the buttons necessary to ensure victory.

"Come on, come on come on." Azure began chanting as he damaged Cardinal's character.

"No, no, no, no." Cardinal began saying as he began to fight back against the onslaught. Seconds felt like minutes as the time ticked down on the clock and the health gauge of both characters seemed to dwindle down.

"K.O. Yoshimitsu wins." The announcer announces. "Yes!" Cardinal lets out a victory cry as he places the controller down on the ground. "Maybe next time bro."

"Yeah, yeah, yeah. You lucky I have to leave or else we would run it back." Azure says while placing his controller down and picking himself off of the floor.

"Your mom is outside already?" Cardinal asked.

"Yeah she just called me so I gotta go." Azure informs as he puts his shoes on his feet.

"Well, I'll come out with you and say hi to mom. I wanna see if I can come over sometime next week since we are on summer break." Cardinal confessed.

"Yeah man that would be pretty cool." Azure exclaimed. Cardinal ran to his room to find a pair of shoes that he could slide on quickly. Cardinal's mother threatened that if he was to go outside again without wearing shoes she would give him a spanking, and Cardinal could not afford to get one of his mother's beatings. He found two shoes that did not match and slid them on and started down the hallway towards the front door. As he reached the end of the hallway, he nearly collides with his mother Omega.

"What have I told you about running in the house?" Omega asks.

"I know I'm sorry, I just want to say hello to Mom, she is here to pick up Azure." Cardinal confessed with guilt attempting to curb her frustration.

"Yeah, I'm headed out there now to talk with her." Omega said to Cardinal.

Cardinal reached his room where he found a pair of old sneakers, that he had thus converted into a pair of work shoes, with the shoes in hand he rushed back to the front door to put the shoes on his feet. He slides his right foot into the shoe and then the left foot. He stomped down with the attempt to forcefully grant his foot full access into the shoe, but all he was able to do was step down on the back of the shoes and thus cave the back in. He did not care. Cardinal then opened the door and began to run outside to say hello to Carolina.

"Hey what have I told you about walking around on the back of your shoes!?" Omega yelled out of the door. With Fear gripping his heart and speed bag punching it Cardinal quickly adjusted his shoes. Once he seemed safe Cardinal then completed his journey to reach the van.

"Hiiiiiii mom!" Cardinal exclaimed with excitement.

"Hello handsome, how are you doing today?" Carolina asked.

"Good. Thank you for letting Azure come over today, it really made today awesome." Cardinal thanked with appreciation.

"It's no problem. He was the one that wanted to come over. You two are truly the best of friends. We will have to make sure that you guys still see each other even though you will not be going to the same high school. Say where is your mom?" Carolina asked.

"She is inside she said that she was coming out to say hi to you." Cardinal informed.

"Oh there she is, Hi Momma!" Carolina let out with excitement.

"Hey there Momma." Omega let out with equal excitement. Omega had finally reached the car and they began to talk. All the while Cardinal and Azure continued to talk about how different things would be now that they would be attending separate schools. A few minutes went by and it was time to say their goodbyes for the day.

"Ight man I'll see you later. I will try and go over to your house next week or something. If my mom lets me." Cardinal states.

"Yeah man you will definitely have to cause we just got a trampoline and it is so fun flipping on it." Azure informs.

"Dude no way! I definitely gotta come over now." Cardinal lets out.

"Alright now Momma I'll see you later." Carolina says while putting the car in drive.

"I'll see you later. Come on Cardinal." Omega orders.

Cardinal waves at both Azure and Carolina as they drove away. Cardinal and Omega both walk back towards the house. The sun had begun to go down all the while Consequence had visited Alpha.

Alpha was on his computer while Azure and Cardinal were playing video games and kept seeing ads pop up on his computer regarding sexuality. He could not understand why this started happening all of a sudden, so he searched through his computer files to see what could have caused this problem. In some of the searches of his firewall he saw that there were pornographic sites visited. When Alpha saw the sites that were visited and the duration of time spent on each site he freaked out. He then looked to see if there were any correlations between the time of day and the days these sites were frequented. He noticed that the sites were only visited during the night time and more so only during the weekdays. He had a theory of who could have looked through these videos but he was not holistically sure. At that moment he knew that once Azure left, he would have to confront everyone simultaneously, in an attempt to snuff out the evildoer.

Cardinal and Omega entered the house and it was completely silent. Out of nowhere came the bellowing of Alpha from the back of the house, "Omega! Cardinal! Come here!"

Cardinal was immensely confused by the stature of his father's voice. He usually did not scream like this unless something was seriously wrong. What could make him this upset? Cardinal turned the corner of the wall to see his sisters both standing behind Alpha at the designated computer station of the home. What were they all doing back there? Cardinal began to think. Fear again gripped Cardinal's heart and played jump rope with his intestines, for he could feel his stomach turning. Cardinal walked slowly to the back where they had gathered, Omega came around the corner rebutting the yelling from Alpha.

"Don't scream in the house." All the while shouting back. "Oh." Omega said in shock.

The entire family was staring at a computer screen with pornographic images and videos going on. It was not just one screen but it was about 7 tabs opened each on a different site broadcasting pornography. At that moment Cardinal knew his secret had been discovered. Blood rushed through his body at what seemed like the speed of light, his head got light and dizzy. He could feel stress gripping him by the throat. They were clearly trying to kill him. All the while Truth and Conviction, The hoodies, stood by the side of Cardinal and urged him to be honest and transparent. Before Cardinal could say anything, Alpha stated.

"Who in the hell has been watching this damnable content on my computer. They clearly know that this is wrong because they were only watching this stuff when it was late at night, during the weekdays, and only for small time periods. So I am only going to ask this once, whoever has been watching these videos please speak up now." Alpha commanded.

Stress still had a clutch around Cardinal's throat and Fear still had his stomach turning. He could not talk. As much as he wanted to just state that it was him who had been watching the videos, he literally could not speak a word. Silence fell over the room. It seemed as if they had been standing in the room for an eternity. All the while Alpha just cycled through the pages and after about 10 seconds of letting the page sit there, he would close it and move to the next one. More time passed and still nothing was said. Out of frustration Alpha began to read the titles of the videos that were on the screen.

"Black girl shaking her booty. Booty bouncers 3. Black booty warrior. Boo…." Before Alpha could even finish reading the rest of the titles Cardinal let out a cry that seemed to bounce off the walls and ears of everyone in attendance for this moment.

"It was me." Cardinal confessed. At that moment Fear and Stress tightened their grip on Cardinal. He began to sweat and hyperventilate.

"So you have been the one watching this filth in my house, around your sisters, around your baby brother. You brought this poison in the house. Is that how you see your mom? Is that how you see your sisters?" Alpha asked.

"No daddy. I'm sorry." Cardinal began to plead.

"Shut Up! Just shut up! You ain't sorry you just caught! But believe me you gon be sorry. You know, I knew it was you. I just wanted to see if you were gonna come forward and say it was you once you seen you were caught, but you are so much of a coward that you almost let your sisters fall for this by not confessing." Alpha aggressively spoke towards Cardinal as he closed each tab. Once each tab was closed, he then closed his laptop and stood up.

"Thank you all for being here to witness what Cardinal had been doing, everyone but him can leave." Alpha instructed.

Each person began to evacuate from the back of the house to the front. Cardinal stood there with little strength to even keep his body standing up. He was so scared that he couldn't even imagine what fate would fall before him. Back at Man's Bosom Porn could clearly see what was about to happen to Cardinal and what that meant for his existence as a Coat.

"Well Abuse this is it, the moment has come for me. I have not only been discovered but I have also been admitted by Cardinal. This is the vision that we have seen." Porn expresses to Abuse.

"Funny, I feel the power in me growing, I know what is about to happen. Alpha is going to punish Cardinal, but he is going to go too far. This is what you were talking about." Abuse admits.

"Yes our neighbors know the historical problems that Alpha has had to endure and it's because of that history that you will become even more powerful and I will be going dormant." Porn confesses. In that moment Porn began to fade from Man's Bosom and reassemble back at the Heart of Man, not as a Coat but as a Suit. His ethereal body warped and changed as he was beginning to disappear. In his transformation Lust, Perversion, and Masturbation emerged into their own states. All the power that Porn had acquired began to resurface. Lust was a very powerful Blazer who in itself had a feminine body. The only thing that was confusing to Abuse was that the body of Lust was not holistically feminine there were parts of Lust that were conceptually masculine. From the muscular arms to the strong facial features. The breast of Lust clearly showed that it was a mixture of both male and female. Lust had a rather small build and looked like a developing child. It would seem as though Porn had capitalized on the consumption of this Blazer when it had not fully reached its maximum potential. To the right of Lust stood Masturbation. Masturbation was rather shy as it hid its face constantly and attempted to separate itself from the gaze of Abuse, Lust, and the last one in the Bosom, Perversion. Masturbation was also rather small in stature but it was evident that when Porn consumed these Blazers, he did so with the idea of collecting the ones that shared similarities to his nature and also to capitalize on the immaturity of them at the time. The last one Perversion stood tall and mature. Its body was fully developed and full as its shoulders seemed to fill the blazer it wore to the extent of showing every muscle that formed. As powerful as Perversion looked it was missing something, one of its eyes were gone.

"Wow these are all the Blazers that Porn had consumed through the time he has existed in this body. This is incredible. I have only had the ability to consume one and I'm this powerful, with Porn consuming these three I can see the potential for just how powerful I can become. Two of the three weren't even fully matured yet. Maybe I should consume them now." Abuse thought to himself.

"Hey you what's going on here. Why have we diverged from the oneness of our master?" Perversion asks Abuse.

"It's because for the time being I am being sent back to my lowest state. I imagined that I would go dormant but it would appear that there was something I may have miscalculated. No matter, if I am getting demoted and not purged then that just means that my time here is not over. I will see you all again very soon. Oh and Perversion I will be keeping that eye." Porn spoke just before vanishing for good.

"So I guess you are our new master then." Perversion stated. "I am not going back into anyone else; I want to become a Coat for myself." Masturbation proclaimed.

"You all can chill out, my desire is not to consume you but to use all of your talents, I believe that in and of yourselves you have skills that can help in the grand scheme of pleasing the Tuxedo." Abuse informs the three.

"So we still do not know why we have been released from our consumption." snarks.

"It will all make sense in a moment. For now let's go up to Cardinals eyes so you can see the consequences of his decisions." Abuse instructs, as the four of them instantly transmit themselves up to obtain the answers they were looking for.

The moment Cardinals mother left the room Alpha grabbed Cardinal by the back of the neck and aggressively squeezed and ushered him to the back door. He was leading him to the backyard. Alpha grabbed the door handle and swung open the door with might and force. The door swung open with unimaginable speed and collided with the wall on the outside of the house. The darkness of the night looked even more menacing tonight than it usually looked. The cool summer air struck Cardinal in the face with little consideration for the emotion that was welling up inside of Cardinals eyes. Alpha pushed and shoved Cardinal outside until they were both engulfed into the darkness of the night. Alpha let go of Cardinal and stepped back inside the house, not because he was done with Cardinal, but to illuminate the backyard for what would soon transpire. Cardinal with no energy left in his body dropped to his knees. Weak and terrified he kneeled there with tears streaming down his face. Fear and Stress had broken his spirit and Cardinal was completely vulnerable. Abuse could feel Selfishness rising in power on his Coat. At that moment it dawned on Abuse why Porn was so powerful. He turned and looked at Lust, Perversion, and Masturbation as they stood there looking at the Rage in Alpha's face quickly approaching Cardinal's lifeless body. Porn had strategically consumed these three because each moment Cardinal would interact in pornographic activity it would grow the power of the consumed Blazer thus growing the power of Porn himself. Alpha reached the lifeless body of Cardinal kneeling on the cold concrete and screamed,

"Get up! Now!"

"Please daddy! I am sorry!" Cardinal cried and pleaded to prevent Alpha from doing whatever he was planning on doing next.

"Get up!" Alpha yelled even more forcefully. Cardinal raising his head from the ground to finally look his father in the face was instantly terrified when he saw the expression of disdain, disgust, and rage in his father's eyes.

Abuse could also see Rage and the history of the Coat in the eyes of Alpha. In that instance Rage and Abuse stared at each other. Rage uttered to Abuse and in that moment, he knew exactly what he had to do.

"Hey guys I have to go do something. I'll be right back." Abuse informed before disappearing into the heart of man.

Cardinal mustered up the energy to get off the ground. As soon as he stood on his feet Alpha cocked back his balled up fist, and turned his hips through as his fist followed. Cardinal could see the impact coming, not for his face but for the center of his chest. He could not stop it and he could not defend against it; he was far too weak to do anything. 3, 2, 1 impact. The fist collided with Cardinal's sternum. A strange feeling erupted from that spot. It felt like Cardinal's chest had been caved in, like the ability to breathe was something foreign. He gasped for breath, but before he could take another gasp for breath, he saw another fist coming around except this one was not aimed at his chest this one was aimed at his face. After the blow he just experienced there was no way he could take a blow like that again. Cardinal put up his arms to protect his face from the next onslaught. Impact. The force pushed Cardinals weak arms against the side of his face and he inadvertently smacked himself in the face. There was no time although to consider the implications of what just happened because in less than 3 seconds another fist came from the left side and that one collided with the defensive stance that Cardinal was in. Another inadvertent blow to the face. In between the small window in Cardinals defensive stance, he could see another fist winding up from the right. All he could do was sit there with the expectation of the next blow and contain himself the best way he could.

All while this was going on, Abuse retreated to the Heart of Man to fulfill the utterance of Rage.

"Hey Violence, do you know what is going on right now?" Abuse spoke into the empty void.

From the darkness a voice responded, "Yes. It is marvelous." Violence responded.

"I have something for you, something that was extended to me, something that I know you will appreciate." Abuse spoke to violence.

"Oh yeah? And what's that?" Violence asked. "Ascension." Abuse responded.

"What are you talking about?" Violence asked.

"I am talking about a grand opportunity to level up your influence. A chance to become a superior. A chance to be more than a mere Blazer, a chance at becoming a Coat." Abuse informed.

"I am definitely intrigued. Tell me what I have to do." Violence questioned.

"Join my ranks and I will make it possible." Abuse instructs.

Blow after blow ensued as Cardinal kept his guard up. After what seemed like a lifetime Cardinal's father Alpha screamed in frustration.

"Stop crying and take it like a man. Take it like a man."

Cardinal instantly stopped crying and looked through his window of defense to see the final blow coming toward his head. With his father's fatigue, the blow came much slower and with less power. Impact. After the blow landed Alpha yelled out.

"Now go to your room. And I better not see you the rest of the day. And you better not look like you got a problem with anyone in here or we can get back to it."

Cardinal whipped around quickly and retreated back to his room. He ran through the home so quickly, he felt as though he was going to be pulling the carpet from the foundation. He turned the corner passing the kitchen, then the living room. Sitting on the couch in the living room was his family. They noticed him as he flew by, passing from room to room. All anyone of them could honestly do was express deep concern and love for the hurt boy. Cardinal slipped down what seemed like an endless hallway and entered his room. With all the strength exhausted from his body, Cardinal collapsed on the ground. No tears streamed down his face even though he was clearly hurt from the initial blow to the chest. No sadness ensued, in fact only rage brewed in his heart. A melodic and devastating hymn rang out from Cardinals mind the whole time he sat still in the middle of the floor.

"Stop Crying. Take it like a man. Stop Crying. Take it like a man. Stop Crying. Take it like a man. Stop Crying. Take it like a man." Over and over on repeat in his mind. He could feel his jaw clenching, he could feel his temperature rising and he could feel his eyes burning as he learned very clearly that day how to deal with pain. He learned how to deal with confrontation. Cardinal reached his hand out to the faceless being sitting in the room with him. This time Cardinal did not cower away from the faceless creature, no this time he intentionally reached out and invited this new Coat into his heart. Cardinal willfully and emotionally welcomed Rage into his heart.

At the gates of the Heart of Man, Abuse stood there with arms crossed waiting as Rage suddenly appeared.

"Rage. I got your message and I am here to welcome you to your new home. Hey how did you know that this event would generate a generational curse?" Abuse asked.

"I have not the slightest idea what you are talking about.

Who are you anyways?" Rage asked.

"My name is Abuse, evidently being brought here you have not retained your memory, so I will remind you of the message you uttered to me while you were at Alpha's eyes about the transference of generational curses. It appears that here in Cardinals heart you are minimized to a mere Blazer but I intend to get you promoted that way you can show me the powers that your former self have wielded. I do believe that you are the only one that Cardinal willfully selected to bond with. You are going to do amazing things here." Abuse said.

"I have a feeling that Cardinal and I will be together forever." Rage proclaimed.

Abuse and Rage both walked back into the Heart of Man and Abuse began to inform Rage why he had been summoned. Cardinal sat still in the middle of his bedroom floor and stared at one spot at the wall the entire night.

"Stop Crying. Take it like a man. I WILL NEVER CRY AGAIN!" Cardinal thought.

"Hmmm. This is going better than I expected." the Tuxedo thought.

RAGE

"You asked me when I first appeared a question. You asked me why I uttered instructions to you earlier. Answer me this. Why would I say anything to you when I do not know you?" Rage asked.

"Look I could go into what happened but it would not make a difference, I do not believe you possess the level of mental prowess to be able to maneuver through thoughts. So it would be in your best interest to just stick with me and I will be able to help you attain not only greater power but information and power. What we need to do is set up a meeting with The Tuxedo and have you elevated to a Blazer. I am going to need you on my team." Abuse informed.

"And what is this team you are speaking of?" Rage asked.

"It's my legion." Abuse responded.

Rage and Abuse walked through the Heart of Man until they reached the Stairway of Ascension where Abuse would call for The Tuxedo to have an immediate meeting about the emergence of Rage and what that would mean for Cardinal. All the while in the Land of the Neutrals several of the Neutrals sat at their table and began to converse about the severity of Porn threatening to consume one of them.

"Has no one considered what Porn was saying he would try and do? Again." Consequence panicked.

"Consequence it is not like you to be so flustered, that's one of my characteristics." Emotion joked.

"The Fact of the matter is there is no way that a Coat or a Blazer could possibly consume one of us. They are not nearly powerful enough to do that, and in this land, we are protected by the Seraphim. We exist as a balance through all the chaos in this world. The only way that one of those demons could even come close to consuming one of us would have to be if we were misplaced and that could only happen in the event that we were in the world of humans. That would be so improbable though because not only would we be unprotected but the Blazer and the Coat would be subjecting themselves to become neutralized instantly. It would not be conducive for their existence." Death the Reaper spoke.

"What I am worried about is that Porn seldomly speaks metaphorically. I believe he was planning on doing something to obstruct our existence if even for the possibility of being stronger. Not every one of those Blazers and Coats are leveled you know." Consequence spoke with concern.

"Well look Consequence there is really no need to be so fearful when we enter into the world of the humans, we are under contract we have missions so we are never just there like the hoodies and the legions are. So they would have to know specifically what we are there for to catch us slipping." Emotion said.

"Catch us slipping? With that type of slang, it would appear that someone has been amongst the humans a little too frequently." Life joked.

"Whatever. I hope we are done here. I have something I have to go do. Cardinal needs me." Emotion proclaimed.

"Be Careful." Consequence urged.

"Relax. I'll be fine." Emotion calmly spoke before vanishing.

"Look everyone there is no need to be all up in arms over the zealous actions of one Coat who tried to consume one of us in our own home. Not to mention a Blazer who has, since a few days ago, become a mere seed of a Suit. And if that does not calm you down let this comfort you, no one knows how to consume one of us, but us. We are completely safe. Just continue to do your jobs." Death the Reaper authoritatively spoke.

It had been a few days since the incident with Cardinal and Alpha. Cardinal had been in his room for a few days. No one spoke to him, no one engaged him, no one showed any interest in his mental wellbeing. Alpha had placed Cardinal on a strict diet of Top Ramen, a piece of bread and water. That was all Cardinal could eat and he could only eat it once a day. This was no longer a home for Cardinal, this was a prison. It was after all Cardinal's fault, if he had not watched all that porn on his father's computer, disrespecting his parents and demoralizing his sisters and mother, well life in the house would be so much better. To Cardinal, he could understand the fact that this living situation was all his fault but what he could not get out of his mind was the physical abuse he had just gone through and the demand by his father to "Be a man…Stop crying". This is what it took to be a man, now he would have to live out his sentence and hopefully, with good behavior he could get out early and get back to the general population.

"Why did he beat me like that? I definitely was wrong but did he need to beat me up like that? What if I would have fought back? I could have hit him. Does he hate me now?" All these thoughts began to cycle through Cardinal's mind and as he thought tears began to well up in his eyes.

"NO! NO! MEN DO NOT CRY! SUCK IT UP, YOU COWARD! SUCK IT UP! WE ARE NOT GOING TO CRY!" Cardinal began to tell himself. All the while Emotion was sitting right with Cardinal as he began to figure out what he needed to feel in this moment. Cardinal was so confused. He could feel the pain in his chest but he could not release it because crying was not manly, what was he to do. It was in that moment that Cardinal remembered the partnership that he made the other day with that Suit. Cardinal then knew what he had to replace his overwhelming emotion with. He would now use Rage to cope with his problems. No more tears.

A few minutes before Cardinal's destructive thoughts back at the Heart of Man, Abuse and Rage stood at the bottom of the Stairway of Ascension waiting for The Tuxedo to endow Rage with the intellect and power to level up into a Blazer.

"Usually there is a whole promotion for Suits to gain a new level but under the circumstances, we have to move quickly." Abuse informed.

"What circumstances? I feel there is something you are not telling me." Rage uttered with aggression.

"I'm glad you are getting worked up, that will be very good for what is about to happen in a few minutes." Abuse let on.

"What is about to happen in a few minutes and why is me becoming a Blazer that important?" Rage aggressively questions again.

"Well since it's about to happen I guess it would be no harm to just come out with it. So in the next few minutes, Cardinal is going to denounce his use for emotions and use you primarily for a coping mechanism. This is inherently good for you because that means you can become a very strong Suit to do the bidding of your officer. You see there is something that we are going to do to make you even more powerful though. In the moment that you become Cardinal's primary mechanism, Emotion will be around and you are going to weaken Emotion enough to consume her. You will not be able to do it in the state that you are in now, this is why I have called for this meeting with The Tuxedo. If I can get you leveled up quickly then you will be just strong enough to defeat the Neutral and have a gripling ordinance over Cardinal." Abuse informs.

"How do you know all of this?" Rage asks confused.

"You see, being a Coat I have a lot more reign over Cardinal. I am in his thoughts and I can hear what he is thinking. He is reliving the accounts of yesterday, just like he constantly relives what happened to him when he was 6 years young. His thoughts are becoming very detrimental and any moment now he is going to convince himself that his emotions make him weak, and that will be the opportunity you need." Abuse informs more.

"Now what about this thing you said earlier about generational curses?" Rage asks.

"That will have to wait. Our master is here." Abuse states while kneeling.

"I know what you are up to Abuse and I must say I am very pleased with the plan that you have put together. I believe that this is the best plan that anyone of the Blazers or Coats have ever brought to me. Go Rage, take this power, go consume that Neutral. Now make sure you do it while she is in the world of humans because if you do not, she will take you back to her realm and I cannot do anything to protect you there." The Tuxedo said while simultaneously placing the illumination on Rage's face. In that moment Rage's eyes appeared.

"Wow so this is the power that you were talking about all this time. I am really feeling like I could do something here" Rage confessed.

"Yes and the time has come for you to journey to Cardinal's home and consume that Neutral." Abuse commands.

"I have no combat training. How am I supposed to war against a Neutral?" Rage asks.

"I'm sure you will do just fine; in fact you have inherent skills you will find will emerge only when tested. Believe me, I defeated a Coat with no combat training at all." Abuse confesses.

"Now go! You will only have a moment to strike, if you don't leave now you will likely never get another chance like this again." The Tuxedo spoke.

"I wonder why that Tuxedo guy never shows his face." Rage thinks while preparing himself for the world of the humans.

It was in that moment that Cardinal remembered the partnership that he made the other day with that Suit. Cardinal then knew what he had to replace his overwhelming emotion with. He would now use.... Instantly Rage appeared and Cardinal could feel his sadness minimize and his anger rise. Sitting on the other side of Cardinal was Emotion. Emotion could feel the reluctance of Cardinal to embrace his human feelings and this began to strip power from Emotion and Rage could see this. He knew that this was the perfect time to strike. Rage lunged across the room to where Emotion was and grabbed her by the neck. He locked both hands around her delicate neck and began to squeeze. He squeezed with all the might that he could. He could feel the energy beginning to leave as he advanced.

"I hope you are prepared to be consumed today." Rage let out with confidence.

"Well I hope that you are prepared to be neutralized." Emotion spoke from the other side of the room.

"When did you get over there? I have literally been looking at you this whole time." Rage asked confused.

"I knew you would be here; I could feel your presence on Cardinal's being. He has accepted you into his life. A mistake that I plan on rectifying today. He has made a decision that he believes was made out of logic but was really made out of emotion. This is why you will be defeated by me today. I know his true intention and this case is likened to my being. Now I know I'm not supposed to get involved in the human experience but I can definitely take out the trash before I go back home." Emotion boasts.

"Well look at this you have gotten me passed pissed. Prepare! To be torn! Asunder!" Rage yells.

At that moment, Rage lets go of the dummy that he had his hands around and he charges at Emotion who had been sitting in the corner. Cardinal, completely aware of what was going on in this moment, watched as he could see the humanoid figure charging at what seemed to be a winged warrior. Emotion deflects the charge from Rage and grabs him by the back of the head and slams him into the ground. His face collides with the carpet in Cardinal's room, the impact not causing any physical damage but from what Cardinal can see a shockwave of energy emitting from the ground. The energy wave ripples out violently across the floor and travels up the walls. The energy from Rage does not go down with this attack; In fact with this blow, it sends Rage into a chaotic state of destruction. Rage rolls his eye up to look into the face of the winged warrior and yells, "I'M GOING TO KILL YOU FOR THAT!" Rage screams.

Rage places both his hands on the ground and forces his body from the ground, and with a fit of rage lets out a blood thirsty scream and charges at Emotion again. Emotion steps back to avoid the fists coming toward her face. She knows that all she has to do is wait just a few minutes before she can return back to the Land of the Neutrals. If she gets back there then she can relocate Rage back there and because of the law, she can do away with him for good. She bounds around the room like a professional boxer evading the attacks of an opponent. Swing after swing, punch after punch Rage throws blow after blow with the intention of knocking Emotion out.

"Why don't you stop dancing around and fight me!" Rage yells

"I do not need to fight you all I have to do is beat you and in order to do that I just have to wait for clear passage back to my Land. I only have 30 more seconds to fool around with you." Emotion informs.

At this point Rage knows that with his combat experience, there is no way that he will do anything fatal to Emotion to finally consume her. He needs something to change in his favor. Ten seconds go by and no damage has been done to Emotion, the only thing that Rage was successfully able to do is grab a feather that had fallen from the wing of Emotion.

"Dang it. I need help." Rage confesses.

"All you had to do is ask." Cardinal responds.

"Cardinal, why are you doing this? There is no need for you to get involved." Emotion questions shocked and confused.

"You do not know why I have purposely decided to take on Rage as my coping mechanism do you, you winged witch." Cardinal scoffed.

"Cardinal you cannot get involved in this. I am a Neutral and I cannot get involved in human affairs like this. If you want to be subject to Rage there is nothing I can do to change your mind but aiding in its side to defeat me, that is not conducive to the human condition. Do not do this." Emotion pleaded.

"You know for the last 8 years I have been seeing things around town, around my family, next to my friends, but I have never seen one of you before. To be quite honest with you I just want you to leave me alone. I heard what you told Rage you cannot go back home for another 20 seconds, well that is more than enough time for me to get you out of here." Cardinal proclaimed with aggression.

"Cardinal, please do not do this." Emotion pleaded once more.

"Stop talking to me it's useless." Cardinal growled.

"When I'm done with you, I will make Cardinal a man." Rage projects to

Emotion.

"13 more seconds and I'm home free, there really is nothing that Cardinal can do since he cannot infer from our realm." Emotion spoke to herself.

In that moment Cardinal reached out his hand and grabbed the wing of Emotion and as he grabbed her, he could feel the weight of the wings. They felt as if they were heavier than a bus, but they were soft and gentle. As he grabbed one, Emotion stood there in disbelief. Rage saw the guard of Emotion was down and knew this was the moment that he was waiting on. He lunges forward with light speed in an attempt to seize this opportunity. Emotion's gaze was not on Rage but on the face of Cardinal. With the touch of her wing, she noticed something that she had not seen before. With horror written on her face Emotion looks into the eyes of Cardinal and says the words, "It's you."

Cardinal was still grasping the wings of Emotion as Rage rushed forward with a blow mighty enough to deplete all of the energy from Emotion. Emotion struck in the head fell slowly as her wings began to curl and slowly wither like the rose pedals on a delicate flower, and as a pedal of a delicate flower the wing of Emotion fell off. Cardinal still holding the wing from Emotion falls suddenly under the strain of trying to hold such a heavy burden.

"How could she fly around with these things and what did she mean when she said it's you? How does she know me? Why didn't she announce that when she first arrived?" Cardinal pondered. As Cardinal picked himself off of the ground Rage walked over quickly to the lifeless looking Emotion and stood over top of her with what looked like a smile on his face. Cardinal couldn't tell because there were only eyes on this being.

"Hey you, the last time I met you, you did not have a face now you have eyes, what happened to you?" Cardinal asked.

Don't worry about that Cardinal just some aesthetics to make me look better for the ladies. As for right now I have something I need to do with this gal and I only have about 5 seconds left, but don't worry we will be seeing each other again real soon. In the meantime, I know what you are feeling and I have the solution for you. Me." Rage announced before vanishing with Emotion.

"Here I am alone again…….I hate my father. The fact that he would even do this to me. I'll be in this room all summer. Dang it. Uuugggghhhh!!!!" Cardinal expressed in an instant. He stomped around his bedroom in a circle as dismay and anger overtook him. Cardinal fell victim to the Rage in his heart.

Back at the Heart of Man Rage, Abuse, and Emotion were gathered together as Rage inquired about how his consumption of Emotion would take place.

"Now look, you told me all I had to do was defeat Emotion in enough time and then I would be able to consume her, I have defeated her and I have tried to consume her but look I do not have the ability to consume anything in my current state." Rage condescendingly expresses.

"I did watch that exchange and I must say I did not think that Cardinal was going to intervene on your behalf you must have truly had a substantial impact on his heart." Abuse utters.

"That's beside the point don't we have a time limit with this thing?" Rage states while pointing to the wingless Neutral.

"No we are good for now. Neutrals are not allowed into the Heart of Man because they exist outside of the human experience. They can only be, not interfere. So as long as she stays in here, we are good to go. Also the Seraphims are not allowed in here so no back up is coming for her." Abuse informs with a smile on his face.

"Well I can certainly see what you are saying but don't I need a mouth to consume this thing?" Rage becoming more and more aggravated.

"Hey….." The lifeless looking Emotion uttered.

"Shut up! You should have nothing to say." Rage barked. "You are making a huge mistake. You have a better chance at life if you just remain as you are. This is not a good idea; I can assure you." Emotion informs.

"Hurry up and grant me the ability to consume this thing before I lose it." Rage expresses while grabbing his head.

"The end for you all is closer than you think." Emotion still speaking with weakness. While Emotion laid with her face planted on the ground, she mustered up just enough energy to look up at the last few moments she would have before being destroyed. Her eyes met the eyes of Abuse and in that moment, she could see the expression of concern written all over his face as she spoke.

"You know what I am saying is true, you may not be able to see your own demise but I can guarantee you by consuming me you have just expedited your death." Emotion informed.

"You keep quiet you idiot. You really think just because you deal with the emotion of men you can create some uprising in me. Please. I am certain that your consumption will not only grant Rage with great power, but in you becoming one with him this will be the perfect opportunity for Rage to be even more useful to me. Once he becomes one with you he will have the Neutral DNA which will allow him to become a conduit between our heart and your land. We will take the Land of the Neutrals and we will consume every one of you until there is nothing left. Cardinal will be destroyed forever and our work here will be done. Onto the next victim." Abuse said with a devious smile.

"Well then, you will do what you have to, make it quick." Emotion dropping her head spoke.

"I'll be right back." Abuse informed before vanishing. Rage stood there in the void with Emotion. Rage paced back and forth with anticipation. Back and forth back and forth, in this timeless void, it seemed as if time ticked very slowly. As quickly as he disappeared Abuse came back. In his hand he held the sharp mouth of Rage. This mouth was different from many of the other Coats, his mouth was encased in iron.

"What's the deal with these teeth, how come they do not look like yours?" Rage asked.

"Well I went to go see the boss and he said that this would be the best set for you. You will be the first Blazer to ever consume a Neutral and he wants to make sure that you can accomplish this goal without any screw-ups. So he custom designed this set of teeth specifically for you. Be grateful." Abuse spoke.

"Believe me I am eternally grateful in fact once I have consumed her, I will go thank him myself." Rage exclaims.

Rage then accepted the new teeth from Abuse and placed them on his face. Instantly he could feel a sensation he never felt before. A lusting for more power swarmed his being and he liked how he felt. He smiled wide and hard as he turned to the downed Emotion and walked toward her. Step after step he closed in on her. Emotion looked up at Rage and smiled wide back at him. A teardrop rolled from her right eye. Bizarre. That tear flowed until it reached her chin and the moment it fell from her chin Emotion let out a bright light from her eyes illuminating the entire room. Blinded, frightened, enraged and confused Rage lunged at her with his mouth open. His teeth sharp as razors clamped down over the body of Emotion.

Clank With a swift swallow Emotion was gone and Rage could feel no difference in his power. Even more confused than the light Emotion just emitted Rage turned to Abuse and questioned,

"I thought after consuming her something would happen? I thought I was supposed to gain some great power? I do not feel any different than I did before, and I don't even look any different than before. Maybe we did something wrong."

"No, we weren't wrong, do you not see what just happened to you." Abuse stated with wide eyes.

Rage not only looked different but now there was a massive hole in the center of his body. His attire changed as well. He went from being a Blazer to becoming a Coat but with a particular difference, this coat had a long cape attached.

"What is this hole for? What did she do to me?!" Rage panicking.

"I believe that this is necessary, how else would you become a conduit from worlds if there was not some sort of portal for us to use. I did not imagine that you would literally become hallowed out. This is not quite what I had expected, but, nonetheless, this is necessary for the advancement of Cardinals demise." Abuse informed.

With this new transformation, Abuse readied his team for preparation to invade the Land of the Neutrals and enact the plan of consuming as many neutrals within the time limit allotted.

WAR BETWEEN WORLDS

"Hey did you hear what the new guy just did?" Stress asked Fear.

"Yeah some taboo, did he even consider the ramifications to consuming her, and of all beings, her. He gon suffer with some type of bipolar disorder for that one." Fear chuckled.

"Personally, I like him, I feel that him and I could be long lost brothers, I definitely need to teach him how to handle himself in combat because that display was embarrassing to our ranks." Violence furthered.

"Y'all know I am standing right here right?" Rage questioned.

"Look it's all fun and games relax a little. Hey does anyone know what plan Abuse has for us?" Ignorance asks.

"I know it has something to do with the new transformation of Rage." Addiction added.

"Well how long do we have to wait for him cause the school year is coming back around I want to make sure to create as many mental blockades as I can in Cardinal's mind so that it will be difficult for him to cope with reality." Stress exclaimed.

While the rest of the blazers conversed with one another trying to understand the grand scheme of Abuse, Rage just stood there blank faced thinking about what Emotion did to him just before she was consumed. He was still so puzzled by the action she took. Why in the world would she try and defend herself especially if she knew she was getting ready to die. Why didn't she get up and try and fight, what was the light for, why didn't she try running, what was the teardrop for? Rage pondered the answers to these questions as he just stared at the members of the room continue their conversation.

"And that's why he has the cape." Fear completes her statement.

"What about my cape?" Rage asks.

"Why do you have one anyway? You know it looks very tacky." Fear states.

"Look I do not know why I look the way I look, all I know is I consumed a Neutral, an accomplishment that not one of you were able to do before and if this is the finality of that decision then I am content with the outcome. You jealous or something?" Rage fires back.

"Oiu, Oiu, Oiu it's okay man no need to get so defensive these are just jokes. You are going to have to learn how to get along with the rest of the team if you want to survive long here." Fear states.

"Where is Abuse?" Stress asks.

In that moment Abuse appeared in the room with some papers rolled up in his hands.

"Sorry I am late guys but I was trying to make sure that this plan will actually work. I would hate for us to do this and not get anything in return, I also had to check in with the boss to see if he would allow us to be gone for a moment to enact this mission. I have to warn you all this will be extremely dangerous but if you do this, I can guarantee you powers that you never could have imagined before." Abuse started explaining.

"Are you referring to the powers that Rage got from consuming that neutral Emotion?" Addiction questioned.

"Wait…are you trying to use Rage as a portal to infiltrate the land of the neutrals and wage war with the Neutrals?" Fear asked concerned.

"Well that has something to do with what I want to do, but not a war what we are merely going to do is go in there like a thief in the night. Rage now has this portal between both worlds. This power and ability was in fact ascertained when he consumed Emotion, and because of this new ability, we can now infiltrate them without their knowledge. There will be no war because all we will do is sneak in grab a few neutrals, transport them back here, and while they are here, we will have the ability to do as we please. There are some ground rules no one can consume Death the Reaper or Life. They are far too powerful for any of us to handle anyone else is fair game. This is a mission primarily based on timing. We cannot be in there too long, because the longer we are there the more that our presence will be known the seraphim in the outer realm, and we do not want them waking up. As long as we are in and out, we should be good." Abuse informed his legion.

"How do you know that the neutrals don't already know that we are planning to go by there? What makes you think they don't know that Emotion is gone? I think you have sincerely and respectfully lost your mind.

That place is a fortress and how could you truly know the location of every neutral in their land? If we were to go there right now what would keep us from wasting our time checking irrelevant locations, or worse, a location with Death the reaper in it?" Fear asked.

"Fear I understand your perspective, your nature is built around it, but I do not need your pessimism I need you to be confident in what I am telling you." Abuse stated. As he spoke this to his legion, he took the rolled up paper that was in his hand and began to spread it across the table thus showing the blueprints of the neutrals building.

"How did you get that?" Stress asked in disbelief.

"Like I said I just need to know if you are all on board with this plan." Abuse repeated himself, this time with more authority.

"If I am going to be the portal between the land of the neutrals and the heart of man then I am not going with you right?" Rage asked.

"No, I need you to stay here and grant us passage. You are the most vital piece to our plan, because if you fail then we all fail. If for some reason we are not able to get back through you then one of two things is going to happen. Either we will have to cross back through the Seraphim territory, which will mean certain annihilation, or we get obliterated by the neutrals in their land. One way or another we will no longer exist. You are the key to everything. Do you think you can handle the strain of transporting us?" Abuse asks.

"How will I know where to transport you? It's not like I have ever been to their land before." Rage points out.

"You do have Emotion and she has been there forever. Use her insight to get us there." Abuse encourages.

"You still have not reassured me that this plan is foolproof. How do we know for sure that when we get there, they are all not ready to destroy us?" Fear asked.

"Because Fear this type of phenomenon has never happened before, as far as those neutrals know Emotion is still working. Look everyone ready up, we leave now. Rage open the portal." Abuse orders.

At the land of neutrals the day emotion was consumed... "Death the Reaper do you see what's going on down there. Rage is fighting Emotion." Relationship notices.

"Well, it would appear that they are, no need to intervene it's not like Rage will win, after all he is just a pup and Emotion is a highly skilled contender. No chance she will lose." Death the reaper responds with confidence.

"This is true that Emotion is far more advanced in combat than Rage is but we should still keep watch at what's going on down there." Life states.

"Life you do know that emotion won't be down there for more than a minute, I'm sure in that minute she will be back here." Death responds.

"Wait something is happening, I think Cardinal is going to intervene in this battle." Consequence pointed out.

"Why in the world would he do that?" Death the reaper asked.

"I don't think he is doing it own his fruition I think that he is being manipulated." Relationship notices Cardinal uttering to Rage.

"Emotion has just pleaded against Cardinal intervening in the battle." Life now invested in the situation.

"Well, this is certainly unexpected." Death the reaper now seeing how this will unfold.

At this point Cardinal had helped Rage get off the ground and prepared to do battle against Emotion with Rage.

"Has this ever happened in history. A human aiding a Blazer?" Esteem asked.

"Not like this, we may have to do something about this. We cannot just sit idly by as one of our own gets destroyed." Death the reaper states.

"Sir, I think it's a little too late for that, Cardinal has just ripped the wings off of Emotion and Rage and Emotion have both vanished." Relationship says.

"Vanished you say? Well that could mean one thing. They have taken her back to the heart of man and are going to try and extract some information from her. Too bad for them Emotion is one of the ones that would never talk even if tortured. She is a brave strong neutral." Death the Reaper states with confidence.

"Sir, is there even anything we can do about her absence." Esteem asked.

"Unfortunately no, after the ordinance went into place, we cannot frequent the heart of man and they cannot frequent our gates either. Thankfully Emotion does have a failsafe; she cannot exist outside of this land for too long, she will just be transported back to our lobby after a minute." Death the reaper informs.

As the moments began to slip by the neutrals waited for Emotion to appear back in the lobby Neutral HQ, this minute seemed like a lifetime as they stood in the lobby.

"Sir, has it not been a minute already?" Relationship asked.

"A few more seconds guys." Life stated.

In that moment a flash of light emitted from the center of the lobby of Neutral HQ. The light was bright and blinding but to no avail, no one came out of the light. Emotion was gone.

"What….what...what does this mean? Sir? What does this mean?" Esteem asks.

"This could only mean one thing. Emotion has been consumed. She is not coming back." Consequence answered.

"Everyone suit up and get ready for battle. Now!" Death the Reaper instructed.

"Death what's going on?" Life asks "Sir?" Consequence seconds.

"Don't tell me you all didn't see what happened after the light appeared. You all were so wrapped up in the answer to the problem you didn't look beyond. Even after Emotion left us a dying hint of what was to come. The teardrop? She was telling us that she was consumed but the water exposed the ripple effects of the decision that Rage made and the outcome of her consumption." Death explained frantically.

"Sir are you sure you saw that?" Relationship asked concerned.

"Of course I saw what I saw. Father Time will validate this with his vision. Father, are you there?" Death the Reaper called out.

"What do you need?" The voice of Father Time called out from a distance.

"Can you please show everyone what I just saw in slow motion please?" Death the Reaper pleaded.

"Of course. Everyone, look at the lobby wall. I will replay the events of the blinding light." Father Time time echoed while rewinding back time to what had recently just happened. All of the neutrals looked on the wall and could see the events played back in slower time. The blinding light flashed and lit up the entire room. They all reacted to the light by squinting so as not to be too affected by the effect, while they all looked away from the light a drop of water hit the floor of the lobby. That water droplet very quickly outlined the lifespan of the HQ, Rage, and Cardinal. The events even with slowed time still went by far too quickly for anyone to make out anything except for just a few key moments. One moment, in particular, stood out to everyone, and that was the transformation of Rage and what the plan of the

Blazers and Coats now was with the new power they had just claimed.

"I can see it now!" Consequence exclaims "Me too!" Relationship seconds.

"How are they going to be able to transport themselves over here with the current declaration we have going on?" Esteem asks.

"They will not have to travel through our gates, with the power that they have just gained from consuming Emotion they will be transported exactly where she was supposed to be a few moments ago. Right here in this lobby." Death the Reaper responds.

"We need to revoke the access of Emotion to this location before they get here." Life commands.

"Wait, why are you all so stressed we have the upper hand here. In this world we are far more powerful, a couple of blazers and a few coats wouldn't stand a chance against us." Consequence expresses.

"The problem is we do not know how many they are bringing and if they outnumber us even if we are more powerful then we will be over run. Lastly all they would need to do is overpower you enough to get you into their portal. Once you are in the Heart of Man then there is no saving you. Now everyone prepare for battle." Death the Reaper commands.

This time each neutral went to their designated arrears and prepared for war.

Death the Reaper switched out his dagger for his scythe. He would need overwhelming power in order to defend his territory from the Blazers and Coats. Life suited himself in armor from head to toe. A golden chest plate, a golden helmet, a golden shield, and golden gauntlets. Consequence, Esteem, Pain, Relationship, Time all were fighters who required only chainlink on their wrists and hands for they were not fully trained for combat. The neutrals were primarily peaceful as they relied on the Seraphim and the knowledge of impending doom to keep the peace between worlds. After each one of the Neutrals were prepared for the battle that was going to take place in their home, they all went back to the lobby to meet with Life and Death the Reaper. Life and Death the Reaper stood in the center of the lobby fitted and ready for battle. Life saw the looks on everyone's face and decided this was the perfect opportunity to give a speech to encourage everyone.

"Now I know that we are all shocked by the recent discovery of our fallen comrade, and moreover by the hands of not just a Blazer but by a human. I know that this information is unsettling and I know that you were not at all prepared to defend our world against an attack today but I have to let you all know that we will not let you fall. One thing that we have on our side is the element of surprise. I am certain that the Blazers and the Coats have no idea what that light was that they saw, and I am 100 percent sure that they did not see the timeline that we recently just saw. One thing that I saw in the ripple of time is that we will win this battle. Be brave. We will overcome." Life spoke with authority and passion.

When he had finished speaking, he could see that hope showing in everyone's eyes and that was the moment that Death the Reaper knew that he would have to give instructions for how they would have to fight this battle.

"Now this is what we are going to need to do. I need Consequence, Relationship, and Esteem to be here in the lobby. You 3 will be our first line against the attack it is important that we hold them here in the lobby but just in case a few get through the primary forces it is important that they do not get past the secondary forces. The secondary forces will consist of Pain and Father Time you two will make sure they do not get to the directory because if they get to that then they will in turn know where everything is located here and they may steal information. If all else fails then Life and I will be keeping them from doing any further damage. We are the final forces because we are the only ones that can revoke access to this place from Emotion. Does everyone understand what is required of you?" Death the Reaper asked.

"Yes!" they all yelled out.

"Perfect. Since we have this moment of solitude, we need to get to Eden to revoke Emotion's access. Now get in formation. Let's go, Life." Death the Reaper orders before getting ready to disappear to Eden with Life. Just before they vanished to Eden a portal to the center of their headquarters opened up. Each Neutral knew at this point what to expect. War.

The black void spun in circular pattern sucking the light out of the room and attempting to draw in the neutrals standing close by. The portal sought after the beings who had created the rift of transportation thus the neutrals next to the blackness had to withdrawal to prevent from being pulled in. When the portal was wide enough a sinister smile emerged from the darkness, and eyes as malicious and toxic as a radioactive isotope shone through the blackness. From the darkness stepped forth Abuse and his blazers Fear, Stress, Addiction, Violence, and Ignorance. On his left side stood Lust and on his right Perversion, two other coats.

"We did not account for their being 3 coats here." Life secretly says to Death the Reaper

"Nonetheless we do not have the time nor the energy to fight them here this time we must hurry to Eden, we must trust that they can handle this." Death the Reaper urges life with a pull on the arm. In that instant they disappeared to Eden.

"So. It looks like Death and Life have decided to leave you all here to die, how fitting of Death." Ignorance boastfully proclaimed.

"You all know what to do, take them back to the Heart of Man. Go!" Abuse ordered. Abuse rushed straight for Relationship with Addiction close by his side. Rage hung back at the Heart of Man holding the portal open as long as he could. Stress and Fear jumped into action with Lust going after Consequence and Esteem. Lastly Perversion rushed into battle with Violence and Ignorance and they engaged Time and Pain.

As the battles began downstairs of the Headquarters Death the Reaper and Life made it to Eden to revoke the access so that the portal would close thus trapping all of the Coats and Blazers in their land.

Both Death and Life knew the process for revoking access to a Neutral even though they never had to do it before. The process was somewhat lengthy but under the circumstances they had to hurry. Normally they would need the documentation of the Neutral, the reasoning in writing for why the Neutral was being revoked, then that would be submitted for review by the upper courts, and then they would then be able to take access and power from the Neutral. That Neutral would be forced to live out the rest of its existence a solitude, foot soldier in the war between Nephilim and Seraphim. Death the Reaper and Life did not have the appropriate documentation for Emotion because they are required to carry their credentials on them especially when traveling human territory. Since emotion was consumed, that access was inadvertently given to Rage. So they then had to go before the upper courts with the plea to revoke the access of Emotion without creating a lifetime of servitude to the war, primarily because if they were to do that with Rage existing in the heart of Cardinal this would be instant death for Cardinal. A Neutral's job was to exist in the midst of the humans but never to take their choice from them and this gesture would surely go against what they stood for. Cardinal would die for the simple fact that ripping away a neutral and a coat from the heart of man would take a piece of the man and thus would trap the soul of the man in the zone between heart and land of neutrals. Death and Life could not let this happen.

"So have you brought the necessary documentation for why you need to revoke access to Emotion from your land. As you know your home is under siege." The voice spoke from the blinding light.

"Oh great and wise one, we do not have the necessary documentation to revoke the access from emotion for as you already know when we frequent the human world, we take our access cards with us. What I am here to plead is not to revoke her access but to temporarily suspend access until we can figure out how we can revoke her access without killing Cardinal." Life explained.

"Yes. I do know what you were expecting me to do in regard to your situation but consider that I make the rules for the reason, I need what is required in order to even do anything for you. Imagine if some Coats were to come here and ask me to do something for them would I be able to merely just grant their wants and desires just because they asked me to do it. No, I could not. If some Hoodies were to come here and ask me to do something for them, would I just be able to do it for them just because they asked me. No, I cannot. Not because I do not have the power to do it, it's because I cannot go against my word. I am just. So Life, Death I am sorry but I can do nothing for you." The blinding light spoke out.

"But father we do have to consider what happened to Emotion she was bested by a human. This is something that has never happened before. Beyond that she was consumed by one of those wretched Blazers. Father, I know we abide by a code, we rule according to what we have already set in place but what is happening is nothing like it should be. This young boy Cardinal has dynamically altered the reality of why and what we do, Father I believe we should hear what they have to say." Another voice from the blinding light spoke.

"So tell me exactly what you need done." The first voice from the blinding light spoke.

"We do not need you to revoke access to Emotion, we just need you to temporarily suspend her access so that we can close that portal that's open in our land so that we can trap those Coats and blazers inside. If we can trap them then they can be enslaved to serve out the rest of their lives among the Nephilim. With a little bit of time, we will figure out a way to save Emotion but we need to close that portal first. We just need some time, but ironically, we do not have much time." Death Pleaded.

"Let me have a word with the council." The blinding light spoke.

Death and Life stood there as the light dimmed.

"Do you think we will have favor and they will grant us the time we need?" Life asked Death.

"It really does not matter what I think, all that matters is what is. We made this journey here so we need this, otherwise many of the neutrals fighting down there may not be strong enough to hold out against those Coats and Blazers." Death rebutted.

Just as soon as Death and Life began discussing the decision the light sparked bright again and the voice came back booming and boisterous.

"We have made a decision and we have decided that because of the situation that has recently transpired. Cardinal taking the side of his Blazer and aiding in the defeat, capture, and consumption of Emotion has drastically altered the dynamics of how interaction should be with you and the humans. Emotions capture has created a battle between your land and the Heart that has never happened before. This event is problematic because this rift can create further problems for not just you but my humbled and obedient seraphim. We are not only allowing for temporary suspension of Emotion from your land, we are also going to rework the access of the Blazers and Coats because they have overstepped by trying to access greater power and consume you. With that being said, call us when you are back in the lobby and we will seal your land and suspend the access of Emotion." The light commanded before dimming again.

"Thank you for everything or wise ones." Death and Life bowed and reverenced before making their way back to their land.

While Death and Life were both at Eden the battle waged between the Coats and the Neutrals. Relationship seemed to gain a substantial advantage over Abuse and Addiction who were trying hard to pull Relationship back to the portal.

"You know you should really just give up now and head back to the darkness you crawled out of. There is no way you are going to defeat me here in my home, and beyond that, your portal is looking awfully small there." Relationship informed while pointing at the void closing up back at the entrance of the tower.

"Great it looks like Death and Life were successful at getting Emotion's access revoked here." Consequence exclaimed.

"Shoot that means Death and Life are heading back here now. We do not have the means to deal with both of them, we need to abandon this mission." Abuse stated to Addiction.

"We cannot just leave without accomplishing anything here. I am almost certain that if we do not take one of them here, we will never get an opportunity like this again. WE NEED TO DO SOMETHING!" Addiction rebutted.

"You really think I came here without a contingency plan. Of course, we are not leaving out of here empty handed." Abuse calmly engages.

"There is literally nothing y'all could do here so I just recommend you leave out of here before you get hurt." Relationship warns.

In that moment Abuse telepathically transmits the contingency plan to each one of the Coats and Blazers in the land. In the midst of everyone's battle they all stopped what they were doing and turned and looked at Addiction and Abuse. The team of Neutrals stood there looking at their enemies in disbelief as they all stood very still looking at their leader.

"Hey what's going on here." Consequence let out in confusion.

In that exact moment Death and Life descended back to the lobby from Eden. The two of them looked to the phone to engage with the light to inform them it was time to revoke access to Emotion. The moment Life moved in the direction of the phone to broadcast their arrival Abuse let out a one word command and all the Blazers and Coats moved.

"Go!" Abuse yelled out.

Abuse, Addiction, Stress, Fear, Lust, Perversion, Violence, and ignorance all converged onto one target. Relationship. All eight of them moved in uniscene from every angle towards Relationship limiting the escape path for him. Once all the other neutrals realized what was going on they all rushed after each one of the enemies they were just fighting.

"Hurry Life, they are trying to take Relationship." Time pleaded.

Relationship assessed the angles that each Coat and Blazer was coming from and deduced that the only way he would potentially get out of this situation is he would have to take out one of the weaker ones and create a hole, and maybe one of his Neutrals would get there in enough time to save him. Relationship knew that there was no way that he would be able to take on all eight of them and saw an opportunity lunging at Fear. Relationship immediately cocked back his arm and charged at Fear to land a blow heavy enough to send him back to the black portal. Life accelerated towards the phone with even more urgency understanding the severity of the situation they were in now. Death the Reaper could also foresee the great loss they would endure rushed towards the group as they converged on Relationship even closer now. Death the reaper removed his dagger from its sheathe and pointed it in the direction of the strongest Coat in the lobby, Abuse. Everything seemed to move in slow motion as everything began to transpire. Relationship hit his mark and landed a powerful blow to the face of the enemy he sought out. After relaxing that this blow did not send his enemy back into the portal, he realized that something was wrong, Fear had not been blown back because his twin Stress was holding his hand. They took the force of the blow from Relationship and converted it into energy for a shockwave. This shockwave was so powerful that it was able to push back every neutral in the lobby. The help that Relationship was expecting had been thwarted by his own hand. Panic began to set into Relationship. Was this the end? He began to think. "No." he thought "Life is so close to broadcasting to Eden that they can revoke access to Emotion. There is no way they are going to be able to take me back to the Heart of Man. I just can't make it easy for them." Relationship rationalized in his mind. Relationship took back his fist and looked at the next best Blazer to throw a punch at and realized that the closest in his swing space was actually Abuse. He knew that a blow to Abuse would not be strong enough to send him back to the portal but maybe this blow will be strong enough to discombobulate their attempt to work in unisense. Relationship cocked back again and twisted his body in the direction he remembered Abuse was coming at him before. When he finally reached the angle, he remembered seeing Abuse his memory deceived him, for what he saw was not Abuse but nothing. An empty space. An escape path. It was towards the portal but Relationship began to think that he could adjust his movements as he got close enough to the portal, he would just need to be cognizant that the portal could pull him in. Relationship then took the energy conserved in his fist and relocated it to his feet to lunge in the direction of the small empty area. As Relationship committed to the action of springing forward in his peripheral, he saw Abuse within arms reach of him and that's when he realized what transpired. It was not his memory that failed him, for Abuse was just there but when that shockwave went out from Stress and Fear, Abuse must have used the shockwave to relocate himself to one of his blind spots. Relationship was in danger. He could see Death the Reaper lunging in his direction, unaffected by the shockwave, but he was not close enough to close the gap between the Coats and Blazers and his body.

Relationship then realized what they had planned to do, they set him up. They led him to believe that he had a chance to escape, they gave him the perception that he would make it. This perception created the opportunity for relationships to go on the defensive rather than battling. This defensive tactic was what they were going to capitalize on, because Relationship was already moving in the direction of the portal then they were going to use that momentum to drive him into the portal and there was nothing to Relationship could do to stop it. With the last bit of energy that Relationship had left he turned his head to look in the direction of the phone just to see if Life could maybe save him. He saw that Life had literally just reached the phone and, in that moment, he felt a hand on the back of his head, Abuse had gotten him. He instantly felt multiple hands grab his body simultaneously and push his body in the same direction he was headed to. His body quickly accelerated towards the portal. This was it. Either Life was going to reach the phone or they were going to get him into the portal before the call was made. Inch by inch the group moved closer and closer to the portal and every moment closer hope began to fade for Relationship. Just as he could see into the darkness of the portal, he heard a small voice from the distance.

"We are here, revoke her access!" Life left out loudly, but due to the distance Relationship could only hear an utterance of the command.

Just then the portal began to shrink and Relationship could hear the groaning of Rage from the other side of the portal. His strain came from his inability to keep the portal open for the 8 of the legions headed back.

"I cannot keep this open any longer." Rage let out.

Abuse seeing that they literally only had a fraction a second left urged everyone to push harder. With a final burst of speed, the 8 exhausted all of their energy as they rushed towards the portal that was once the size of a doorway was now minimized to the size of a domestic cat. All of the Neutrals stood in anticipation as the portal began to close, each one hoping that they were able to claim victory and keep the Coats and Blazers stranded in their land. Death moving closer to the group with anticipation to neutralize the closest Blazer or Coat. Smaller and Smaller the portal closed until everyone in the room began to realize that they had made a crucial mistake and dropped their guard. Relationship had gone through the portal and disappeared. One by one each Blazer and Coat entered into the portal that was now the size of a quarter. Finally, there was one Blazer left and as half of the body of Addiction entered the portal it closed, thus trapping one half in the Land of the Neutral and one half in the Heart of Man. This was very dangerous for Addiction because typically a Blazer could regenerate its body once in the Heart of Man with enough time but because its body was trapped there then the remaining portion of her body may be eradicated or enslaved. Unbeknownst to Abuse and the rest of the legion of the state that Addiction was in they began to celebrate their victory over the neutrals.

"Great job guys, we were able to get a neutral and bring them back here unscathed." Abuse exclaimed with excitement. "Now it's a shame that you all won't have the chance to consume a neutral of your own but at least with the power I will soon have we will be able to cease Cardinal Wolf forever." Abuse decrees.

"I AM NOT WHOLE!" Addiction lets out in a panicked cry. Abuse sensing the disorder emitting from Addiction he turns around to see half of Addiction missing. In complete disbelief and shock Abuse lets out a tormented scream in disbelief to what he was seeing.

"Hahahahaha Y'all really thought you were going to come out of there unscathed. You really thought that your plan was full proof. That you were going to consume most of us and gain some immeasurable power. Now look at you broken and in half. Hilarious." Relationship humorously proclaimed.

"Someone shut him up!" Abuse roars.

The blazers and coats that had been gathered around grabbed Relationship by the arm and began taking him away when in the midst of the confusion an idea sparked into Abuse's mind.

"Wait. In fact, leave him here. I know what we are going to do." Abuse ordered the team.

The blazers and coats then grabbed Relationship and brought him back to where the fading Addiction and Abuse laid side by side.

"You think it's so funny that my sister is laying here half alive. You really should be less observant about what we got going on and more concerned about what is about to happen to you. We won. We may not have achieved our ultimate goal but we won. You were brought back here and I know exactly what you will be used for. Originally I was going to consume you all to myself but then I thought, you could actually be of great service to my sister here. Allow me to introduce you to her. Her name is Addiction and you see what you are going to do is be ripped in half. Just like she was. I am going to fuse you with her and you two will become one. The other half of your being will be consumed by myself and I will assure you right now you will feel everything." Abuse maniacally informed.

"Well let me tell you a little something about our design. We were constructed and designed not to feel. We are neutrals for a reason. Unlike you foolish and despicable beings we only exist to add balance. We can feel no pain, we can fear nothing, we just are. Understand this, no matter what you do to me will make no difference, but things always find a balance. Heed my words you do not want to do this. Let me go and you will have a better chance at survival." Relationship rebuts.

"You must really be desperate. Trying to plead for your life I see. Well, it's too late you are already dead." Abuse states while quickly turning around and plunging his hands towards the center of Relationships body. His hands were swift and lethal. As both of his hands went completely through Relationship's body they tore and separated one side from the other. Once both hands had torn through his being he separated the halves and without even taking a second, he consumed one half of Relationships body. Before swallowing the body, he had just ingested he grabbed the weakened body of his sister Addiction and the other half of Relationship and fused them together with strength and precision. Once Addiction and Relationship were a whole body Abuse swallowed the half that he placed in his mouth. Both Abuse and Addiction could feel the overwhelming power overtake them as the power of the Neutrals began to engulf their bodies. Unlike what happened to Rage there was no portal between the land of the neutrals and the heart of man because the blinding light in the midst of the war decided to include an automatic shut off to prevent immediate retaliation from one place to the other. Abuse turns to his sister and asks, "How do you feel now?"

"I feel complete in a way but I also feel as though my body is sinking into a pit. That's the best way I can explain it. I think it's from my half being trapped in the other dimension." Addiction informed.

"With this new power we no longer have to fear being neutralized. We cannot be neutralized with the power of a neutral in our being. We have a victory on our side. Let's take this opportunity and get back to work on Cardinal. I think it's about time we made more partnerships with him." Abuse ordered while walking back to Man's bosom.

All before Abuse had determined what to do in the Heart of man the neutrals were gathered around the flailing body of Addiction in the middle of their lobby. Each neutral looked down in disbelief that they had lost the battle that they were so confident that they would win. Out of nowhere the flopping body let out a scream "I AM NOT WHOLE!" The half conscious body let out. "Death, do you see that? She is clinging on to the little bit of life she has left." Life obviously points out.

"We are seeing a rift from the other side. She is expressing herself in the heart of man similarly. There is no need to do anything because she will be eradicated in a few moments." Death the Reaper informed in disdain.

"But sir what if they use Relationship to restore her body.

She may actually survive." Pain informed.

"Well if that happens then this half will die. I know just what to do with this half. When I get back we need to discuss what just happened here. If you have assignments, please complete them now." Death states while reaching down and grabbing the body of the fading Blazer. Just before opening the door and walking out to enslave Addiction, Death the Reaper remembers the tear that fell in the lobby and tried to make sense of what he saw. He saw a victory, why did it seem like they were the ones that lost this battle. He kept replaying it over and over in his mind and he could not see how they won. Then it hit him, his victory was not in the battle but in the war. He was co concerned with winning the war when the tear drop might have been outlining more than current events but future events that synced more with the design of the creator. Timeless providence. Death with a satisfied mind of the events that transpired took the body to the edge of the land and tossed it into the void where the seraphim lived. This was a place that a Blazer would never be able to ascertain its body again, and Death had also realized that by throwing the body in the void even if there was a bonding with Relationship, Addiction could never absolve itself. She would be tormented. This was a conclusion that Death could live with. Once the body disappeared Death turned back around and entered into the lobby of Neutral Land and ascended back up to the top of the tower and rested from the day's events.

All the while in the world of humans Cardinal had experienced a few weeks and it was time for his first day of high school.

FIRST DAY OF HIGH SCHOOL

Ring Ring Ring went the sound of the alarm clock informing Cardinal that it was time to experience his first day of high school. Cardinal was immersed in excitement.

The days preceding this blaring alarm he had gone back to school shopping with his granddaddy and his father Alpha. This did not consist of much for at this point in Cardinal's life his parents did not make enough money for him to dress in all the designer clothing and multiple outfits. All they had money for was a few outfits, a new book bag, some pencils and notebooks, and one brand new pair of shoes. Basketball shoes are what was constituted as prime fashion during Cardinal's time as an adolescent. Michael Jordan was one of the greatest basketball players to ever play the game, and because he was so iconic his shoes were held to high regard as well. They cost a few hundred dollars in order to own a pair, but this price was far beyond what his parents of 7 children could afford at this time. There were a few different basketball players that had a shoe line come out during this time, but from years past Cardinal knew wearing these shoes were taboo and would ultimately turn him into a target for verbal bullying. Being in a new place he could not afford to be the guy people ganged up on for his fashion, for his esteem was far too brittle.

There was another basketball player that had played basketball during this time who Cardinal had heard a lot about. Allen Iverson. This guy was gritty and had extreme skill and success in his basketball career. His shoes looked nice and were more affordable. These were the shoes that Cardinal wanted, and because they were all black, they were discreet enough to wear every day and no one would notice that he only had one pair of shoes.

The night before Cardinal would rise to the sound of the loud alarm clock, he made sure all his stuff was packed for the next day. In his shopping he acquired a black track suit that he really clock, liked. It was black with white and grey stripes coming down the side of the leg and the arms. The jacket was a short sleeved one and was the apple of his eye. With his new black shoes and a blank white tee shirt Cardinal knew he would be easily welcomed into the folds of all the well dressed and popular people at this new school. He packed all of his school supplies in his new book bag and made his lunch for the next day and placed it in the refrigerator. He was ready.

The excitement rushed through Cardinals entire body as he jumped out of bed ready to not only be at a new school but meet some new people. He was still a little bit sad by the fact that his best friend would not accompany him to the new school but this would be a new fresh start. He rushed to the bathroom to brush his teeth; he knew that if he did not get up before his sisters, he would have to wait in a long line to use the bathroom. Once inside he brushed his teeth and as he brushed, he looked deep into his reflection and began to speak about what he wanted to accomplish during the day.

"Okay look Cardinal it's your first day in a foreign land. You will probably not know anyone but this just means that you have a lot of potential and opportunity. We are gonna stunt on em with the outfit you picked out., you are gonna be super smooth, and who knows maybe we will meet a fine lady to be our crush on the first day. That would be crazy." Cardinal speaking solely to himself. After he was done brushing his teeth, he cupped his hands to rinse out his mouth. Once the water swished around his mouth enough to remove the toothpaste, he bent over to spit the residue into the sink. When he was satisfied with the completion of his hygiene, he looked into the mirror again and when he looked, he saw his legion of suits, coats, and blazers looking back at him through the reflection. Cardinal had accepted the plight he was living among them and was no longer horrified by their presence. He gathered himself and stepped out of the bathroom back to his bedroom to put on his school clothes. All the while he realized that his sisters had not gotten out of the bed yet. Just before he could think to bypass his room to go wake up his sisters, Omega opens the door to her room and instructs Cardinal to go wake up his sisters or they will be late on their first day. Cardinal walked into the room and gave Aurelia a good shake.

"Come on, Aurelia, it's time to get up. If you don't get up, we will be late." Cardinal's excitement intensified.

"Look, you are all excited now but this is no different than any other school experience you faced before. 5 more minutes." Aurelia pleads.

"No. Mom said you gotta get up now. No more sleep. Get up." Cardinal commands.

"Jade. Time to get up. Same thing Mom said if you don't get up and if she gotta come in here she is gonna start whopping people and I don't want that to happen to you." Cardinal informs. He stepped back and it appeared that his siblings were starting to wake up so he walked out of their bedroom and went back to his bedroom to get dressed for school. He put on his freshly ironed white tee shirt. Slid on his black track pants, he made sure to sag his pants a little bit because that was the style. Then he threw on his track suit jacket over the top of the white tee shirt. He sat on the side of his bed and slid his feet into some brand new white socks. Then he put on his black Iversons. Cardinal walked out his room feeling super confident about how he looked. He knew he was fresh to death. Once he had everything on, he swung his book bag over his right shoulder and walked out of the bedroom. He walked down the hallway just passing by his sister Aurelia heading to the bathroom.

"Hey you might wanna just wear the pants and the white tee shirt and leave the jacket here." She advised.

"Why? The jacket goes with the outfit." Cardinal responded with confusion.

"Because high school is a much different beast. You look like an old man wearing that track suit with the sleeves off. I'm telling you the boys up at that school will embarrass you. And....you are gonna be getting out the car with me and I don't want my image being tarnished because you decided to go up there looking like that. Just wear the tee shirt and the track pants." Aurelia explained. Aurelia was one year older than Cardinal and as such she had attended high school already and had already seen what the adolescent boys were wearing and she cared for her brother's self esteem thus she gave him insight that he did not value at the time.

"No. I really like this outfit. This is what I am wearing to school. Enough said." Cardinal committed to what he had put on. He was confident that his outfit was prime fashion.

Once both of Cardinal's sisters were ready to leave the house, Omega came out of her room dressed with her purse over her shoulder and made one decree to each of them sitting in the living room.

"2 minutes and I'm pulling out of the driveway if you are not ready you are getting left." Omega informed while running in the kitchen to make herself her morning tea. Cardinal, Jade, and Aurelia got off the couch in the living room and walked out the front door to the car where they waited for Omega.

The sky was completely grey and overcasted. It looked as if it might rain, but that was normal for the environment they lived in. The bay area waters would roll in fog typically every morning but the summer sun would burn it out by the afternoon. So it was a bit chilly outside. Cardinal could feel the moisture of the air on his bare forearms. Just before the shivering set in Omega stepped out of the house and unlocked the car door for the 3 of them to jump in. They all sat down in their designated seats and put their seatbelts on and Omega pulled out of the driveway.

On the way to the school Omega began to pray for their day.

"Father God in the name of Jesus, I thank you lord for waking us up this morning and starting us on our way. I pray that in your infinite wisdom and all knowingness that you will aid my children in their day at their new school. That you will unite the hearts of my son and daughters with some kind young people. I pray that they have a friendship that will get them through school. Lastly, I pray that they stress not and enjoy the new subjects that they have been enrolled in. In the name of Jesus we pray. Thank you father. Amen." Omega concluded.

"Amen." Aurelia, Jade, and Cardinal all responded in unison. All the while Omega had pulled up to the last stop light where the kids could see the school on the hill and all the students walking up to it. At this point Cardinal could feel his heart pounding as the anticipation grew to be on a new campus, meeting new people, learning new subjects. All the while he was still a little bit sad that he would not be able to experience this new lot in life with his best friend, Azure. Omega went through the green light and turned right into the parking lot of the campus. Cardinal could see the sea of young people walking into the gates of the school that had plastered the name of the new institution Cardinal would be doing 4 years at. Century High School. It seemed as though there were hundreds of chariots pulling into this vast parking lot and at that time Cardinal could feel the overwhelming effects of anxiety setting in. The irony he began to think. Right after his mother prayed for him, he could feel and see Anxiety with his knee on his throat keeping him from breathing normally. Omega slowly pulled up to the front of the campus and unlocked the door for the Wolf 's to exit. Cardinal and Aurelia got out the car and waved back at their mother and little sister who were still sitting in the car. As soon as they both started walking into the campus Omega and Jade drove off in the van. Now Fear gripping Cardinal's heart he panics and asks Aurelia several questions about what he was going to have to do for the day.

"Hey, so where do I get my schedule from?" Cardinal asks.

"Right over there. It literally says freshman schedules A-F, G-M, N-T, U-Z over there." Aurelia answered while pointing to what looked like a theatre kiosk at the far corner of the courtyard. "Go over there and tell them your last name and they should have a schedule for you. On that schedule you will find your classes with the building numbers and letters on them. Each building here has a letter and a number right on the side of it. In order to find which class is yours you will need to look for the corresponding letter and number. It is literally that easy. Stop panicking and go do what you need to do. I cannot go with you because I will be late for my classes so go over there and do exactly what I instructed you to do. I'm sure you will figure it out, and if you cannot figure it out all you have to do is go up to one of those people driving around in the golf carts and they should be able to point you in the right direction of where you need to go. Ok. Bye." Aurelia finished and then turned and walked into the sea of people entering into the gate of the campus. Cardinal turned to the kiosk and began to walk in that direction. Once he got there, he went to the section labeled U-Z and stood in line behind the three people in front of him. Once they were all served, he saw the look of a very kind looking woman who with a soft and securing voice asked.

"What's your last name sweetheart?"

"Wolf. That's W.O.L.F" Cardinal spelled it out for her. "Thank you young man." The kind lady responded. She flipped through the various pages of student schedules until she got to his name.

"Are you Cardinal?" The kind lady asked. "I am Cardinal Wolf." Cardinal responded.

"Okay here you go honey. Do you know where your first class is?" She asked.

"I have no idea where anything is here." Cardinal honestly admitted.

"No worries." She responded while turning over his schedule to showcase a map of the entire campus. "Your first class is history at P100. That's in the back. So what you wanna do is enter through these gates here and walk straight back. Once you get past the lockers on your left you will see the P building just slightly on your right. 100 should be the first door on the right side of the building. You got that?" The kind lady asked.

"Yes." Cardinal confirmed. "Thank you so much." Cardinal thanked her before walking away.

"No problem honey. Now hurry along before you are late to class." The kind lady stated while looking down the line to the next student who looked as concerned and spooked as Cardinal did. Cardinal did just as the lady described to him to do while keeping an eye on the map so that he did not miss anything. He walked past all the buildings and he could see that they all were basic in design and uniform. All the letters for the buildings looked as if they were in the same spot for each of the buildings. At this time the worry Cardinal had stored seemed to settle. Cardinal came up to the lockers on the left just like the kind lady spoke about. He looked slightly right and he could see the P marked on the building and the first door he could see was P100.

"Perfect, this is my first class. History." Cardinal thought to himself. He strutted over to the door and opened it up with confidence. He could feel that maybe he was over analyzing what he thought would happen.

"I just need to live in the now." Cardinal thought to himself. He then walked through the door and he saw a dozen or so students looking up at the door. The little bit of confidence he thought he had suddenly left his body and he began to panic again. He could see Fear enter through the door with him and quickly sucking the strength from his legs. He tried to walk to an open chair but he no longer had the strength to move his legs. Before matters got any worse his professor asked, "Before you sit in any chair, what is your name, because I have a seating chart which will give you your assigned seat." The professor asked.

"My last name is Wo...Wolf." Cardinal stuttered.

"Wolf? Ok ok ok. Ah Wolf yes your seat is right here sir, please take a seat we will be starting class soon." The professor instructed.

"Cardinal, slightly relieved that he had a place, walked over to his desk right next to several young men that seemed to know each other. As he neared his desk, he could see what looked like two of the young boys that knew each other constantly looking at each other, peering back at cardinal and giggling. Cardinal once again became self conscious.

"Are they giggling at me?" Cardinal thought. He got to his seat and dropped his backpack right next to his desk and sat down in his desk. The two young men began laughing rather than giggling and it made Cardinal very uncomfortable.

"Maybe they are laughing at a joke that they had told each other just moments before I came here. Perhaps they are not laughing at me, perhaps it is something else." Cardinal began to assure himself. Just before the assurance set in for Cardinal one of the young boys tried getting Cardinal's attention.

"Pssss. Pssss. Aye yo. Hey." The boy began to pester. Since Cardinal had not turned the boy reached out and tapped Cardinal on the shoulder. Cardinal turned around quickly with a smile on his face, thinking this might be the start of a friendship.

"Hey man, what's your name?" the young boy asked. "Cardinal Wolf." Cardinal answered. What's yours?" Cardinal rebutted.

"You hear him. Cardinal Wolf." The young boy mimicked Cardinal's voice. All the while the other young boy snickered under his breath. "Me and my mans were talking about how bold and proud of yourself you gotta be to come to school looking like someone's grandfather at a senior center with that two piece track suit you got on. You ain't even get the one with the full sleeve you went and got the one with the short sleeve." The young boy badgered.

The other young boy interrupted. "Hol'up you ain't even peep the shoes he got on. He got on the Big 7 specials on his feet. OHHH NOOOO." The other young boy stated.

"I didn't even get these shoes from Big 7; I got these shoes from Shoe Haven. And this is an expensive jumpsuit." Cardinal tried to fight back the tears, but all this did was cause more fuel for the boy to poke fun at.

"I know he didn't just say Shoe Haven, like that was a better store. This boy out here shopping at the goodwill for track suits and buying busted Iversons. There ain't no way in the world THAT track suit is worth anything especially if you are out there shopping at Shoe Haven for your shoes. I bet that track suit was expensive like 50 years ago when my grandpa was going to school. This boy looks Goofy. I bet that white tee is from a combo pack from Walmart." The first young boy continued. Just when Cardinal didn't think the embarrassment couldn't get any worse another kid walked through the door and the two young men threw up theirs arms and yelled out,

"D! Oh snap you got this class too. This semester is going to be dope."

"Q what up baby. B what's up." D responded.

Cardinal now knew the identities of the ones that persecuted him. The first young boy that started to make fun of Cardinal was named Q and the second one was named B.

"Aye bruh you gotta come over here and see what this boy got on it got us cracking up." Q loudly announced to not only his friend D but all the other students as well.

"Check out this boys' shoes." B added.

"Hol'up lemme see." D stated while making his way over to the other side of the room. Cardinal's heart began to flutter and he went from a state of embarrassment to a state of rage. Cardinal wanted violence to the extent of death on one if not all three of these boys.

"He isn't serious." Violence stated.

"He could really want to do something Violence. Why are you just sitting idly by." Fear questioned.

"There are two reasons. One is his reverence for his parents and their rules that they have indoctrinated him with. They specifically told him since he was a little boy not to cause trouble at school for any reason. If at any point they would have to come up to his school for something he did then there would be a price to pay for his actions. This has enslaved him to a "do good" mentality which will not allow him to cause any trouble, but he also lives by a creed that if any act of violence be done unto him then it is his obligation to finish it. This creed collaborates with the dealings of his parents as well, they believe that if an act of violence be carried out against him and if he does not do anything then he will have to deal with the repercussions from Alpha and Omega. The other reason I know that he is not serious about conducting violence against these bullies is because of his exposure to martial arts at a young age. He knows that he could really injure one of these boys and he was trained to never use his skills unless he needs them. So even though he is fantasizing about what he could do to these boys he is not at all serious about it." Violence explained. "My time is coming though I can sense it." Violence finished.

At this point D made his way over to the other side of the room and looked down at Cardinals shoes and began to laugh. Before he could get the words out to start talking smack the teacher finally notices the social genocide being conducted and decides this would be the best time to create a new seating chart.

"D your seat is located on this side of the room. Please come over to your desk and have a seat. I am seeing now that this will be a long semester if I do not separate you two boys so Q you sit over here and B you sit over here, please." The professor instructs while pointing to polar opposite corners of the room. B and Q got their stuff up from their desk and began to move from their current seat to their new desk on the other side of the room. Before getting up Q looked at Cardinal and could see the rage in his eyes. Before moving Q tapped Cardinal's shoulder and said.

"Hey man, it's all jokes, relax. My name is Q. That is B and he is D. You gon have to learn how to cap back otherwise your time is gonna be ugly." Q then walks to the desk in the back of the classroom.

"Okay kids welcome to history 101….." The professor began to give his introduction about the class and some background about himself but Cardinal's ears could not receive anything that he was saying because his mind was still captivated on the onslaught that he fantasized. Toxic thoughts ran through his mind that poisoned his mood. The kind Cardinal had gone away. He made a decision in that moment that in order for him to survive high school he was going to need to shapeshift and become. Become what? That was something that he could not figure out just yet but that was something he would have to determine in order to keep himself safe. The teacher finished his introduction and passed around the rubric for the semester.

"Ok now it's time to get to know each one of you, so let's go around the room and introduce each other. So we will start on this side of the room and when it's your turn just announce your name and one fun fact about you." The professor instructed while pointing at the first kid sitting in the front. Each kid announced their name and a fun fact about them. Cardinal, seeing that his time was soon coming, knew that he would have to say something and do something to not be seen as a nerd. First thing he did was take off the short sleeve tracksuit that he was wearing.

"Okay, next we have." The professor led.

"My name is Cardinal Wolf. A fun fact about me is I know martial arts and started fighting when I was 6."

"Hiyaaaa." Q yelled out from the back of the room. The classroom let out a small chuckle.

"Settle down now." The professor ordered.

It was at that moment that it did not matter what he said or what he did, these boys were going to pick on him because he gave them too much power already. He should not have shown emotion and he would have gotten rid of them. Now Cardinal would have to consciously think about every outfit worn and everything that he did to prevent from being singled out. The rest of the classroom finished giving their introductions which left only a few moments before the bell would ring to dismiss everyone.

"With just a few moments left of this first period, I'm going to pass out your book's homework as the first chapter. Make sure you read it because tomorrow we are going to be working out of the workbook. I believe that is all I have for you today. You have a few moments to speak with the person sitting next to you, introduce yourself because that is the person you will be sitting next to for the rest of the semester." The professor instructed. Cardinal decided to make himself look so busy as to distract himself from the pretty girl sitting next to him. He knew she was a witness to the verbal onslaught he took moments ago from the two bullies and he did not want to embarrass himself by conversing with her. That 2 minutes seemed like a millennium as he distracted himself, but the 2 minutes did eventually end and the bell rang.

"See you all tomorrow, don't forget to do the reading." The professor stated before the room was empty. Cardinal stuffed his backpack with all his new stuff and put the shoulder straps on over his shoulders and walked out of the door. One foot followed the other as he kept his mind focused on walking and not starting any trouble. As hard as he tried to keep his mind on his current tasks he was still stuck inside of the classroom and his next classroom experience was like a dream. He could not hear the words of the teacher and he could not remember anything from the class. All he could think about was the rage that he had bottled up. It was almost like someone was imparting thoughts into Cardinal's mind because at this point, he began to think of all kinds of harmful and debilitating things to say to the boys the next day.

"That's why your father left your mom to fend for yourself. Do you even know who your father is? How many boyfriends has your mama had anyways?" These were the thoughts that ran through Cardinal's mind as he sat in class listening to the next teacher talk about the lesson plan for the year.

"Looks like you got Cardinal in a snare." Abuse spoke with admiration.

Rage turning around shocked that someone else was present responded, "Well, this is the best that I can do at this moment because Violence is not doing its job today. I instructed him to push Cardinal, and by doing so we might be able to get him to use some of that Karate that he learned when he was a kid. Violence keeps saying it is not his time, he is not serious, you know stuff like that. So all I can do is throw these ideas in his mind and hopefully get him to act out on them tomorrow." Rage informed.

"So that's why you are up here?" Abuse asked.

"That's right I find that if I stir up some trouble in his amygdala then I can maybe throw his emotions out for good and he will have no choice but to listen to me, and if that happens then logic will go out the window. I have been around here looking for his hippocampus so that I can alter his memories and ideals from his childhood but for some reason I cannot get in there. The entrance is blocked by some pretty dangerous looking figures. So this is the best I can do." Rage informed.

"Indeed you cannot go in there and alter memories because you were not present in his memories for long you are new here. I think what you are doing is very powerful work though. If you keep doing what you are doing you will eventually disrupt Cardinal's way of dealing with situations. Good Job." Abuse congratulated while walking towards the hippocampus.

"Wait, how is it that you are going over there? And what are you even doing up here. I thought you had to be closer to the Bosom especially after everything that has been going on around here?" Rage questioned.

"Rage, I need you to be aware of one thing. Do not just go around here doing whatever you want. The master will demote you if he sees fit. I have the liberty to move around Cardinal's body because of how important I am at diminishing his life. You are new here, and although you have done a great job at helping us acquire new power you are not in a position to scout about and make moves without letting me know. The only reason I am not court marshaling you now is because you just so happen to be doing something that I was going to position you into anyways. This is your first and final warning. As far as what I'm doing, I'm going to stop into Cardinal's hippocampus and pay some of his memories a visit. Cardinal needs an awakening. Thanks to you I am teaming up with Neutral power as well. There is one relationship that I need to distort in Cardinal's memory, and with all the stress you are putting on him and all the pressures he will be dealing with from school I can resurrect my mentor Porn from the miserable state he is in now." Abuse informs Rage as he moves out of the Amygdala.

Abuse slowly walks over to the hippocampus where the guardians of memory sat at the gate. The memory guardians were ferocious creatures. They stood on four legs and they had fur like fire. Guardian 1 burned with reddish orange fire and the guardian 2 burned with a blackish blue flame. Their eyes were bright and piercing, burning with conviction, they stared down any who would find themselves foolish enough to come there. They embodied the physical archetype of a wild wolf. They were created to preserve the memories of man and keep the rulers of the dark and the light from imposing their wills on what was sacred to a man. Their memory. Abuse understood how they worked and how to appease their existence. Abuse strolled over to the gate and the Memory guardians stood tall and looked at Abuse and snarled. Unshaken and unmoved, Abuse put up his hands and shrugged his shoulders and spoke very calmly and very lowly.

"Good day oh powerful Guardians. Do not be alarmed I am not that idiot Rage it is I. Abuse. I am here because I hold a very dear memory of Cardinals and I just need to go and see to it that the memory is still intact. I understand that you are here to protect the memories of mankind and I am here to do what you are created to do, ensure my memory has not been tampered." Abuse cautiously informs still creeping to the gate.

"That's enough, do not take another step towards this gate or we will permanently get you removed." Guardian number 1 stated boldly.

"We'll rip your throat out if you come in here trying to propagate Cardinal." Guardian number 2 interjected. Both now showing their sharp fangs and getting in a stance to lung at Abuse who was now in reach to attack.

"Fellas, Fellas please this does not have to get nasty. Look." Abuse pointing up over the gate. They all looked up to the influx of information pouring into Cardinal's memory. "Cardinal is already under so much stress with all that is going on with this school and all this information will be lost if you don't start to filter out what stuff needs to stay in here and what stuff does not. I'm literally here to check on one memory guys. Look, I know you don't want me touching anything else, how about one of you can escort me to the memory. Once I see that it is still there you can escort me back out. Pleeeeaaaasssseee…" Abuse pleaded while on his knees with his face now on the ground and the back of his neck exposed.

Both of the guardians looked at the vulnerable area he displayed, snarled one last time, then looked at one another. They spoke briefly inaudibly for a second and agreed that Abuse could go in and see to the one memory that he had with Cardinal, once that request was fulfilled, he would have to leave. Abuse sensing that they had made a decision got off his face and Guardian 1 said,

"We have agreed to let you go in, 2 is going to accompany you to the memory you are looking for. Once you have checked in on that memory you are not to do anything else you are to leave this place. Next time follow the rules and send up your request and we will check to see the status of a memory for you." Guardian 1 informed Abuse.

"Thank you oh powerful Guardians. I promise I will be quick." Abuse thankfully administered before walking through the now open gates with 2.

"What memory do you want to see?" 2 asked.

"I would like to see the conception of me." Abuse stated.

"That is an ancient memory we are going to have to go way back in the archives to see that one. You are standing here with me now, should be proof enough that you are still in Cardinal's memory. Why do you need to see that memory?" 2 asked.

"It's not the fact that I am present that I need to check in on that memory, I need to see it to see if Cardinal still has details about the day we met that is important."

"That is not up to you to alter." 2 rebutted.

"Again I won't be making any changes, I just need to look at something." Abuse continued.

"Well since we are already here, I will show you that memory, do not touch anything or I will purge you right here." 2 addressed.

They moved through the database of Cardinal memories, memory after memory flew through the mind of Cardinal until they reached the memory that Abuse was looking for. As the memory played Abuse could see Cardinal walking into the back of the house with his cousin Jay. This was a time where he was able to travel around without having to worry about detection. The door closed to the room and Jay started his charade of confusing the young Cardinal. Some moments of the historical event went by and Abuse became noticeable to Cardinal in the corner of the room. 2 showing signs of impatience Abuse leaned in more to view the memory in more detail. He realized that while he was in the back of the house, he did not take into account who else was in the bedroom. Upon deeper investigation, he could see exactly who he was looking for. His mentor. Dwelling over the shoulder of Jay Porn stood strong and powerful. When Cardinal's eyes had become open to seeing the Suits, Abuse considered that he was the only one that tormented the mind of Cardinal, but he had not considered that there was a much more frightening being in there. This memory was what he needed

Cardinal to see again to get Porn back, and by playing the memory over this would trigger a delayed reaction for Cardinal to see it at some point during the day. With Cardinal being under immense duress from the stresses of school this would accelerate the memory to the forefront of his mind.

"Okay thank you so much for showing me that we can go now." Abuse thanked 2 while starting to walk back towards the exit.

"Wait, I have to put everything back to the way it was before I can escort you out." 2 informed.

"That's okay. I understand you have some work to do. I'll just leave through the same door we walked through." Abuse said while continuing to an exit.

"I need to see you out!" 2 yelled out.

"No it's okay." Abuse completely out of sight stated. Abuse knowing now that he could not be seen by 2 knew that he had one chance to complete his mission in the hippocampus looking for all the memories in the database labeled father. Once he acquired all the memories labeled father, he placed his DNA in the mix of the memories as to corrupt the memory Cardinal had with his father Alpha. He knew he would be able to fuse with this memory because after he consumed Relationship, every relationship Cardinal made could now be overwritten with the DNA of Abuse. Abuse knew that he could not wait for all the memories to be altered and he could not risk the guardians finding him so with the little bit of work he was able to accomplish he began leaving the hippocampus. He got out to the front and he could see 1 waiting at the gate still curating the information that was flowing into Cardinal's brain.

"Alrighty then I will see you late number 1." Abuse waved as he passed through the gate. "Wait, where is 2?" 1 asked.

"Oh he told me that I was free to come back out alone because he had to revert Cardinal's memory bank back to the way it was." Abuse deceptively informed 1.

1 detecting that there was something wrong with the story that Abuse was giving him ran around to the final exit to prevent Abuse from leaving.

"That does make a lot of sense. It really does. The problem is that there were specific instructions relayed between the two of us that you were to be escorted in and escorted out. The fact that you were not escorted out is very concerning to me, so you are going to wait right here until 2 comes out to verify that story." 1 ordered snarling and showing his teeth.

"You cannot keep me here, in fact if you do not get out of my way then I will make you move." Abuse threatened.

"You think you can do something to me here in my domain you have got to be out of your mind." 1 chuckled.

"I'll give you to the count of three to get out of my way." Abuse began counting down.

"One…..two…..three." Abuse concluded the count and just before lunging out at 1, 2 comes running out of the hippocampus shouting.

"Hey didn't I tell you to wait for me. I should trap you in the dungeon for that." 2 yelled out.

"2 are you okay?" 1 asked.

"I'm fine." 2 running to the side of 1." I told him to wait for me and he just left." 2 informed 1.

"Why did you lie to me?!" 1 furious at this point.

"Relax." Abuse laughing at the anger displayed by 1. "Yall are too serious, I was just having some fun with you all, but honestly you are doing a very poor job siphoning through all this new information coming in here. Cardinal is seriously not going to remember anything today." Abuse said with a devious smile on his face.

"If you did anything in his hippocampus we will find out. Memories that you are not a part of will correct themselves and when they do, they will show what was altered in them. You will be found out, and when you are found out you will have no choice but to be dismembered and destroyed." 2 warned.

"OOO I'm so scared. Well considering that all I needed was to inspect a memory of Cardinals and determine some important information then there really is nothing for you two to worry about. Now if it is okay with you I would very much like to get out of here. There are some things I must attend to. Thank you." Abuse states while walking through the small gap between guardian 1 and guardian. They both snarled and glared as Abuse walked through the exit of the hippocampus.

In the world of the humans, Cardinal had gone through most of his day and could not figure out why for most of the day he could not shake the rage he felt and why he kept thinking about the abuse he was exposed to when he was child. This frustrated him. So much so that he could not focus in his class. The visions soared through his mind and he became more and more enraged. The final bell from the school rang thus dismissing all the kids from their classrooms. Cardinal for the last time of the day packed his backpack with his books and binders and placed the shoulder straps over his shoulders and exited the classroom. It seemed that the whole day elapsed quickly and nothing stuck out in Cardinal's memory from the day except what had happened in his first period class. Cardinal knew now what he had to become in order to survive in this new world, he had to become someone who stayed out of the way but one that did not take any lip from anyone. When someone would talk about the way he looked he would then find their weakness, exploit it and dig so deep that it would prevent them from ever talking about him again. He would also need to become a chameleon. He had to adapt to the way everyone looked, how everyone talked, the customs of the world. This is the person he knew he could be. Cardinal made his mind up while he placed his books into his locker. He remembered that his sister planned to meet him back at the front of the school by the theatre so he began to walk to the front of the school. Cardinal walked through the courtyard of the school where he saw groups of people talking and the school drumline preparing for the coming football game. Cardinal passed through the gates and looked to the right to see the theatre, the one place that gifted him a kind welcome to this hellish facility. He stood there and waited for his sister and his father to pick them up from school. As he stood and waited, he could see all the groups of kids walking out of the gates to the parking lot where many of them hopped into their own cars, and some hopped onto the bus that would take them back to their homes. Cardinal watched carefully as each guy walked out of the school, what they were wearing, how they were walking, what they were saying, how they acted. To him this was going to be his homework assignment for the next week. He studied all that he could until his sister passed through the gates.

"Hey Cardinal, how was your first day baby brother." Aurellia asked.

"It was fantastic. I learned a lot, how was your first day of your second year? Cardinal asked.

"It was good seeing all my friends again, come on we have to talk back to that light post because that is where dad has been picking me up for the past year." Aurellia instructed.

"Okay." Cardinal responded walking beside Aurellia. They both walked through the parking lot, passing the variety of cars and people until they reached the back of the parking lot where Alpha was indeed waiting for them to come.

"Y'all are late!" Alpha seemed irritated.

"Dad it's the first day and Cardinal did not know where to go in regards to meeting you and my last class is PE so I had to get changed, then I had to go to my locker to gather my books so it took a while for me to get all my stuff." Aurellia informed Alpha.

"Well I will let it slide today because it is your first day of school but do not make this a habit. If yall ain't present here within 10 minutes of the bell ringing then yall can walk home. Test me if you want to." Alpha seemingly threatens.

"Ok." Both Aurellia and Cardinal respond.

Alpha hearing their responses starts driving out of the parking lot of the campus. He began their descent down the winding road that led up to the school. Cardinal realized that he had not said a word to both his siblings sitting in their seats in the middle section of the minivan. He sits up slightly to allow access to the car seats and greets the younger baby girl and his little brother. Alpha, sensing that his sternness might have left the kids feeling upset, decided to start having a conversation with Cardinal and Aurellia.

"So how was y'all first day of school? Learn anything?" Alpha asked.

"It was ight, I mean I didn't really learn anything. The teachers just handed out all the rubrics and paperwork for the year so they did not really teach anything." Cardinal exposes.

"My day was normal. I got to see all my friends again. They said that they all had a pretty rad summer and did not wanna come back to school but such is life." Aurellia states.

"Cardinal, were you able to make any friends?" Alpha asked.

"Yeah, I got a bunch of friends. In fact I met 3 guys from my first period and they seemed like cool guys, they were pretty funny." Cardinal responded.

"Oh that's great. Did you hang out with your sister at all?" Alpha asked.

"What?! EW!" Cardinal interjects.

"Wow. Well you don't have to say it like that. I am right here!" Aurellia responds.

Alpha cracks a smile, then looking in the rear view mirror notices that Cardinal was missing something.

"Hey Cardinal, where is your jacket? It is a little cold outside." Alpha asked.

"Dad it's a short sleeve so it's not like it would keep me warm anyways, but it is in my backpack." Cardinal answers.

"Well if it won't make a difference between you being warm or not why would you wear it out this morning without grabbing a coat but then not wear it now?" Alpha investigated.

"Cause I just don't wanna wear it right now that's all." Cardinal became seemingly irritated by the line of questioning he was receiving from Alpha.

"Were people talking about you today son?" Alpha asked concerned.

"Are you kidding me, of course they weren't. I look fly. It's just I wanted to switch it up, you know, do something a little bit different." Cardinal stated.

"Okay just asking." Alpha responded.

Cardinal now fully convinced by the toxic perceptions circulating his mind about the relationship he has with his father made this interaction less of an interaction between child and concerned parent and more of an interrogation. Cardinal despised the fact that Alpha was all in his business. He began to despise Alpha even more because his father was probably the type of kid in high school to throw jokes around at the nerds and poorly dressed kids also. He had heard stories that his dad came from a household where his Granddaddy would leave money on the table every week for him and he would go out and buy the latest fashion.

"He gon ask me about my wardrobe like he could even relate to what I just went through. Who does he think he is? He was the thug that did to others what those three boys were doing to me in class today. I really cannot stand him." These were the thoughts that ran through Cardinal's mind, the same caliber of intention that occurred during his time at school.

At this point Alpha had gotten to the next school to pick up Jade from middle school. Jade understood where she should be standing because Aurellia and Cardinal had both stood in the same place for years. Jade, seeing the minivan runs up to the street and slides the door open and hops into the back seat. Before she could even sit down and get the seat belt on Alpha pulled off to the adjacent street to drive back home. Jade fully inside the vehicle places her seat belt on and Cardinal looking at her asks.

"Hey little sister, how are you? How was your first day of your last year in middle school?"

"It was cool seeing all my friends again but I did miss seeing you there. I also miss having you as my escort to walk me to my classes. Mr. Nixon told me to tell you hello and that he wished you the best." Jade relayed.

"Oh man, Mr. Nixon was my man. Well I appreciate him for that." Cardinal responded.

The sounds of a talk radio station played in the background as Alpha continued the drive back to the house. A few left turns and a couple rights and they were back in the driveway of their house. While Alpha grabbed the carrier for the little baby Cardinal let Omepha out on the other side of the van. He let him down and Omepha ran into the house.

"Before yall make yourselves a snack or do any homework yall need to get your chores done. If you do not have them done before your mother gets home there will be hell to pay." Alpha warned.

Jade, Aurellia, and Cardinal dashed to their respective places to knock out their chores as not to be disciplined by Alpha who was considered heavy handed when it came to belt lashings. Cardinal rushed over to the trash cans and took the bag out along with all the plastic bottles on the kitchen counter outside to the respective bins that they were supposed to be in. When he got back into the house he replaced the bag in the trash can and swept around the floor to get the debris that fell out. Once that task was completed, he moved through the entire house picking up shoes, trash, socks, anything that would hinder the vacuum cleaner from doing its job properly. Once he had completed that task he walked over to the closet where the vacuum cleaner was housed and pulled it out to complete his last chore. Jade during that time walked into the bathrooms and emptied the trash into a bigger bag for Cardinal to take out later. She wiped down the toilets, sink, and tub. Aurellia did not have any work to do for her job consisted solely of cleaning the kitchen once dinner had been cooked. So she began making herself a snack before committing herself to her studies. Cardinal quickly moved through each room with the vacuum cleaner until he got to the final room in the back of the house. While the hum of the vacuum reprobated off the walls in the room a still small voice spoke out to Cardinal.

"Do you miss me?" The voice asked.

Cardinal could not understand why he knew the frequency of this voice but was unable to determine who the voice belonged to. Before his mind could begin to search his database on the voice heard images run through Cardinals' mind. Images of naked women, naked men, scenes from videos that he had watched that summer. At this moment a couple gripped Cardinal's heart Fear and Lust. The Lust that had his heart gave him a deep yearning to go on the computer in the back of the house and go watch some videos. The Fear that gripped his heart revolved around what would happen to him if he were to be found out again. He had just recently gotten let off of punishment because he was back in school and he could not afford to just go back to punishment especially after spending over 2 months locked up with a diet of top ramen every day.

"Fear you're going to have to let up on Cardinal, otherwise I have no chance of convincing him to invoke my practices." Porn advises Fear.

"Understand something Porn you are not ranked enough to be able to tell me what to do." Fear responded.

"Yeah and if you think that I will aid you in this pursuit then you have another thing coming, you don't remember what you did to me? Maybe this would be the opportune time for me to do the same thing you did to me back to you." Lust Seconds

"Hey now no need to get all uptight and bring up the past, we can work through this." Porn jokingly exclaims.

"You are in no position to even be consulting with us, just because Abuse revived you does not mean you do not have to follow protocol in here, you are beneath us, and if you want to prevent yourself from getting annihilated then I suggest you go somewhere." Stress ordered.

"The reason he is here is because my brother needs him to be here." Addiction informs them.

"Well he is the boss after all." Stress submitted.

"Porn cannot do anything except make suggestions like he has been doing. Cardinal will have to decide if he wants to accept you back." Fear admits.

"You know it would be in your best interest to let up, Fear. let me inform you why. If I am allowed back, then I will be stronger than I was before. Cardinal will live in a perpetual state of Fear and Stress. Not only from being found out by Alpha but when I am used more and more you two grow naturally. So we should actually be working together not against each other. We all have the same goal here." Porn educates Fear and Stress.

Cardinal was overcome with so much anxiety behind the decision that he knew he should not be making, but he felt compelled that after the day he just had a release would be all that he would need to get his mind back focused on his work, after all, sexual desire was something healthy. It would only be right for him to exercise a natural urge. Cardinal continued his chore of vacuuming the back of the house, once he completed his task, he slowly started to roll up the cord of the vacuum around the machine, all the while he could hear whispers emitting from where the computer sat. He knew it had to be one of his suits, but which one was this one. It couldn't be Rage because he had a strong stern voice. This one was small and seemed sweet.

"Come on Cardinal, I have everything you need right here." Porn beckons like a siren leading a sailor to its demise.

Cardinal leaned the Vacuum to its back wheels and began to roll it out of the back of the house to the living room closet where it rested until it needed to be used again. As he rolled past the computer, he glanced in the direction of the computer just to see what was speaking to him so sweetly. He looked but could not see anything there. Slightly paranoid that he was now just hearing voices Cardinal turned his attention back towards pushing the vacuum back into the living room, but Porn could sense the yearning of Cardinal to know who was speaking to him so just before Cardinal stepped over the threshold to go into the next room Porn stepped from behind to computer and again spoke out to Cardinal, because of his small stature he was not seen so easily.

"Cardinal, I know you were looking for me. Here I am." Porn says fully exposed on the keyboard of the computer.

"I knew I heard something." Cardinal now relieved that he was not just hearing things "Tell me who are you. I met your superior a few months ago his name was Rage, and upon meeting Rage I have come to an understanding about how I have to behave in this life in order to survive. I come to feel that you are here to help me in some way, so tell me why do I feel as though I know you?" Cardinal asks.

"I DO NOT HAVE A SUPERIOR!" Porn aggressively lets out before realizing that he was far too emotional about the comment that Cardinal made. Cardinal slightly taken back by the tone and agitation of Porn steps back slightly to create some distance. Porn seeing that he is not doing a good job at ascertaining Cardinal's trust readjusts, and says, "I apologize for raising my voice but things like "superiors" do not really exist where I am from. I am just a smaller stature because I have not fully matured yet. You know me because you and I have had a lot of great times together. I am Pornography." Porn introduces himself.

"Wait a minute. You are what all those boys were talking about in middle school. You are what I got beat and put on punishment for. Do you even know how long it took for me to be able to breathe without my chest hurting from my father punching me in the chest? You say you have everything that I need but it was because of you that I lost my sense of self, it was because of you that I was beat, it was because of you…" Cardinal began to list things before porn abruptly stopped him from continuing.

"Come on Cardinal this is not all my fault. I mean come on and think about it. I had nothing to do with what happened to you, what happened to you happened because you were not successful in keeping this secret of ours under wraps." Porn chuckles. "It's not funny but honestly if you would have come to me and asked for my assistance then none of this would have happened to you. Do you think that this is my first rodeo? What? Do you think that after my existence all this time that I do not have contingencies to keep you low profile? I have existed for years and have dealt with boys and girls alike. Why do you think that your buddy in middle school Seltzer was able to keep his secret so well?" Porn asked.

"Wait, so are you saying that Seltzer could see and talk to you as well?" Cardinal asked now confused.

"No dear boy. What I am saying is this. That is because Seltzer and even your father have yielded to me then my strategies and way of life become skills to them. Something as simple as borrowing a tape or a magazine from some of your friends so that you can indulge off the grid of your father. This will keep you low jack for a while and then once things begin to settle down in the home and your father and mother forget about the little act you were doing you can use the cell phone, he got you to download videos at school and just watch them here. See. Simple strategy. All this you would have known had you trusted yourself to me." Porn concludes.

"Did you say my father?" Cardinal stood there in complete disbelief.

"Of course your father. What? You thought that he did not have friendships with us as well. Like I keep trying to tell you Cardinal. We are friends. I can understand the mistrust you may have in me considering what happened to you." Porn chuckling again. "But honestly, we all are just here to help you maneuver through this life. It is hard enough already, like for instance what happened to you today at school. It's such a shame that those young boys were picking on you and you did nothing but try to be their friends. It's such a shame that you had to experience that feeling of isolation from being repudiated. I am with you all the time and I see how special you are and the fact that they could not see how special you are is a loss to them because they will never be able to see you the way I do. That's why I am here, to give you a release from the irritation from the day and to relieve the God given desire that you have to want sex. Now look based on what just recently happened over the summer I think it would be in your best interest to not get on this computer and look for me through the screen." Porn concluded.

"Wait after telling me all of that you want to end by saying I shouldn't go online and try and find you. Then what are you doing here then?" Cardinal asked.

"Cardinal, you have consumed enough videos and pictures in the last few months that your mind will be able to regurgitate all the content you have consumed. All I am asking you to do is listen and trust me like you have yielded your trust to Rage. I need that same level of intimacy." Porn pleads.

"So you just want me to think about that stuff that I had already seen?" Cardinal asked.

"Exactly! All you have to do is go somewhere quiet and close your eyes and think about what you saw and I will help in re-engaging the things that you once saw." Porn informs.

"Not gonna lie to you, you are making a lot of sense, and the thing is I'm sure I have the ability to recount what I saw but because of what I just went through I do not think that my mind will allow me to review that type of content, if you say that you are here to help me and keep me happy, I need a solution that will allow me to see something without getting me into trouble." Cardinal ordered.

"So it looks like you are willing to trust me." Porn acknowledges.

"To an extent. We did have some great times together that is true, but I cannot afford to get beaten like I did before." Cardinal confessed.

"I know Cardinal. I know. And believe me I have something that you can do that will help you get all that you will need to pleasure yourself." Porn advocated and before letting too much time go by began to instruct Cardinal on what he needed to do.

"So what you need to do is rather than go on hardcore porn sites because those typically have some extreme and obvious names to them do what Seltzen did." Porn instructed.

"The anime sites?" Cardinal questioned. "Exactly." Porn acknowledged.

Cardinal shook his head with understanding and finished towards the front of the house to put up the vacuum cleaner and prepare himself for the mission of the night. This would be tricky but not as impossible as before specifically because he now had a way to explain what he was doing on the computer. As Cardinal completed his homework his brain began to circle around the fact that Alpha literally beat him for the same friendships and actions that he himself committed and this made Cardinal more than angry but resentful and Enmity towards his father began to fester. Abuse, completely satisfied with the turn of events that transpired between Cardinal and Porn visited Porn at the heart of man as the day for the humans began to end.

"I like how you brought up the father to create a more distraught relationship between him and his father. That was the cherry on top of all the work that I committed today up in the hippocampus. Now I can see why even though you did not have much action in Cardinals life you were still considered a Coat." Abuse congratulated Porn.

"Believe me, my intention was not just to stir up more problems with him and Alpha, my goal was to get him to trust me inherently like he trusted Rage. Rage has taken a part of him that I do not believe that he will ever change because Cardinal feels that in order for him to survive, he has to utilize him. I want that same level of dependence from him. Once I get that then I will become immortalized in his heart and will never lose my rank again." Porn confessed.

"That brings me to why I am here. I do not believe that you being in this lowly rank is going to benefit you at all so I have done my due diligence to speak to the boss and get you advanced to becoming a blazer, but this is all contingent on whether Cardinal follows through with his act with you tonight." Abuse informs.

"Don't you worry about that. Cardinal will do just what I said." Porn confidently confirms.

"Everyone wash your hands so you can eat." Omega bellowed from the kitchen across the house. Cardinal, Aurelia, Jade, and Omepha all rushed to the bathroom to clean their hands so they could sit down at the table and eat together. Alpha and Omega made a point to have the kids sit down with them after the day so that each individual could talk about how their day went.

"Aurelia, can you please come in here and help me put the plates on the table." Omega asked while handing one plate to her. "This one is for your father. Go put it at the head of the table." Omega commands. Aurelia takes the first plate over and places it exactly where Omega instructed, after the placement of that plate she returns back to the kitchen to place the other 6 plates on the table.

"Cardinal, could you place Omepha in his booster seat please." Omega asks.

"Sure mom." Cardinal responds. Cardinal walks over to Omepha and lifts him into his assigned seat at the table. Once he placed him the seat he looked to the other side of the table where he was assigned to sit and, in the moment, he began to think about the assigned seating he encountered at his school today. Frustration began to rush through his body as he took his seat behind his plate. Everyone else sat down and Alpha asked everyone to bow their heads as they said grace over their food.

"Thank you Jesus for this food that we are about to receive. I pray that you will bless it for the nutrition of our body and our mind. Seek first the kingdom of God and all his righteousness and all things will be added unto you. If there is anything in this food that should not be we pray that you will remove it in the name of Jesus. Thank you for the hands that prepared this food. In Jesus' name we pray. Thank you God. Amen." Alpha concluded.

"Amen." They all responded in unison.

"Okay let's go around the table and talk about our days.

Alpha how was your day?" Omega asked.

As the family began to talk the conversation seemed to fade as Cardinal lost himself in the flavorful food. Spoonful after spoonful he ate while taking little to no breaks in between bites. Each bite made him feel as though the harshness of the day was not as bad as it may have seemed.

"Cardinal your turn. How was your day?" Omega asked. Cardinal did not want to alarm anyone about how his day went and the torment that he went through so he opened his mouth and said, "My day was fine. I got my classes. I learned absolutely nothing today considering that the teachers were just trying to get us acclimated to the rigmarole of high school and how this was somehow much more different than middle school. To be completely honest it was not all that much more different than middle school, except for the fact that people were much more prone to cliques. Other than that observation and the limited work today was just fine and dandy." Cardinal concluded.

"Did you find a Clique that you fit in with?" Omega asked. "Yeah we got our own little gang." Cardinal lied.

"That's good to hear." Omega responded. "Okay so I'll tell you all about my day." Omega immediately followed up. As she began talking about her day Cardinal drifted back into his world of bliss experiencing the flavor of the food on the plate in front of him, until there was nothing left on his plate.

"...and that's when traffic got so bad, I thought I wasn't gonna get home. Cardinal, did you even chew your food. Goodness!" Omega shockingly exclaimed. "Would you like some more food?" Omega asked.

"No, it's okay, I'm good." Cardinal responded standing up to put his plate in the kitchen."

"Ah ah ah. Sit down you know you don't get up from the table until everyone is done eating and you are dismissed." Alpha interjected his action. Cardinal instantly annoyed by the voice of his hypocritical father, looked over at him with a face of disgust and disdain then sat back down at the table.

"What?! You bad now?" Alpha asked menacingly.

"Nah I'm good." Cardinal responded slightly concerned. "Don't get snatched up in here!" Alpha responded.

"Ok ok everyone just relax." Omega interjected. "Now is everyone done eating?" Omega asked.

"Yes." Aurelia answered. "Yup." Jade responded. "Yeah." Cardinal answered.

"I'm done too." Alpha admitted still glaring at Cardinal from across the table.

"Ok so Alpha do you think it's fair to say that everyone is dismissed from the table?" Omega asked.

"Yes dear. Everyone get your plates from the table. Scrape the remnants into the trash can and rinse off your plate. Cardinal don't forget to take out the trash so it's not stinking. Aurelia knock them dishes out now. Jade if you haven't finished your homework you need to go finish that." Alpha ordered just before standing up and walking into the living room to go watch TV.

Each one of the Wolf 's got up from the table and proceeded to their designated tasks so they could conclude their day.

Hours went by as the young Wolf 's completed their assigned chores and completed their preliminary work for their classes, and at this point it was far beyond their bed time. Aurelia had gone to bed after getting her supplies ready for what tomorrow would bring her. Jade completed her homework and went to bed with Aurelia, since they shared the same bedroom, it only made sense that they would go to bed at the same time. Omepha had been escorted to bed by Omega hours ago. Cardinal stayed awake for a little while after everyone had gone to sleep because he was excited for the experience that he believed he needed, especially after the hectic day he just experienced. Once Omega had gone to bed Cardinal went to the computer to watch an episode of his favorite anime which in and of itself was taboo for the Wolf household. Alpha and Omega specifically ruled that there would be no TV watching during the school days so Cardinal could not just go watch this show while Alpha was awake, he would have to wait until his dad had gone to bed.

"I'm going to bed now, good night dad." Cardinal said. "Goodnight Cardinal." Alpha responded.

Cardinal went to his bed and laid there with his eyes wide open as he lay awake waiting for Alpha to finally go to bed. The longer that Cardinal laid in his bed the more that he thought about what Porn had told him about his father. He was an individual that had befriended this suit that he got beat for. How could he be so hypocritical?

"Don't cry be a man." were the echoes of Alpha replaying in Cardinals' brain. "Suck it up." more word echoed in Cardinal's head, and the frustration began to build to the extent that Rage could feel his presence becoming more felt. Cardinal continued to lay there until he heard the TV cease to project sound and the light in the living room turn off. This would be the opportunity he was looking for. Cardinal rolled to his side to view the hallway from his bed, he was waiting to view Alpha walk by his bedroom to his own, and just like he expected Alpha walked right by and closed the door to his bedroom. Cardinal saw this was the opportunity he had been waiting for and got up out of the bed and tiptoed to the back of the house so that he could turn on the computer.

"That's its Cardinal let me be your escape from the stress of the day." Porn spoke softly into Cardinal's ear as he navigated through the browser to get to an anime site that showed risqué photos and videos. Once he opened the page Cardinal could feel a twisting in his stomach, it felt as though he were going to throw up. Cardinal looked down and he could see a chain going through his torso and slowly reeling itself back into his body with Porn present on the other side of the chain. Cardinal now starting to panic not just because he was not quite sold that his dad would not find out about what he was doing but also because of the feeling that he started to feel.

"What are you doing to me?" Cardinal asked.

Porn responded, "I want to be as close as you and rage were when he first entered into your life you felt as though you could not orchestrate yourself through this life without him and I am completing the same cycle you have with him. Cardinal, I love you." Porn uttered as Cardinal fell back into his habit. Once Cardinal had finished watching his video, he stayed up for a few more hours going through numerous safer websites so the ones that he did look at did not just stand out in a query if his father were to look again.

"Well that felt good, now I have a better hold on Cardinal." Porn confessed. Porn feeling accomplished from chaining Cardinal walked about the Heart of Man with another purpose on his mind. He needed to regain the power that he lost when he vanished. There was one thing that he kept that would dynamically help him regain the power he lost; it was Perversion's eye. Keeping Perversion's eye would allow Porn to not only easily locate Perversion in an instance, but it would also expose Porn to some of his old skills. As he reached into his pocket to pull out the eyeball, Abuse materialized directly in front of Porn to have a conversation about the recent accomplishment.

"Great job today. Your acquisition into Cardinal's bosom was exquisite. I saw the methodologies that you used to ensnare him. Now before I got here, I noticed you were digging into your pocket, what were you getting?" Abuse asked.

"The truth of the matter is that I cannot fully do the work I need to with Cardinal unless I am fully empowered. My ascension to power is predicated on consuming the Blazers that I once had. Perversion, Masturbation, and Lust. Before I consumed Perversion the first time, we battled. The battle was fierce and in the midst of the battle I was able to knock the eye out of him. At that point he became weak enough for me to consume and I acquired immense power by consuming him. I kept his eye in the event that he was to ever pull away from me. His eyeball will draw out his location to me and will also reengage some of the skills that I lost when Perversion was stripped from me." Porn informs.

"Normally I wouldn't care much for your endeavors, especially because I am the one who got you released from the prison that you were in. The reason that I am going to help you is because you helped me when I first came into power. You showed me around Man's Bosom and I am grateful to you for that. So let's get you that power, I will need you for the next plan that Tux has for Cardinal's life.

POWERFUL PORN

Porn reached back into his suit to find the eyeball of Perversion. He took the eyeball out and inserted the eye into his head to acquire the power of the Blazer's without having to go through an extensive ceremony or ask Tux for permission for momentary power. Porn knew that if he wanted to ascend back to his ranks of being a Coat then he would need to make this process quick. The eyeball sat in the center of his head like a cyclops. Porn understood that now that the eyeball had been removed from the veil of darkness Perversion would now know where his other eye was and would seek it out with great persecution. Porn did not currently have the physicality nor the raw power to do war with a Blazer, thus he needed help.

"Now when you said you were going to help me, what did you mean by that?" Porn asked.

"Well, I clearly understand that you will be absolutely useless against the power of a Blazer, especially one that had been sitting in the rank for longer than you had been a Coat. I am going to have to engage in battle with you." Abuse answered.

"Then I best describe what is going to happen momentarily. I just placed this eyeball into my head, which means that Perversion now knows where his other eyeball was this entire time. By taking it out of my pocket I have unveiled the darkness that it was susceptible to, thus Perversion knows it's in my head and he will be coming back here to ensure that he regains what he had been looking for ever since he was released from me." Porn informs.

"I wouldn't worry too much about Perversion rushing back to do something to you Porn, I currently have him on a very important mission in the hippocampus of Cardinal. You see, in order to get you back here I had to alter some of Cardinal's memories. By doing that, it allowed you to resurface in his heart. My consumption of relationship allowed me to frequent some of his relational memories with his father and create a narrative that will be impossible for Cardinal to break free from. Perversion is up there to further ensure that we pervert his ideals and memories even more. I found out that the guardians up there will let you into the mind if you have a valid reason to be there, and I gave Perversion the perfect alibi." Abuse informs.

"Now that you mention it, I can see both of the Guardians now, through the eye of Perversion. Looks like he is being met with major hostility." Porn states.

At Cardinal's hippocampus, Perversion stood tall and unafraid with conviction. The two guardians of memory stood in front of the gate snarling and preventing Perversion from getting into Cardinal's memory.

"Great guardians. You know that you cannot forbid me from entering into Cardinal's memory especially when I have a valid reason to be here." Perversion states

"You have yet to state your reason for being here." Guardian 1 stated.

"Isn't it strange brother that we were frequented by another one of those disgusting creatures not too long ago." Guardian 2 added.

"The reason that I am here is because there are some core memories that Cardinal has that I am involved in that need my attention. You both know that if there are core memories stored up in the hippocampus, I have the freedom to access them." Perversion states as he begins to walk to the gate. Guardian 2 rushes towards Perversion as he attempts to walk by them guarding the gate. He leaps at him with his mouth wide open, his sharp teeth showing, and the flame from his body now glowing brighter than it had before. Guardian 2 clamps his mouth down around the shoulder of Perversion, the force of the blow puts him on his back. Perversion now freaked out asks,

"What is the meaning of this? I thought you were supposed to be peacekeepers?"

"Our job is to keep the peace, but with extreme prejudice. If we did not use force then your kind would be up here wreaking havoc any chance you got. Now you imposed that you would just be able to access any memory that you are aligned with and that is your mistake. You most certainly can access that memory, IF WE ALLOW IT!" Guardian 1 roared. At this point Guardian 2 had sunk his teeth deep enough into Perversion's shoulder to rip apart his arm.

"For the level of disrespect you have just displayed we will be keeping that arm." Guardian 1 stated. Guardian 2 ripped the arm off of Perversion and carried it back to Guardian 1 and dropped it on the floor. Perversion rolled around on the ground screaming in agony.

"Now get yourself together and tell us what core memory you would like to see. After what has just transpired with Abuse, we are not letting anyone past this gate. If there is a core memory that you would like to see then we will bring it out to you." Guardian 2 states.

Perversion gets off of the ground and grabs the stub of where his arm was just ripped off. He lifts his eye to now look at the two guardians and the arm that was laid out on the ground. Wrath began to swirl in his being. He mustered up the energy to tell them the memory that he was sent there to look at, but before the words came out of his mouth both of the guardians crouched into a defensive stance in anticipation for what they assumed that Perversion was going to do next.

"I need to see the memory of Cardinal and Alpha." Perversion mentioned.

"There are far too many of those memories stored up in the hippocampus, we need something more specific than that." Guardian 2 snarled.

Perversion began to think of a specific memory that he knew he would be able to pervert. He knew because of the work that Abuse had successfully accomplished that really any memory would infect the others but he needed something important, something revered in Cardinal's mind.

"The memory that I need to see is the memory of Cardinal and Alpha in the bed watching Karate movies together when he was little." Perversion ordered.

"What are you trying to pull? I can guarantee that memory has nothing to do with you Perversion." Guardian 1 refuted.

"I can assure you I was there at the time." Perversion responded with fear now gripping his being.

"Brother, go bring that memory out for him. Let me inform you that when he pulls that memory out here and you are not involved in it, we are both going to rip you to shreds. Do you want to reconsider? This is your last chance." Guardian 1 spoke.

"Please, do what I asked and bring out that memory." Perversion seconds. Both guardians snarled at the order. Guardian 1 looked at Guardian 2, they both nodded and Guardian 2 instructed.

"Brother, why don't you go get the memory instead, I will stay out here and watch over the arm that I tore from his body. When you come back with that memory, we will surely eradicate him."

"That works for me. I'll be right back." Guardian 1 agreed. At that moment Guardian 1 turned around and walked through the gate into where the memories were stored in the hippocampus. While Guardian 1 was gone Perversion realized something that was not evident to him before. It seemed as though one side of his face that was always shrouded with darkness had finally come from its hiding spot. He could see through both eyes again. As elated as Perversion became equally in that moment he was confused. Why was it that his eye was observing Abuse and where had the eye been all this time? Who was the eye attached to at this point? These were questions that he knew he would not gain the answer to unless he made it out of the brain. Leaving the brain was not going to be an easy task especially with the Guardians being overprotective about the memories. As Perversion stood there trying to figure out everything going on, Guardian 1 emerged from beyond the gate with the core memory that Perversion asked for. Guardian 1 looked angry and wrathful, for every step that he took out of the gate his body emitted a stronger and stronger flame.

"Brother, what has you disturbed?" Guardian 2 asked.

"We have been foolish and it is because of our ignorance and stupidity that we allowed these disgusting creatures to play us." Guardian 1 states while releasing the core memory from his mouth. When the core memory hit the ground, it illuminated the surrounding sky and Perversion and Guardians could see the core memory play out. The moment the core memory started playing both of the Guardians began to shine brighter and brighter as their anger intensified. Perversion watching the core memory understood completely why they were upset. When Abuse implanted his DNA into these memories, he did not do a good job of making it discrete, so when the Guardians looked at the memory, they could clearly see that the memory had been tampered with. Rather than a Suit being easily identifiable it was like darkness was present in the room, a darkness so dark that it was impossible for them to tell who was present in the room. They both snarled and began to circle Perversion. Perversion, now immensely concerned about what they would do, began to speak in an attempt to save himself, for he was unsure that they would not kill him as soon as there was an opening.

"Oh gracious guardians…"

"You can save it with the formalities. How did you know about this? How many more of Cardinal's memories have been corrupted like this?" Guardian 1 asked, still circling his body.

"Look I don't know what you both are talking about I was clearly present in the memory, look that is me over in the corner, you can't see me standing there?" Perversion asked.

"You're not going to trick us; we both saw the image. It's distorted and corrupted there is no way for us to tell who was in there…..It was Abuse. After he left the memory I took him to look at, he was not in my sight for a little while. That small gap of time was all he needed to distort Cardinal's memory." Guardian 2 realized.

"Look if that is truly the case, I don't know anything about that. All I know is that I am present in that memory that you brought out, just turn around for a moment and look." Perversion urged pointing at the sky. Both of the Guardians looked at each other and decided that they could in fact take a glance before ripping the head from Perversion. They turned and looked up to the core memory that was playing and they both could now see Perversion standing in the corner. Noticing this now created even more discomfort and anger in the Guardians, they became so full of wrath that they both turned and pounced on Perversion to the point that he was looking up at both of their faces.

"Brother, should we just kill him?" Guardian 1 asked.

"I don't see a reason why that would be a problem. We should have killed Abuse while he was up here too." Guardian 2 responded.

"Now I understand that you are upset for something that you may or may not have been privy to while Abuse was here, honestly you killing me is not the answer and if I may say it's wrong. You are going to chastise me for the issue someone else may or may not have caused. All I know is that I am present in that memory and both of you killing me for that would be against protocol. Can I just do what I need to do and leave you both alone. I will definitely never come back up here." Perversion persuaded.

"Do what you need to do." Guardian 1 reluctantly agreed "But we are keeping this arm." Guardian 2 stated.

"Thank you." Perversion thanked. Both Guardians removed themselves from Perversion and he got up from the ground. Perversion began to think back to what he had not really considered during this time, what was going on with the eye that had recently surfaced. He attempted to look through the eye again but his attempt was futile as his eye was shrouded in darkness again. What was going on with Abuse? Why did his eye get shrouded again? He needed answers and these were answers that he would not get until he left the brain. Perversion walked over to the core memory and inserted himself into the location he observed himself while he was laying with the guardians on his chest. He materialized into the memory and from the corner of the room he could see Cardinal and Alpha in the bed watching karate movies. This was the same bed that Jay had laid Cardinal down in and done unspeakable sexual acts weeks before. Perversion looked over at the smiling Cardinal and reached over Alpha's head and wrapped his hands around Cardinal's neck. Suffocation began to set in on Cardinal as he physically sat in class attempting to do his work. Once Perversion realized that he had made an impression on Cardinal's memory he knew that he could now go and pursue the eye that had revealed itself. He walked out of the memory, but just before he left he made sure that he left an impression on Cardinal's physical body, one that would feel uneasy about any male interaction. Any time a man touched Cardinal unbeknownst to him, Fear would settle in. Any time someone would crowd his space, irritation and Anxiety would rule him. body. Whenever he would think about this moment in his life then Perversion would be there. Once he considered his mission complete, he left the memory and appeared before the 2 Guardians watching the entry to the gate. Perversion crossed the threshold and passed both of the upset Guardians. They both turned their heads to look at him as he passed by them.

"Have you done all that you need to do?" Guardian 1 asked.

"I am done. As promised, I will never return here. If I do then you have every right to kill me." Perversion responded.

"We will. Like we stated this arm stays here with us, if you even think of coming back here, we will know." Guardian 2 threatened.

"Understood." Perversion responded. Perversion turned around to where his back faced the guardians and he disappeared from the hippocampus back to the Heart of Man where he last saw his eye's visual. He looked around but to no avail, there was no one in sight.

Just moments before Perversion left the hippocampus to return to the Heart of Man, Abuse and Porn both discussed a plan to successfully ascertain the power necessary for Porn.

"It looks like Perversion is going to be in the brain for a long time, it appears that the guardians are not letting him get through the gate because of something that you may have done when you were up there." Porn pauses. "They just ripped his arm off! Did you know that this was going to happen?" Porn asked.

"I had no idea he would be met with hostility. I believed that I did a good enough job to keep the guardians off my track but it would seem that I will not be able to return back to the brain to further any more of my future plans." Abuse responded.

"So what do you devise that we do?" Porn asked.

"I believe that what you should do is put that eye away. Shroud it back in darkness because we do not want Perversion to know where we are going, you will probably need it though when you go to consume Masturbation and Lust." Abuse advised.

"So you think it would be a better idea to consume them before going after Perversion. I mean, Perversion has just lost an arm, I think that we can probably take him now." Porn remarked.

"That is a chance I do not want to take. You will come to find that I do not like taking chances. I have seen my demise, it may seem, and I don't want anything falling to chance. We are going to first go after Masturbation and after that we take down Lust. We save Perversion for last. Now, put that eye away." Abuse commanded.

"As you wish." Porn responded. He removed the eye from his head and placed it back into his suit pocket, shrouded from detection.

"So how do we find Masturbation?" Porn asks.

"Finding him is going to be a bit challenging considering he is a very shy Blazer. The last time I remember seeing him he was sitting by the Stairway of Ascension. I believe he likes feeling close to Tuxedo but he is too shy to actually be in his presence. So let's try there." Abuse advocated. In that moment Abuse and Porn both vanished and transported themselves over to the foot of the Stairway of Ascension, this was just moments before Perversion appeared where they were forming their plan.

At the foot of the Stairway of Ascension Masturbation sat in the middle of the floor with his Blazer folded over his head. He wished to not be seen amongst the rest of the Blazers because of a self contrived idea of how he looked. He sat in the middle of the floor doodling in the ground, figures and shapes to entertain himself. At that moment Abuse and Porn appeared before him.

"Abuse is that you? Who do you have with you?" Masturbation asked.

"Why don't you pull that Blazer from your head and find out!" Porn commanded.

"Wait a minute I know that voice. Porn is that you?" Masturbation asked.

"Yes, it is me." Porn paused in that moment to remove the eye that was resting inside of his suit pocket and placed it in his head. "I am here to take what is rightfully mine, the power that you owe me. I am here to get my quirk back from you." Porn confessed. At that moment Masturbation removed the back of the Blazer from his head so that he could see what was going on. He looked up to find Abuse and Porn standing in front of him, with Porn having the one eye placed in the center of his head. Masturbation immediately erupted into laughter as he saw how incomplete and powerless that Porn looked.

"Wait a minute. First and foremost, what is in the middle of your head? When you ascend in power Tuxedo is supposed to endow you with 2 eyes, why is it that you ridiculously only have one? You also said something about consuming me, how are you gonna do that without the temporary power granted from the master? It would appear that you have drastically over-estimated your expectations!" Masturbation states. Realizing that he has nothing to worry about, Masturbation takes the back of his Blazer and places it back over his head and sits back in the middle of the floor. Porn looks over at Abuse and shrugs his shoulders in amazement that Masturbation is making their mission much easier because he is not taking this situation seriously. Porn then looks back down at Masturbation sitting in the middle of the floor with the Blazer over his head, then looks back at Abuse and says,

"Well, we don't have much time because it appears that Perversion is currently standing in the same place that we stood before we came here. It is only a matter of time before he finds out where we are. We need to make quick work of Masturbation; can you grant me the temporary power that I'm going to need in order to consume Masturbation?" Porn pointing to where his mouth would go. Masturbation, now fully understanding why Abuse was there, removes the Blazer from his eyes, just to find Abuse endowing Porn with a mouth to consume him.

"Abuse what are you doing?" Masturbation remarks in panic. "You said that I was pivotal in your plans, how am I to accomplish anything if you are going to have Porn consume me? Again!" Masturbation now on guard speaks.

"What you need to know about me is I do what I need to in order to ensure my survival. You are not competent, confident, or even strong enough to prevent what is going to happen here someday." Abuse retorts.

"Then why not feed Porn to me? I will be much stronger if Porn resides in me!" Masturbation offers the suggestion. Abuse considers maybe this would be a better option, he turns around to look at Porn who now had the ability to devour Masturbation. Porn realizes that Abuse may be considering another option, attempts to try and reason with him.

"Look I understand that you could go either way with this thing, but do I need to remind you that I was the one that had Masturbation as a quirk before, and I would be better equipped in the long run to ensure your stay here. Remember how I took you to the Land of the Neutral and consulted with Consequence in order to keep myself from being purged. Do you really think someone as shy and aloof as Masturbation would have been able to do something like that. I am telling you I am the best suited for your plan. Lastly it won't be long until Perversion shows up here, if we are to get me back into power then we need to move swiftly." Porn argues.

"Porn, I risked my livelihood to get you back into this heart. There is no way that I am going to undermine my success and have you consumed by Masturbation, in fact…" At that moment Abuse turns and looks over at Masturbation, and without hesitation, Abuse punched Masturbation in the throat. Masturbation immediately grasped his throat in agony. Porn did not hesitate either, the moment that he saw that Masturbation reached up to guard his neck Porn opened his mouth wide and consumed Masturbation. Instantly Porn could feel an increase in strength and familiarity that he longed for. The badge that had once been on his coat had returned and Masturbation showed up where he was supposed to.

"Thank you for your assistance, Abuse. We have 1 Blazer down, just two more to go. Should we take the opportunity to wait for Perversion to get here or should we go find Lust?" Porn asked.

"I think the first thing that you should do is place that eye into your Coat pocket. Now that you have ascended in power you are not going to need to use that. We are going to go after Lust now. It's just as I said before, we are going to save Perversion for later. Do not destroy that eye because I'm sure that he is probably confused as to who just consumed his partner." Abuse instructed.

"That sounds like a wonderful idea." Porn agreed. He removed the eye from his head and placed it in his coat pocket and instantly his own eyes formed on his head. Elated to be back in the power that he once had Porn let out a celebratory scream, just before Abuse and him disappeared to another location in the Heart of Man.

Just before Masturbation was consumed Perversion stood immobilized by his eye coming back from the darkness it was shrouded in. The first thing that Perversion was able to see was Masturbation sitting in the middle of the floor with the back of his blazer over his head. Perversion chuckled because this was something that Masturbation liked to do.

"He is so self conscious about the way he looks to everyone. It's sickening." Perversion stated to himself. Perversion stood there still observing what was going on through the eye of the mystery suit with his eye. The next thing that he saw was Abuse again. Perversion became confused again.

"Who is this person traveling around with Abuse? It has to be a Blazer or a Coat." Perversion thought with surety. He continued watching as the events played out in front of him. Instantly he noticed that something was wrong, Masturbation seemed very upset and looked as if he were ready to do battle. Then Abuse very quickly punched him in the throat.

"What?! Why would he do that?!" Perversion quickly began to think. As quickly as that thought surfaced in Perversion's mind was as quickly as he saw Masturbation consumed by what looked like him.

"Wait a minute, someone with my eye just consumed Masturbation?! I need to go there now and figure out who this is!" Perversion let out with aggression. He immediately relocated to the foot of the Stairway of Ascension just to find that there was no one there. He was too late.

"Dang it! I'm too late again. Where could they be going now?" Perversion thought to himself. The moment that the thoughts began to run through Perversion's mind Abuse and Porn relocated into the Bosom of Man.

"So what is your plan on finding Lust?" Porn asked. "Well, it's obvious we hold an advantage here, we can clearly inhabit the Bosom, and Perversion cannot. The only way that he would be allowed to exit the heart is if he were able to gain the power of a Coat or if he was summoned here. That is precisely how we are going to get Lust; we are going to summon them." Abuse answered.

"Perfect, I will summon them now." Porn remedied. "Don't be foolish, if you were to summon them here, they would be fully aware of the act you committed and your opportunity to consume would be next to impossible....I will summon them." Abuse recommended. Abuse disappeared from the Bosom of Man to the world of human's where Cardinal had just left school and started his 2 mile walk back to his home. Abuse materialized beside Cardinal in the midst of his walk and startled him.

"Hey Cardinal." Abuse said.

"Yo, you can't be just popping up and talking bout hey. You dang near had me release my soul." Cardinal admitted.

"Then my mission would be complete." Abuse thought to himself. "Hey so have you seen Lust around today?" Abuse questioned.

"From my interaction with Rage I have come to find that you guys have some type of ranking, how do you not know where your subordinate is?" Cardinal asked.

"Simply because Lust is not my subordinate. I figured that they might have been around you today because I could sense that you had an urging to satisfy your sexual urges." Abuse responded.

"Why did you say "they "? I only saw 1 person. Also, yeah I seen him....her....I couldn't really tell what it was. I have been curious, yall look a lot like humans and evidently take on their sexual makeup, why is that?" Cardinal asked.

"Look Cardinal, the fact of the matter is I do not currently have the time to divulge that information to you right now. As for Lust, you have seen them. When?" Abuse responded.

"I would have to say sometime around lunch, so like 2 hours ago." Cardinal responded.

"So they must have gone back to the Heart of Man to prepare for your interaction today with Porn." Abuse mentioned.

"I mean, I guess. Porn did some weird stuff a while ago. Something with a chain and talking about being as close to me as Rage and I were. What was that about? It felt kinda weird." Cardinal asked.

"Look Cardinal, there is nothing to worry about. Porn was just endowing you with more power so that nothing would happen to you like it did before. We all want to make sure that you thrive. The only way that you will thrive is that you are closer to us because we can grant you power." Abuse answered.

"If you say so." Cardinal responded.

"I have to go back to the Heart of Man and speak with Lust. See you later Cardinal." Abuse informed just before vanishing back to the Heart of Man. Lust had implanted a few thoughts into Cardinal's mind that day to intensify his longing for sexual intimacy, but Lust's goal was not just to get Cardinal to continually look at pornographic images, what they wanted was for Cardinal to engage with a man or a woman. This would help Lust elevate and ultimately consume Porn. This would ultimately take time but because of the situation that Porn was in, time was on their side. Lust paced back and forth in the depths of the Heart of Man waiting for the perfect opportunity to strike and take down Porn. While Lust lay and wait Abuse appeared before them and demanded them to come back with him to the Bosom of Man in order to go over some strategy regarding Cardinal and the ascension into higher power. Lust sensing that there was no ill will and foul play decided that this invitation to the bosom was ideal to pass the time until Cardinal got home, as well as position the idea of consuming Porn to Abuse, considering Abuse was present when they got their bodies back. Abuse walked over to Lust and placed his hand on their shoulder and transported them back to the Bosom of Man, due to the position that Lust held they were unable to travel there without the assistance of a Coat. The moment they both appeared in the bosom Lust wasted no time to break down their plan.

"Abuse, do you remember what you told me when I was released from the body of Porn. you told me that you were not my superior and that you needed me, Perversion, and Masturbation in order to achieve your goals. Well, I have a proposition for you." Lust started to explain.

"Oh….tell me what your plan is?" Abuse curiously asked.

"Porn has just made it back into the Heart of Man because you traveled up to the brain to revitalize him. Honestly, Porn is not doing anything new, and on top of that can we really trust and believe that Porn is going to make a lasting impression on Cardinal considering what his father, Alpha, did to him the last time. Here is what I am thinking….I am making some pretty good headway on Cardinal's heart and on top of that my power existed in humanity longer than Porn. Let me have the temporary power of a Coat and I will be able to consume Porn, and the two of us will run amuck in here. What do you think?" Lust asked. When the plan had fully been divulged Porn stepped out of the darkness with a big smile on his face. Lust became instantly shocked and concerned by the emergence of Porn. Lust looked at Porn intensively to find that there was a badge on his Coat, it was Masturbation, and it was at that moment that Lust fully understood why Abuse had relocated them there.

"Abuse?! What is the meaning of this?! Did you bring me here to get consumed by Porn?! Again?!" Lust asked.

"You know it's funny because Masturbation asked the same thing just before I gorged on him. Believe me when I tell you this Lust you are going to be no different." Porn confidently informed Lust.

"Answer me this Abuse, did you help him?" Lust asked.

"I do what I need to do in order to secure my legacy." Abuse responded.

"So let me ask you another question, are you going to help him now?" Lust asks while getting into a defensive stance. Before Lust could get his left hand up to protect his face, Abuse lunged at him with his hand balled up in a fist. Abuse cocked back to throw a punch but Lust was expecting the punch and turned its face to prevent from getting hit. The punch grazed its chin and Abuse followed through with the punch, Porn saw that the punch grazed their chin and saw it fit to rush Lust. Lust saw that Porn was jumping into action and cocked back his leg for a kick to Porns head. Porn was unable to see the kick being thrown because his attention was trying to consume him. Porn opened his mouth in order to finish off Lust, and the moment his mouth opened Lust flung a lightning fast kick that connected with his jaw. The impact let off a sound that was as loud as thunder clapping. Porn flew across the bosom and fell against the wall, Abuse reeled back in his failed attempt at knocking Lust out and bounded back to where Porn had fallen.

"Whoa, you didn't see that coming, did you Porn?" Abuse asked.

"That stupid thing over there broke my jaw, look at me." Porn scoffed while pointing at his hanging jaw.

"Yeah they did kick you really good. You think you can finish the task and consume Lust?" Abuse asked.

"Oh yeah. My jaw should heal back any moment now." Porn admitted and after a couple of seconds Porn's jaw snapped back into place. Porn moved his jaw around a little to become comfortable with the realignment. Lust stood at the opposite side of the bosom in a defensive stance ready for the oncoming onslaught of both Porn and Abuse. Porn and Abuse rushed forwards pacing towards Lust with aggression and malice. Porn decided to circle around to the left of Lust and Abuse went right. Lust tracked their movements with their eyes and knew that if one of them was able to get behind them it would be over quickly, so they devised to go after the weaker Coat. Lust lunged out at Porn who had decided to go left and slung another kick that would do more damage than the kick that they had thrown before. Porn was fully focused on the battle so he was able to see the kick being flung and raised his arm to block the kick. Once the kick had been blocked Porn threw a kick on his own. Lust saw the kick coming and blocked that one. They began to consistently throw punches and kicks in a flurry, all the while Abuse decided to refrain from rushing into the fight again, he figured that this would be the perfect opportunity to sit back and observe the fight. Lust saw from the corner of their eye that Abuse was no longer pursuing the fight and felt a bit more comfortable with how the outcome of the battle would go.

"Hey Abuse, since you are not going to be joining the fight, how about this…." Lust began to speak but paused once they had successfully landed a strong punch to the face of Porn thus dislocating his jaw again. "Why don't you give me the ability of a Coat, I'm telling you I could be a better asset to you than Porn could. And Porn, the only reason that you defeated me before is because you consumed me when I was in my infancy stage in Cardinal's heart, I am much more powerful now. You do not stand a chance against me." Lust gawks.

"I'm not going to lie to you, those last few blows hurt, but one thing you did not consider is that I have the eye or Perversion and once I place this in my head this little game will cease." Porn confessed.

"Wait. That's not fair. Abuse stop him." Lust urged.

"Please…I could care less what means you go through to obtain victory as long as this gets wrapped up soon, I am at my wits end watching you too fight." Abuse stated. At that moment Porn pulled the eyeball of Perversion from his pocket and placed it in the center of his forehead. The moment the eyeball was secured immense power reprobated from the body of Porn. Lust stood across the battlefield in shock and fear because it appeared that now there was no chance of winning the battle.

Back at the bottom of the Stairway of Ascension, Perversion finally could see through the other eyeball that had surfaced from the pocket of Porn. Perversion stood there confused as the room that he was looking at was none other than the Bosom of Man.

"Now why would my eye have gone from the Heart of Man to the bottom of the Stairway of Ascension, to the Bosom of Man? This doesn't make sense. Who has my eye? Who are they fighting?" Perversion began to ponder as he tried to make out the person standing across from the unknown thief of his eye. Porn rushed in on Lust at incredible speed, the engagement was so fast that even Perversion was shocked by how closely the Blazer appeared before his eye. It was at that moment that Perversion knew who was standing in front of his other eye. It was Lust, and off to the side he could also see Abuse.

"Why is Lust in combat, and why is Abuse just standing there watching this happen?" Perversion began to think. Perversion watched as Lust got punched and kicked across the vast space in the Bosom of Man. Lust became tired and fatigued from battle and laid in the middle of the floor as Perversion could see his eye getting closer to the lifeless looking body of Lust. Lust turned and looked into the eye and mouthed the words, "Just make it quick." Perversion understood exactly what was said and witnessed as Lust was consumed inside what he knew was a Coat. Perversion stood there in complete silence as his other eye stared at the ground. A couple of seconds went by and Perversion saw two fingers reach up for his eye and grab it. The fingers then placed the eye in the middle of the room and turned it to look at the one who had been using his energy to consume two of his partners.

"Finally, I will get the answers to my questions." Perversion began to think. The eye staring at the 2 feet of the being responsible began to reveal more and more of the body of the individual as they began to back away from the eye they placed in the center of the room. It was evident who the perpetrator was who had taken his eye and used it to gain power to consume his partners. Perversion stood in disbelief as the eye revealed that the one who had consumed both Masturbation and Lust was none other than Porn. Perversion witnessed as Porn mouthed something to the eyeball. Perversion iterated what he believed the mouth was saying in his head, "I'm coming for you." Perversion thought to himself. Porn pointed to the eyeball as he mouthed the words to the phrase that Perversion was able to make out. Just as Porn had finished making the claim to the eyeball, he walked away from it and went over to speak to Abuse. Abuse stood in the center of the room unbothered and unafraid of what Porn's intentions were now with him. Porn now immersed with so much power thought it wise to now defeat Abuse but consume him as well, he cocked back his fist in an attempt to defeat Abuse in just one punch. Abuse now fully aware of what Porn was planning instantly disappeared. Porn looked throughout the room to find out where he went, but his movements were so fast that his eyes could not keep up with his movements. Just before Porn could drop the hand he cocked back, Abuse appeared back in front of him but this time Abuse had grabbed Porn's arm and placed the fist right on his cheek. Porn stood there in amazement as

Abuse seemingly was going to allow him to destroy him. Porn began to smile and just before he could step into the punch and release all the power that he amassed; Abuse warned him.

"I know that you probably think that with the power you have amassed that you would definitely have the upper hand against me, but let me assure you, not only could you not defeat me but it would be in your best interest to not push your luck."

"Why is that?" Porn asked.

"The first thing is, no one, and I mean no one has ever embellished you simply because of you, most of the time it is me or the one you just consumed, Lust, that would allow you to even be here. You are probably thinking if you consume me then the narrative for you would change, but again that is a big mistake.... When I freed you from Cardinal's memory, I did not do a sloppy job like you may have thought I did. In fact the reason that Perversion was met with so much hostility when he went up there is because when I altered his relational memory of his father, I placed some contingencies in his mind. If it were to come to a point that you lust for power was to have you consume me then the memory of what happened to Cardinal that day, he received sight would undoubtedly revive me from you and ultimately destroy you. This is why the Guardians were so upset when Perversion was up there.... You have one shot to accomplish this goal of yours to defeat me but understand that you do not nearly have the power to defeat me, and any attempt that you make will just make me angry." Abuse informed with confidence and assurity. Porn now fully aware of what he was up against dropped his balled up fist from the face of Abuse and smiled.

"Hey man, I was just kidding. I was more making a fist to pound your fist for not helping with Lust. I appreciate the fact that you allowed me to enjoy the fruits of my labor by consuming Lust without your help." Porn jokingly accounts.

"Wise decision." Abuse responds. "Now what do you plan on doing with Perversion, are you bringing him here or do you want to consume him and the bottom of the Stairway of Ascension?" Abuse asks.

"I think it would be best to allow him to see what Bosom of Man looks like before he becomes another badge." Porn states.

"Then you hold up here and I will retrieve Perversion." Abuse orders. Abuse disappears from the Bosom of Man and appears directly in front of Perversion at the bottom of the Stairway of Ascension. Perversion, now shocked by Abuse's presence, dropped to his knees and became enraged by his immediate appearance.

"How could you show your face here after all that you told us after we were freed from Porn. You told us that you needed us and our skills, you said that you had a plan for us but now you are having each one of us get picked off by Porn. Why? Why would you do this to us? Even after everything that I did for you. I risked my body to advance your vision. The Guardians now have one of my arms because of you, why then would you give Porn the opportunity to consume me?" Perversion rambled.

"Simply put Perversion, I have my own goals and my purpose here far exceeds your existence. I say what I need to say, I do what I need to do, and if Porn grants me a better chance of being in this body longer then I will exploit that opportunity every time. It is not personal." Abuse answers. Abuse walks closer to the still kneeling Perversion and places his hand on his shoulder.

"Now time to embrace your purpose." Abuse states while transporting the both of them to the Bosom of Man where Porn stood waiting for their return.

"Welcome to your reunification." Porn states as soon as Perversion materialized.

"There is no way I stand a chance against you, especially because I do not have an arm and you have been using my eye." Perversion confessed.

"Now come on don't be like that, this is going to be less fun if you don't fight back. Look, I was originally going to smash your eye the moment you got here for dramatic purposes, but how about you just take your eye back. That should give you some power. Clearly not enough to defeat me, but it should be enough to make this interesting. What do you say Perversion?" Porn asked.

"I watched you completely defeat both Masturbation and Lust. You had some trouble with Lust but after consuming both of them there is no way I even remotely stand a chance of fighting you. This is the only opportunity to not give you what you want. I am not going to fight you and as far as my eye goes, it was perverted by going into your nasty face. I will never use that eye again. Just consume me and be done with it." Perversion ordered. At that moment Porn became enraged.

"Who are you to tell me what you will and will not do?! You do what I tell you to do! You think that in your dying wish you can just acquire autonomy! You are putting this eye in your face and you are going to fight me!" Porn yelled.

Perversion sat down and crossed his legs. He was not going to fight Porn. Abuse observing the entire interaction interrupted the conversation and urged that Porn hurry with consuming Perversion because they had things to do.

"Look, Perversion has already admitted that he is not going to fight you, so just consume him and let's continue our work on Cardinal." Abuse ordered. Porn reached down for the eyeball on the floor and rushed over to the sitting Perversion and with great speed smashed the eye back into Perversion's face. Perversion rolled around on the floor in pain screaming because of the smack he received from Porn.

"Now look at what I had to do, you could have been consumed with honor and dignity, but now I have to consume you rolling around looking like an idiot. If only you would have just done what I asked you to do. Now, become a part of your destiny." Porn remarked. Porn opened up his mouth wide and clamped his teeth around Perversion. Another badge popped up on the coat of Porn and he felt just as complete as he did just before he was temporarily removed from Cardinal's heart. Porn now fully satisfied with the help that Abuse lent, attempted to say his goodbyes so he could wreak havoc on Cardinal but Abuse stopped him just before he could leave.

"Before you go thinking that you have freed yourself from me, allow me to fill you in on some pertinent information. You are now indebted to me for getting you back here, and let me be clear to you, the Blazers that you consumed were given the same speech. The only reason you are here is to assist me in my bidding, you work for me now. Your ambitions and goals now coincide with mine. When I need you to do something to Cardinal you are to do it. Do you understand?" Abuse ordered.

"First of all, we are the same rank. You cannot tell me what to do." Porn responded.

"Our destiny is now intertwined, If I get exposed so do you, if I get purged so will you. Your existence is dependent on my success that is why I brought you back, whether or not you want to accept it, the fact of the matter is you and I are now linked." Abuse reiterated.

"I have to assume that you have planned this thing out deeper than I am giving you credit for so I'll submit for now. What do you have planned?" Porn asks.

"I spoke to you before about the vision I once saw of my demise, well that vision is becoming more and more vivid. I still do not know when this demise will come about, but what I do know is that it is coming. I believe that our work together can maybe sway our future if we play our cards right. For now, let's just continue to keep Cardinal uncomfortable and snared in his passions and lusts." Abuse commanded.

"Understood." Porn acknowledged.

HOODIES

It seemed just as quickly as Cardinal entered into high school the time he spent there came and went and he was in his Senior year. Nothing Changed much for him while he was there. He settled into a friend group that mirrored certain elements of his life that he was relatively comfortable with. He coasted through his classes every year and even joined a few clubs to gain some experience for college, but one thing that did change for Cardinal was the fact that his attachment to his Suits, Coats, and Blazers did grow substantially since the last resonance with Porn and his legion.

"Does anyone else notice that Cardinal is not making any genuine connections anymore, in fact most of his friends and connections are superficial and abstract. I don't know about yall but I do not understand why life for us is like this." Friendship admitted.

"We do not have the same privileges as the Tuxedos have with their legion of minions." Patience stated.

"I tell you, all this power that we have and we cannot even use it because of the condition that we have been "Blessed" with." Self-control air quoted.

"What exactly are you all so frustrated about?" Kindness questioned.

"See here we go, just because you are utilized more than any of us on a daily basis does not mean you have to be so oblivious Kindness." Patience responded.

Each one of the hoodies sat around a table in a room filled to the brim with illuminating bright vibrant lights. Their home was called Eden. In every direction, there was so much light that there was no place for a shadow to even grow. This was the purest place in existence and this was a place where all Hoodies were born and trained. Their connection to Earth was one that was complicated because they were created with the mission to make humanity better, the problem with their mission is that they did not have the same basic interaction that the Tuxedos, Blazers, Coats, and Suits had. They did not inherently exist with humans, in order to be utilized by humanity, people had to choose them and that's what made their existence and plight very difficult.

"I'm telling you the longer we have to wait on Cardinal the more I'm starting to think he has just sided with them and he is out of touch with himself. I mean the writing is on the wall." Generosity admitted.

"You know I am finding all of this very hard to believe coming from you both. You know that this is not a Cardinal thing but a humanity thing. This is nothing new. We have had to wait for humans to make up their minds when it comes to us making their lives better, the only reason that this is different is because Cardinal has the ability to see us and that is usually not granted to anyone until they are passing away." Faithfulness said.

"Everyone please, if I can have your attention." Light spoke. "Yes, your majesty." All in uniscene while simultaneously kneeling in reference.

"We have had some unusual circumstances occur recently and I want to make sure that you all are taking this whole ordeal seriously. I have heard a lot of groveling about the plight of humanity and even more so about this child Cardinal. Can someone explain to me what seems to be the problem, so that I can inform you all what is about to happen." Light spoke.

"If I may, your excellency." Joy volunteered. "You may speak." Light accepted.

"Thank you, your grace. May I add that you are truly the most awesome and gracious and you look as good as you always do." Joy added.

"Thank you, my child. Now what about Cardinal." Light asked.

"Yes. Some of us are a bit unsettled because of the power that Cardinal has, your excellency he can see us. Typically, humans can only see us right before they are going to die. Cardinal's choice and allegiance with the nefarious creatures in the Heart of Man is nothing uncommon but it is troubling because of the boy's eyes of discernment. Not to mention that those demons literally did something recently that they never have before, they invaded the Land of the Neutrals and they have consumed two Neutrals. They are getting more and more devious. You have coats going in and altering perceptions in memories and on top of that Cardinal does not seem to be wanting to use any of us freely anymore. Lastly, your excellency, Cardinal is not a child anymore, statistically we have seen that the patterns that young boys get in around this age will typically be practices they are ensnared to for the rest of their lives. Your grace, we just feel that we are running out of time and we do not know what to do." Joy explained in a panic.

"Is that the consensus throughout?" Light asked. "Yes." They all responded unanimously.

"Okay, so I have to let you all know and remind you that I am the only one that knows all and I can tell you that there is nothing to worry about. Cardinal is an anomaly but things are changing, there are more and more people that are starting to have discerning eyes, in the Land of the Neutrals we had a victory. Rage, Abuse, and Addiction were the ones that were able to consume a Neutral and they are the ones that believe that they have attained a power that is world shattering and from what you all were saying it sounds like you are all concerned with this new found power as well. Understand that this power that was attained will ultimately be what starts the downfall of the Heart of Man. What those mindless little imps did not consider is that once a Neutral is consumed the "genetic makeup" if you will, never gets eradicated. In fact Emotion and Relationship are still very much alive and because they are coexisting in Cardinal right now it will actually draw him closer to me. You all will have a very pivotal role to play when Cardinal decides to utilize your help to overcome. The memories that have been altered is something that Cardinal is going to have to work through. I know that each one of you has been training and waiting for your time to go and help Cardinal and I am so proud of each and every one of you that you are so called to purpose that you are frustrated about what is going on in his life and you want to help. Keep that same energy because before the year is over Cardinal is going to need you to lend your strength for his heart." Light divulged to the Hoodies.

"Master! Are you saying that we are getting ready to go to war for Cardinal's heart?" Peace asked.

"That is correct." Light responded. With the response of Light the hoodies began to celebrate with cries and shouts of excitement and also for the anticipation of war. Each one of them understood that in order to win Cardinal's heart they would have to fight the entire legion that has taken refuge in Cardinal's heart since he was a child and that would be a very tough battle to fight. They all partied and prepared for what would come in a short time. The hoodies were all unaware of when the time of Cardinal's redemption would come for only Light knew that, but nonetheless, they were getting ready.

On planet Earth Cardinal's day by day went by like it normally did. He woke up went to all his classes and came back home. Now that he was a senior in high school, he had more to think about than the simplicity of just going to class. He had to consider what he was going to do when he left high school. Was it college? Was it the workforce? Was it pro sports? Cardinal was convinced that his plight would yield him going into college and studying business because he had grown accustomed to it in school. Many young people would have to experience the confusion of the final year in high school.

Cardinal applied to many colleges with no clear direction to where he actually wanted to go. The only thing that Cardinal knew for sure was that he wanted to go to a college that was far enough away from his father and mother that he could do whatever he wanted to do without the notion that they could just stop in on him, but yet he wanted to be close enough to his home just in case his father had any health issues that would require him to come back home. He had to also consider that his Granddaddy was getting older and that he may not be around for much longer and he wanted to be close enough that he could go back home in case he was starting to see fewer days. All of the colleges that Cardinal applied to were either in southern California or they were in a conjoining state.

Day after day passed by and Cardinal and his family had heard nothing about whether Cardinal had gotten into his school of choice or if he had been rejected and the pressure was starting to settle in. Aurelia, the previous year, had been accepted and attended a prestigious private university in southern California and Alpha and Omega were very proud of her for her accomplishments; however, the standard had been set for all Wolf children after she had gone to college. Day after day and nothing, no mention of acceptance or rejection. At some point during the wait, Omega had become impatient and began to question whether Cardinal had even applied to any schools.

"Cardinal. Did you put your applications in late for the schools you chose? At this point we should be getting some type of correspondence from the schools and we have gotten nothing." Omega attacked.

"I applied before the deadline. I'm sure we should be getting something soon." Cardinal responded nervously that he may have done something wrong.

"Well if we do not hear anything from any of the colleges you applied to by the end of next week, I am gonna have you call up to each and every school and you will ask them about your application status. This is getting ridiculous. Don't let me find out that you took the money I gave you for your applications and spent it on something else. I will beat the black off of you." Omega threatened.

"I didn't mom. The acceptance letters should be coming in any day now." Cardinal again responded nervously. Alpha walked into the room as the conversation was taking place.

"For your sake they better because if they don't, I will personally tear your behind up." Alpha echoed Omega's intensity.

"Ok." Cardinal responded with disdain and irritation.

A few more days went by and just before the week could end a letter from one of the schools Cardinal applied to came in the mail. Plastered along the top of the letter was the name of the school and behind the plastic square read Cardinal Wolf.

"CARDINAL ITS FOR YOU!" Omega yelled from the other side of the house.

"What is it?" Cardinal asked.

"It's one of the schools you applied to in LA." Omega responded.

Cardinal's heart began to pump fast not because this was the school he really wanted to get into, but because this was his first letter. He began to feel that the response that he would get from this school would set the precedence for what to expect from all the other colleges that he applied to. He took the letter out of his mother's hand and began to walk to the other side of the house. Omega instantly reached out and grabbed Cardinal by the shoulder.

"Where do you think you are going?" Omega asked.

"I'm going to my room to open the letter?" Cardinal responded.

"No, you don't. I had to pay in order for you to send off those applications. I am just as invested in this response as you are. You are going to stand right here and read it out loud." Omega quickly refuted Cardinal's action to retreat to his room. Cardinal could see from the look on his mother's face that she was serious about this decision, he was not going to be able to leave. He stood there and ran his finger between the seams on the envelope to tear an opening to receive the letter. Once the letter was opened Cardinal pulled the letter out and opened the nicely tri-folded letter and began to read.

"Dear Cardinal. Congratulations, it is with great pleasure to offer you admission into Stanislaus state university for our business program for the class of 2009." Cardinal halted reading and looked up at his mom's face. He could see that she was overcome with joy and pride. Cardinal could see the hoodie Joy standing there 7 feet tall arms folded smiling with his mom, that made him feel good. Cardinal was excited that at bare minimum he had a college he could attend if all else failed.

"LET'S GOOOOOOOO!!!!!" Cardinal let out a great scream as he ran outside the house and began doing laps around the front yard. Joy began to fill Cardinal's heart. He felt accomplished.

At the Heart of Man Porn, Abuse, and their legions began to party for the accomplishments of Cardinal because they imagined that with this new elevation in Cardinal's life there would be some new development for some of the suits that had been patiently waiting to invade and elevate to new ranks.

"What's all the rave?" Rage asked.

"I would imagine you probably wouldn't know what is going on because Cardinal is embracing Joy which would in turn make you blind but Cardinal just got accepted into a university." Abuse informed.

"So why are all y'all so hyped for that?" Rage asked again.

"Because now that Cardinal will be out of this home then there will be no covering for him. He will be out there in the world all by himself. This is the perfect scenario for us. Typically when a young boy or girl leaves the tutelage of their parents, we have an opportunity to really run them into the ground. Now usually this would be a favorable situation for us because normally humans cannot see us, but this is a special case because Cardinal can see us and has chosen our side in many instances. I believe that we can literally enslave him to us and he will never be whole again. No more prying Alpha and no more praying Omega, just Cardinal and us" Porn spoke.

"I don't know what all the commotion was about, Cardinal doing away with us. He has literally been our agent." Abuse stated.

"What are you talking about Abuse? That seems like a pretty weird thing to say considering we are all celebrating the accomplishments and progression of Cardinal. Who said anything about going away?" Fear asked.

"Back when I was a lowly Suit, I remember seeing something that I did not understand, and it was that we were to be conquered and ran out of Cardinals heart. The thing is that when I saw this vision, I did not have all the power and the influence that I currently have so the vision I had must have been some type of insecurity or motivation to get me to where I am now." Abuse responded.

"Yes, that's right I do remember you asking Stress and I to aid you in a pursuit to ensnare Cardinal a bit more because you were the one Fearful of being purged, and look at you know. Large and in charge. You really leveled yourself up, Abuse." Fear congratulated Abuse.

"Look at us now, on our way to glory. Cardinal may have his eyes of discernment but he has used those eyes to help create a more prosperous life for all of us." Abuse proudly acknowledged.

"Don't get too cocky and relaxed, some things are going to get tough around here pretty soon." A voice emitted from the stairway of ascension.

"Master, what are you doing here amongst us?" Abuse asked.

"I heard the commotion from the celebratory party you were all throwing and I had to come down here and let all of you know that we have a war on our hands." The voice amplifying as the figure walked down the stairs closer to Abuse. Once all of the Suits, Coats, and Blazers realized that their master Tuxedo was descending down from the Stairway of Ascension they all stopped their partying and kneeled. None of them looked up from fear that they would all become killed if they did.

"Everyone, I need you all to understand something very crucial here. Please rise and hear me." Tuxedo briefly paused to let them all get to their feet. At that moment they all looked up and saw their master standing before them. Tuxedo stood tall wearing a pinstripe tuxedo. The base color of the tux was black and the pinstripes running down the suit were red. His face was shrouded by the shadow of a black colored panama hat with what looked like a feather from a bird but was in fact the scale of an otherworldly creature. The scale fluttered as if it was alive. Each individual in attendance noticed something that seemed familiar about the appearance of Tuxedo, although none could determine what the familiarity came from.

"Listen. I understand that each one of you is probably shocked by my appearance today. I have materialized myself to a form that is most comfortable for me. Normally I would not show myself but what is soon to come is pivotal for even my existence here." Tuxedo paused briefly to gather his thoughts. "There is going to be a coming war to the Heart of Man." He concluded. In the moment many in the legion began speaking amongst each other and panicking because of the new found information.

"Master, if you are concerned, then does this mean you already know the outcome of this battle." One of the suits let out from one side of the heart.

"That would be impossible for me to know." Tuxedo quickly answered. Abuse now slightly concerned, because this would corroborate the vision had when Cardinal was little, spoke with conviction.

"You say that we have to be made aware of some battle that is going to ravage through the Heart of Man, but I think you may have forgotten that we invaded the Land of the Neutrals and we were able to absorb power from them. I think you have forgotten that I have set in motion contingencies to keep us from being overrun with the likes of some lowly Hoodies. I think you are just concerned because you do not have the power to do anything in this situation. If you don't have the strength to…" Abuse spoke until he was suddenly stopped. Tuxedo instantaneously traveled between the space between him and Abuse standing at the bottom of the stairway of ascension. Tuxedo's hand wrapped so quickly around the throat of Abuse that no one in the place could even register what had happened until Abuse began gagging.

"How dare you speak out of order! If I don't have the strength! How about I show you who is really in charge here, you worthless piece of trash! I have seen you growing in power and I have allowed it but I think you have misunderstood the power you have acquired with divine authority!" Tuxedo screamed while tightening his grasp around the neck of Abuse.

"Sir…… Please…… I was wrong…. You are omnipotent……. I forgot my place." Abuse let out slowly through the little bit of breath that he grabbed from being choked.

"Should have considered that before you spoke up." Tuxedo said back to Abuse.

"Master, I understand your rage, but you cannot purge him, he has the power of one of the neutrals. Not only that he has altered the perception of Cardinal and if he is purged then this may change some things for Cardinal." Rage spoke out.

"If it is not one thing it's another. You all are speaking to me like I'm an idiot. Do you really think I do not know what goes on around in this body? I run this body. I am in every fiber, in every organ, in every memory, in every cell. I am not like you tragic imperfections. Every move that any of you has ever made has been because I have allowed it. I know exactly what Abuse has done and I know the essence of why he has done it; nonetheless, you are correct. I cannot let myself get wrapped up in all this rage because then I would be like you, and we surely cannot have that. I will not purge you Abuse due to your consumption of that neutral. Next time though, I will not hesitate to take your head off." Tuxedo iterated to Abuse. He removed his grip from around the throat of Abuse and instantaneously traveled back to the top of the stairway of ascension. Abuse fell to his knees and began coughing and gasping for breath.

"Like I was saying there is going to be a battle here in this place and the reason I am here to tell you this versus giving this assignment to one of your superiors to tell you is because this greatly affects my existence as well. Cardinal has the eyes of discernment which makes this situation very difficult for all of you, and as powerful as I am, I cannot govern this place if all of you have been purged. If you have all been purged this will weaken me and in turn make it easier for me to get expelled by those Hoodies. What concerns me is that I do not know what will happen with Cardinal having the power he has." Tuxedo said.

"Master, what are you saying?" Fear asked.

"I have a really strong feeling that the eyes of discernment will give Cardinal the ability to come here to the Heart of Man and uproot me from my throne and that I cannot have. That being said, for the time being I need everyone to strengthen the borders and the first sight of a Hoodie I want to be informed because they will not be alone." Tuxedo voiced.

"Yes sir. We will obey." They all announced in unison.

After Cardinal had completed yelling and running around the outside of his house he walked back inside and sat down with his parents. They both looked at him with so much pride in their eyes and hope.

"See, I told yall that I had it under control. But honestly this is just one of the schools that I want to go to, it is not The One. I really want to go to a college out of the state." Cardinal confessed to his parents sitting across from him at the dinner table.

"Well son you will have options so just make sure you end off this year strong. You only have a couple of months left in school. Make sure you complete all of your senior projects and solidify your GPA cause what you don't want to have happen is your GPA drop and the scholarships you would have gotten get revoked." Omega stated.

"I know mom. Like I said, I have it all under control. I will make sure to close off the year strong." Cardinal responded.

"You better make sure you do cause you can't stay here if you don't." Alpha proclaimed.

"Sure thing dad." Cardinal acknowledged the statement loosely. Cardinal walked away from both parents with a sense of accomplishment knowing that he had done enough in the past 4 years to get accepted into a college. He went to his room to finish reading the rest of the letter in his bedroom. Once he completed reading it, he folded the letter and placed it on his desk and walked out of his room to finish his chores. After he completed his chores and his homework he went to bed. Peace began to comfort Cardinal as he slept because now he would not have to worry about what he was going to do when he graduated.

ADMISSION

Week had gone by since Cardinal had received his first admission letter from the school in LA and he had received many more acceptance letters from other schools that he applied to. The school that Omega wanted him to apply to had rejected him from their business program, but this did not upset Cardinal because he wanted to go to a school of his choosing, not one that his mother chose for him. It had come to a point where with all of the applications in he would have to make a decision about where he was going to go. Many of the schools that he had been accepted into were schools in California but a few of them were out of state. One was in Arizona, another one was in Florida, and another in Iowa. Cardinals' rationale of thinking was to go to a school that was far enough away from home to where his parents could never just drop in and check up on him like he was a child, but he also wanted to be close enough to be able to come back home just in case his father's health became compromised again. Also his grandfather was slipping away and he wanted to be close enough to come see his grandfather before he passed away. Cardinal automatically segregated the California schools into the category of last choice, his first choice was ASU because this school was revered as having a fantastic golf program, many of the elite golfers on the tour were alumni from this school, and lastly it was the most exciting party campus in the whole country. Cardinal knew this was indeed where he wanted to go; he just had to make sure that he could get financial backing from the government and the school in order to attend.

As the weeks of school came to a very quick close Cardinal fully placed his energy into filling out the necessary paperwork to receive financial aid. He got into contact with the people in charge of the Professional Golf Program for ASU and introduced himself with the hope that they could further help out with granting some funds to be able to attend the school.

Cardinal became aware that the reason that he had to pay so much money to go to this school was because he was an out of state student and was incurring more fees which made it more difficult to get the money that he needed. When the time came for the government and the school to release the money, they would allocate to Cardinal he was shocked to see that the money that the schools in California, ASU, and Florida state were all relatively close in value but not in dollar amount. The out of state schools gave more money in order to account for the out of state fees, but all the schools still requested a substantial investment for Cardinal to attend their schools. Cardinal knew that at this point he was going to have to try and convince Omega and Alpha to let him go to ASU because he knew that they would probably try and make him go to a school in California. He would have to wait for his parents to be in a good mood to have this conversation because he knew with all the trouble he had been getting into regarding his grades his parents were ultimately going to be authoritative and demanding about where he would go. Day in and day out Cardinal observed the behavior of his mother and father, not just to him, but also how they behaved to one another. Cardinal knew that his deadline to choose which college he would go to was right around the corner which meant that he would have to have that difficult conversation with his parents sooner rather than later. He felt that he had been behaving well enough to have that conversation where they could all speak without it becoming a dictatorship. Omega came home from work one evening and Cardinal, before dinner was served, asked to speak to both Omega and Alpha after dinner was over. They ate dinner and what took 20 minutes felt like 20 years to Cardinal because he was so anxious about the outcome of that conversation.

All the while Anxiety suffocated Cardinal's heart and altered chemicals in his brain to keep him unstable. Fear closed in on Cardinal's subconscious mind and created thoughts that would ultimately cripple Cardinal from being honest.

Omega and Alpha finished their plates and ushered Cardinal into the back of the house where they would have the conversation Cardinal asked them for. He searched for his breath but it was far off. His brain began to race about a story he could conjure to further strengthen his case about going to ASU. Alpha and Omega sat down on the couch next to one another and Cardinal sat in the seat right in front of them, with sweat pouring down his brow. Just before he could work up the might to open his mouth to say anything Omega interjected.

"This is it, are you all ready to save Cardinal from himself!" Light let out to the hoodies gathered in Eden.

"Yes Master!" They all responded back with as much vigor as Light.

At the Heart of Man Tuxedo could feel that there was something off about this meeting and could feel that Light was up to something. With urgency Tuxedo shouts.

"Anxiety! Fear! Both of you back to the Heart of Man! Now! Something is happening, I think that my premonition about a coming battle was correct. I believe we are going to be invaded by Light and his goons today. I need you to be in fighting shape!" Tuxedo orders.

"That goes for all of you! Ready up!" Tuxedo seconds. "Yes sir!" the legion responds in unison.

"Son, has everything been okay with you lately? You walk around the house like you are lost. You don't have the same goofy and excited spirit that you usually have and your father has sensed some hostility from you and he cannot understand where this comes from. We want to know before you have a conversation with us what is going on with you." Omega asked concerningly.

Cardinal could not believe what he was hearing. Was this sincere, especially what she had said about Alpha? Was he really concerned about him?

"Well yeah, everything is okay. I just have a lot going on with trying to get ready for college and also trying to finish out this final year of high school has put a lot of stress on me. That's all." Cardinal responded.

"Well why do you walk around here and don't even speak to me, you treat me like an enemy or a roommate what is that all about?" Alpha asked.

"Honestly it's nothing. I think that stress from school and everything is making me shut down. I treat everyone here the same way. Which ironically is what I need to speak to you both about. I have to make a decision on the college I want to go to by the end of the week. That in and of itself is not the problem, the problem is that I have to decide which school I want to go to because that will be the university that I compile my financial aid portfolio for. I know you would probably want me to go to the school that is in California because then I would not have to pay for out-of-state fees but I really want to go to ASU. I know it is a little bit more money to go there but I promise that if you help me to go there then I will get on the dean's list and obtain the grant that will pay for the rest of my bills but I just need you all to trust me." Cardinal pleaded.

"How much?" Alpha asked.

"The California schools are asking me to invest an additional 7 grand to pay for one year of schooling and ASU is asking to invest an additional 10 grand to pay for 1 year of school." Cardinal responded.

"This boy has lost his mind!" Alpha responded "Where are we supposed to come up with that type of money for your schooling?! This is why we told you to get good grades because if you would have gotten better grades then they would have given you more money, now you are in a bind and you are asking us to pay for it for you. If you would have done what you were supposed to do then you wouldn't be here now. This is really your fault." Alpha responded.

"Sweetie, that is not necessarily true. The amount of money he was awarded from the government was maxed out because of our financial situation. Cardinal got the most money that he could in that department, he did obtain a few scholarships and grants because of his grade but that is true had he did better he could have gotten some additional funding." Omega explained. All the while Cardinal tried to stop the tears from forming in his eyes. He was feeling disappointed in himself because his father was right, had he done better on his own then he wouldn't need his parent's help right now. He also felt rage from the way Alpha just lashed out at him, especially when all he did was ask for help. Before Cardinal could start to think any further about what was going on Omega insisted that they all pray together.

"We should all take this time and pray because ultimately what sounds good and what doesn't is really irrelevant. In the grand scheme of what needs to happen, God is really the only one that can order your steps Cardinal. So let's table this conversation. Cardinal thank you for coming to us with this information, but let's all just pray." Omega said.

"You know what baby that is an excellent idea. let's do that." Alpha agreed.

"Get on your knees Cardinal." Omega instructed as she descended to her knees.

Cardinal got up from the seat he was sitting on and descended to his knees as well. The moment his knees hit the carpet he could feel an overwhelming sense of emotion hit his heart and his body felt heavy. It felt as if there was a mink coat on him. His mother began to pray.

"Father, God, in the name of Jesus. We come before you today completely humbled and transparent before you. Lord, we come to you about our son Cardinal. Lord be a healer and a way maker for him today. I come against any demonic infestation that would try and take over his spirit. You are not welcome here Satan and by the blood of the lamb you have to perish. We thank you Lord for all that you are doing in and through our lives. If it had not been for you then we would be nothing. We would have nothing. You have been so gracious to us and so good to this family. Lord give direction, give clarity, give life, in the name of Jesus." Omega prayed.

"Do you hear what is going on out there? Something is happening with Cardinal." Fear let out.

"I know. Something is definitely wrong with me; I am having a hard time keeping Emotion under wraps here. I have not had to deal with Emotion trying to rip away from me but I think with all this commotion from Cardinal, he is causing some kind of rift." Rage said with a panic in his voice.

Abuse stood there in the void shocked and worried because he could feel what he had felt all those years ago. He could feel the cold nothingness of being purged. He knew that this was the vision he momentarily saw when Cardinal was a child, the vision of his own demise.

"This is what I saw." Abuse whispered "What?!" Rage lashed out.

"We are all screwed." Abuse continued whispering in disbelief.

"Speak up!" Rage yelled. Abuse finally broke his blank stare and looked over at Rage with fearful eyes.

"We need to inform Tuxedo about what is going on!" Abuse let out in a panic.

"Don't be stupid. You really think that Tuxedo doesn't know what is happening here. This is his place. He has a plan that if we are to be calm, we will be victorious, we just cannot lose it. So I am going to need you to calm down because the way that you are acting now is erratic and that will literally spoil all of our plans. Chill out." Rage ordered.

Abuse still worked up, put on a fake smile to indicate that he had everything under control. The Heart of Man began to shake and the gate that was locked around the borders began to fall.

"Lord God invade our hearts and overwhelm us with your presence, lord. I pray that your power would begin to uproot any form of evil that has attached itself to us. I pray now that truth would begin to set us free now, lord." Omega continued her prayer for another 5 minutes. Cardinal at some point lost track of time and every word that Omega prayed seemed to fade out of Cardinal's world. He knelt presently in the room with his eyes closed but Cardinal perceived that he was no longer in the room with his parents. He opened his eyes and he was blinded by the light that overtook him. He raised his hands, shielding his eyes from the overwhelming presence he was in.

"Cardinal Wolf." someone from the light spoke out. "Yeah, that's me." Cardinal responded.

"I have watched you for a long time. I have seen the struggles of your life and I am fully aware of the power that you possess and how you have used that power to empower the rulers of your heart. I want to tell you that I am proud of you for exploring this very powerful gift and power that I have granted you with." the person from the light spoke.

"Wait, you are the one that cursed me with this power. Step out of the light so that I may see you." Cardinal demanded.

"Cardinal, I wish I could do that for you but understand that the glory that I am is the light that you see. You can call me Light. I am the master and ruler of this place and I know that I may be something new to you but I want you to take a look around and you may see someone here that you may recognize" Light instructed.

Cardinal diverted his eyes away from light and looked in the whiteness of the room he was in and he saw a hooded individual standing to his left with its arms out looking as if it were looking to give a hug. Cardinal realized now that this was the same hooded individual he had met when he befriended Azure.

"Hey I know you, you're Friendship aren't you?" Cardinal asked "That is correct Cardinal, I am the one that attempted to point you in the right direction when you were a young boy. I have seen you grow since that day into a young man, full of purpose and confusion and I am so pleased to see you standing before us today." Friendship stated.

"What am I even doing here?" Cardinal asked. "I was just back at my parent's house; my mom was praying and then I ended up here." Cardinal continued.

"I brought you here because this is going to be a pivotal point in your life, Cardinal. You are going to have to decide how you want to use this gift I have given you." Light explained.

"This is not a gift; this is a curse. Ever since I was sexually assaulted, I started seeing all this stuff. You said that you gave me a gift? Then that lets me know that you were watching me when my cousin did what he did to me and you did not stop him. What kind of "Light" would allow that to happen to someone. On top of that you cursed me to have to see the suits every day. I cannot see how you could do that to someone. Why? Answer that. Why?" Cardinal asked.

"Cardinal. Cardinal. Cardinal. I am sorry. I am but you have to understand this is not what I had intended for humanity when I created them. I created them with the intention of sharing a life with them fully and truly. My vision was to share all the power and the omnipotence with them on their own little planet but you know what happened, man got greedy and wanted something that I instructed them not to have. They partook of a power I did not want them to have and because of that now bad stuff happens to everyone. You are so concerned about the pain that I did not cease from you but did you ever consider what your cousin went through?" Light asked.

"What do you mean what he went through?" Cardinal asked.

"Allow me to show you." Light responded. Light then shined so bright that Cardinal had to shield his eyes completely from the increase. The light began to dim and Cardinal found himself looking at an individual that looked like his cousin Jay just really young. He looked like he was about 7 years old. Cardinal, suddenly confused about what was going on, asked.

"Hey Light, what is going on? Where are we?"

"We are with Jay when he was your age, and where we are is a crack house." Light informed.

"A Crack House?! Why are we here? Why is he here?" Cardinal asked.

"You asked me why this happened to you and in order for you to fully understand why this happened to you I have to show you. Jay is sitting in a Crack House because his mother is addicted to crack. What you are seeing is the effects of a fallen world. Jay was a very troubled boy because of this plight. Now what is going to happen is Jay's mother is not going to have enough money to pay for her fix so she is going to use the only currency that she has. Her body. When her body is not enough to get her fix then she will use the only other form of currency she has. Her son. You see Cardinal, Jay went through exactly the same thing you went through, but he had it worse than you did. He was assaulted and not only that, he was assaulted because the one person in this world that you are supposed to trust used him so that she could escape the reality that she created for herself. This was not the only time that this happened, in fact this happened for years to him, so much so that it crippled his mind and poisoned it to believe the same thing that you did. This was all a game. You know Jay asked me the same thing in his twenties. Why? This is the question I get asked from every walk of life, from every group of people, from every generation. Why would I, could I allow this type of evil to exist and now you can see the depth of the question you just asked me. Jay was in a sense rescued by the kindness of your father Alpha who took him in and tried to show him a better life than what he had. You were a casualty of that perversion that Jay was introduced to as a young boy. When he saw you, he could see the Hoodies and he could see the legion of Suits as well. He had the eyes of discernment; the problem was that he would not overcome. He was given the same opportunity you got but he declined the offer, and because of that he did to you what was done to him. Cardinal, I am truly sorry for what happened to you just as I am truly sorry for what happened to Jay." Light explained. Light then shined brightly and relocated Cardinal back to the white room they were standing in before. Cardinal covered his eyes until he felt that it was safe to reopen them.

"Wait where are we now?" Cardinal asked.

"We are in a place called Eden." Light responded. "Does that mean I have died?" Cardinal asked.

"No son, you are still very much alive. I just have something that I want to offer you, an opportunity, that is why I have brought you here." Light responded.

"Why didn't you just come down to earth then." Cardinal asked.

"I tried that once and let's just say that I was killed for no reason." Light responded.

"You mean Jesus?" Cardinal asked.

"You know for someone who was raised in church you don't seem to know much about me." Light jokingly responded.

"I mean, I know but I just gotta say it's not every day you actually get to meet the person that created everything." Cardinal said with a smirk on his face.

"Cardinal, I need to know if you want to go to the Heart of Man and confront the legion that has been causing you so much grief. Do you want to conquer and grow or do you want to forsake this gift and this power and forget all this that you have seen and just go through life?" Light asked.

"When you say forget everything that I have seen, what do you mean by that? Cardinal asked.

"Do you remember the day after you gained the eyes of discernment?" Light asked.

"Yes I do. I attempted to tell Jay what I was seeing and he wrote me off as having a vivid imagination. There was nothing following me around and that I needed to stop talking about what I was seeing." Cardinal responded.

"Well the reason that Jay was saying that to you was not that he didn't believe you it is because he had lost all recollection of everything that he had seen prior. So the description you gave him of the suit you were seeing was the same one that he saw years ago, the issue is his body and his brain have been dissociated in a way. Similar to him you will be able to comprehend what is going on but you will not be able to experience any of its full glory. You will become more susceptible to carnal ideology." Light explained.

"So I can either be like everyone else or I can be unique?" Cardinal asked.

"That is correct." Light agreed.

"I cannot imagine why I would ever go back to life before this gift. This is all I know. I mean since I was 7 years old, I have had this gift. More than half my life has been experienced with this "eyes of discernment," I believe that is what you called it. I am concerned about confronting this legion though, how am I supposed to fight a whole legion alone?" Cardinal asked.

"Cardinal, I am so pleased to hear that you are willing to confront the very issues that have been holding you down all this time. As for how you will battle them, I have that taken care of." Light informed.

"Wait. Battle? You said confront, you didn't say anything about a battle." Cardinal announced in shock at this new information.

"Cardinal, I can understand that you are nervous but do not be fearful especially not in a place like this, for fear cannot live here. Now as I was saying, I have taken the liberty to have an army at your disposal for this endeavor. I had something planned for you just in case you decided to confront Tuxedo." Light stated.

"Wow, a whole army! That is amazing. So I won't be alone, but I don't really know how to neutralize, annihilate, destroy, kill, I don't know what the jargon is for these suit things." Cardinal immediately responded.

"You would be purging the Suits, Coats, and Blazers from the Heart of Man." Light answered.

"I noticed you didn't bring up Tuxedo when you said purging. Why is that?" Cardinal asked.

"Cardinal, I appreciate the fact that you ask a lot of questions; unfortunately, I cannot give you the answer to every question that you ask because our time is coming to a close. This is what I will need you to do in order to prepare yourself for this war. I need you to set the ball in motion by weakening the enemy forces by exposing them to your parents. I need you to tell your parents what happened to you as a young boy. Not only that, I need you to let this part of your life be a testimony to many other young boys that never opened their mouths to expose the siege that is on their hearts. By doing this you will have purged evil from your heart. After you expose the evil in your heart, I need you to go somewhere quiet and desolate. This will be your battle ground. I need you in a place where you cannot be disturbed. Once you are in your quiet space just sit down, close your eyes, and look to where your help comes from and say my name and I will come with my army." Light instructed.

"Woooow. That is a lot to ask. Are you sure that I have the strength to do all this that you ask?" Cardinal asked.

"100 percent positive. Now go, I will see you again. Soon." Light said while fading away. As quickly as Cardinal was Eden was as quickly as he was back present in the room with his parents praying. Cardinal looked up at the clock and not a second had elapsed.

"How could this be? I know I was gone for at least a few hours?" Cardinal thought. Then Cardinal ascertained the answer to his question. In Eden the construct of time does not exist. Cardinal's mother continued her prayer for another 5 minutes before closing it out with

"Amen." Omega finished.

"Amen." Cardinal and Alpha agreed in unison. All three of them got off their knees simultaneously. As Cardinal ascended from his knees the heavy nature that he was filling immediately vanished. It was like a heavy burden was lifted from him. He felt light and joyous now. He looked around and all he could see was a room full of Hoodies shining as bright as Light did.

"Thank you Light." Cardinal thanked in his head. "Hey mom and dad there is something that I need to tell y'all." Cardinal confessed.

"What is it?" Omega and Alpha asked.

"I have to tell you about something that happened to me as a young boy while we lived in Grandaddy's house." Cardinal started. He went from twiddling his thumbs to looking up and seeing the pain on his parent's face. It was almost as if they knew what he was going to say.

"While we were living in Grandaddy's house, my cousin Jay used to play this game with me. He would play this game after school before anyone else got home. He would say to me that if I wanted him to buy me some ice cream or candy then I would have to play this game with him. The number one rule of this game is to never tell anyone about the game because if I told anyone then he would have to kill them and he would never buy me ice cream and candy anymore. This was the game. Jay would take me to the back of the house to your old room and he would turn on the TV and he would let me watch all the cartoons that I wanted. He forced me to lay on my stomach and he would take my pants off. He would force himself on to me until he won the game. He would make me clean up after him and then he would go buy me ice cream and candy from the ice cream truck. Sometimes he did not force me to lay down, he would have me use my mouth. I hated that. Now you know why I was so excited to get my own room when we moved here because I did not have to share a room with him. I have been desperately wanting to tell you all this for the longest of times but I couldn't say anything because I was scared." Cardinal stated.

Omega and Alpha sat in their seats in complete disbelief. Their eyes filled with tears and their bodies lifeless. Cardinal could feel the tears well up in his eyes as he looked at the pain that his parents were showcasing. Time seemed to go on forever as they just sat there in the silence of the room.

"It all makes sense now. I knew there was something wrong, I just knew it. There was a time I was going to the grocery store and I left you all at the house and you begged and pleaded with me not to leave you three there with him. I did not know why you were all so frantic about being there with Jay and now I know why!" Omega wailed with pain in her eyes. "Why did we have to bring him into our home?! Why?!" Omega continued. Alpha still sitting in his seat with tears now streaming down his face. Omega stood up and began to pace back and forth as her breathing began to increase and the weeping turned into full hysteria.

"If I knew where he was right now, I would kill him. To think I tried to do something for him. Change his life. Take him out of the slums, clean him up after going to jail, take care of him just to come here and do this to my son. It must truly be a work of God that he is not in this house anymore because if he was here then they would be putting me in jail for what I would do to him. AAAAAHHHHH!" Alpha finally releasing the tension in his heart.

"Guys, I can understand how you feel. I have had to deal with this for a long time now. I have even had to cope with the idea that maybe I liked it and that is why maybe I did not tell anyone about what was happening. I had to take into account that maybe I am gay and I like men. I have had to deal with so much behind this experience and after seeing some things recently all I want to tell you is that I forgive him for what he did to me. I forgive him because I know that his life may not have been easy, I forgive him because he went through the same trauma that I went through and worse, I forgive him because I cannot let the toxicity of hatred forever engulf my heart. I know that it may be hard for you to do what I have done because you have not had the time to grasp and contend with this news, but please, don't let this information change you for the worse. Let this new information revive you and create a heart that can forgive even him." Cardinal confessed with now his own set of tears streaming down his face.

"Cardinal, I am so sorry. I am so sorry. I don't even know what to say but I am sorry. I did not ever want this to happen to you. I was so vigilant of the little girls that I didn't consider that he may do something like this to you. I am so sorry. I have let you down as a father because I was put here to protect you and I couldn't do my job. Can you forgive me?" Alpha asked.

"Dad, I never even thought of this being your fault at all. I forgive you. Please don't put this burden on yourself. You should have a talk with Jade and Arellia about all this." Cardinal advocated. Omega and Alpha both stood up and wrapped their arms around Cardinal and cried until no more tears would form. Once everyone had exhausted their emotions Cardinal jokingly stated "Sooooo……about the college situation?"

Alpha and omega both appreciating the lightheartedness of Cardinal grinned. They gathered themselves and walked out of the back of the house to their bedroom where they stayed for the rest of the night. Cardinal, fully remembering the instructions given from that night, fell asleep anticipating the mission he would embark on when he woke up. It was time for Cardinal to meet the one in charge.

WAR OF THE HEART PT.1

Cardinal slept peacefully through the night. His mind was at ease even though he had not gotten an answer about his financial aid situation. Before falling asleep he could hear his mother and father in their bedroom having a deliberation about whether they should vocalize the information they just heard to the rest of the family, and about what to do now. Cardinal could not help the way they felt and could not change the decision they would have to make about learning what happened to him, all he knew was that the burden was no longer his to carry. The sun rose over the house across the street from their house glowing beams of light through the window awakening Cardinal to a brand new day. Cardinal arose from his bed feeling lighter and more purposeful than before. This was the day that Light would meet with him and instruct him on how he would even enter into his own heart. Cardinal got out of bed and went towards the bathroom to brush his teeth and wash his face. On the way to the bathroom the door to his parent's room opened and at the door was his father, Alpha. Cardinal turned and greeted him with a calm and loving, "Good morning, Dad." Alpha, still in shock from what he heard last night, simply looked at him and began to tear up. Before Cardinal could turn around and walk into the bathroom Alpha beckoned him to the bedroom with a wave. Cardinal, seeing that he wanted to speak, walked into the bedroom. Once he crossed the threshold of the doorway Alpha closed the door so that it was just Omega, Alpha, and Cardinal all in the room together. Cardinal looked at both of them and waited for one of them to explain why he was in there.

"Son, the reason that your father has asked you in here is because we talked a lot about last night. Your father and I both had a hard time falling asleep. One of the reasons was because I was furious with your father for bringing Jay here because I did not fully agree with the decision to have your cousin live with us. I'm sure you can understand the feeling of us being ashamed and disappointed in ourselves for letting that happen to you. But the other reason is because we do not know if it should be us that tell your sisters about what happened to you. We honestly believe you should be the one that should tell them about your past. It is your story after all, and to be honest we are just to hurt right now to fully give that accord. Do it at your own time though." Omega unveiled.

"I understand mom, dad, and I know that I cannot tell you how to feel about this because prior to yesterday this was all new information that you did not know, but you have to try and let these feelings go. Understand that this happened to me 10 plus years ago, and not only that but you have other children that you have to protect and guide and I can imagine it would be hard to do that if you are so worked up about what happened to me." Cardinal stated.

"You're right son, and we hear you but do not be so insensitive to what your mother and I are feeling because you have had 10 years to work through the emotions and reality of this, we have had less than 24 hours. We understand you are just trying to make sure we mature from this and be righteous but you have to give us adequate time to work through this. Don't worry about our parenting, you just make sure that you handle your business at school and do what you need to do." Alpha instructed.

"Will do dad. Hey, can someone drop me off at the golf course when you are finally up?" Cardinal asked.

"Yeah your dad can do it, I have to get these girls up so that they can clean up this house." Omega answered.

"Yeah I'll take you once I finish brushing my teeth. Remember you are supposed to be cutting the grass this weekend so you can either do that before you go to the golf course or after, but either way I want that done today." Alpha stated.

"I'll do it when I get back from the golf course, I have some really important practice I have to get into up there." Cardinal answered.

"Ok." Alpha responded. Cardinal realizing that his parents were done talking, walked over to the door and opened it. He turned his head around to see if his parents were still sitting on the bed and he noticed both of them getting up. He turned back around and went straight for the bathroom so he could accomplish his preliminary daily activity. He brushed his teeth and exited the bathroom and walked straight back to his room so that he could get dressed for the golf course. Just before he turned the corner to get into his room Jade creeped out of her bedroom rubbing the sleep from her eyes. Cardinal stepped in front of Jade to stop her from continuing her pursuit to the bathroom.

"What do you want?" Jade asked with a little irritation in her voice.

"I want to tell you good morning and give you a hug." Cardinal responded while simultaneously grabbing Jade and throwing her into his arms.

"You're so gross and weird." Jade immediately cringes.

"Hey, just accept the hug and go about your day." Cardinal rebuts letting go of his sister. Cardinal smiled and left Jade in the hallway and walked into his bedroom so that he could get dressed. He rummaged through his messy shirt drawer until he came to his favorite red and gray golfing shirt. While Cardinal slipped his shirt over his face Porn materialized in front of Cardinal. Cardinal finally clearing his face from the shirt is surprised by the Blazer sitting in front of him.

"Oh my goodness you scared me." Cardinal confessed "Cardinal, what happened to you last night? You know we were all so worried about you." Porn asked and consoled.

"What do you mean what happened to me and who is all?" Cardinal asked.

"Well, "all" are your guardians, Cardinal. Silly. And you were nowhere to be found. It was like your heart was beating but you were no longer present in your body. What happened last night." Porn asked, inching closer to Cardinal.

"Oh nothing, just my mom praying you know nothing major. So we still on for tonight?" Cardinal asked.

"Cardinal you are acting a little bit weird, you weren't with Light were you." Porn pried even more.

"Light. Who is that? Is that some type of new rapper or something?" Cardinal now panicking.

"I knew you had compromised us! That is why we couldn't see you nor formulate what you were doing with your parents last night, it was like you were speaking a foreign language! You have compromised us and have sided with that deceiver! Cardinal after everything we did for you this is how you repay us! I bet he did not tell you why you were given the ability to see us! You will greatly pay for your treachery! By the time we are through with you, you are gonna wish that you were dead!" Porn screamed before vanishing.

Cardinal now completely freaked out about what just happened, just stood there focusing on his breathing. At that time Fear came in and attempted to soothe Cardinal by stroking his head but the minute that Fear touched Cardinal his hand burned. Realizing now that he could do nothing, Fear vanished as well. Peace entered the room and spoke clearly and sternly to Cardinal.

"Lift your eyes to the hills, that is where your help comes from." Peace instructs.

Cardinal looked up and almost instantly the feeling of fear subsided and Cardinal felt rejuvenated and at peace. Understanding that Peace was responsible for this newfound zen looked around to see if he was around and realized that Peace abounded not among the room but literally in it. Cardinal opened the drawer to his pants and found his favorite pair of black pants and slid one leg into them at a time. Cardinal then gathered the rest of his stuff and prepared to leave for the golf course. Alpha exited his room. He walked down the hallway to the kitchen where he looked for his keys, Cardinal already fully prepared yelled out.

"I have your keys; I'm headed to the car!" "Okay I'll be out in just a sec." Alpha responded.

Cardinal walked around to the back of the van and opened the door. He placed his golf bag gently down in the back of the van and closed the trunk door. He pressed the button several times to ensure that the car was unlocked and opened the passenger door and entered the car and started the engine. He then placed his headphones in his ears and proceeded to wait for Alpha. After a couple of minutes Alpha came out of the house and entered into the car and off they went to the golf course. All while this was happening a huge uproar came from the Heart of Man about what had just transpired.

"I know what happened last night!" Porn yelled out in the Heart of Man.

"Tell me! Tell me! Tell me!" Abuse immediately appeared in front of him.

"Cardinal saw Light." Porn confessed.

"I knew it. I knew that this was the vision that I had years ago, I just knew it." Abuse panicked. "Did you at least figure out what was said?" Abuse asked.

"No. The moment I found out what happened I freaked Cardinal out and retreated back here, but I'm sure that I left him in a pretty defeated state, I'm sure that Fear won't have a problem altering Cardinal." Porn stated with confidence.

"That's a negative. The moment that I tried to mess with Cardinal's mind my hand got burned. There is something pretty powerful encompassing him to keep him from being manipulated." Fear said fearfully.

"So that's why the gates all fell last night because we are getting ready to be invaded. This is exactly what Tuxedo was talking about, well if it's a war they want then it's a war they will get." Abuse now full of rage expresses.

"You know I could use some action." Violence interrupts. "What are you doing here, aren't you supposed to be on the front lines?" Abuse asked authoritatively.

"Slow your road turbo. I don't answer to you anymore. Tuxedo says that it would be more beneficial for all of us to lose rank. Considering that we are all about to fight for our stay here. Also because of the outcry that you let out at the last party he thinks that all of this ranking stuff has made things complicated. So, he has ranked us all suits until after this war ends and he will allocate rankings afterwards." Violence explained.

"Wait, why do you know this and not I?" Abuse questioned. "Because I'm me and you're you." Violence responded now with his guard up.

"I need to go see Tuxedo. He doesn't know what he is doing." Abuse urged.

"Yeah I don't think you want to do that. Because we have all been repurposed to Suits you can't even go up the stairway of ascension anymore, and even if you could I don't think he would want to see you. I think what he would like for you to do is prepare yourself for war." Violence advocated.

"When does this demotion go into effect?" Porn asked "It's already happened." Violence responded.

"How? We still look exactly the same." Fear responded.

"Yeah I think that is because you were not at the rally I just left from." Violence informed.

"What rally?" Abuse, Porn, and Fear all asked.

"There was a rally that took place because of what happened last night. Tuxedo had us all put on some new gear and gave us orders for the battle. He did say something in regards to having a special meeting in play for a few of us but I'm not sure who he was referring to." Violence spoke candidly. While they were talking, they did not recognize that Rage had melodramatically walked into the room and sat down. Just before they could turn to look at Rage, Tuxedo popped up in front of the 4 of them.

"Thank you, Violence, for your assistance, now I need you to go back to your spot on the frontlines." Tuxedo thanked.

"Yes master." Violence agreed before vanishing.

"Tuxedo what is the meaning of this change? Do you understand what will happen to us Coats if we are based with the Suits." Abuse let out.

"Abuse you never cease to abuse your power. This is one of the reasons for my decision. There needs to be only one in charge for what is coming to this heart and that is me. If there are too many people controlling and calling shots then things will get complex and out of hand. I don't need that here in my home. I am fully aware that if you are a suit then you will lose much of the power that you have acquired through the years. But worry not, I am not stripping you of your power, for if I did that not only would you lose the Suits and Blazers you have consumed, but the two of you, the neutrals that you have acquired as well. We wouldn't want a war between light and the Neutrals here would we. Also, it is more of an aesthetic for me too. When this war takes place and I am standing about my throne I want to be able to fortify this visual forever. Cardinal is mine and no amount of gifts, Hoodies, or help from Light will ever change that. As for why I did not inform you 3 of the rally being had is because you three will be my personal dogs. You will be by my side for the entirety of this battle. You are equal to all the Suits on the battlefield so do not get any ideas about favoritism, for I could have chosen anyone. The reason it is you three is because you are the most desperate. I can use that. Go get your new gear and wait for me at the Stairway of Ascension and I will come and get you. Do not come up unless I come get you. Is that clear?" Tuxedo asks.

With Abuse, Porn, and Fear all completely speechless about what they just heard; they just nodded their heads. Tuxedo, not satisfied with the response that he just received, asked again just more sternly.

"Is. That. Clear?" Tuxedo asks one last time. "Yes master!" All three respond with vigor.

"Fantastic, now Abuse I must ask you, where is your sister Addiction? If my memory serves me well she has fused with half of that neutral Relationship? Correct?" Tuxedo asks.

"That is correct she did fuse with the other half of the neutral but it was to save her from being cast out." Abuse responded.

"I need you to find her and bring her with you to the Stairway of Ascension." Tuxedo commands just before vanishing and leaving the three of them there. Rage sitting in the corner gets up and walks out the room completely undetected and unbothered by the information he had just heard. Abuse went forth through the heart of man in search of his sister Addiction. He searched every place he knew she would potentially frequent, he searched the brain, the bosom, and eye gate but to no avail. He was unsuccessful in finding her. Rather than get hung up on searching for her and losing his opportunity to show Tuxedo how valuable he was in battle, Abuse went back to the bottom of the stairway of ascension to wait.

Cardinal and Alpha finally arrived at the golf course and Alpha looked at Cardinal in the eyes before encouraging him with some words about seizing the day. Cardinal, with the encouragement from his father, gets out of the passenger seat and goes around to the back of the car to get his clubs. He slams the trunk shut and begins to walk down to the practice facility. Before he got too far away from the car Alpha rolls the window down and screams,

"Practice hard! Sustain mental Fortitude! I will pick you up at 4! I Love you son!"

"Sure thing! Love you too!" Cardinal yelled back. He turned back around and walked to the practice facility. Alpha drove out of the parking lot thus leaving the golf course. Cardinal focused on the walk to the other side of the facility to get to a spot where he felt he was being led to. A place that was slightly secluded from the rest of the golf course. A quiet place, to meet with Light. Step after step his heart began to flutter, not from Anxiety but from excitement. What was going to happen? How would Light help him fight a battle within himself? How long would this last? What is the big secret with Tuxedo? These were all the questions that floated through Cardinal's mind as he got closer to the secluded area of the golf course to work on his short game. When he felt that he finally arrived he pulled out a few clubs and began stretching so that he could practice. He stretched out his legs and his arms for about 5 minutes but Light never showed up. "Maybe this was not going to happen today." Cardinal's mind began to think, but just before his thoughts could formulate disappointment a small inaudible voice spoke through the thoughts in Cardinal's head.

"I see that you have arrived just as I knew you would." Light said.

Cardinal, shocked and surprised by the voice, answered, "Well of course I would be here. You enticed me with an opportunity that I would be foolish to turn down. How are you today, Light?" Cardinal asked.

"I am pleasant and perfect. Are you ready for the journey you are about to undergo?" Light asked.

"Yes I am, but I do have a question about how this is going to work." Cardinal consented with hesitancy.

"What's that?" Light responded.

"If we are going to be traveling to my heart then how will I be aware of what is going on out here?" Cardinal asked.

"This is why I have asked you to go to a place that was desolate and where you could not be disturbed. You do not have the ability just yet to be present with your heart and present in this world at the same time. What is going to happen is you are going to be somewhat disassociated from reality and this realm. You will have what you may know as an out of the body experience." Light informed.

"So when people say that, they are actually really experiencing that?" Cardinal asked.

"That's correct. Most of the time they have these experiences with drugs or alcohol which can sometimes be enlightening but most times frighten the individual. What you are going to experience may seem like hours, but will only really be a few seconds in the real world. Because you will be standing outside of this reality, the construct of time will not apply. Your willingness to continue your battle will all be up to you. Now take a seat and close your eyes." Light instructed. Cardinal sat on the bench that was in the corner of the grassy field. He dropped his head and closed his eyes like he was instructed to do last night. The moment he closed his eyes the darkness that he normally saw from shutting his eyes from the sun was not there. This time when he shut his eyes, he saw Light and the Army of Hoodies standing in front of him. "Are we back in Eden?" Cardinal asked.

"We are actually still on Earth. If you turn around then you can see your body on the bench there." Light stated. Cardinal turned around to find himself sitting on the bench with his head down and eyes closed. Cardinal was completely confused about where he was and why things were like this, so he asked.

"If we are not in Eden why is everything so bright here?

Am I an angel?" Cardinal asked.

"We are out in my creation. Life is abundant. You are at a golf course and the entire field that you sit in is my glory. You are looking beyond the lens and eyes of a man. This is what mankind would have been seeing had they not chosen evil. You are not an Angel nor are you Human, you are ethereal. Cardinal this army will only go as far as you will allow them to go.

They are fully capable of clearing your heart but understand you have to be willing for this. Do you understand?" Light asked.

"Sure. If I didn't want that I would not have showed up today. Why is it that they all have swords and spears but I have nothing?" Cardinal asked.

"All that was required of you was to arrive and you did." Light interjected. "As for your weapon and your gear I have prepared that all for you. Here." Light formed the armor and weapon in an instant right in front of Cardinal.

"This is your helmet. Its name is Salvation. This is your shield. Its name is Faith This is your breastplate. Its name is righteousness. This is your sword. Its name is Spirit. This is what you will be taking into battle, Cardinal. It is custom fitted specifically to you." Light explained. The armor and weapon were forged from gold and glistened brightly against the light that Light was giving off. Cardinal looked at the armor and felt much more confident about his assignment.

"Whoa baby!" Cardinal exclaimed with great excitement. He reached out to grab the armor but before he could touch it the Armor ascended and engulfed Cardinal with great speed. Before Cardinal could even begin to formulate what was happening, he realized that his body was covered in the golden gear he was reaching out for. The only thing that was still in front of him was the sword. Cardinal reached forth and pulled the sword from the ground. He was in shock how light the armor was. He could move freely and swing around the sword without hesitation. Cardinal then realized that he was swinging a sword freely and masterfully and he had never trained with it before. Confused he asked.

"Light. Why is it that I am able to wield this sword with mastery and ease?"

"The reason is because you are actually not swinging the sword at all, it is more that the sword is symbiotically swinging itself through you. Remember that the weapon's name is Spirit. You wield my spirit." Light informed.

"That makes a lot of sense." Cardinal responded. He turned around and looked at his body again. When his eyes saw his body, he was astounded to be staring at a body that he could no longer recognize. His body did not look like his own for his body had been shrouded with darkness as if his silhouette had embodied his essence. Cardinal took a few steps back, alerted by what he was looking at and was only calmed by the hand of Peace who had been standing close to Cardinal.

"No need to fear Cardinal. What you see is normal." Peace soothed him.

"That is correct. In fact Cardinal how you are viewing yourself is precisely how I view you every time I look at you, but there is no need to fear because we are going inside to clean you up." Light seconded. Light in that instant began to form himself into a body. His features were larger than all the other Hoodies that were standing in wait to storm the heart. He was tall and majestic. He was just as bright as he was before. His face was shrouded by the cloak that he was wearing. A perfectly white colored cloak tapered with gold draped the body of Light and a sword similar to the one Cardinal was holding hung from his hip. All Cardinal could see was the mouth of the newly formed Light. A bright smile gleamed through the bronze like complexion of Light. Cardinal's worry turned quickly to confidence. Light now fully prepared to enter Cardinal's heart stepped towards the body and the rest of the warriors followed. Every Hoodie closely in pursuit of Light began to make a loud clank as they clapped their swords against their armor. Just before light crossed the threshold of Cardinal's lifeless dark body he let out a loud cry.

"TO VICTORY!"

"YEEEEEAAAAHHHHH!!!" All of the Hoodies cried out directly after. Cardinal feeling the power from the cry of Light joined in with the Hoodies.

WAR OF THE HEART PT.2

Moments before the invasion from Light, Tuxedo descended down the Stairway of Ascension back to where Fear, Abuse, and Porn stood.

"The time has come, the time for us to stand tall and battle for our home. This is time to show me how valuable you three are to me. Now to the front, we need to ready the troops." Tuxedo stated. "Abuse, where is Addiction?" Tuxedo asked.

"I searched all over this wretched body and was unsuccessful in finding her sir." Abuse answered.

"There is no time to go searching for her, we need to leave immediately." Tuxedo commanded. The 4 of them all quickly moved to the front of the heart of man where all the gates had fallen from the previous night. Tuxedo stood tall on the gate post with Porn, Abuse, and Fear standing next to him. Down below were the legion of Suits ready and prepared for battle. Tuxedo slammed his fist against his open hand to get the attention of all the suits who were casually talking amongst each other. The loud noise traveled amongst the void and all of the suits turned and looked up at the gate post.

"Today will be the day that we fight to defend our home. As you all know Cardinal has removed himself from his physical body with the help of Light and very soon we will be invaded. This is the moment that I warned you all about. Do not waver. Do not falter. I can sense it now; Light has transformed into a form that would not destroy Cardinal's body upon entrance into the Heart of Man. This is all perfect for our victory. Stand strong and we will prevail!" Tuxedo commanded loudly.

"Sir! Yes sir!" the legion screamed back with vigor. Satisfied by the response of the legion, Tuxedo teleported to the back of the battlefield, up the Stairway of Ascension with Porn, Abuse, and Fear. He had a perfect view of the battlefield from his throne. In that moment a bright light formed in the darkness of the Heart of Man. The legion of suits became fearful as the piercing light illuminated the heart to the point that the darkness fled. Each frontline suit took a step back away from the gates as their confidence about the battle began to dwindle. As they were all stepping back, a hoodie stepped through the portal. His golden armor glistened just as bright as the light projected from the void. It was Family. Next walked in Friendship, then Peace, Kindness, Love, Destiny, Conviction, Truth, Self control, Generosity, Patience, Joy, Mercy, and Grace. The 14 of them stood at the entrance of the Heart of Man with their hands on their weapons looking around at the vast empty space and the powerful Suits they would have to do battle with. Lastly Cardinal walked through the bright portal with Light walking directly on the other side of his body. The moment he crossed the threshold into his heart, he was taken back by the amount of Suits living there.

"How could my heart be this overrun with evil?" Cardinal thought to himself. As he scanned the now illuminated void, he noticed some of the suits that he had come into contact with personally. Rage was in the second line of defense. At the back of the legion Cardinal could see an ominous figure sitting atop a throne with a Panama hat masking his face.

"That must be Tuxedo." Cardinal thought.

"That is indeed Tuxedo, do not fight him without me." Light instructed.

"You can hear my thoughts?" Cardinal thought.

"Of course I can, this is how communication works here, although these evil suits will not be able to comprehend what you are saying because you are speaking a language they cannot understand. My hoodies already know what their task is here. They will take care of the weaker frontline suits. You and I will purge the stronger ones. They are the ones with fully defined facial features. Do you understand?" Light commanded

"I understand. Hey I know this might be bad timing for this question but why do these suits look so human?" Cardinal asked.

"It's because they were a creation of mine that rebelled. They were the human prototype. Now let's go!" Light commanded.

"Aaaaahhh!" The army of Hoodies let out as they charged straight for the frontline of Suits.

"Aaaaaaahhhhhhhh!" The legion of Suits let out as they charged for the 14 hoodies. They ran out towards each other but Light and Cardinal did not run directly into battle, they walked down the battlefield. They knew that their battle would only come into effect after the smaller suits had been purged. In no time the army of Hoodies had reached the frontline of suits. Conviction quickly removed his sword from his sheath and with a mighty swing unleashed a forceful slash which single handedly eradicated a large fraction of Suits. As they were directly hit from the shockwave of Conviction's swing, they let out a grimacing cry and disappeared. As they disappeared from the heart, they left behind little pieces of light that further illuminated Cardinal's heart. Love, Peace, Grace and Kindness were Hoodies that attacked from a distance. Rather than attacking the small legion with massive swings from swords they threw axes and knives. Tuxedo watched from above as his legion quickly lost valuable numbers. Family, Friendship, Destiny, and Self control were not as powerful as conviction was but they were super fast and attacked their suits with precision. Truth, Generosity, Patience, and Mercy were long range combatants and focused on using weapons like arrows and explosives to deal damage to the suits. Every arrow hit its mark and every explosive effectively dwindled the number of suits down. Conviction was not the only power wielding Hoodie; Joy was the last of the Hoodies that wielded a longsword that with one swing annihilated numerous suits. The remaining suits stood there in disbelief as they witnessed firsthand the power from the Hoodies. As fear began to set in, they stepped back to prevent themselves from getting purged, but their hesitancy did not stop the battalion of Hoodies from attacking them as they backed up. Violence who had been waiting for the numbers to dwindle, saw this as an opportunity to showcase his powers to Tuxedo. He jumped from the back of the legion and threw his fists into the long sword of Conviction and Joy. They both saw the attack coming and they held up their long swords to block the flying fist from hitting them. Violence collided with their swords and smiled. He let out a maniacal laugh because his excitement for the battle began to rise.

"You guys messed up, my name is Violence and I am the strongest combatant here in the heart. If you can get rid of me then you can consider this heart yours. If you fail and become defeated then you can forget about claiming this heart." Violence said after creating space from the punch that he threw earlier. Conviction and Joy both understanding that this would be a difficult battle yelled out to the rest of the squad.

"We will take care of him, the rest of you keep pressing forward, get Light and Cardinal to the stairway of Ascension and complete the mission."

"We're on it." The rest of the Hoodies responded. They continued to press forward into the heart, rushing past Conviction and Joy. Violence knew he could not let them pass and turned his attention toward the hoard of Hoodies, but the moment he looked away Conviction and Joy both let out a whirlwind of slashes, that grazed Violence on the cheek.

"Your battle is with us." Conviction stated, putting his long sword across his back.

"You will be purged now." Joy iterated.

"I guess I better focus on you, otherwise I'll end up like the rest of my comrades. Let's begin." Violence said afterwards charged right at both of them with aggression. While Conviction and Joy were fighting with Violence, Light and Cardinal continued making their way to the stairway of Ascension.

Rage observed everything that was happening from the shadows of the heart. With his presence completely undetectable he could see from the side of the battlefield that Cardinal and Light were completely vulnerable, and with his power from the neutral Emotion he knew that he would have the upper hand fighting Light. Rage seizing the opportunity inches in closer to Light and Cardinal who were unaware of the doom making its way across the battlefield. Rage slithered and crawled through the darkness until he knew he was close enough to apply a deadly blow to Cardinal. He figured if he could take Cardinal out then all he would have to worry about was taking care of Light. Rage lunges out like a tiger to unexpecting prey, but because of the awareness of Light before Rage could deal his blow to Cardinal Light intercepts the blow and becomes immobilized. Cardinal stops walking and turns around to see that Light had been fatally wounded by an attack that was meant for him. Cardinal in complete disbelief that Light could even be bested by one of the Suits in his heart stood looking in complete shock. Light grabbed the hand of Rage and slowly removed it from his chest, Rage also in complete shock that he was able to deal a fatal blow to Light fought the force of Light removing his hand from his chest. Light's power and strength began to fade and Rage's hand pressed deeper through the heart of Light. Cardinal, now becoming less paralyzed by the situation, snapped and hurled his shield at Rage. Rage, now sensing that he may be in danger from the blow that Cardinal would land, removed his hand from the chest of Light and retreated back. Cardinal looked into the face of the fading life of Light, his emotions began to rise and he could not keep himself from holding back the tears welling in his eyes.

"Why did you allow yourself to be injured?" Cardinal frantically expresses.

"Cardinal, it is my job to protect you, I have no doubt that you will be more than capable to handle this heart alone, after all, this is your heart and you can definitely handle Rage. You have seen how he fights so this shouldn't be a challenge for you." Light expressed with little energy.

"Ha. I can't believe that the all powerful Light could be so weak and vulnerable. I bet that Tuxedo will have me at his side after he hears what I have accomplished." Rage expressed with a smile on his face.

"Please Light you can't be like this. I cannot do this without you." Cardinal admitted.

"My dear Cardinal, you will never be alone. I will be with you always. Even in your darkest of days I will be there. You can do this." Light expressed with the energy he had left before fading and vanishing. Rage began to laugh only to suddenly stop and look down at his stomach in confusion. Rage began to twitch and move around erratically and uncontrollably. Confusion began to set in on the face of Rage.

"Wait what the heck is happening to me?" Rage asked. Rage began to gyrate and convulse uncontrollably to the point that he became fearful. His body shook fiercely and his belly grew as if pregnant. It then became very evident what was happening to him, Rage was losing control of Emotion, because of Cardinal's release of tears from the damage that Light took the Neutral, Emotion began fighting its way from the hold Rage had on her.

"No, no, no. I have worked too hard to get you in here and I refuse to let you just escape like this." Rage grunted.

"I will not let you get away with this!" Cardinal yelled out emotionally. In that moment Cardinal threw his shield across the created space that Rage had made earlier. It moved at great speed until it closed the gap and hit Rage right in the stomach. The collision caused Rage to convulse and shake. He dropped his head and his eyes closed strongly. He grasped his stomach and his mouth in an attempt to keep from throwing up the fighting Emotion in his gut. The moment that he opened his eyes and lifted his head, Cardinal closed the gap between him and rage and drew his sword, The Spirit. As the sword came from the sheath an immense light shined and blinded Rage. Cardinal pulled the sword out so fast the sound of thunder clapped from the metallic sheath and the sword slid through the stomach of Rage. Rage, completely shocked that his former colleague bested him, looked back down to see the sword cutting through his stomach and Emotion sliding out onto the floor. Cardinal followed through with his slash then turned the sword around to perform his final attack, but Rage, not fully discombobulated by the first attack, threw a kick at Cardinal's head to get him off of him. To Cardinal the kick moved in slow motion. He tried to dodge it but because he was already fully committed to throwing a final slash, he knew that he would have to take the damage from the kick. Cardinal turned his head to prevent being hit harder than he needed to be. The kick smacked him right across the face and sent him flying backwards. He regained the distance that Rage had created earlier but no more than a small scratch landed on his face, Cardinal was barely fazed by the previous attack. Emotion rose from the ground and bounded over to Cardinal; Rage stood in his place not fearful but waiting for his body to heal from the previous disembodiment. Emotion looked over at Cardinal and smiled,

"Thank you, Cardinal, for setting me free. I would stay here and help you fight Rage but the fact of the matter is this battle does not concern me. I cannot break the code that was put in place and fight a battle on your behalf. I can grant you a bit of information before I head back to my land. Rage obtained all his power from consuming me, now that he has lost me, he will lose much of the power that he acquired. I also do not hate you for how you reacted by helping Rage. You acted as I would have expected a confused human to act. Now I have to get back home. Make sure to free Relationship from Abuse and Addiction." Emotion stated.

"Relationship was consumed by Abuse and Addiction?" Cardinal asked.

"That's correct, I can feel him. Half of him is at the foot of the throne of Tuxedo. The other half has been running since the walls fell in this place last night. I doubt that you will be able to do anything with Addiction now, but I assure you there will be a time for her as well. Thank you again Cardinal." Emotion thanks just before floating in the air then vanishing back to the Land of the Neutrals.

While Cardinal thought about what the once enslaved Emotion just stated, Rage healed completely and with malice charged at Cardinal to get back at him for removing the Neutral that he worked so hard to obtain. Cardinal observing the motion of Rage heading forward prepared himself for the onslaught of the completely illogical and impulsive Rage. As Cardinal gripped his sword tightly, he noticed that Rage was not moving like he was previously, he was moving much slower and not just that but Cardinal could recall these movements from when Rage had fought Emotion the first time. Rage galloped on all fours like a beast, until he finally closed the gap between him and Cardinal. He jumped forward and with a loud yell lashed out at Cardinal with claws as sharp as daggers. Cardinal completely aware and perceptive to the attack coming towards him side stepped the sharp claws plunging towards his face. Rage, missing his mark landed behind Cardinal, turned around and tried for a second time. Cardinal stood where he was without even turning around to see where Rage had landed and prepared himself for the next attack. Cardinal squatted and gripped his sword once again. Rage cocked his hand back and drew forth as much strength as he could to behead the seemingly unaware Cardinal.

"This is the end!" Rage yelled out as his sharp claws closed in on Cardinal's neck. Just before Rage was able to fully reach Cardinal, Cardinal vanished. Rage swiped the air now in front of him, losing his balance he tumbled over. Rage regained himself and stood and looked around in an attempt to find Cardinal.

"Where have you gone you Coward?!" Rage screamed. "Show yourself!" he continued.

"Here I am." Cardinal responded. Appearing inches from Rage's face. Rage stunned and surprised by the immediate arrival of Cardinal, reached out with both arms to grab the seemingly quicker Cardinal. Just before Rage could wrap his arms around Cardinal, Cardinal used the hilt of his sword to hit Rage in both arms rendering them useless in the battle. Rage let out the scream, one so loud and twisted it rivaled that of a lion in distress. Cardinal squatted low and the immediate gripped the handle of the sword and under his breath whispered.

"That was for everything you did to me. And this…." Cardinal removed The Spirit from the sheath. "This is for Light!" Cardinal yelled and in one movement slashed straight through Rage and ended up on the other side of him. Rage in complete disbelief attempted to turn and look at Cardinal who instantaneously ended up behind him, but as he began to turn, he noticed that his body began to disappear. Rage panicked and lashed out at Cardinal in hopes that just before completely disappearing he could land a blow on Cardinal. Cardinal, not phased by Rage's desperate attempt to injure him, walked toward Rage with complete confidence.

"Cardinal!" Rage yelled out as his voice began to fade into the void. Just as his sharp claws got closer and closer to Cardinal's face, the rest of his body vanished. Cardinal sheathed The Spirit and looked back towards the Stairway of Ascension and began to make his way back in that direction. Even though

Light had protected Cardinal from the attack of Rage, and told Cardinal not to go fight Tuxedo by himself he could not see any other alternative than to finish this journey alone. Cardinal ran towards the Stairway of Ascension as Tuxedo looked down on him.

"Here he comes prepare yourselves for battle." Tuxedo warned Abuse, Porn, and Fear. The three of them all jumped in front of Tuxedo and took a fighting stance. Cardinal rushed across the battlefield, moving past numerous suits. As Cardinal moved at great speed through the chaos a suit attempted to stop Cardinal by jumping in his path and challenging him to combat. Cardinal drew The Spirit and vanquished the suit easily. Many of the suits now seeing that Cardinal was still heading to the Stairway turned from their battles with the Hoodies and began to make their way over to Cardinal. The brainless and senseless mob abandoned their fights and lashed out at Cardinal. Cardinal again unsheathed The Spirit made quick work of the mob of Suits. From every direction they closed in on Cardinal, Cardinal starting to feel the effects of the battle began to slow down. His slashes became weakened and his speed drastically decreased. The Hoodies, now noticing Cardinal's fatigue thrusted themselves in between Cardinal and the mob to fight off the legion. Family, Friendship, Destiny, Self Control, Love, Peace, and Grace all appeared instantaneously to protect Cardinal from the Suits that sought to destroy Cardinal. With the combined force of the 7 of the Hoodies they made quick work of the small legion.

"Don't worry Cardinal, we will protect you and ensure that you make it to the Stairway of Ascension. We saw what happened to Light, it is not your Fault, that is just his nature. Conserve your energy because your battle is coming, for we cannot make it up the Stairway, that is a journey you must make on your own but we will guarantee your success in getting there." Destiny informed. Cardinal placed The Spirit back in its sheath and took a few deep breaths and continued forward to the Stairway. As they continued to press forward the number of suits that formed at the base of the stairway began to grow to prevent Cardinal from making it up. Cardinal figured that the reason the Suits were so adamant about keeping Cardinal from going up the stairway is because they themselves could not make it up, much like the Hoodies. Cardinal smiled and continued to press forward with one thing on his mind, make it to the first stair and everything else would be up to him. The 8 of them rushed towards the legion with speed and purpose.

Joy and Conviction continued their clash with Violence as their swords hit his gauntlets. Maniacal laughter emitted from their battle as Joy and Conviction both hurled their large swords with speed and force. Violence continuously blocked the blows but the mere force of the attacks still managed to hit home by cutting Violence up. Violence enjoyed what was happening and seemed to grow stronger every cut that he got and every second the battle carried on. Joy and Conviction could not understand after the amount of time that they had been fighting Violence why he seemed to get stronger and stronger. They created space while Violence continued to laugh and smile.

"Come on guys please don't stop, I am really starting to have some fun here. It has been such a long time since I had this much fun." Violence pleaded.

"Why does it seem like he is getting stronger?" Joy asked Conviction.

"There has to be something we are missing here." Conviction stated.

""Come on, fight me!" Violence screamed out as he lunged towards Conviction with great speed. Conviction held his sword up to prevent from getting hit by the gauntlets. As the gauntlets smashed into his sword and sparks emitted, Joy swung his sword around and attempted to slash Violence, but he could see the attack coming and jumped out of the path of the sword. Violence landed and lunged back at the two of them and began a flurry of attacks toward Conviction and Joy. Conviction and Joy blocked and protected themselves from the blows being directed to their faces.

"Why is this suit so autonomous and not like the rest of them that are mindlessly heading over to protect the stairway?" Joy asked.

"It would have to be because…" At that moment it all made sense to Conviction why Violence did not seek to prevent Cardinal from getting to the Stairway of Ascension. Violence was violence, he thrived and became empowered off the battle he was having with both of them. Every slash of the sword, every swing from his gauntlets fueled him and made him stronger. That was why Violence desperately wanted to continue the battle. It all made sense at this point. Violence ceased his onslaught and backed up to engulf himself with more of the power he gained from the continued battle.

"Joy, he is fighting us because he is Violence. He is getting stronger because we are fighting him. We have to stop fighting him." Conviction stated.

"But if we stop fighting him then we will get pummeled, we have to fight him to prevent from getting destroyed." Joy responded concerningly.

"Look at how Violence fights and the weapon he chose to fight with us. It is not something to eradicate us swiftly; he chose gauntlets. I believe that he chose them because it is his nature to be violent. We need to stop fighting him, but just because we stop fighting him doesn't mean that there is not another way to defeat him. I think what we need to do is get him to the other side of the battlefield where our entry portal is located, for the light shown through that portal will be enough to purge him." Conviction ordered Joy.

"That makes sense, let's try that." Joy responded.

"What are you two over there talking about, come over here and fight me!" Violence yelled.

"Here we come!" Conviction let out. "Let's go!" Joy seconded.

"Yeeeesssss!" Violence excitedly yelled while bringing his gauntlets up to throw another punch. Just as Conviction and Joy dashed over to Violence, they both raised their swords as if to attack Violence. As Violence anticipated this attack from them, he reached up to intercept the blades headed toward his head. Violence nearly grabbed the blades but Joy and Conviction both disappeared instantly. Violence confused looked around to figure out where they had gone. He spotted them running through the destroyed battlefield filled with light shards. Violence knew at that moment what they were trying to do, they were trying to go back to their home and regain power to destroy him.

"Ha, trying to get more power are you? Well, I'll never let you get the chance." Violence yelled out and started his pursuit of Conviction and Joy. At this point in their battle Conviction and Joy had both become much slower than Violence and they knew it, which is why they relied on the element of surprise to gain some distance between them and Violence. They continued through the battlefield of light shards and Violence pursued them closely. To prevent Violence from getting too close Conviction and Joy picked up some of the axes and knives laying around from their comrades and began to toss them at Violence. Even though Violence had gained so much power even he wouldn't risk getting hit with one of these weapons because that would decrease his power. Violence raised his guard to allow the weapons to hit his Gauntlets.

"You think these little knives and axes will keep me from you, when I get my hands on you, I will pummel you both to smithereens." Violence yelled out. Conviction and Joy continued working toward the portal which was now close enough for them to use the light to purge Violence. They stopped running and turned around to look at Violence in his pursuit.

"It's about time you cowards stopped running." Violence stating while lunging at both Conviction and Joy. Conviction and Joy waited until Violence had fully committed to throwing the punches at them and once that moment came, they dropped their swords and grabbed both of Violence's arms. Violence completely confused, began to scream.

"Let go of me! Let Gooooooo!" He screamed and fought to break their grasp.

"When I break free, I am going to suffocate the both of you." Conviction and Joy walked with the fighting Violence in their arms.

"Wait where are we going?" Violence asked. As the three of them turned around, Violence then noticed what they were trying to do, they were going to carry him out of Cardinal's heart into Eden. Violence began to panic because he knew that if he got carried in that portal, he would be just like all the suits before him. Purged.

"No! No! Noooooooooooo! Stop! Please Stop!" Violence begged and pleaded. Conviction and Joy both began to recite words from the ancient text simultaneously.

"Yea, though I walk through the valley of the shadow of death, I will fear no evil: for thou art with me; thy rod and thy staff they comfort me. Thou preparest a table before me in the presence of mine enemies: thou anointest my head with oil; my cup runneth over. Surely goodness and mercy shall follow me all the days of my life: and I will dwell in the house of the Lord forever."

"Please stop it! Just fight me!" Violence flopped and dead weighing himself tried to prevent himself from being carried in. It was useless Conviction and Joy again began to recite the words they had just uttered.

"Yea, though I walk through the valley of the shadow of death, I will fear no evil: for thou art with me; thy rod and thy staff they comfort me. Thou preparest a table before me in the presence of mine enemies: thou anointest my head with oil; my cup runneth over. Surely goodness and mercy shall follow me all the days of my life: and I will dwell in the house of the Lord forever." They were now within a few steps of entering the portal and Violence could feel himself disappearing. His gauntlets are completely gone now and his body fading.

"Nooooo!....." Violence let out one last yell before the light from the portal finally took him out. Conviction and Joy, victorious from their battle knew that this was only the beginning of what they needed to do. Conviction yelled out to the other Hoodies that had not accompanied Cardinal to the stairway.

"Truth, Generosity, Patience, and Mercy you can stop firing arrows into the legion, your other 7 comrades should be able to get Cardinal into the Stairway. In the meantime, I need you 4 to come with me. Light gave me specific instructions before he was vanquished. We need to allow the light from our land to expand into Cardinal's heart. We can only expand it to the areas where there are no suits. Once we have cleared out the remaining suits, we will be able to encompass Cardinal's entire heart with this marvelous light. Help me spread this light please." Conviction ordered.

"Let's do it." The 4 of them answered in unison.

"We will not allow you to do what you want here." A voice called out from the darkness.

"Why don't you come forward and show us who you are." Patience ordered while drawing an arrow and aiming it in the general direction the voice came from.

"Why? Why?" The voice became louder and louder. "Why did he choose my twin but leave me down here." The once small voice grew louder. Patience and Mercy sensing where the voice was coming from shot an arrow into the area the voice spoke.

"Ooooowwwwww that hurt! Ooooowwww!" The giant suit screamed as he rushed towards Patience and Mercy. The light began to illuminate the figure who had conformed to the darkness. It was Stress. Mercy and Patience hit their marks as when Stress became fully visible 2 arrows protruded from the massive muscular arm of Stress.

"We need to bring this beast down!" Generosity claimed while loading an explosive tipped arrow in his bow.

"We need to surround it and aim for the head. Don't get hit by that massive arm." Truth informed while loading an explosive arrow.

"Everyone aim, on 3 we fire. One, two, three." Patience counted down, but just before the word three was uttered another voice let out from the darkness.

"You're dead." Mercy and Truth heard this just before firing their arrows into the head of Stress and repositioned their arrows to the voice that spoke behind them. As their eyes began to focus on the darkness, an open mouth with teeth sharper than blades accelerated towards the body of Mercy with incredible speed.

"Mercy look out!" Truth yelled out. Truth swung his arrow toward Mercy and with amazing precision Truth fired off his arrow, it flew with great speed hitting the beast right in the stomach, but because the beast was wearing chain linked armor the arrow did not penetrate it. The damage that Mercy was going to take was inevitable simply because Truth had drawn an explosive arrow into his bow and the explosion from the impact would affect both the beastly suit and Mercy. The other 2 arrows flew and hit their mark but not directly in the head of Stress because the voice shocked the 4 of them. Rather the arrows from Generosity and Patience hit Stress in the chest. Conviction and Joy emerged from the portal they had walked through to find Generosity, Mercy, Truth, and Patience fending off 2 odd looking suits.

"What is going on here?" Conviction asks just as the words left his lips all of the arrows fired hit their marks. Truth's arrow hit the stomach of the beast Suit sending it and Mercy flying backwards. Joy observing Mercy flying through the air flies over to catch him so he would not suffer any fall damage.

"I got you buddy." says Joy.

"Hey Truth, thanks dude, it almost got me there." Mercy emphatically thanked. Joy floating down to the ground placed Mercy on his feet to prepare for the coming battle.

The beast looking Suit hit the ground on its back but quickly got up and ran over to Stress.

"The master is not going to be very happy with us if we do not take out these warriors." Ignorance states.

"Why would the master separate me from my twin? I don't like this one bit." Stress continues to complain.

"Stress, I need you to focus, otherwise we will be purged here and there will be no coming back. Is that what you want?" Ignorance asks.

"No, that is not what I want." Stress responded.

"We can meet up with your twin once we are done here." Ignorance informs. Instantly Stress changes his demeanor and becomes more battle hungry and determined than when he first arrived.

"Let's kill them all, Ignorance!" Stress yells. Stress then reached up and removed the arrows from his chest and his arm and threw them to the ground.

"Be careful everyone they are getting ready to charge." Conviction yells out.

"Joy, cover me while I load this next arrow. I'm going to need some time because what that beast Suit is wearing a normal arrow isn't going to purge it. Give me a minute and I guarantee you I will put that animal down." Mercy promised.

"You got it." Joy acknowledged.

In that moment Ignorance galloped over on all fours towards where mercy was creating an arrow to destroy him. Joy, seeing that his attention was primarily focused on Mercy, placed herself in front of Mercy to stop the attack from Ignorance. Stress began spinning in a circular motion with the speed and destruction of a tornado. His precision was better than that of a trained assassin. He spun into the direction that the 3 other archers were standing with his massive muscular arm swinging out to hit a suspecting target.

"Remember we have to hit him in the head in order to purge him. Here he comes. Everyone move!" Generosity ordered.

"Don't worry, I'll handle this." Conviction states while cocking his sword back. The three of the archers jump to the side and Stress continues spinning, now heading in the direction of Conviction. Conviction prepares himself for impact but just before the massive arm of Stress collides with Conviction's sword Stress stops short. He continues spinning but does not press forward. What was he planning on doing?

"Now Ignorance!" Stress yells

In that moment Ignorance stops his rush towards Joy and leaps directly towards where Stress was idly spinning. The timing, precision, and speed were perfect. While in motion towards Stress, Ignorance balls himself up and Stress opens up his massive hand. Ignorance lands in Stress's hand and just as quickly as he got there was as quickly as he was thrown from Stress's hand. The speed that emitted from the body of Ignorance was so fast that Conviction could barely see him. Ignorance emerged from the ball he was in and opens his mouth wide in an attempt to bite Conviction.

"So fast, there's no way I can…." Conviction began to utter. But before he could finish his sentence Ignorance clamped his mouth shut and completely shattered his sword and his upper body. The only thing left standing was the lower half of Conviction's body.

"Conviction!" Joy yelled out.

Ignorance took a few chews of the body and spat it out. "Disgusting." Ignorance grimaced. "If we keep doing what we just did, there is no way this battalion will be able to take us out." Ignorance claimed with great confidence.

"Well that's why your name is Ignorance, because you lack understanding. Now take this!" Mercy expressed while releasing the arrow that he had been creating. The arrow was as bright as the sun and as quick as a lightning bolt. The bolt of light traveled bright and quick across the battlefield until it completely obliterated the head of Ignorance. Ignorance fell to the ground with a mighty thump. His body began to deteriorate quickly and a light shard was left in the place where he was bested. Stress began to fear the impending doom that he could see was inevitable. Rather than stay and fight a battle that seemed grim, Stress turned from the archers and began to run. What Stress did not take into account was that while Mercy was creating that arrow for Ignorance the rest of the archers had gotten into place to take him out.

"Hey up here ugly!" Generosity yelled out. Stress looked up to see that Generosity had flipped over his head. In the midst of the flip Generosity had an arrow drown down at his head ready to purge him. Generosity lets the arrow fly with great precision but because Stress was aware of the coming attack, used his massive arm to shield himself from being purged. In that same moment Stress swiped at the airborne Hoodie and knocked her across the battlefield.

"She almost killed me." Stress whispered.

"Try this on for size!" Joy yelled while dragging his sword behind him as he ran up to Stress. Stress sensing that he could no longer run from the team pursuing him, prepared to do battle with Joy. Joy, now finally within range to strike, lifts his long sword from the ground and swings with exuberant force. Stress now privy to this pattern of battle from watching Joy and Conviction fight Violence anticipates the swing from the sword and grabs it with his massive arm. The chainlink on his hands prevented him from getting sliced.

"I observed your fight with Violence there is nothing that you can do to defeat me!" Stress informs.

"I'm not trying to defeat you; I'm just keeping that massive arm out of the way." Joy stated with a smile.

"What?!" Stress questioned now in a panic.

"Gotcha." Both Patience and Truth stated from polar opposite sides of Stress. Stress then understood what had happened. When he turned to run away both Patience and truth and split up and one gave chase and the other stayed back and followed him with an arrow drawn. When the one that chased got into position that was when Joy engaged. Joy just a distraction just like Generosity was a distraction. Their true plan was to surround him and shoot him from both sides. They let their arrows fly at the same time, and just before they closed in on Stress's head his last words were, "Twin, Help, I'm Scared." At that moment both of the arrows hit their mark and stress was purged. A light shard was left in the place where he once stood.

"Great job team." Joy congratulated. "Now let's finish up the mission that Conviction put before us before he fell in battle. Let's spread the light throughout Cardinal's heart. I will go back to Eden and get some pure light. You can use the light shards from all the purged suits."

"We're on it." They all responded in unison.

Joy took the light from Eden and the archers spread the light from the purged suits and began to include it in Cardinal's heart. Tuxedo Watching from the Stairway of Ascension became very angry because his plan was not working. He now had Cardinal being rushed forward towards the stairway and 6 other hoodies spreading light in his home. He was losing. As quickly as he became angry, he began to smile and chuckle.

"Master what is so funny we are losing." Porn asked, now concerned. "Porn, do you not see it? Through the sacrifice of our dear Rage we were able to eradicate Light. The hardest part of this was getting rid of him and he is gone. All that is left now is to have Cardinal submit to me, and once I have him in submission, I will rule over his flesh forever. Let him come up, Without light's help he will be easy work for you three." Tuxedo responded.

"Master, you are right. This is not a loss for us, this is a great victory. We have bested him." Abuse amusingly exclaimed.

"Now don't get too excited because you still have work to do." Tuxedo reminded him.

"Yes master." Abuse responded.

"Why didn't you bring my twin up here with us? I would have been stronger with him here, now he is gone!" Fear expressed.

"Watch your mouth and mind who you're talking to! I specifically told all of you that you are not important to me. The only reason you are here is because you are the most desperate. Your twin was more loyal to you than he was to me. He was a necessary pawn to slow down the forces. If you miss him so bad…." Tuxedo paused and grabbed Fear by the throat and began to squeeze. "I can send you to meet him." Tuxedo grimaced.

"No master.......I am content where I am at." Fear responded, grasping for breath.

"I don't want to hear anything else about your twin, you got it?" Tuxedo asked.

"Got it." Fear answered.

Cardinal continued forward toward the stairway with the 7 Hoodies surrounding him. The 7 Hoodies engaged in combat with the legion holding the line at the stairway. Sparks flew and weapons went flying. Cardinal continued to press forward with the team. He saw a small opening made from the attack of the Hoodies.

"Go Cardinal now is your chance!" Love commanded.

"I see it!" Cardinal responded with gratitude and new energy. He jetted towards the opening the Hoodies made for him. Once he removed himself from the protective circle the Hoodies made for him the Suits all unified turned to look at Cardinal and attempted to thwart him from reaching the stairway. Just as they turned to prevent Cardinal from making it to the Stairway the 7 hoodies used their combined force to let out a strong attack that wiped the remaining legion out. A large group of axes, knives, and katanas rushed forward like a whirlwind. Every suit became purged and as quickly as that whirlwind swept through and whipped out the remaining suits the light from Eden illuminated the Heart of Man all the way to the bottom of the stairway. The purity of the light strengthened Cardinal as he took his first stop on the stairway. The immense darkness emitted from the stairway was heavy as if a thousand pounds sat on Cardinal's back. He struggled to get his bearings together but he remembered what Light said just before he vanished.

"I will always be with you even in your darkest moments." Echoed in his mind.

Cardinal fought the darkness attempting to put him on his knees and he continued to walk up the stairway. The 14 hoodies, understanding that their battle was now over, placed their weapons back in their sheaths, pockets, and holster and walked back into their portal home. Tuxedo watched from above as Cardinal ascended the stairway.

CHIMERA

The moment Cardinal began to walk up the stairway of ascension he no longer was Ethereal, he opened his eyes and became one with his human body.

His mind began to ponder and think about what was going on. He knew that the battle still continued but why was he here? Light had told him that he did not have the ability yet to be able to fight in his heart and still be present in this world so why was he back here. "Was I too weak to continue with the mission? Did I only accomplish what I could and that was it? Where was Light?" These were all the questions that began to run through Cardinal's mind. Before doubt could even start to well up in Cardinal's mind it was like a bolt of electricity aggressed Cardinal's mind. Confidence and surety abound, Cardinal somehow knew that things would be okay.

"How's it going Cardinal, you wanna come out and play 18 holes with us?" The twosome golfers asked as they passed Cardinal sitting on the bench.

"Maybe later, I'm going to practice on my short game for a little bit." Cardinal responded. Cardinal, now sensing a bit lighter in his heart from the battle that just transpired, stood up and grabbed a golf club and began swinging it rhythmically back and forth.

The head of the club brushed the grass flinging the dew from the grass across the green foliage. Cardinal removed a few golf balls from his bag and positioned them in front of him and took a relaxed athletic stance. He rehearsed the same rhythmic swing he had just practiced and once he felt comfortable, he approached one of the balls that he had previously thrown down. He placed the head of the golf club behind the white ball and conducted the same rhythmic swing. Click went the sound of the golf ball as it connected to the head of the club. The ball bounced and rolled toward the small hole in the ground. Cardinal watched intensively as the ball rolled toward its mark. The ball rolled into the hole and Cardinal celebrated with a rise of his fist towards the sky. Again he placed a ball in front of him and again he practiced his swing, all the while he could feel slightly disconnected from the world of the living. He could feel his ethereal body was still in his heart. Cardinal confidently interpreted that the reason he was present in this world now was because the power that was latent in his body must have been awakened when Light, the Hoodies, and himself wiped the Suits from his heart; nonetheless, Cardinal's physical body felt weakened from the journey his ethereal body was taking up the stairway of ascension. He continued swinging his golf clubs rhythmically through the grass while his Ethereal kept ascending up the staircase. Ethereal Cardinal endured mocking by the Tuxedo and the 3 coats at the top.

"YOU REALLY THINK THAT JUST BECAUSE YOU DEFEATED ALL THOSE GRUNTS YOU ARE ANY MATCH FOR ME AND MY 3 SOLDIERS!" A strong voice bellowed from the top of the stairway. Cardinal kept on walking up the stairway. The words echoed through the emptiness of the heart as there was no longer anything left there.

"IT'S TOO BAD LIGHT LEFT YOU IN HERE TO DIE, THERE IS NO WAY YOU CAN DO ANYTHING ALONE! YOU'RE SO SMALL AND INSIGNIFICANT!"

The voice continued to let out from the top of the stairway. Cardinal did not let the voice stop him from what he came here to do, nor did he let the fact that Light was no longer here affect his goal. Light had enough faith in him to sacrifice himself to have him continue.

"I can make it." Cardinal said to himself. Step after step Cardinal pressed on to the top of the Stairway.

"Master worry not we will put an end to Cardinal the moment he comes up here." Abuse stated.

"Yes my king he is clearly no match for the three of us." Porn responded.

"I know you three can handle this, what we need to do is trap him here. If we can take control of his Ethereal, I will forever rule his body. He will be mine. Just weaken him, then leave the rest to me." Tuxedo instructed.

As Cardinal got closer to the top of the stairway the weight of darkness became heavier and heavier. But below his feet the light from his successful battle gave him strength to battle the darkness. Cardinal took another step forward and was instantly shocked that there were no more steps going up, it had appeared that Cardinal had reached the top of the stairway of ascension. He stood there looking out in the rage of the darkness which any other time would frighten him, but because he had Spirit in his hand, he lifted it and slashed through the thickness of the darkness creating an opening in what was now visibly a hallway to a door. The door was massive and Cardinal could now see where the loud monstrous voice was coming from. He walked forward slowly and carefully on guard for he did not know what could come for him.

"CARDINAL THIS IS YOUR LAST CHANCE TO LEAVE THIS PLACE. AS MUCH AS I WOULD LIKE TO COMPLETELY TAKE OVER YOUR BODY YOU CAN JUST LEAVE AND GO THROUGH LIFE WITH ME AS YOUR ALLY! YOU DON'T HAVE TO DO THIS!"

The voice loudly announced from the other side of the door. Cardinal felt more courageous now that he could see. He found it fitting to respond to the voice that had been yelling at him since he stepped on the stairway.

"YOU MUST BE TERRIFIED OF WHAT I'M ABOUT TO DO TO YOU. I WILL PUT YOU BENEATH ME AND YOU WILL NEVER IMPART ANYTHING IN ME AGAIN!" Cardinal responded. Silence fell in the hallway as Cardinal now closed in on the door. Just before he could open the door, an immense laugh broke out.

"HAHAHAHAHAHAHAHAHAHAHAHAHAHAHA- HA! YOU KNOW NOTHING IF THAT IS WHAT YOU THINK! PLEASE COME FORTH!" The voice from the other side of the door beckoned. Cardinal reached out with both hands and with great strength flung both of the doors open. Cardinal was shocked by the size of the three suits standing in front of him in this massive room, they were like giants.

"Cardinal, if you could do me a favor and shut the door behind you, that light you are letting into the room is really messing up the feng shui." Tuxedo commanded from beside the giant suits. Cardinal gripped his sword tightly and took an offensive stance against the enemies in front of him.

"Before we completely destroy you and steal your body from you there is something you should know, aside from the fact that there is nothing you can do to prevent me from doing it, is...." instantly Tuxedo vanished and appeared right behind Cardinal. Cardinal, noticing the speed and trajectory of Tuxedo, swung his sword in a reflex and slashed behind him. His sword clashed against the blade of another weapon. Cardinal peaked over his shoulder to see sparks flying from the sword in Tuxedo's hand. Cardinal grunted as he could feel that he would become overwhelmed by the power of Tuxedo threw a punch at his face. Just before the blow landed Tuxedo vanished again but rather than completely retreat to his previous location his hat slowly descended to the ground. Cardinal looked instinctively into the face of Tuxedo expecting to see an empty faced individual like what he had been battling before but rather he was shocked to see the feature on the face of Tuxedo. The face mirrored his own.

"What is this trickery?" Cardinal asked in confusion. "Cardinal, it is a bit rude to interrupt someone from finishing. Like I was saying you should know that I am you." Tuxedo completing his previous statement.

"What do you mean you are me? Why do you look like me?" Cardinal began to panic.

"Isn't it obvious, I am all the unflattering, diabolical, unrighteous essence of you. I am who you really are. Since the day you are born we are there with you. No one knows you better than I do. Let's not make this messy, just submit and I'll do you a favor and keep you from ever having to remember what your cousin did to you. Isn't that what Light said he would do for you." Tuxedo began to pry.

"I mean where is he now anyways? All powerful am I right? Haha." Tuxedo stated sarcastically. "All that power and he fell victim to one of my weakest grunts. It would have been nice to plunge my blade into him but as it were, it doesn't really matter." Tuxedo continued. Cardinal remembered the conversation he had with Light last night and the question that he asked him. Cardinal instantly remembered that he did not answer anything regarding Tuxedo and this might have been the reason. There was only one thing Cardinal wanted to know.

"Can you be purged like the suits?" Cardinal asked, raising his sword to point at Tuxedo.

"Hahaha is that what Light told you? No you wouldn't be asking that question if Light would have told you, you are asking because you really don't know. Hahaha well why don't you use that sword and figure it out?" Tuxedo remarked while putting his guard down.

"Why wouldn't Light tell me about you?" Cardinal began to think now gripping Spirit more tightly than before.

"You know what. As much as I would love to blow your mind with everything you don't know, I don't see it in my best interest to do so. Porn. Fear. Abuse. Take care of him." Tuxedo ordered as he turned his back and began to walk to a throne in the back of the large room. Porn, Fear and Abuse walked towards the center of the room and turned towards one another. They looked to the sky and began to shapeshift into one another. Their bodies twisted and turned unnaturally and their heads all formed on the body of one beast. Claws began to form sharp as daggers and the eyes of the monster shown red as a blood stained moon. Teeth that would rival the veracity of the fiercest dragon. The three headed monster no longer favored the image of a humanoid this monster looked like something out of the nightmares of a demented child, truly the things of horror. Porn the once strong and masculine by nature transformed into a feminine wench. The face of Porn now looked more menacing than any of the other faces of the monster, the chimera. Her hair sharp as thorns and her skin reptilian, yet she still had an enticing appeal. Fear took on the image of a ghoulish goblin with large ears and snaggleteeth. Abuse purposefully took the face of Jay as to create the same victimized feeling Cardinal had when he was a young boy. The body of the chimera was now larger than the original bodies of the suits that were once in the room. Once they had finished their transformation, they all let out a horrendous howl that even darkness itself shivered a bit. Each one of the heads of the Chimera looked down at Cardinal with great hate and disdain. Cardinal gripped the Spirit and leaped into battle against the giant chimera. He swung his sword through not only the darkness but also attempting to behead the giant chimera. The problem was as equally as the chimera was large it was fast. Cardinal was unsuccessful at hitting the chimera and because he missed, he left himself wide open for a counter attack. The chimera jumped into the air at the moment Cardinal swung his sword and its hand was cocked back to completely annihilate anything on the receiving end. Cardinal anticipated the counter attack because even though the chimera was quick it was not nearly as quick as Tuxedo was. He parried the attack but the impact of the claw of the Chimera with Spirit blew Cardinal back a few feet. Cardinal was astounded with the amount of force emitting from it, considering that he had just blocked a blow from Tuxedo. The chimera did not waste any time, the moment Cardinal regained his footing the face of Fear opened its mouth wide and let out a deafening scream. The sound wave of the scream cracked the helmet of salvation that Cardinal was wearing and disoriented Cardinal to the point that he could no longer see straight. He was now seeing 3 different chimeras. Cardinal staggered around just before the other head of the chimera Porn unleashed her long reptilian tongue to ensnare Cardinal. Porn reeled him back in to consume him but while she drugged him in, Cardinal regained what little bit of strength he had left and took the sword and sliced the tongue right out of Porn's mouth. She let out a horrifying cry of agony. Cardinal lay in the middle of the floor still trying to regain his energy from the last scream of Fear. Abuse saw this as an ideal situation to capitalize on Cardinal being weaker and unleashed an array of words that he knew would be effective considering they were things that Cardinal idolized and identified with.

"YOU'RE DUMB! YOU'RE RETARDED YOU'RE NOTHING!" Each word formed itself into a deadly array of projectile weapons that flew through the darkness with great speed and precision. Cardinal tried his best to counter the words but they sliced him deeply. He did not prepare himself for the onslaught that he was being dealt by this chimera. Abuse, sensing how effective his warfare was, continued to hurl more weaponry at Cardinal.

"YOU'RE A MISTAKE TO THE WORLD! YOU WON'T AMOUNT TO ANYTHING! YOU WILL ACCOMPLISH NOTHING! SLAVE! YOU SHOULD HAVE NEVER BEEN BORN! JUST KILL YOURSELF! DISAPPOINTMENT!"

Each statement and word sharper than the last cut through the golden armor that Cardinal wore, it did not protect him because it wasn't strong enough to do so, it was becoming less effective at protecting him because Cardinal started losing faith. Porn began to administer her own attack of computer and cell phone screens rich with images and videos that Cardinal had watched over the years. Fear continued its deafening scream. Each attack became more and more effective as the armor ripped right from the ethereal body of Cardinal.

"You see it's no use. If you can't best them then you surely cannot do anything against me." Tuxedo mockingly stated from his throne. Cardinal realizing that he would not last long against the chimera and Tuxedo decided to throw a desperate final attack at Tuxedo. Cardinal staggered to his feet and with the little bit of energy he had left he leapt at the throne with Spirit and slashes at the neck of Tuxedo. Cardinal, watching the blade move swiftly towards its mark, became somewhat relieved because the shocking expression on the face of Tuxedo fulfilled that he did not expect him to throw this last ditch attack at him. The blade connects with the neck of Tuxedo and passes completely through, decapitating Tuxedo.

"Huh." Cardinal let out a sigh of relief as the head rolled off the shoulders of Tuxedo. Cardinal began to put spirit back in its sheath but while the sword was halfway put away Cardinal felt that something weird was going on. When he had purged all the suits down on the battlefield they all just disappeared, why was it that Tuxedo was still here. He removed the Spirt again and slashed multiple times at the body of Tuxedo until he was in pieces. The feeling of uneasiness still did not go away. Cardinal stood there confused, but he also forgot about the Chimera that was behind him. The large Claw of the chimera smacked Cardinal hard across the room creating space between him and the throne of Tuxedo.

"Y O U . . . . J U S T . . . . . R U I N E D . . . . M Y . . . . GEEEEEAAAAAAAR!" Tuxedo exclaimed full of rage. All of a sudden the once slashed up pieces and decapitated head of Tuxedo formed back into a full body. Cardinal lost every bit of hope he had left, considering that he used all the energy and faith he had left to try and end this battle by attacking Tuxedo.

"If you will excuse me, I need to change." Tuxedo remarked before disappearing and then returning not too long after disappearing with a burgundy tux this time.

"I know you're shocked but you wanted to know the answer to that question. Can I be purged? Well clearly you can see I cannot. See that's the problem with Light he won't tell you everything and because of that you humans are in the state you are in now, nonetheless, this is a very exciting day. This is the day that I take over your body. Don't worry it won't be like anything where you won't know who you are. After all, I am you. What will happen is more like you will go through life hedonistically, you will enjoy it, I mean of course because I love this world. You will forget all this virtue stuff, you will lose all of your abilities, I will be in control. Now if you don't mind, hold still so that we can make this quick, we all we got now." Tuxedo explained. He formed his hand into a fist and threw it right towards where the heart would be for the ethereal body, right before he could pierce through his body to control his human body a lightning bolt shot through the darkness of the room and sliced the arm off of Tuxedo. Cardinal in complete disbelief looked up to see what had saved him from being harvested, and it was Light. Light had returned to save Cardinal from himself. With tears welling up in his eyes Cardinal could not help but welp and ask.

"Where have you been? I literally thought that you were dead?" Cardinal asked, all the while he looked back at the light trail that was still shining and noticed that it had gone through the belly of the beast. The chimera doubled over in pain and began to fade away as Light's immense speed had dealt more than enough damage to purge them.

"My son, like I told you, I will never leave you or forsake you. I sacrificed myself to give you independence for one, and for two because I had to transform you by renewing your mind. Abuse had taken the time to rewire some of your programming and some of your memories in your hippocampus, if I had not dealt with restructuring your mind you would not be truly free from everything that happened to you. I also had to unplug all of those monitors broadcasting all that noise of defeat, faithlessness, porn, and nothingness. I knew that this battle would be something you would struggle with but I was never going to let you fall." Light informed.

"Why didn't you tell me that Tuxedo couldn't be purged?" Cardinal asked.

"When you are a baby, it would be unsafe to feed you a steak dinner. Even though a steak dinner is nutritious and delicious, giving that type of food to you that young would be irresponsible of me as a parent. Similarly, it would have been dangerous for me to give you that information before it was time to give it to you." Light answered.

"Um hello that was my arm you just removed." Tuxedo calmly mentioned.

"I am well aware." Light responded.

"Hang on there Light, I thought you couldn't inhabit these unclean vessels for it would destroy them, and not only that I literally saw Rage destroy you. I thought you had to limit yourself in order to be here." Tuxedo questioned.

"That's your problem, you are always looking to know everything. Like you Tux I cannot be purged. But unlike you, you can be evicted, I cannot." Light rebutted.

"So what are we going to do with him?" Cardinal asked. "Cardinal it is now important for you to know that Tuxedo's cannot be purged, but they can be cast out. This was his kingdom but because you have chosen to live amongst virtues then your heart will be filled with light and goodness. While they are here, he cannot live here. He will be tethered to you constantly trying to force his way back into your heart but as long as you choose to live in righteousness then he will not be able to inhabit your heart. This tether is only for a season. As for what we are going to do with him, that is something I cannot tell you, just know that you have done great today, you are free." Light explained.

"When you say for a season does that mean that I will someday never have to deal with Tux again? Or do I have to wait until the day I die?" Cardinal asked.

"Cardinal, I know that you are a very inquisitive individual and that you listen to every word said, that is something that is very special about you. I can tell you this, a war is coming, very soon. I cannot tell you when, just know that when it comes you need to be distinguishable from them." Light stated pointing at the Tuxedo. "Cardinal, bask in this freedom. I love you." Light said.

"If you think that you have won you are sadly mistaken. I will be back. You haven't heard the last of me, Cardinal Wolf. After all, we are one and the same." Tuxedo remarked with confidence. At that moment it was like Cardinal was completely back. The weakness that he felt earlier was gone, in fact he felt empowered and strong. He picked up his golf balls and placed them in his bag and slid his golf clubs back in his bag. He placed the straps over his shoulders and walked over to the first tee to play a round of golf. Joy rose up in his heart so strong that Cardinal could not stop smiling. He walked tall and proud with immense light shining from him. He walked to the top of the hill where the first tee was, and there were a couple of guys standing there waiting to play as well. Cardinal seeing them wait to play sat his bag down in an attempt to wait for them to finish so he could play. One of the guys on the tee box turns around and looks at him and asks,

"It's only the two of us, you can join us if you want. We are only playing 9 holes anyways."

"Sure." Cardinal responded walking up to the first tee extending his hand out to the gentlemen. "My name is Carindal."

"Nice to meet you Cardinal, my name is Jay and this is here is Christopher." The first gentleman reciprocated the salutation. When Cardinal heard the name Jay his heart seemed to have skipped a beat, but rather than worry and Fear gripping his heart he felt Peace abound about him. He released Jay's hand and grabbed his club and began to practice swing.

Cardinal played with the 2 gentlemen the whole 9 holes and when the last putt dropped in the hole, they all removed their hats and went to shake each other's hand. Jay looked Cardinal in the eyes and said.

"It was nice meeting you today young man. There is no doubt in my mind that you will do amazing things in this world. Keep your head up and stay focused."

"Yeah man what Jay said. You have an amazing swing and a great countenance. Keep up the good work." Christopher reiterated.

"Thank you fellas, I really appreciate the kind words and I will keep progressing and getting better." Cardinal responded with great admiration. The three of them walked to the parking lot and Jay and Christopher got into their sports cars and drove away. Cardinal waited around for his father to come and pick him up, he did not wait long for his father showed up the minute the sports car turned onto the main road. Alpha circled the parking lot until he came to the end of the turnabout to pick up Cardinal. Cardinal placed his golf bag down in the trunk and rushed to the front seat with the exciting news about how well he played today. The moment he sat down in the car Alpha looked over at him and asked.

"How'd you play?"

"Oh my goodness dad I played so well. I shot a 38 on 9 holes!" Cardinal responded excitingly.

"A 38?! No way you shot that! How many balls did you use? How many strokes did you not count?" Alpha asked skeptically while driving out of the parking lot.

"None, in fact I played some guys that just drove out of here just before you arrived." Cardinal responded.

"Wow, that's amazing! Great job Card. Keep up the good work and you will be on the PGA tour in no time." Alpha admitted.

"Yessir." Cardinal responded as the car drove back home.

Several months had passed by since the day on the golf course and Cardinal was shocked to not have heard anything from his Tuxedo. No correspondence at all. It was almost like he just disappeared. Cardinal did not care, nor did he want him to return for he was having the best few months that he ever had being free from all the baggage that he had been carrying for all that time. The summer time had finally come to an end and it was time for Cardinal to go off to school. He jam packed all of his clothes and shoes in the back seat of the SUV his parents rented to drive him to school. That day was saddening for Omega for she was hurt to see her young man leaving for another state. When Cardinal finished putting all his clothes in the car he went to embrace his mother who started to let the tears run down her face.

"It's okay mom, I am seriously not even that far away, I am literally 1 state away if you miss me so much just come out and see me." Cardinal assured.

"Ok as long as you promise I can see you." Omega sniffled. "Of course mom, okay I have to leave now. Goodbye mama." Cardinal hugged tighter.

"Goodbye Card, I love you and I am so proud of you." said Omega with emotion Cardinal got into the SUV and closed the door and just before Alpha entered the car Cardinal heard a child like voice behind him.

"Hey Cardinal, you miss me?" Cardinal turned around to see a smaller, more feeble version of his Tuxedo.

THE END?

Back in the year 2019, Cardinal prepared himself to take the drive to Mariano City. He took the keys off of the kitchen counter and began making his way to the front door, but before he left he made his way back to the other side of the house to see if his grandmother needed anything. As he walked past the various bedrooms he looked into the bedroom where Jay and him played a game years ago and he saw Suits sitting on the bed and standing around. He passed the bedroom and continued to his grandmother's room.

"Hey Mamama, I'm headed over to Mariano City to see my Parents Alpha and Omega, I'll be gone for a little bit do you need me to pick you up anything while I'm out?" Cardinal asked.

"It's okay baby, I'll be alright. Say hello to your mom and dad for me okay. Oh, and give your brother and sisters a hug for me now, okay." Mamama asked.

"Will do Mamama. I'll be back soon, try not to over exert yourself while I'm gone." Cardinal ordered.

"Now you are a little too young to be telling me what to do. Lemme tell you something, I'm old enough to know what to do and young enough to still do it. Go on to your parents' house. I'll see you when you get back."

Mamama responded with authority.

"Okay Mamama, I'll see you in a bit." Cardinal said waving to her and closing her door.

"Okay baby, make sure when you get back you hang up all them suits in that room you got them sprawled everywhere." Mamama replied as the door closed. Cardinal's face immediately converted to complete fear hearing what he heard from his grandmother; he immediately reopened the door very slowly to his grandmother sitting in the same spot looking at a suit in the bedroom. Under her breathe she softly says, "Cause I don't care who you are and what you think you are about to do in here you have no authority in here and you gon get me to do nothing, understand that."

Cardinal closed the door and walked outside Fear now gripping his heart fully after what he had just heard from his grandmother. He fumbled through his keys shakingly until he gained control of the fob. He clicked the unlock button on the car fob until he heard the door to his car unlock. He reached down to the car door and opened the door, when he saw the entrance that he made for himself to sit he flopped in the driver's seat and closed the door directly behind him. He put the key in the ignition of the car and turned it over. Cardinal rushed to grab his phone and pair the Bluetooth with that of his vehicle so that he could turn on his music and drown out the voices of the Suits that began to call out his name now even louder than before. "BOOP" went the chime of the vehicle as the phone became connected, cardinal quickly rushed over to some music and played it loud. A song that he had not previously finished came on loud over the speaker of the car and filled it with a gratifying and overwhelming peace that Cardinal had not felt since that morning. Now relaxed, Cardinal placed his car in reverse and reversed into the street to start his short drive to Mariano City. The drive was much like any other one considering that his parents only lived about 15 minutes from his grandmother and himself. Cardinal traversed through the streets, across the bridge, and through the stop signs until he pulled up to his parent's house. Since he did not see any room in the driveway to park his car Cardinal parked on the street in front of his parent's house. He reached for the volume dial to turn the music down but just before he was able to do so his mother stormed out of the house waving her arms signaling him to turn his music down. Cardinal immediately turned off the car with a guilty look on his face because he remembered the last conversation, he had with his mother about driving up the block playing music loud like that. Cardinal opened the car door entering the street and turning towards his mother.

"Hi mom." Cardinal greeted her softly so as to not get her worked up about the music.

"Hello Card. How many times have I told you about the music?" Omega asked.

"More than once, I'm sorry I just got a lot on my mind." Cardinal responded.

"Oh, what's going on son?" She asked.

"It's a lot, can we go inside?" Cardinal asked.

"Sure. You are just in time; the kids are getting home from school. They will be happy to see their big brother." Omega stated. They both embraced for a hug and then they disappeared into the house. Alpha sat on the couch in the living room of the house, when Cardinal walked in, he stood up and said,

"Wassup boy. How you doing?"

"Man. Actually there was something I wanted to speak to you and mom about. Is it cool if we sit down so I can tell yall all about what has been going through my mind and everything that is happening with me." Cardinal spoke in desperation.

"Yeah, absolutely this sounds serious, sit down." Alpha Instructed. The three of them sat down on the living room furniture.

"Okay tell me what's been going on." Alpha asked. Cardinal took a deep breathe and said, "Well this all started 20 days ago."

About Kharis Publishing:

Kharis Publishing, an imprint of Kharis Media LLC, is a leading Christian and inspirational book publisher based in Aurora, Chicago metropolitan area, Illinois. Kharis' dual mission is to give voice to under-represented writers (including women and first-time authors) and equip orphans in developing countries with literacy tools. That is why, for each book sold, the publisher channels some of the proceeds into providing books and computers for orphanages in developing countries so that these kids may learn to read, dream, and grow. For a limited time, Kharis Publishing is accepting unsolicited queries for nonfiction (Christian, self-help, memoirs, business, health and wellness) from qualified leaders, professionals, pastors, and ministers. Learn more at: https://kharispublishing.com/

www.ingramcontent.com/pod-product-compliance
Lightning Source LLC
Chambersburg PA
CBHW070633310726
48982CB00001B/272

* 9 7 8 1 6 3 7 4 6 2 2 7 0 *